Dawnbreaker
A.B. Charles

Banned & Burned Publishing

Second Edition 2024

ISBN: 979-8-9884757-6-7

Cover Art and Design by Laura Charles

Yeah, this book is dedicated to all the teachers that told me I'd amount to some-
thin'

When nations grow old, the Arts grow cold,
And commerce settles on every tree

William Blake

Contents

Preface   VII

Acknowledgements   X

"What's past is prologue."   1

1. "The abyss gazes also into you."   11

2. "Do not go gentle..."   31

3. "...sincerest form of flattery..."   39

4. "...a house that tries to be haunted."   48

5. "...the crag of Scylla and dire Charybdis' vortex..."   59

6. "...straight on till morning."   61

7. "...six impossible things before breakfast."   68

8. "...let the theory go."   76

9. "...eddying darkness seemed to swim round me..."   86

10. "A warrior will sooner die than live a life of shame."   101

11. "It isn't what we say or think that defines us..."   116

12. "...that dare not speak its name."   126

13. "Ships that pass in the night..."   138

14. "...barefoot from distant travel..."   152

15. "...making the darkness conscious."   162

16. "...awoke one morning from uneasy dreams..." — 180

17. "I defy you, stars!" — 192

18. "Unfortunately the cave contained a lion." — 202

19. "What hath night to do with sleep?" — 221

20. "...this bitter world where vice is king..." — 233

21. "How did I escape? With difficulty." — 249

22. "...then in the following one it should be fired." — 265

23. "...brains do not make one happy." — 286

"What can one make of such a denouement?" — 298

Chapter Title Reference — 302

The Orb Mongers — 304

About the author — 333

Preface

Hey, here's a bunch of crap you can choose to ignore because it isn't why you picked up this book.

Oh, you're still here? Well, this is kind of awkward. Why don't I tell you why I wrote this book then?

For as long as I can remember I wanted to be a writer. It was one of two things I wanted to be when I graduated high school. Life didn't initially take me down that road though. I had a lot of pragmatic voices in my life that stressed the importance of money to live. I was also of the mind at the time that nobody wanted to hear stories from someone who didn't have any life experience; at least I didn't. So I went the pragmatic route and got into tech. It was good for a while. It was where my aptitudes lay. This doesn't mean that I still didn't write on the side. I have so many novels that I started on but never escaped the first act. This was usually because I'd encounter too much stress from the rigors of my day job and the abuse of a not-so-nice boss(that's putting it mildly). Self-doubt would creep in. I'd start to think what I had written was garbage and run the manuscripts through the digital shredder. Don't worry, I've saved the really good ideas.

My work-life balance eventually degraded into a state of unsustainability and I started to look for a way out. I'd had a couple of other escape attempts over the years but every time I was ready to leave, I'd start to think that that not-so-nice boss was capable of change and would stick around a little longer. Fast forward to Covid, and things got a lot worse. That boss doubled down on being not-so-nice while trying to have a "we're all in this together" personality. As anyone paying attention to mandates because of the compassion they have for others knows, it's hard to have that "we're all in this together" feeling when you're forced to be apart.

I'd taken to going on long walks in the woods to relieve the stress from work and the sense of impending doom from the pandemic. It was on one of these walks that I had had a particularly revelatory experience. I cracked the code of a story I had been noodling on for a while; the very one in this book. I became super excited. I also decided that things weren't getting better at work and that it was time to follow a dream. After all, I was now old enough and had enough life experience that people might want to read something I'd written. I put in my notice the following Monday.

I was going to take a month off to decompress but didn't make it a week. I pounded out six thousand words in the first few days. They weren't good words and there are barely any of those early ideas in this book. I didn't care though. I had a breakthrough. I knew I could make those words better and I did. Are they great? I don't know; that's not for me to say. They're at the very least up to a standard where I'm not embarrassed for them to be read by you. If you knew me, you'd know that that is an almost impossible bar to reach. I'm not just saying, "This is good enough for the rubes."

I had glibly chosen this story as the one I was going to tell first. It seemed like the story that had the highest potential for the kind of commercial success that would allow me to keep writing full-time. I hadn't anticipated falling so in love with the story and the characters that tell it. I hadn't anticipated how much I would learn about myself. This may be a work of fiction but there is a lot about this book that is autobiographical. I was working through some issues while putting it together and I think a lot of that is reflected in the struggles that Marnie and company face.

I am very proud of this work and hope you enjoy reading it as much as I enjoyed writing it.

-A.B. Charles - July 2023

***

Addendum

In celebration of the launch of Banned & Burned Publishing, this 2nd edition contains the prequel story BEFORE THE BREAK OF DAWN: THE ORB MONGERS which was written after the main novel. It tells the story of what a couple of our main character's new friends were doing right before the events of this book. I recommend reading it after DAWNBREAKER but the choice is entirely yours to make. I'll also key you into the fact that the prologue of this book was originally written as a separate prequel story called THE FLOOD but it meshed so well with the over-arching narrative that I included it in the original printing of this novel. I don't know why you needed to know that but here we are.

-A.B. Charles – May 2024

Acknowledgements

I'd like to thank the following people:

Laura for dealing with my dumb writer quirks and being a good editor.

Kathryn, Jake, Kim, and Josh for reading through the rougher versions of this book and claiming that they liked it.

Heidi for letting me know when I was projecting darkness rather than dealing with it.

The real Marnie for never restricting the words that could be used as long as they served the story.

"What's past is prologue."

“**W**hat you're talking about is suicide.”

“If there was any other way, I assure you, we'd be doing things differently. Why do you think I didn't tell you? I was trying to avoid this,” said the man known as the Vagabond Master to his cloaked apprentice.

“I can't—I can't let you go through with this,” replied the young man, his eyes already starting to show signs of mourning.

“The choice is not yours to make. This is a bed I alone must lie in,” the Master said. “The only thing that should concern you now, is getting him to safety. He is the only thing that matters. We can't risk letting her have him.”

The apprentice opened his mouth in an attempt to lodge another protest. What the Master was asking him to do may have looked like the lesser sacrifice but on the scales they were using, it could be debated.

The Vagabond was quick to cut him off, “You have the map, correct?”

The apprentice looked at him, seeing a face set and unwavering, “Yes. I know where I must go...and what I must do.”

“Good, that just leaves one last thing,” the Master said as he walked up to his pupil. “I'm sorry, but this has to be done. Much too dangerous for you to have where you're going.” He rested his hand upon his student's head. A violet light pulsed in waves through the apprentice's veins. The apprentice's once purple blood vessels morphed to a dark blue as his power was pulled into the Master's hands. A vital piece of his essence had been extracted. The apprentice could feel the modifications being made in his brain...something being locked away. It felt like a violation. He would have objected had the circumstances not been so dire. In a matter of moments, the feeling faded. The apprentice was left with no recollection of the Master's intrusion.

“What do I do if he wakes?” the apprentice asked.

"With what he's been through this night, he won't," The Vagabond replied. "Now we have one shot at this. You must get him to that door before the Lonely Sister hits her apex. He cannot know that this world exists."

The apprentice stared at the Vagabond in silence, waiting for further instruction.

"Go!" the Master shouted, casting his hand toward the darkened path and the pale green horse behind them. The leaves that bordered the path sprung to luminescent life.

***

The Vagabond Master watched as his apprentice galloped away on his mount. He waited until he could no longer detect the movement of the beast's glowing tail. He didn't detect any pursuers, deducing that any interlopers would rightfully be watching him instead. The power he had siphoned for his plan was more than enough to draw the forest's attention. "If you only knew where the true power now lay," the Master whispered as he turned his gaze toward the path ahead.

He took up a mount on his own steed as he dropped his last remaining orb into its fuel tank. The hollowed eyes in the machine's oaken figurehead sprung to life, casting two high-intensity beams onto the trail before him. A suspicion that had been growing in his spine was now confirmed, shooting a cold shiver from the bottom of its base up to the back of his neck.

Silent hopelessness tried gripping his heart, but hope was something he no longer gave much quarter. It was a luxury he was unsure he'd recognize at full strength; the last decade of despair had seen to this. The hopelessness that tried to attack him felt like home as a mass of disembodied wings and crimson eyes began to circle. Their numbers seemed to multiply as each passing wave grew in intensity. The Slaugh had arrived.

The Master did still possess the capacity for fear, which the creatures stoked as their circle grew tighter and tighter. The chill in his spine seemed to get colder, ever-growing toward a crescendo of panic. It was at the peak of his terror that the Master closed his eyes and drew in a deep breath. He slowly exhaled out his nostrils before opening his eyes. His body ejected a sudden blinding flash of white light, forcing the encroaching swarm to disband. The Vagabond Master saw his opening and cranked the throttle with an unwavering intention. A cascade of dust and stone spit out from behind as the cycle lunged violently forward through the cloud of wings flocking in front of him.

He waited a few breaths before turning his head to see how much distance he had gained. The swarm was regrouping quicker than he had planned, forming itself into a singular dark mass. He could no longer pick out the individual eyes that formed the black and crimson crescent that pursued him at canopy level behind. It was waiting for him to make one misstep, one mistake that would undo the last year of careful planning. With the throttle cranked as tight as it would go, the Vagabond Master drew his braking hand to the fuel tank and channeled the smallest amount of his siphoned energy into it. The bike tore hell for leather up the path, turning the bordering trees into a glowing blur. Warmth returned to the Vagabond Master's heart with each meter gained on the destroying horde.

The Master was barely able to navigate the forest's twists and turns, trying to stay well enough ahead of the Slaugh to avoid its grasp. He did, however, want to stay close enough to keep its interest, lest it reset its sight on the apprentice. He knew where he must go, focusing his intention on the old Citadel, not quite allowing himself to hope that the Masters Coimín had already broken what remained of the Geddes line, knowing that if they had been lost it would have all been for nothing.

He could see the forest's border in the distance as the amber light of a glow-wheat field started to peek through the trees ahead. Fear once more began to creep up his spine. The absence of the forest's canopy was sure to leave him exposed. For the sake of the mission, the Vagabond Master shoved the feeling down, focusing on the what next instead of the what if.

As the surrounding forest faded into grass, the Master was able to hear the sound of the Slaugh behind him. The trees had muted its wailing but now it echoed across the rolling hills of the fields ahead. The sound was eerie. Its shrieks seemed to dampen the light emanating from the ears of the nearby grain stalks.

The Vagabond didn't let the attempts to stoke despair seep in, keeping the throttle pegged as he could see the top of the Citadel creeping over the city wall. He looked back once more to confirm the swarm was still in pursuit, that the cries weren't of a herd of beasts losing whatever hope was left to be extracted. The Slaugh's course hadn't diverted. This would be the last time the Master looked back as he once more charged the cycle, setting his eyes back on the fortress in the distance.

***

The apprentice had made his way to the designated forest clearing with his unconscious traveling companion. He peered around at the edges. The forest was dark these days and had only become darker with the Vagabond drawing out the essences needed for his plan. Still, the moons in the sky shined enough light to allow for reflection in the eyes of the creatures that came to observe, the ones that could smell the unconscious boy, this boy who had become the focus of his mission.

The apprentice climbed down off his horse and lowered the boy to the ground. He removed the supplies he had packed and unburdened the animal of its tack. The remaining light in the horse was pulsing, sensing the beings in the shadows. The apprentice patted his companion to calm it. He then faced it to look it in the eyes. The horse was in a state of anticipation, already nodding its head to offer a goodbye. The apprentice rested his hand on the creature's snout as a final gesture before uttering a low, "Go."

The horse turned toward the trail and sprinted away, thankful it wouldn't also have to hold watch until the witching hours.

The apprentice looked on as the beast galloped away, glancing around at the shadows to see if any of the watching eyes had given chase. He almost allowed himself to be disappointed that none had, catching himself halfway through the thought, instead thinking back to how loyal his steed had been. He then walked over to his gear and picked up a scabbard from which he unsheathed a sword smithed from cold iron. He took a stance with it before spinning around, brandishing it to his observers as a warning. He then rotated it around the outside of his wrist before raising it up and firmly planting it in the ground.

The apprentice went over to the boy to pick him up and carried him to a monolithic stone that had been toppled and now served as an altar. He looked at the carvings on the stone as he set the boy's sleeping body on top of it. They were recent, lacking the patina of the upright menhirs he had seen in other clearings.

The etchings showed no sign of weathering, still allowing an observer to make out the chisel marks that had been visited upon it by the sculptor.

The apprentice picked up and placed all of his gear on the slab before grabbing his sword and climbing up to accompany the boy's unconscious body. He began to recite and repeat the instruction the Master had given him as his fear continued to grow. The watching eyes had begun to advance.

***

The Master slowed slightly as he approached the western gate, noticing that the guard posts had been emptied. "The line has been broken," he thought, crossing under an open portcullis.

As he entered the city, he spotted multiple pockets of orange glow. The glow wasn't from the fruit of the trees that normally lined the western road but was one of burning embers. The Master took a deep breath, his nostrils were invaded by the smell of black smoke. He could barely make out the sound of iron hitting iron over the howl of rushing wind. The Vagabond had brought the Geddes war home to roost.

The Master covered the distance between the gate and the Citadel swiftly and observed the destruction as he prayed that it had all been worth it. As he approached the ivy-coated building, he veered to the right, circling it to the rear.

The Master had an accomplice waiting for him, someone on the inside who was able to get him where he needed to go. "Are you sure you weren't spotted?" he asked.

"Who exactly do you think you're talking to?" the young woman responded.

"Oh...right," the Master said.

"I unlocked the doors. The path should be clear to the Wellspring," the woman replied. "It's a real shitshow out there, everything's a mess. Don't expect you'll be running into much resistance...You remember how to get there?"

"Think I'll manage," the Master stated as he glanced over her shoulder and through the doorway, already following his mental map, "...Hey, before I go, I just wanted to say I'm sorry for..."

"Don't..." the woman cut him off, "They were evil...needed to be stopped. I won't be mourning them and neither should you."

The Vagabond considered her words, almost wishing that his own children thought of him in the same light, hoping to spare them the grief they would have to endure. Looking to the woman as an almost surrogate for his children, he said, "Don't 'spect we'll have another occasion to meet after this."

"'Spectin' not," the young woman responded as she looked somberly at the Master, "Don't worry, I'm not going to try and talk you out of it."

The Master looked at her, hoping he hadn't condemned her to a fate worse than his. He offered, "I know you have your gifts but if you need a place to lie low for a bit, the Cloister's doors will be open to you."

"Thanks. Think I might have to take you up on that," she said as her heart warmed to the thought of being welcomed in by someone after the events of the last decade. "Guess this is goodbye."

The Vagabond Master nodded and headed into the darkness beyond the Citadel's doorway, his image dissipated into the blackness.

The woman turned to make her way into the city when she heard the Master's voice add, "Hey."

She turned around to see a set of keys gliding out of the dark. The young woman snatched them from the air with an Adept's instinct and glanced over to the Master's magnificent steed.

"Take the bike...Not going to need it where I'm going."

***

The apprentice continued to watch the eyes, not daring to leave his perch. Their stirrings appeared to be coordinated. Shadowy figures had started to exit the forest into the clearing. He couldn't identify what kind of creature the glowing orbs belonged to. This left him unsettled, unsure how to prepare. He clenched tighter at the hilt in his hands, hard enough to feel pain from the leather-wrapped iron digging into his palms. The pain became a focus, a place to hide his fear.

The figures were moving forward deliberately, ploddingly, closing off his exits. The only thing the apprentice could do now was hope; hope that the Vagabond would go through with what he had proposed. He shuddered to think that his chances for survival rested on the Master's self-destruction.

The apprentice glanced up to the sky, seeing the face of the red moon closing in on its zenith. He then looked at the figures with their red eyes, planting himself into a defensive stance.

***

The Vagabond Master navigated the rear corridors of the Citadel. His mind was working on instinct. This wasn't the first time he had had occasion to sneak through the passageways of the fortress. This wasn't even the first time in the last week. The extraction of the Master Wordsmith from the dungeons was the purpose of his previous visit. Her essence was one of the last that required collection. He didn't want to risk her death in the siege or his plan would have met its premature end.

The Master found his way to the black wellspring pool at the center of a cylindrical atrium prison. He glanced around the room at the near countless number of cell grates that encircled him. He could hear the unlocking and slamming of grates all around him from the liberation taking place. He then drew his gaze to the two-meter tall wall that circled the wellspring in front of him and made his way to the steps of a wooden catwalk that surrounded it.

He walked up the steps and around the walkway to the platform that propped up the room's focal piece. A six-meter tall slab of black onyx was perched at the edge of the thirty-meter-wide pool. He studied the visage that had been carved out of it with appreciation. He didn't detect so much as a misplaced chisel mark in the intricate layers of leaves and vines that formed the face etched upon it. His thoughts then drifted to the door's dark purpose, snapping him back to reality. The Master looked up to the ceiling port hole that let the moonlight in. The red glow of the Lonely Sister moon was shining through the round compluvium above. He could make out the moon's face and prayed that his apprentice had reached his destination, that his sacrifice wouldn't be for naught. He could hear the Slaugh approaching. It had picked up his scent. The red glow of the Lonely Sister moon was being eclipsed as shrieks started to echo down the atrium.

The Vagabond Master turned his thoughts to the loved ones he was leaving behind, his wife and two children, wishing he possessed the ability to make them forget; to spare them the pain his absence would inflict. He shut his eyes and tried to carve their faces out of the blackness before him, to get one last look, finally allowing himself to embrace hope; hope that they could forgive him; hope that they find a way to move on. He said his final goodbyes to the lifeless facsimiles.

A familiar feeling crept up his spine, exploding through the synapses in his brain, easing his pain as he opened himself, pulling in the last remnants of light the world possessed before releasing it all in a singular, blinding ejection.

***

The shadowed figures drew ever closer. The apprentice, through his terror, could see why he wasn't able to detect the nature of their being. They possessed no discernible features. They were shrouded apparitions with red glowing eyes. He looked at where their feet should be, seeing only ground. He then drew his gaze to their hands, seeing only clouds of black smoke pooling out from the ends of tattered wraith-like robes. Their numbers were uncountable as they continued their plodding advance to within swords reach.

The beings stopped suddenly. The apprentice couldn't see the ground in any direction as he snapped his head around, desperately trying to search for a possible exit. There was no escape to be had. He turned to face the direction of the Citadel, hoping to catch a glimpse of the Vagabond's plan coming to fruition.

The shadowed abominations started to reach out. Clawing with their incorporeal hands toward the boy at his feet. The apprentice slashed at the limbs and watched them dissipate into nothingness before reassembling to reach out once more. The apprentice looked to the sky, finally seeing the Lonely Sister reach her peak. He drew his eye back to the direction of the Citadel, ready to give up hope and resign himself to an unknown fate.

There was an explosion of white light. The apprentice watched as more than a thousand sets of eyes turned their attention to the city behind them. As the blast wave approached, a nervousness grew within him. He desperately hoped he wasn't trading one demise for another.

The apprentice continued to watch. Time seemed to slow as the wave approached. One by one the wraith-like creatures were lifted and consumed by the light as it passed over the clearing. The surrounding forests and grasses became illuminated with a glow his eyes hadn't seen since he was a small child. As he took in the view, relieved he was still alive, the boy at his feet began to stir. The apprentice glanced down seeing the cracks in the menhir altar radiating with light as it traced its way from the child's small body and down the sides of the stone.

Then as suddenly as the wave had passed through him, he found himself pulled down into a silent blackness. The apprentice knew at that moment that the Vagabond Master was no more.

Chapter One
"The abyss gazes also into you."

"Where do you think ideas come from?"

"What do you mean?"

"You ever think that your thoughts aren't your own? Like you've stolen every good idea you've ever had from someone or somewhere else."

"When have I ever had a good idea? If I had good ideas I wouldn't be following you around every night. Would I?"

"What's that supposed to mean?"

"It means, what we're doing is illegal. The longer we're out here, the more likely we're going to get caught."

"It's three in the morning...Third-shift cops don't like to run. But I digress...I think we are light-bulbs tapped into a collective unconscious, working as a hive mind, generating novelty. Ripening it for harvest. That's the real reason we work at night, less competition for the reaping." Scot Murphy loved the spark of an idea more than its execution. To him, even these micro epiphanous moments were a thing to be savored, never getting the recognition they deserved.

David Almánzar rolled his eyes, getting ready to entertain Scot's musings, "Your woo woo bullshit aside...Sounds ridiculous coming through that respirator by the way...It's not like you're coming up with these ideas on the fly and just throwing them up. You need time to develop the concept. You have stencils to cut. You have to cop the spray. You ask me, you've been breathing in too many fumes."

Scot paused to consider his friend's rebuttal. He conceded, "Okay so maybe it's mostly the third shift pigs...My best ideas do come at night though...after everyone is asleep. Take what we are doing tonight. The Green Man, a symbol of death and rebirth, stenciled and free-handed on the side of this 7-Eleven. A 7-Eleven which was once a Pizza Hut. What was new became old and is new again.

It takes a special sort to make these connections, harvest the ideas, separate the wheat from the chaff, and lay down something as sick as this."

"That is some serious conceit," David replied.

"I was just being an asshole," Scot responded. "Could you imagine if I thought that highly of myself? Could you imagine if anyone thought that highly of themselves? I just think Green Men are dope."

"I should think so," said David. "You do them enough."

The piece that Scot was stenciling was a six-foot-tall Green Man head. Using a forearm-length oak leaf stencil and a can of vibrant green paint he had worked to create a wreath. The leaf points created the appearance of hair as he took the stencil in turn, orienting it to produce the appearance of ears and a beard.

After surveying his progress, he used the stencil to add additional layers of browns and darker greens, giving the piece additional depth as he worked his way inward. He was sure to radiate the leaves out from the center, switching to a smaller stencil as he moved toward the middle. He roughed in the appearance of a brow, a nose, and a mouth before further defining the beard and the ears.. Parts of the massive face started to look like they were popping out of the wall.

Next to him, David shifted nervously. "Mooch, would you hurry up? It's been forty-five minutes already. You're gonna get us caught." Forty-five minutes might as well have been an eternity working at street level.

"Settle down. I'm almost done," replied Scot before attempting to ease David's mind, "Besides, you're my good luck charm. Cops have never rolled up with you on watch."

At this point, the face on the wall was a more than passable representation of a foliate Green Man, one of three major types of Green Men and Women which could be seen adorning antique furniture, door knockers, and cathedral grotesques.

The only things missing were the eyes. To fill the voids where they should be, Scot brought along a crescent moon stencil and a can of amber-colored paint. With quick motions, he free-handed two circles in the middle of the empty ocular cavities. Then using the crescent stencil with points up he shot in a second layer. Finally, with two short bursts of dark green paint, he added in pupils.

Scot and David stood back to admire the piece. The visage was truly haunting, having an almost three-dimensional appearance, as if at any second it would stick its tongue out and swallow them whole. "It's almost like the eyes are watching me, penetrating me," remarked David. "Like he wants to know my deepest darkest secrets."

"I'd watch my phrasing on that one," Scot replied, picking up David's unintended innuendo.

"I'm being serious, this one feels different from the others, somehow elevated," David said. He had always admired Scot's work but there was a level of mastery in this piece which his others had merely been reaching for.

"I've been working on my layering a bit more," Scot responded.

David cocked his head to the side, trying to get a glimpse of what Scot was describing. "Yeah, maybe that's it." He wasn't sure.

"Somehow, it doesn't feel finished," said Scot. "I wish I'd remembered the silver. More accents would have made this one pop... I'm gonna come back Saturday and finish it off."

"Are you sure that's a good idea?" David asked. "Looks finished to me. Spot's gonna be burned for at least a week. Surely some of those 'third shift pigs' want a collar like you on their record. Help them get off third shift. The notorious Mooch, purveyor of fine graffiti Green Men across the city."

"Don't you see? That's exactly why it's a good idea," Scot responded, "We've never hit the same spot twice. Won't suspect it. Do it tomorrow but my sister's coming over. S'posed to help her with a project...Prolly gonna take all night."

Scot took off his respirator and threw it in his backpack along with the spent cans of paint. He folded up his stencils and tucked them by his reference sketchbook in his backpack's unneeded laptop pocket. Scot gave the piece a final look, mentally noting that he would only need silver and another five, maybe ten minutes. It would almost be worth coming back in an hour but they had already been there too long. It was time to go.

***

Scot and David made the half-a-block walk back to David's inconspicuous purple Ford Ranger pickup. David would tell you it was blue if you asked him. They then made the ten-minute drive back to Scot's artist loft in the South Wedge.

David asked if he could crash for the night. Scot obliged, it was the least he could do. David had always been a reliable friend and never discussed their witching hour activities with outsiders. Scot had known David since the time just after his family was forced to move to a new neighborhood due to the sudden disappearance of their patriarch.

Scot's father Declan had been an artist not unlike his son. He was a sculptor, specializing in the carving of stone and wood. One of those "the figure is already there it's just my job to reveal it" types. He wasn't without his eccentricities, giving him a bit of a mystique in the art community and heightening his local celebrity. His long grayish-brown hair and beard made him look like a wizard, which only added to the image, an image he fully embraced and exploited.

Declan's works focused on ornate doorways and arches, featuring natural elements like laurels, all manner of flowers, and the occasional animal. His main claim to fame was his grotesques, most of which were Green Men. There are many churches and gardens around the city still adorned with his creations.

Scot had access to his father's old sketchbooks and often used them to derive inspiration for his own works. He truly idolized his father or at least his memory of his father. To others, Declan could have been considered a 'bit of a prick', that is at least until you came to know him. But many didn't know him, he liked to keep people past arms reach.

The story behind Declan's disappearance was the subject of constant debate among those who still talked about him. He wasn't known to participate in illicit activities and didn't have any known enemies. The most common theory was that it was a mugging gone wrong. Declan liked to do his outside work at night when there was less chance of being bothered by passers-by, leaving him exposed and vulnerable. His disappearance also coincided with a rash of unsolved robberies. The local police had even gone so far as to dredge parts of the Genesee River looking for a body. There had never been a credible sighting or shred of evidence to explain what had happened. It was as if he had vanished into thin air.

Scot's mother, Diane, was only able to hold out hope of his return for so long. She took his disappearance in stride as much as she could. This process was helped along with Scot stepping up to become 'the man of the house', a role that was desperately needed. Raising a four-year-old while working a day job was enough stress without constantly having to look after a teenager as well. On one hand, Scot harbored a bit of resentment against his father for leaving them like he did, forcing him to grow up sooner than expected. But, on the other hand, he relished the latitudes of freedom that came with the additional responsibilities but also gave him freedoms his peers didn't have: lack of curfew, access to a car, and minimal parental oversight. But if it meant having his father back, Scot would have traded in the extra freedom in a heartbeat.

In the first few months after Declan's disappearance, Diane could no longer afford the mortgage on a house in the more affluent part of the city. They had had a fairly comfortable lifestyle but Declan had a lust for the finer things and liked to keep up appearances. He did have a mystique to cultivate; being an eccentric was rarely cheap. Despite the appearance of his prematurely graying hair, Declan was young enough and worked what he considered a low-enough-risk job that he had yet to consider life insurance.

Diane ended up having to sell their old Victorian and move with her two children into a modest house in the South Wedge. She put all of Declan's unsold sculptures and sketches in storage. The new dwelling was a house that a widowed mother working as a mid-level law clerk could afford, an eleven hundred square foot late nineteenth-century colonial. It was the kind of house that was rubber-stamped into the residential areas of cities during that era. It wasn't anything special but to Diane, it was home. She even grew to prefer this new house over the one Declan had insisted on when he had started to make what he considered to be decent money.

In the ten years subsequent to Declan's disappearance and due to the mystery surrounding it, the value of his pieces had increased. Their worth became further elevated when he was declared legally dead, so much so that they allowed Scot and his mother the ability to rent out a gallery after selling a few pieces through a broker. The gallery space featured some of Declan's sculptures and framed copies of his sketches. They sold, on average, four sculptures a year, bringing in enough money to cover the rent and eventually purchase the building outright.

The gallery also featured a space for a rotating selection of local artists which provided additional profit. Scot featured some work of his own as well. It was street art inspired but not the same style as his illicit nighttime activities and definitely nothing to do with a Green Man. The building also contained the flat where, ten years removed from his father's disappearance, Scot now resided.

***

The following day began the way most of Scot's Fridays did. He awoke at nine-thirty, which was quite the feat after his nighttime activities. He checked to see if David was still on the couch. He wasn't. He then took a shower, ran a comb through his long black hair, and trimmed down his wispy beard to a point just over what could be considered stubble. Scot hardly ever ate breakfast. This day was no exception. He started the kettle in anticipation of a morning cup of tea and by the time he had finished his first, he was ready to start his day.

The virtue of living above the gallery was that he had a short commute. Normally it opened at ten. This day however it was closer to ten-thirty. Owing to this erratic opening schedule it was rare they ever had a potential customer before eleven and today was no exception. The gallery didn't require much in the way of daily setup. After emptying the waste bin and straightening the business cards he took his seat behind the desk. He then opened his sketchbook and began to draw.

***

The front of the gallery featured an installation by the artist Maxine Gladwell, a neo-pop artist. The show being featured in 'The Murph' was called 'Hype' and consisted entirely of advertisements for itself. The works in the show were large acrylic paintings done in various advertising styles from the past hundred years. Among the pieces were ones in the style of World War I Art Deco, Broadway Playbills, and punk rock fliers. There was even one that looked like a page from an old Sears catalog advertising all of the other works in the show. The originals were used to produce prints which were posted on telephone poles and empty walls across the city. In time, the prints used as advertisements would be worth quite a bit of money on their own. They were all part of a numbered single run and most of them were lost to the weather. The opening for the show had occurred the previous weekend and was well received, with half of the paintings having already been sold.

The back of the gallery was divided into two sections, the larger of which featured Declan's work. Currently on display were a series of five tree-men he had produced in the year prior to his disappearance. The tree-men were essentially golems with the faces of human beings. The pieces were all carved from single pieces of wood harvested from deadfall. All of the figures were male in appearance, standing between five and six feet tall. Each of the tree-men featured giant beards reaching down to their chests, much the same as their creator. Their skin was chiseled to look like the bark of the wood that the figures were carved from. Behind each of the figures was a framed sketch of the tree-man in front of it. The pieces had originally lined a small ballroom in the Victorian that the Murphys used to live in. There were originally eight in the set but three of them had been sold as part of other shows.

The smaller of the two sections featured Scot's work. The works on display were part of a series that combined photography with acrylic renditions of street art. Scot would create these works by going out and taking photographs of nature which he would then have printed on canvas. The canvas would be stretched over a wooden frame and he would paint on top of it. The fan-favorite piece in this display was of a mighty white oak whose branches were painted over to look like the wavy arm men used to advertise car dealerships. Scot didn't understand what exactly it was about the wavy-armed man that was supposed to draw in customers.

The series Scot put up could have been seen as a juxtaposition between either Maxine's or his father's work but stood to complement them both as a whole and added cohesion to the gallery. The statement he was trying to make with the show was the fact that people's eyes weren't drawn to what he considered to be truly important. People were too distracted by upgrading their possessions to be newer, better, and faster when they could be beholding the wonder of the natural world, a world that was growing smaller due to the resource requirements of making said things newer, better, and faster. It was a spin on the themes of his father's work, which Scot had interpreted as trying to bring a bit of the natural world into urban environments. He called the show, 'Force Nature'.

Near the desk, there were a couple of racks containing prints of sketches and photographs of many of Declan's works along with prints of Scot's and Maxine's past and present works. Sales from these prints provided Scot with what he liked to call 'walking around money'.

***

Scot had a slow morning but things started to pick up early in the afternoon. Several characters in the local scene would make their rounds of the local galleries every week or so. Scot had given them the nickname 'the patrons'. There was Margo who styled herself after Edith Head if Edith Head had red hair and a little more meat on her bones. She affected an accent that Scot could never place. This was likely because the accent didn't actually exist. There was Gregor who liked to wear very colorful, very loud suits. He was known for his boisterousness at openings across the city. He was the kind of guy who knew a great deal about art and wanted you to know that he knew a great deal about art. Scot wasn't sure what Margo or Gregor did for a living. He suspected they were from old money but felt it impolite to ask. These were people that Declan had tolerated but silently judged, thinking that their personae were a tad pretentious and false. Perhaps they were holding up too big a mirror to the parts of his persona that were a put on.

There was also Martin, a fellow artist who worked primarily in oils. A devotee of Vermeer who was consumed with trying to replicate his methods. He was a student of tradition, dealing mostly with still life and landscapes. Martin came off as aloof to most; his deadpan sense of dry humor often left people confused. This always left him thoroughly amused. While being a decade and change his junior, he was one of Declan's true friends. One of the ones that 'got me' and 'got it' as he would say.

Scot revered these people, particularly Martin, whom he looked to as an almost surrogate father figure, someone who was truly looking out for him. The patrons had adopted him into the Rochester art scene after his father's disappearance and became valuable resources when he started to produce work of his own. Gregor and Martin were reliable providers of consultation when Scot was experimenting with methods and mediums. Margo provided instruction in navigating the local culture and provided introductions to many of the artists featured in his gallery. Having once owned a gallery herself, she was able to provide guidance in the proper pricing of pieces and management of the business end.

Their visits were generally social calls, preferring that their rare purchases be made in public at openings. The talk of the day was that of the Green Man which had popped up over the previous evening. Gossip travels fast in the scene.

The Green Men had started to appear two years prior and initially, they had assumed that Scot was creating them. Scot was always playfully evasive about them, insisting that he doesn't work in stencils and found them to be cheap and lacking substance. While being a position that Martin respected, it was also a lie but a good enough lie for them. Scot had never featured a stenciled piece of his own work in the gallery.

"Have you seen the new Mooch?" Margo opened. "It is simply…divine." The affectation on 'divine' was especially amusing to Scot today.

"Yeah, I checked it out this morning. I don't know, it seems like it's missing something," Scot replied.

"Are you sure it isn't your doing?" questioned Gregor. "The subject is so similar to yours and your father's."

"I think I would know if it was me. They say imitation is flattery but it's not even my style. Stencils seem so lazy," Scot replied, knowing full well they weren't. The skill with them is as much in the prep as the execution. One has to strike the correct balance of positive and negative space, with the latter being arguably more important. It works parts of the brain that many traditional mediums do not. At least in Scot's mind, it did.

Martin jumped in, "Scot's work typically has something to say. While well executed, what is this piece saying, Gregor? Scot's not one to live in his father's shadow like that."

"It says, 'Come to the Murphy gallery'," Gregor shot back. "But I'm only teasing. So, any new pieces my dear Scot? And are they speaking?"

Martin's last line cut Scot to the bone. Scot looked up to Martin in much the same way that Martin looked up to Declan when he was Scot's age. There was truth in what Martin had said, while he did enjoy painting the Green Men, Scot always felt a bit like a sham when anyone praised them or drew comparisons to his absent father.

Scot led the trio over to a piece he had installed earlier in the week. It was an addendum piece to his show, filling in a blank spot caused by a sale. The buyer insisted on breaking protocol and taking the piece with her before the end of the exhibition. Rather than replace it with an older piece, Scot opted to create a new one out of some unused photo canvases.

He had two forest scenes which he hadn't originally had a use for. The larger one contained a late spring forest where everything was a lush green. The smaller canvas contained the same forest only earlier in winter when all the leaves had fallen and the ground looked yellow and decayed. Scot had stretched the larger image over wood framing and the smaller one over a piece of plywood. The smaller piece was glued to the middle of the large canvas leaving a substantial border. He then painted in a large projection TV of the type that had been popular in the late nineties and early aughts to frame the smaller piece. Scot applied a tinted lacquer to the screen section of the painting to give it a dark mirror-like finish, reminiscent of a powered-off TV. Around the base of the TV he had painted in an old tire and the bottom part of a discarded toilet.

The patrons were complimentary of his new work. Scot was never sure if they were being genuine or not. In the end, he decided it didn't really matter and he should just accept the compliments at face. With that, the group bid him a collective adieu and went about their day. Despite some of his father's opinions, Scot had thought them all to be good people.

There was one thing Gregor was right about. One of the reasons Scot performed his midnight escapades was that it did actually bring in extra foot traffic to the gallery. There was a small local legend that had started when the Green Men began popping up that Declan was alive and was letting people know he was still there.

***

Not all foot traffic was welcome, however. A little over an hour after Scot's patrons left, one of Rochester's 'finest' walked through the door. Officer Dobry was a frequent visitor to the gallery over the last two years, starting when Scot's Mooch persona had begun to put up the Green Men. Dobry was wrongly convinced that solving the 'vandalism' issue would put him on the detective track. Nobody downtown cared about the Green Men. If anything they were appreciative that it wasn't the normal phalli and racial slurs that traditionally adorned the overpasses and walls around town. It was more of a harassment campaign against, who Dobry deemed, the only logical suspect.

The visit went as most visits did. Dobry performed a round of the gallery and took a few seconds at each piece. He then proceeded to low-key insult the works in the gallery while also trying to display what little art knowledge he had.

Dobry stopped at one of Maxine's pieces, "This is pretty good but I think Warhol did it better."

"Which do you prefer, the 'Ads Portfolio' or the 'Campbell's Soup Cans?'" Scot replied with disdain, knowing that Dobry's only exposure had probably been the cans.

Dobry took a moment to consider and was opening his mouth to reply when Scot cut him off, "So what are you trying to accuse me of today?" Scot used to be afraid of cops but over the years he had started to approach the conversations contemptuously, a trait he had learned from his mother.

"I'm not here to accuse you of anything," Dobry said defensively. "I just know you have connections in the art scene and was wondering if you had seen the new tag by Mooch."

"Who the hell is Mooch and why should I give a shit about some dickhead signing their name somewhere?" Scot asked, slyly calling out Dobry's misuse of the word 'tag' to describe the Green Man. "Or do you mean the guy that is trying to get some clout by aping my father's style? There are so many up-and-coming artists out there. I can't keep them all straight."

Dobry knew he wasn't going to get anywhere. Like the patrons, he was also putting in his weekly rounds. "You still have my card right? Please give me a call if you hear anything, yeah."

"Roger Roger," Scot replied mockingly. With that, Dobry was on his way.

***

After work, Diane brought Scot's sister by the gallery. Always the thoughtful mother, she had picked up a pizza on her way. Marnie headed up to the loft to get her project unpacked and Diane stayed behind to have a quick word with her son.

"I saw your handiwork on the side of the 7-Eleven," she said. "I really wish you would stop doing that. I don't want you ending up like your father."

"I don't know what you're talking about," Scot replied.

"Don't bullshit me," Diane said. "Your father couldn't lie to me and you got your graces from him." The tone she used was one of concern.

"The patrons and Dobry seemed to buy it," Scot responded.

21

"Those coots just want a good story. And Dobry...Dobry couldn't investigate his way out of a wet paper bag. Do you know how many cases we get from him that I would be better off running through the shredder than trying to prosecute?"

In the years between Declan's disappearance and Scot's ascension in the scene, Diane had experienced her own rise. She had worked her way from law clerk to becoming the assistant district attorney for Monroe County.

"Stop worrying," Scot replied. "I'm careful. I have a lookout."

"Your father thought he was careful...and look where that got him," Diane rebutted. "And why...why do you have to get David involved? He is such a sweet boy."

"If I thought there was any risk, I wouldn't do it," Scot replied. "Besides, it's the best advertising the gallery's had in years."

Diane considered Scot's words, then sighed heavily, "Well can you at least think of me and my work? Do you know how many cases cross my desk when one of your pieces grabs some eyeballs? There are a lot of copycats in the city."

"I thought the DA's office didn't prosecute graffiti," said Scot.

"We don't. But we do have to at least attempt to prosecute the cops who get a little too rough with the artists," Dianne replied. "Not everyone is as 'careful' as you."

"Okay, okay. I'll tone it down for a while," Scot evaded, knowing that he still needed to finish the piece that had become the latest focus of his mother's ire.

"And Scot...promise me that you won't get your sister involved," his mother implored, a tone of concern shading her words once more.

"I wouldn't dream of it Mom," Scot responded.

Scot locked the front door to the gallery, put up the 'Closed' sign, and headed upstairs to family dinner with his mother and sister.

***

Scot, Diane, and Marnie situated themselves around Scot's table. It was a long counter-height table made of reclaimed butcher block and a couple of old wine barrels. Its primary function was as a work table, which was more than apparent upon observing the countless razor cuts and paint splatters from Scot's past creations. The table could be mistaken as a piece of art in its own right but tonight as with most Friday nights it served as a dining room table for his family's pizza night.

"Have you seen the new Mooch piece?" Marnie opened. "It looks incredible. I can't wait to get a closer look."

"I don't know," replied Scot. "Seems like it's missing something."

Diane's eyes shot daggers toward Scot. Already anticipating the glare, his smile had widened to a Cheshire grin. Marnie wasn't aware of the progenitor of the works and Diane wasn't keen on her finding out.

"I agree with Marnie. It seems perfectly fine the way it is. Seems a shame the city will be going through and buffing it next week." Diane's veiled threat landed exactly as she wanted.

The smile crept off of Scot's face. He knew it was well within her power to have someone from the city go through and cover it up.

"What do you mean, missing something?" Marnie chimed in. With Scot being a professional artist, she always tried to glean some perspective to better her art.

"Well dear sister," Scot started, "If you look at it, it is technically a very good piece. Well executed depth, nice use of a limited palette, but lacking flourish." It was this level of self-criticism which, Scot believed, gave him an edge.

"What do you mean by that?" asked Marnie.

Scot echoed the thoughts he had had the previous evening, "There is nothing to make it pop. The people that see it are looking for it because they are trained to look for it. There is nothing about it right now to truly draw the eye of the casual viewer. Right now it just blends into the building."

"So what are you guys working on tonight?" Diane jumped in, hoping to change the subject.

"Nothing special," Marnie said with a tone of self-doubt. "It's just a character design project for Ms. Roberts's class."

Knowingly taking his mother's bait, Scot continued to steer the conversation in the new direction, "Not special?" Scot pushed back. "That's only because you haven't come up with a good idea yet. That's what tonight is for. That's the best part. We are going to eat sugar and watch scary movies until the witching hour. That's when the good ideas happen. Then we can work tomorrow to get this thing knocked out."

Diane started to roll her eyes. Talk of the witching hour was a line of reason she had heard from Declan for many years and something Scot had started to echo when his star started to rise. She never shared this with Scot and was fairly sure Scot had never heard Declan mention it. While she may have made rolling her eyes into a performance, she found it to be a pleasant bit of serendipity, giving her a warm reminder of her lost husband.

"I think it's about time I make my leave," Diane said as she stood up. She readied herself, made her goodbyes, and headed home. As much as she worried about Scot and his nighttime activities, she was much more grateful that he stepped up to fill his father's shoes for Marnie.

***

Marnie, at fourteen years of age, selected 'Alien' for the movie they would be watching. The movie was one of Scot's favorites. To him, the plot was rivaled only by H.R. Giger's creature and ship designs. While unsettling, there was a sleekness and cohesion between organic and mechanical components which he found captivating. For Scot, it also begged the question, "Which string of the collective unconscious was Giger pulling when his creations were birthed into this world?"

Marnie had never seen the movie and was getting slightly annoyed. Her brother made it a point to pause the movie to explain one detail or another every time something 'cool' came into frame.

"Can we just watch the movie?" she begged. "You're ruining the magic."

"Fine...ignore your education," Scot replied. "I don't share these morsels with just anyone you know."

"Sure you do. You are insufferable with them," David shouted across the room as he entered the loft. His presence wasn't entirely unexpected. He was a frequent visitor to the loft on his way back from work and was always ready for a movie night.

Marnie jumped up and ran across the room to give David a welcome hug. She had known David so long he was basically a second brother to her. She also used the moment of movie disruption to excuse herself to the bathroom.

***

Scot's bathroom wasn't anything special. It had a standard toilet, a pedestal sink, and a clawfoot tub. The walls contained prints from some of the gallery's old shows. On the edge of the sink, Scot had inadvertently left one of his planning sketchbooks. He hadn't given himself time to tidy up and had completely forgotten about it. Marnie promptly knocked the book on the floor as she entered.

As she bent over to pick it up, she noticed that it had opened to the layouts for stencil and color tests of a Green Man; one which had popped up three months prior under an overpass on the inner loop. Marnie had a bit of an epiphanous moment. Scot was indeed the artist Mooch. She immediately felt stupid for not putting the pieces together sooner.

Marnie spent the next five minutes skimming through and studying each page. It contained the last year of work by Mooch, including a few pieces she hadn't seen before. The most recent entry was that of the Green Man which had been discussed earlier in the evening.

***

Standing in the dining area, David informed Scot that he had to pick up a closing shift at the bar where he worked, making him unable to be lookout as planned the following night. "Sorry man, it looks like providence has divined that the piece is finished."

"Something keeps nagging me, saying it isn't," replied Scot. "We'll have to do it later tonight after she goes to sleep. It will take me ten minutes. She'll never even know we were gone."

At this point, Marnie had quietly snuck out of the bathroom, sketchbook in hand. "When were you going to tell me about this and what are you going to do when I fall asleep?" she demanded, throwing the sketchbook across the table without considering that David may not know about Scot's alter ego. "You're going to finish it aren't you?"

"Oh shit," fell out of David's mouth in a tone that gave an unneeded confirmation that Scot's secret was out. His right hand jumped up to cover the orifice in an effort to prevent more words from spilling out, further betraying his friend. He had, at that moment, become a spectator.

"You have to take me with you!" Marnie begged, almost shouting. "I'll tell Mom."

"One, Mom already knows and two, she made me swear to never get you involved," Scot replied. "So the answer is no...And as it stands, I've just decided to leave the piece as is."

"But," Marnie started.

"I'll have no further discussion of it," Scot said sharply. "Let's just finish the movie."

"Fine," she huffed.

Scot, Marnie, and David finished watching 'Alien' and jumped right into 'Aliens'. By the end of the sequel, Marnie had come up with the idea of a robot wearing an organic mech suit. It was a twist on Ripley wearing the power loader in 'Aliens', an idea that Marnie thought was a little hack but decided to go along with at Scot's urging. It didn't help that she was also in the middle of tackling a new project. She knew her brother well enough to know he couldn't let a sleeping dog lay. Marnie retired to the guest room having already built the framework of a plan to join her brother when he inevitably decided to complete his work.

***

"So...I guess I'll head out," David said. He had thought there was no way they were going to go and finish the Green Man after the evening's revelations.

"No...I'm still planning on finishing the piece," Scot replied. "This may be the last chance I get before it gets buffed. I don't know what it is but this piece needs to be completed. It will drive me nuts if it isn't."

"Fine, I'll take you...but ten minutes and we're gone," David replied.

"Ten minutes and we're gone."

Scot waited thirty minutes before checking the guest room to make sure Marnie was sleeping and they headed out.

***

"Ten minutes and we're gone," Marnie heard at the door.

On the futon in Scot's guest room, Marnie had laid out a close approximation of what she would look like in a side-sleeping fetal position. She was able to use the clothes she packed and the extra blankets stored in the guest room closet. She was careful to keep quiet but every creek of a floorboard or squeak of a hinge gave her pause.

One stroke of luck she had was that the closet was also where Scot kept his old costumes from Halloween and the various theme parties the art community invited him to every year. Marnie was able to find a long brunette wig which wasn't quite a match for her shoulder-length auburn hair but it did bear a close enough resemblance that it would do for a quick look.

She placed the wig on her pillow and stuffed it with a bit of extra sheet and blanket. She then stood back and admired her handiwork. The ruse would do for a passing glance but would quickly fall apart on closer inspection.

Satisfied, she slid open the window to the fire escape and crawled out onto it, gently closing the window behind her. She sat waiting until she could see the reflection of light peeking through the guest room door. She had smartly anticipated that Scot would want to check on her before heading out.

Once the light blinked out, she moved over to the fire escape's sliding ladder and allowed the force of her weight to carry her down to street level. She had considered how she was going to get back inside and decided she would reveal herself when Scot was almost done with his work. 'Better to ask forgiveness' was a phrase she had often heard come out of his mouth. She reasoned that he wasn't likely to do anything too severe after making such a fuss about their mother not wanting him to get her involved.

She then made her way over to David's truck and crawled into the back, assuming they were going to use it for transportation. Scot always kept his car in the garage and he wouldn't want to risk waking her up with the opening of the door. His car was also a very garish lime green, the conspicuousness of which, wasn't something he had considered when picking it out five years prior.

***

David reluctantly drove Scot the ten minutes to the site of their previous night's work, just off Monroe Avenue. He would have put his foot down in an attempt to make Scot reconsider but knew his friend would have found a way to finish the piece anyway. He would have also been much more reckless about it.

David parked the truck a short way up the road, making sure it was still in sight of the Green Man. He knew with it being a Friday, there would be much more traffic than the previous night. The potential need for a quick exit was foremost on his mind.

Scot walked briskly to the painting and pulled the silver can he brought with him out of his bag. He started to vigorously shake it as he studied the art, figuring out how to accent the piece. There was a single nearby street lamp off to the left. He decided to treat the lamp as a lunar light source and began to add accents on the upper left-side borders of the piece. He then worked inward, accenting random leaf edges to give the appearance that not all edges were facing the same direction. This gave the piece the flourish that Scot had previously felt was missing. At this point, he moved onto the eyes. He sprayed small circular shapes into the upper left corners to make them look like they possessed a reflected moonglow.

"I really see what you mean about the accents," David said as he and Scot took a step back to admire the piece. "I may have been wrong about the completeness of the piece."

"Yeah, it's exactly as I had imagined," Scot replied. "I can be happy with this."

"I meant it before but as I stare at it, it's almost as if it is staring back at me...Into me," David said as his captivation remained steadfast.

"A real student of Nietzsche," quipped Scot, knowing David would be unaware of the provenance surrounding the words he had uttered.

***

It was at this point that Marnie was readying to make her presence known. Her heart was racing, already anticipating her brother's reaction.

Just as she had worked up the nerve to pop out from under the tarp she had used to secret herself, there was a high-pitched shriek accompanied by red and blue strobing lights. She was frozen in fear. All she could do was silently watch what transpired next.

"Rochester Police. Put your hands in the air," a voice commanded. Seconds later a flood light came on, spotlighting Scot and David.

An overzealous officer Dobry stepped out of his patrol car. "Murphy, is that you? I knew it," he crowed. "I knew you were no good. The 'great Mooch' at last." He acted as if he had just solved the crime of the century.

"Dobry, is that you?" Scot asked as he held up his hand to block the bombardment of light. He then taunted, "Did you get relegated to third shift sometime in the last twelve hours?" Scot knew that he may get arrested but it could only be good for business. He did regret the fact that his alias had been burned but figured the added notoriety would likely be worth it.

David nudged Scot with his foot, silently trying to say, "Keep your mouth shut, you're going to make this worse."

"Seriously…You must be the lowest man on the totem pole to have to work a double like this," Scot continued. He knew with his mother's occupation being what it was, Dobry wouldn't be stupid enough to get rough with him. In the midst of his adrenal rush, he hadn't yet had a chance to consider how his arrest may affect her career or even the future of the friend standing next to him. David didn't have the benefit of having a mother in the D.A.'s office.

"Overtime's worth it to bust your ass," Dobry retorted, almost as if he were delivering a hack line in a late-night TV procedural. "Now get up against the wall with your hands above your heads."

Scot and David moved back toward the wall, placing themselves in front of the now-completed Green Man. They put their hands up against the brick as instructed. Their hands became covered in fresh silver paint as they waited for Dobry to approach them. It was at this point that something unexpected occurred. As the pair were leaning against the wall, they could feel vibrations, almost as if the nearby street was being jackhammered. The vibrations were accompanied by a sound that could have easily been mistaken for Mongolian throat singing. David could have sworn the sound was emanating from the Green Man.

"Knock that off," Dobry barked, thinking that Scot was trying to further antagonize him. The noise kept getting louder as it continued its legato-like undulations, eventually reaching a level that caused nearby car alarms to go off. It was at this moment that Dobry pulled out his service pistol, aiming it toward Scot and David. "I said stop that!" The sound continued to grow louder as the vibrations spread to under Dobry's feet.

Then suddenly, the mouth of the Green Man fell agape, and as it did all sound and vibration ceased. The ambient sounds of nearby traffic and crickets had fallen away as well, leaving only the sound of the three men's racing heartbeats to soundtrack the events that followed.

Leafy tendrils constructed from a raw unfeeling darkness began to reach out from the Green Man's mouth in fluid-like motions. Black droplets that reflected no light could be seen raining down from the vine-like appendages. As the drops hit the pavement below, they dissolved into nothingness.

Scot and David tried to swat away these new intruders but their efforts proved to be in vain. The tendrils continued to grow and reach out for them before eventually making contact. The vines weaved their way through the young men's legs and around their arms and torsos with surgical precision, entwining them further and further with each calculated movement. It wasn't long before the pair were completely enveloped. They tried to fight back but each movement in resistance only served to tighten their bonds.

Dobry watched in horror as the pair gradually disappeared, being cocooned before his eyes. He continued to stare, paralyzed in fear, as the mass of vines that encased the young men raised itself off the ground and rested in the air for a few moments. Then with fluid movement, the pair was pulled into the wall.

A haunting silence was left in their wake, one that was quickly filled as the cop fired off five echoless shots. His bullets didn't have the desired effect as new tendrils had started to reach for him. He turned in an attempt to flee and stumbled before falling to the ground, smashing his knee. Dobry tried to ignore the shooting pain as he crawled his way back up to his feet and started to limp away, desperately trying to escape an unknown fate.

The vines stalked him until he crossed the boundary of the vibration beneath his feet. Then just as suddenly as the event began, it was over. The tendrils snapped back into the painting with a singular violent motion. When Dobry turned around, all that was left was the painting and a couple of cans of silver spray paint. He staggered to his cruiser and fled the scene, knowing anything he reported would make him sound insane.

Marnie was left in the back of David's truck, looking on in horror. She would never be the same.

Chapter Two

"Do not go gentle..."

"What I wouldn't give to see some new art in this city," said Marnie.

"Yeah, the scene really dried up after Scot's disappearance," replied Martin, momentarily forgetting who he was talking to. "Oh I'm sorry dear, I didn't mean to bring it up again. I know it has to be painful."

"It's okay, that was a long time ago," Marnie responded.

"There are some wounds time can never heal," Martin said. "You know you always have my ear if you need it."

"I've done enough talking about it. I'm supposed to be moving past it...I finally feel like I might be," Marnie said, calling on the lessons from her last five years of therapy. "More than I can say for my mother."

"She's lost a lot and so have you. First your father and then Scot. It can't be easy," Martin said.

"Yeah but you don't see me taking it out on the entire art community," Marnie shot back. She was young enough when her father disappeared that she only had a few memories of him, which she attributed to the progress she had made over her mother.

In the interval between Scot's disappearance and the present, Diane had become elected District Attorney for Monroe County. She had made it her mission to 'clean up the city' by choosing to prosecute more graffiti crimes. Graffiti had previously not been much of a concern, only being seen as a problem when there was a hate crime involved or someone was caught in the act of defacing public property. Before, it was just an appearance ticket and a small fine, if the property owner even wanted to pursue it. With Diane's intervention, the county started pushing for jail time. They only needed to make a few examples of artists and writers to effectively wipe out the culture.

"I hardly think that's fair," replied Martin. "While I don't agree with what your mother has done to the writers, she didn't wipe out the entire scene."

"Then how do you explain what's happening?" Marnie replied. "I mean, when was the last time you created a new piece or attended a local's show? Hell, it's been two years since the gallery's hosted anything from Toronto...Even New York is starting to dry up."

"Your mother asked me to take over the gallery after what happened. It doesn't exactly leave a lot of room for new art," Martin said, attempting to defend himself.

"Scot made it work," Marnie shot back, "and he was two artists."

"Do you want to twist the knife a little more or are you good?" asked Martin. He knew Marnie was right. There had still been plenty of time to create but in the last two years whenever he had a chance to put brush to canvas, he couldn't make it work. There was no cohesion between his mind and his tools. He even tried shifting into abstract but still came up empty. He found he was perfectly capable of copying his old works and was able to create rough approximations of other artist's work but that was about it. Novelty was the driving force of art and his ability to tap into it had dried up. This was the first time Martin had considered that the block might not just be him.

"Hey, I didn't imply it was just you. Look around. Art is dying a slow death," replied Marnie.

"Then how do you explain cIris?" Martin countered. "She still seems to be doing some pretty heavy stuff."

cIris was the city's last remaining street artist still possessing a level of clout. She specialized in the ridicule of 'big brother'. Most of her works featured a camera with a human eye as the lens. Sometimes it was a surveillance camera, sometimes it was a camera on a cell phone, and other times it was a tourist holding a DSLR. Many in the art community speculated it was apropos of the city being the home to Kodak. The main statement, however, was that someone is always watching. cIris also happened to be Marnie, a fact of which Martin was acutely aware.

"How do you know cIris is a she?" asked Marnie, realizing at that moment that Martin may be on to her and was finally showing his hand.

"The same way I knew your brother was Mooch. You Murphys think you are so very clever," replied Martin, his vocalization lingering an extra half a beat on the word 'so.' "Oh, 'I'm going to do street art using the same conceits as my father and nobody is ever going to notice because my 'legitimate' art uses different mediums and subjects.' Scot may have fooled the plebs but not the artists, especially the ones who knew him. He was able to pull the wool over Margo and Gregor's eyes but like I said...plebs."

Martin continued, "You...you were a bit trickier, I'll give you that. But here's the thing, at this point, I've known you literally your entire life. Your art has its own signature and I don't mean the one you sign. Whether it's a brush stroke or a spray stroke, you always flourish in the same ways. You move across canvas and wall with the same movements. Always drawing and pushing focus in the same directions. Elegant really, but unmistakably you." Martin truly had an appreciation for Marnie's talent in telling entire stories with a single piece. It wasn't a skill he was able to fully master and here she was, this barely adult, doing it unconsciously.

Marnie stared at Martin in disbelief.

"Don't worry it's not just you, your brother was the same way. My art has a signature or did rather. Hell, most if not all artists have one...but most of us aren't trying to hide our identities. But I digress," he said with a pause. "So what is it about you? Where do your ideas come from that my mind has not been able to reach?"

Marnie pondered the question for a moment, then drew back, "My art is mostly shit. It's easy to come up with ideas when everything you do is built from bad ideas and retreads."

"Hey!" Martin said sharply. "What's the rule in here?"

"It's okay to self-criticize, it's not okay to self-deprecate. Sometimes it's the bad ideas that inspire the great ones," Marnie replied with a tone indicative of countless recitations.

"It's not healthy," he replied. This wasn't the first time Martin had to remand Marnie for putting herself down. He normally had a full speech that went along with 'Martin's maxim' but figured he would spare Marnie that particular ear beating for the day. He was much more intrigued by the larger conversation they were having.

Martin continued, "...and now that we have established that fact for the I don't know how many-ith time, you have not presented an adequate answer. Please do try again. Why do you think you get away unscathed from this societal dearth of creativity?"

Marnie knew Martin was correct. Self-doubt and deprecation have been major issues in her life and were things she had been working on. Her therapist had slowly been coming to the conclusion that the likely cause was a minor inferiority complex, caused in part by Marnie feeling like she was walking in the shadows of her successful father and brother. It was a complex made worse by her mother's attempts to push Marnie away from art, whether she was consciously aware she was doing it or not.

"I'm not really sure," she replied. This was, as far as Marnie knew, an honest answer. She had found herself to be living in a city that was becoming a creative black hole and for some reason, she was a ray of light escaping the event horizon.

The abstruse conversation continued for a little over an hour. In the end, there was no consensus on whether Marnie's view on what she dubbed the 'Dying of the Art' was true and if it was, what the source of the issue could be.

It had occurred to Marnie during the conversation that the issue she had brought up may not be limited only to art but anything else requiring novelty or creativity. She racked her brain but was unable to think of any recent innovations or scientific achievements attributable to the city in the last few years.

Martin hadn't been able to either but he countered that the city hadn't really innovated anything of importance since the death of George Eastman. It was a point he knew would cause him trouble in many of the social circles he was a member of.

One thing they were certain of was that a world without creativity wasn't a world they wanted to live in.

***

It had been five years since Scot and David's disappearance. Five years since Marnie walked her way back to the loft, crawled into bed, and tried to wake up from the nightmare. She had never once discussed the circumstances surrounding Scot and David's disappearance, even with her therapist and especially not with her mother.

She had overheard a conversation at her mother's office a few months after they vanished concerning the fate of Officer Dobry. He had committed himself to the city psych center where he was incorrectly diagnosed with schizophrenia. This wasn't a fate Marnie wanted for herself.

Unbeknownst to Marnie, Dobry ended up being discharged after a month but moved away. Rumors surrounding the circumstances of his absence started to circulate his station and nobody wanted to work with someone prone to mental issues; he might be contagious. Dobry had never filed a report on Scot and David and they had remained flagged as missing persons in the years since their disappearance.

Marnie's mother, Diane, had used her previous role as assistant district attorney to put pressure on the cops to locate her son, a move which proved fruitless. Rather than actually start grieving the loss, she ended up dealing with the trauma of her second major loss by further burying herself in her work. Grieving, she thought, was only saying goodbye; that would mean Scot was truly gone.

Diane had amassed a prosecutorial record that was easily exploited to win her the election for the position she currently holds. Not having the time to maintain the gallery and knowing it would be too painful to shut down what had become a living shrine to the two men she had loved most in the world, she enlisted Martin to run it in Scot's stead. Diane rightly figured he was the more level-headed of the 'patrons' and wouldn't do anything too garish with it.

Contrary to what Marnie believed, her mother didn't have a vendetta against the entire art community. She was, however, lashing out at street art, believing it had some semblance of blame in her son's disappearance. Diane had reasoned that, with her crackdown, she may be saving another mother from experiencing the same gnawing grief she had, a grief that may never be sated. Perhaps it would be if she knew what fate had befallen both her husband and son but that was appearing more and more unlikely with each passing year.

Marnie had been working with Martin at the gallery for the past eleven months to earn her own 'walking around money'. She was also attending the nearby University of Rochester.

Diane knew that art ran in Marnie's blood, just as it had with Scot and Declan. And while she didn't wholeheartedly approve of Marnie's selection of an art history degree, she was satisfied that she couldn't get into too much trouble 'studying the masters'. With everything that had happened to them both, Diane just wanted Marnie to experience some semblance of happiness and if art was where she found it, so be it.

***

Marnie and Martin continued to have various versions of the Dying of the Art conversation in the weeks that followed. Other members of the art community joined in. Many of them were doing retreads of their old concepts or working off old test sketches that had previously gone unused. They all agreed that something bad was happening. Novelty was being bled dry and they were just nibbling at scraps, trying to suck out the last bits of marrow from the bones of their past ideas.

When the Green Men started to reappear on the streets almost no one in the larger art community took notice, and if they did, didn't think much of them. The artists were in a weird position. No one was outright stealing but a lot of people were aping the styles and concepts of others. In contrast, Marnie, along with some of the street artists who were bombing at the same time as Scot, was especially aggrieved and had taken great umbrage with her brother's work being reinterpreted.

In the wake of his disappearance, after Scot was revealed to be Mooch, it had become an unwritten rule that the Green Men were off-limits. A rule that may have become lost in the two years following Diane's crippling of the graffiti scene. Someone was now breaking this rule.

Reverence for Scot's work had been such, that efforts were made to preserve his two remaining pieces: the 'Birch Man' and the 'Maple Man'. The 'Oak Man' from the night of the disappearance was buffed almost before anyone knew Scot was missing. There were a couple of pictures posted in an online graffiti blog but none of them were of the finished piece.

***

Marnie had made it her mission to track down the perpetrator of this theft. She would, however, have first to convince her mother that she wasn't the artist behind the pieces. The focus of conversation for Friday night dinner had shifted to this topic.

"So, I'm guessing you've heard about the artwork near where Scot's last painting was...and the one before that?" Diane asked.

"Yeah, I've seen it. Looks fairly amateur," a fact that Marnie wasn't lying about. While not much worse than what she herself could do, Marnie had quickly assessed that it didn't rise to the level of what Scot was capable of. "The colors are all off," she added.

"You wouldn't happen to be the one doing these would you?" Diane pressed further, thinking she had detected a slight bit of evasiveness akin to the type Scot used to deploy when trying to deny his activities as Mooch.

"How can you ask me that?" Marnie replied with mock offense. "I promised I would never walk in his shoes." Marnie's true skill was now peaking out, using the small amount of anger her mother's question begged to help sell the passive lie contained in her active truth. This level of evasiveness was something Scot was never very good at and was why Diane had picked up on his alter ego and not Marnie's.

"I'm sorry. A mother can be concerned for her daughter's safety you know," Diane countered. "I just wanted to be sure."

Marnie, looking to avoid a conversation that risked betraying her true intentions, opted to end the line of questioning by responding with a simple, "It's okay, I get it."

That seemed to satisfy Diane as she once more shifted the conversation. "So I've been thinking about what we talked about last week. About you moving into Scot's old place. Are you sure it wouldn't be too weird for you?"

"Probably a little at first but I can always come home if it feels a bit much...right?" Marnie did indeed have reservations about moving into Scot's old loft. It was a place she hadn't stepped foot into since the night of the disappearance. For that matter Diane hadn't either, save to grab the business files and some information needed to access and close Scot's accounts, a task the lawyer side of her brain wouldn't allow to go uncompleted.

Martin had been the one to make himself responsible for going in and straightening things up. A few weeks after the cops had concluded their initial investigation, he spent a day putting things in order. He performed Scot's last load of laundry and emptied Scot's fridge, throwing away the science experiments that had started to grow. He kept the few beers that were in there for himself. He also performed probably his most considerate act. He checked around for any lewd or lascivious items that Diane or Marnie might find unsavory. He had been shocked to not find so much as a magazine to clutch a pearl at, wondering what was wrong with young artists these days.

It had been five years and save for a few of Martin's lunchtime naps or his occasional need for a nostalgia trip, the place remained untouched.

"Of course, you can," Diane responded. "Can you wait a week and I can see if I can get Martin or someone else to pack up Scot's stuff and take it to the storage building."

"Thanks Mom," Marnie replied excitedly. She was finally going to experience the freedom of living on her own, even if there was a little trepidation about how it was going to be in Scot's old place. There was a small feeling that she might be stepping into his tomb.

The dinner conversation lingered a while longer. There was talk of Marnie's classes and some interesting cases that had passed Diane's desk. At eleven o'clock they both turned in for the evening. Marnie laid awake for a few hours plotting how she was going to trap and unmask the impostor breaking the unwritten rule surrounding Scot's work.

Chapter Three
"...sincerest form of flattery..."

Marnie woke up late in the morning and as she had done every morning since the reemergence of the Green Men, checked the city art blogs. She had a hunch and that hunch hadn't been betrayed. The 'Fern Man' had been recreated on the side of the parks department building near Highland Park.

The fake Mooch started by attempting to recreate the 'Oak Man' from the night of Scot's disappearance. The 'Moss Man' was recreated a few days later. The 'Birch Man' and 'Maple Man', Marnie reasoned, still existed, so the impostor would likely not attempt them. This meant that if one went backward in Mooch's chronology they would be led to the 'Fern Man' and there it was recreated in its original location.

If Marnie was right, that meant the next work was going to be the 'Ivy Woman'. The piece was one of the few that was actually commissioned or at least in Scot's eyes it had been. A business owner had commented in support of Mooch after the 'Democrat and Chronicle' posted an op-ed decrying street art on their social media.

In defiance of the editorial and because Scot wanted to see if the owner truly meant it, he worked up what many referred to as their favorite piece in the series; which, as far as anyone knew, also happened to be the first in the series. Scot had recognized the name of the commenter as a restaurateur who owned a spot he liked to frequent. It was on South Clinton just on the border of the Wedge, not too far from his mother's house.

The old brick building had a lot of vertical space to work with, making it the perfect canvas. Scot always loved the looks of buildings that were covered in climbing vines and thought this one could use a few of its own. His work had often focused on mankind's intrusion into natural spaces and he liked the idea of nature taking a bit back. With this rationale, the 'Ivy Woman' was born.

The piece was Scot's most documented and aside from the currently protected pieces, the one with the longest run time. It was eight months before a young up-and-comer bombed over it in an attempt to gain some clout. Sk1zm had a habit of stepping on the wrong toes, making his tenure in the Rochester street scene short-lived.

Scot didn't mind when this kind of thing happened. To him, his nighttime art was meant to be ephemeral, to be savored while being executed and talked about with an air of mournful nostalgia when it was gone. This was an outlook that Marnie hadn't quite embraced. The losses in her life had caused her to hold on tightly where she could. If only Scot were around to protest, she may have loosened her grip. In her heart, she knew that he would have been disappointed about his works being preserved but she lacked the same hope for future wistfulness.

***

The works that had already been recreated were being reproduced at a rate of one every two to three days. Marnie posited she would be safe if she had skipped her stake out of the spot that evening but didn't want to risk it.

She went to scout the area near the wall before heading to her shift at the gallery and found an arcade bar across the street. The bar had a basement entryway which would serve well to hide her as she stalked her prey.

Marnie reasoned that on a Saturday night, the street would be busy until at least two thirty. A smart writer wouldn't start until after three and a smarter writer would wait until Sunday when the bars and restaurants closed earlier and there was much less activity. Marnie didn't have a grasp on the brazenness of the impostor yet. All she could do was set her trap and wait.

***

Work at the gallery dragged on. Visitation had picked up in the wake of the reemergent Green Men but Marnie's concern was focused more on the exposition of the perpetrator than the exposition of the works on the walls.

Martin stopped by at one point to check on her even though it was his day off. She had been on edge since the Green Men started coming back and he wanted to make sure she was alright. They briefly discussed the 'Fern Man' piece and Marnie's newfound freedom regarding her loft move. He let her know that he would have Scot's stuff removed by the end of the week.

Marnie closed the gallery at six on the dot, rushing the last visitor out of the door. She had a standing game night with some friends from college. The activity had started as a studio group that would get together to work on new art. The group floundered as Marnie soon became annoyed that she was acting as a muse for a group that couldn't readily produce their own ideas; the execution of which often ended up being derivative anyway, even when using the most novel of what was provided.

After a few studio sessions, she pushed the group toward a game night, an activity she thought would take away some of the social pressures and malaise she felt during the previous activity. For her, the change had the desired effect but may have removed too much pressure from the others. The group started with eight but quickly dwindled to just four regulars. In the end, she may have been better off without anyone showing up. When they would play everyone but Marnie would be checked out, scrolling through their phones between moves.

She continued to go at the advice of her therapist. In the wake of Scot's disappearance, Marnie had adopted withdrawing as a coping mechanism, and social activities were supposed to help draw her out. She could feel alone in a room full of people and despite her best efforts, game night had become no different.

***

The meetup lasted until eleven and afterward, she headed back to her mother's house, the same place they had lived in since Declan's disappearance. The South Wedge had experienced a renaissance in the interval between then and now and had become a trendy place to be. Diane saw no reason to move again, even with her greatly increased salary.

Marnie tried to get in a couple of hours of sleep before commencing her stake-out but found her mind to be much too active. Her thoughts were consumed with running through every possible scenario. She didn't yet know how she was going to confront the fraud if they happened to show.

Unfortunately for Marnie, she wouldn't get the chance to find out. She arrived at her spot a little before two thirty as planned, however, there was a large police presence. There had been an armed confrontation at one of the local establishments and the police were trying to track down a potential suspect. The spot was burned for the evening.

Marnie headed home, crawled into bed, and drifted off to sleep, hoping the impostor had the good sense to stay away too.

***

Sunday, for the most part, was uneventful. Marnie rolled out of bed at eleven and immediately checked the blogs. There was no sign of the false Mooch. She had a quick lunch, a conversation with her mother about the move, and sketched in her planning book for a few hours.

Come evening, she had dinner with her mother and Martin. Diane and Martin took turns telling stories about Declan and the odd manner in which he acted at social events, including one about how he had refused to talk in anything but rhetorical questions at one of his openings. They also squared away the final details of the move and the logistics behind the storage of Scot's old stuff.

After Martin left, Diane and Marnie enjoyed a movie. Diane hadn't noticed how distracted Marnie was during the activity, the latter being consumed with thoughts of how the interaction might play out if tonight was the night the impostor decided to show.

At eleven Marnie headed up to bed. She changed into the dark clothes she always wore while out laying down her own work. At midnight she snuck out of the house as she had done a hundred times before. She then headed to the basement stairwell of her chosen hide.

Marnie waited the better part of three hours for the impostor to arrive. There was a brief moment when she had become nervous at a homeless man heading her way. She had neglected to consider that she may be standing in what was normally someone's nighttime home. Luckily for her, he passed by and headed around a corner, avoiding a possible confrontation.

It had been forty more minutes before something more interesting started to happen. Marnie spotted a hooded figure exiting the shadows of a side street. They walked past the predestined wall and around the corner. The figure walked to the end of the block and turned around, pausing momentarily to gaze down each side street and the main road at the intersection. They walked back to the intersection across from Marnie and repeated the process. Satisfied, the figure then walked just out of range of a street lamp and surveyed the spot where the 'Ivy Woman' had once lived.

Marnie thought to herself, "This must be the creep." However, she wasn't entirely unimpressed. The amateur knew a great deal about casing a wall, even if what they put on the wall wasn't a great facsimile.

She found the clothes that the figure was wearing to be odd. Marnie opted for form-fitting clothes that wouldn't bind up and trip her if she needed to make a run for it. From what she could tell, the figure was clothed in something akin to the uniform of a Shaolin monk. On top of the monk-like robes, they wore an additional hooded robe.

The figure also had a drawstring bag which appeared to be made from similar materials. From the bag, the figure produced a folded stencil and a can of spray paint. Completely convinced that this must be her target, Marnie started making her way over to where the figure was making preparations.

Marnie was careful to match her movements to the moments when the paint was hitting the wall, using the noise the spray generated to mask her steps. It took her less than a minute to cover the distance between her vantage point and the figure, quietly creeping to within fifteen feet. She figured this would give her some buffer to run if the interaction turned south.

The impostor was crouched down and was starting to lay down the piece from the bottom. Scot always started his Green Men at the top. This helped to prevent any over-spray drips on the high parts of the piece from running through the low parts. Occasionally Scot would do the opposite as a design element but never on the Green Men. "Amateur," Marnie thought as she worked up the courage to speak.

"Does it feel good walking in the shadow of a dead man?" The words that fell out of her mouth weren't the ones Marnie had been planning. They were directed at the figure but also, somehow, self-critical.

"Oh shit," the figure half shouted. Startled, he instinctively dropped the can and turned to run. He hadn't realized that while crouching to paint the lower portion of the wall, he had inadvertently been standing on the bottom of his outer robe. The figure had become wrapped up in his own vestments and fell over, smashing his head against the pavement. On the ground, he tried to scramble away in a kind of crab walk, his face still obfuscated by the robe's hood.

Marnie assessed that the figure on the ground was more afraid of her than the opposite and continued her advance. "You're taking a big risk trying to ape a legend," she continued, stalking closer and snatching up the can the figure had dropped in case it needed to become a weapon.

"Holy shit...Marnie?!" the figure questioned as he labored his way up to his feet. He pulled back his hood revealing his face.

"David?!"

Marnie stood for a moment in stunned silence, almost forgetting to breathe. She surveyed the unmasked figure. The visage was almost unfamiliar. It had only been five years but his face had the appearance that it had been fifteen. His once coiffed hair had been shorn to the skin. There was now a scar running from his temple around to the back of his skull. The corners of his eyes had started to wrinkle. This figure had the appearance of wisdom in years that the one who had left hadn't possessed. He was different but at once the same. David had found his way back.

"D...David is that you?" Marnie was finally able to manage. "It's been so long," she almost broke down as she went in for a hug.

David responded in kind, opening up his arms. Tears had formed in his eyes and a heat had started emanating from his heart, radiating out through his chest, then down his arms. "It's been too long," he said, reflecting the sentiment.

"Scot..." Marnie started.

"We have much to discuss," David said, cutting her off. "...we should get off the street," the lookout in him now speaking as he gave her one more tight squeeze.

David and Marnie decided to go to the gallery and break into Scot's loft, leaving the 'Ivy Woman' unfinished.

***

Unbeknownst to Marnie, this wasn't David's first visit to the loft since his return. He had broken in the week prior after he reappeared near the site of the 'Fern Man'.

David had surveyed the loft and after checking the garage and seeing Scot's dust-coated bright green Honda Civic, decided it wasn't being lived in. Further confirmation was provided when he scaled the fire escape using skills he had, in part, acquired during Mooch's 'late-night art installations'. The loft was revealed to be more or less in the same state as the night they crossed over.

Upon entry, he looked around in awe as waves of memories started to pour back into his brain. So much time spent watching movies on the couch or plotting their art crimes around the butcher block table. He wandered over to the couch to lie down and contemplate his next move. The day's activities had proved to be too much and he fell asleep soon after his head hit the cushions.

***

In the morning, with a clearer mind, David considered his options. He had, after all, come back to Rochester with a mission. After enduring the trial that was his return trip, he had momentarily entertained the idea of abandoning this mission but his thoughts quickly returned to what was left behind. At this moment he resolved to see it through. This meant that he couldn't go visit the people he had become close with before his previous crossing. He didn't want to risk breaking their hearts a second time.

There was also the distinct possibility that he could end up in the mental hospital or jail. The answers he had wouldn't be enough to satisfy the questions that would surely come his way. There was no way anyone could possibly believe him.

David's next move would be to figure out how to get back to the other side. The powers that brought him back to the city didn't exist in this world, at least not in any way he had the ability to harness. Establishing that he had the ability to cross would make his second objective that much easier.

David reasoned that the Green Man that Scot had painted on the fateful night five years prior had been the key to their crossing. He dug out Scot's old stencils from the flat file where they were kept. Scot had hung on to all of his Green Man materials in the hopes that he may one day incorporate them into a gallery piece, assuming the day came when his secret was finally revealed.

David was busy combing through Scot's belongings when he heard footsteps coming up the stairs to the loft. He abandoned his search for Scot's sketchbook and bolted toward the bathroom where he laid down behind the curtain of the claw-footed tub. His heart was racing.

He heard someone fumbling with a set of keys and the opening of the front door. He heard the unsealing sound of the fridge door, accompanied shortly thereafter by the sound of a bottle opening and the unwrapping of either a sandwich or a fast food burger. Twenty minutes had passed before he heard the crinkling of wrappers and the opening of the trash bin lid. This was followed by the sound of footsteps heading his way.

David heard the footsteps enter the bathroom and the door close behind them, an unneeded action but it was clear that it was out of habit. He tried to still his beating heart, worried the sound of thumping might give away his position. His co-occupant relieved themself, washed their hands, and headed out the door. It was through force of will alone that David didn't also relieve himself at that moment.

He heard the visitor plop down on the couch and he continued to wait. Fifteen minutes had passed but to David, it may as well have been an eternity. He had remained still until he heard the sound of the soft groan one makes when reaching out for a post-nap stretch.

Then as quickly as the visitor had appeared, they were gone. After this experience, David decided the loft wouldn't be the ideal base for his activities and figured it best to make camp in the wooded area of Highland Park.

David eventually found Scot's sketchbook and raided his stash of spray cans, hoping that they hadn't seized up in the five or so years since their last use. He checked the hollowed book that Scot kept valuables in, finding a little under two hundred dollars. David counted the money, hoping it would be enough to sustain him on his, hopefully, short visit to Rochester.

***

David was of the mind that the Green Men acted as a form of ley line. He thought he would need to have the correct ones in place before he moved on to the second phase of his plan. He started with his approximation of the 'Oak Man' before tackling the 'Moss Man' a couple of days later. When he went to reproduce the 'Birch Man' and 'Maple Man' he was surprised to see them intact after all this time. It was at the 'Fern Man' that he was sure he had started to draw attention. He had revisited it a few times after its creation to see that it was being visited by multiple amateur photographers. He hoped that nobody had put together what he had been doing, allowing him to keep a low profile for the remaining work. David had run out of Green Men to reproduce. The 'Ivy Woman' was the sixth in the series and its completion might signal the end of phase one of his plan.

There were two additional 'secret' pieces that David hoped wouldn't prove necessary. They had both been done at a time when Scot was less brazen. He had painted them on buildings that were set to be demolished as a precursor to a new housing development. David knew he couldn't very well bust into a stranger's home and start laying down art on their living room wall. The pieces were long gone by the time the pair passed through the 'Oak Man', leading him to believe they could be safely ignored.

He had to concede to himself that his thoughts on the ley line were part of working theory, a weak one at that but it was the best he had. There weren't many resources on the practical nature of interdimensional travel. His doubts only served to bring forward another theory that had been rolling around in his head since starting the recreations. It was a theory he was trying to suppress. Perhaps the pieces he was recreating weren't close enough to the originals. He was pretty much winging it based on what little he picked up from Scot while he was busy watching their surroundings. David had considered that his lack of skill would prevent him from saving his friend but for Scot, he had to hold out hope as long as he could.

Chapter Four
"...a house that tries to be haunted."

"Why is it fair for you to go and risk your life and I have to stay back here?" Marnie demanded.

Marnie and David were in the midst of a conversation that at this point could easily be confused as an argument. Marnie had little problem with the logical leaps one had to make to believe the fantastical story that David was in the midst of telling her. Most of the 'plebs', as Martin called them, had already looked at her crazy when she attempted to broach the subject of the 'Dying of the Art'. It only took her a few mental steps to meet David where he was.

"There are horrors over there, unspeakable ones, the least of which will be your brother when he finds out that I got young, sweet, Marnie involved," David replied.

"I'm not so young anymore and I was never sweet," Marine fired back. "I will not let you of all people patronize me, David!"

"What's that supposed to mean?" he shot back.

"It means, David, that you have gone around these streets haphazardly throwing up these, not even close approximations of Scot's work. Not giving a second thought to intention or composition or color or...need I keep going?" David looked defeated as Marnie continued the turnabout of patronage. "How much thought did you put into this plan of yours...David?"

David was at a bit of a loss; his thinking hadn't been clear since his return. "I will admit my mind has been a bit fuzzy since I got back," he said, trying to qualify his plan.

Marnie realized that this may be a side effect of the Dying and softened her position a little. A plan to achieve what he was trying to do may require a bit more novel thinking than he might be capable of. She then proceeded to go into detail about the discussions she had been having with Martin on the dearth of creativity. Marnie could see there were connections that David was making in his head, her assumption being that he was drawing them between the Dying and his currently failing plan.

David had drawn those connections and then some. Some of them were to a pain from which he wanted to spare Marnie. He opted at this moment not to reveal all of the information at his disposal.

"So yeah, for some reason, I'm the only one I know that can still come up with 'freshies'," Marnie's cute word for novel ideas. She concluded her pitch, "Like it or not, you're gonna need me."

David still appeared skeptical but couldn't point to a better option, which spoke to the truth in Marnie's words. He conceded, "Okay, I admit I need your help but only until I get through the door...It's much too dangerous."

"Okay...agreed," Marnie said, seemingly making her own concession, knowing that this was an agreement she had no intention of upholding.

"So we have the ley line theory and the throwing shit at the wall theory," she barbed, while also trying to add a little bit of levity to the serious conversation. "Let's take a look at the works for comparison to see if we are missing anything."

Marnie then pulled out her phone and brought up one of the art blogs, 'The Baudelairian', which had posted side-by-sides of each of the pieces. She found the recent post on the 'Oak Man' figuring that the last piece Scot created was likely going to be the key.

Taking a closer look at David's work, she realized that she had perhaps been a little too critical upon first inspection. The color choices were a little off owing to David's deutan color blindness which caused him to have issues with blues and greens; not the greatest affliction to have when producing a Green Man. The layering was mostly correct. The accents left something to be desired and the eyes looked a little off but they were passable. It was by no means a great piece of art but the layest of lay person could be forgiven for accepting this piece as a Mooch.

"Okay, so looking at your work in comparison, the colors are a bit off," Marnie stated.

"They are?" David questioned, only realizing at that moment that his color blindness had struck again.

"Yeah...and I say this knowing I'm not up on my interdimensional gateway architecture, but I have to imagine that color wouldn't matter." She took a pause. "The eyes are a bit off as well. What were you using as source reference for this piece?"

David went over to his pack and produced Scot's sketchbook, the same one that led to Marnie's revelation about Mooch five years prior. "I used this," he said as he slid it across the table half expecting to produce a revelation of his own, though he wasn't sure why. It wasn't as if Marnie would have known it was missing.

Marnie started flipping through the book and arrived at the work-up sketches for the 'Oak Man'. She studied the pages but couldn't discern any additional information.

"I don't know, it just seems like something is missing," she said, parroting a sentiment that was all too familiar to David, a cold reminder of the chain of events that had led to his current predicament.

It was just shy of four in the morning and Marnie was starting to fade. The witching hours were coming to a close and they hadn't made much progress. Marnie reasoned that some sleep may do them both some good. She was running on fumes after the activities of the last few days and was sure David was in no better shape. She resolved with David to pick up the conversation the following evening, taking the sketchbook with her to prevent him from getting any more bright ideas. Marnie headed home after advising David that he should stay in the loft for the rest of the night.

He opted to return to the park, recalling his interaction with the intruder he hadn't known to be Martin just days prior.

***

Marnie arrived home and fell into bed, not even bothering to take her clothes off. After listening to David's tale, shrouded in a cloak of mystery though it may be, finding out that Scot was still alive gave her a feeling of hope she hadn't experienced since before he went missing. She barely had time to mentally comb through all of the new information before sleep took her.

***

Marnie woke up a little after noon feeling mostly rested. Had she had any Monday classes she would have surely skipped them. She had a quick lunch and was out the door.

Marnie's first stop was the 'Oak Man' reproduction. It was a spot she had never been back to, even as cIris. To her, it was hallowed ground and many others in the scene saw it in the same light.

Shortly after the disappearance, Clutch, one of Scot's contemporaries, put up a shrine piece in the style of a POW-MIA flag. He shifted the flag's elements, using Mooch's name instead of the top lettering, a Green Man as the silhouette, and a spray can instead of the guard tower. The piece caused a bit of controversy with war vets and out of respect he self-defaced, replacing it with a more modest cameo framed silhouette. The memorial had a run time of a month before it was buffed. No one had touched the wall again until David.

Marnie took several pictures of David's reproduction and then headed over to the gallery for her Monday shift. Monday's were usually slow which would give her time to think.

***

She had the pictures up on the computer at the front desk and was pouring through Scot's sketchbook when Martin stopped by to check in with her.

"What are you looking at there?" Martin questioned.

"I'm trying to figure out who this low-rent writer is so I can tell them to cut the shit," Marnie said.

Martin wasn't involved in the Rochester graffiti culture but understood enough to know what was being perpetrated by the unknown copycat would be seen as a sign of disrespect. That kind of thing was also frowned upon in his world but was met with a little more civility...depending on who you asked.

"You know I didn't notice this the first time but those eyes..." Martin pondered. "There is something about them, I've seen them before."

"Yeah, they are the same ones Scot had in the original. Look," Marnie said, shoving the sketchbook at Martin. She then flipped back a page, "and here they are in detail."

"No, I mean somewhere else. I know I've seen these before. Hold on a sec," Martin responded. He went to the back office where the safe was kept and returned a moment later with one of Declan's leather-bound sketchbooks.

Martin flipped through the pages until he arrived at the one he was looking for and spun it around to face Marnie. "From one of your father's sketchbooks. Take a look at this page," he said.

Marnie was presented with a page that looked like a sigil set, however, none of them looked familiar in the context of historical societies. She had recently finished a semester of 'symbolism in art' which had a section on runes, sigils, and glyphs, giving her a little bit of expertise in the matter.

"Do you know what he was using these for?" Marnie questioned.

"I believe they are eye tests. Look at this one here. It matches the top of the doorway sketch over there...The one your father was working on when he went...well um," Martin trailed off awkwardly, then trying to cover his misstep, pointed to one of the ornate doorway sketches in Declan's section of the gallery.

The sketch featured a woman with flowing hair running the lengths of the door frame. The hair appeared to have leaves growing out of it, reminiscent of Mooch's 'Ivy Woman'. The eyes appeared to be three concentric quarter moons resting inside each other. "And this one here, this is the one from Scot and the impostor's pieces...except it has an extra moon."

"Let me see," Marnie exclaimed as she pulled back from the book. "Shit, that's it!"

"Shit, that's what?" Martin questioned, puzzled.

"Ooh...oh just something that had been bugging me," Marnie responded. "The piece looked unfinished but I couldn't put my finger on it. The extra moon gives the eye some balance."

"Ahh makes sense," Martin said, accepting Marnie's response. She had often been prone to jovial outbursts when having even the most banal of epiphanous moments, a trait he had observed her brother exhibit as well.

"Do you mind if I take this?" Marnie inquired, referencing the sketchbook.

"As far as I'm concerned, it's yours anyway," Martin replied.

"Hey while I remember it, I've got a guy coming in tomorrow to start moving Scot's old stuff. You should be good to get in there Wednesday, Thursday at the latest," Martin said, pivoting the conversation.

"That's great news...but if it wouldn't be too much trouble, do you think I could crash there tonight?" Marnie responded. "I've been on a real nostalgia trip lately and think this might do me some good. You know just to remember it the way it was before..."

"Say no more," Martin jumped in, cutting her off. "I get it." Of all people, he truly did.

"Thanks, could I get a key? Mom said you had them both," Marnie said, not wanting to have to break in again.

Martin slid the spare key off of his ring, handed it to Marnie, and indicated he would drop the other spare off when the movers were done with Scot's stuff. They engaged in some further small talk and then parted ways.

Marnie called her mother to inform her of the change in plans. Diane had a new indictment coming down and was going to be working late, preempting any possible objection.

***

"So sigils were believed to hold magical powers in ancient times, some people think they still do. I thought it was woo-woo bullshit but here you are," Marnie said, biting into a slice of pizza in the middle of giving David a mini-lecture on symbols.

"I think this is what we need to concentrate on," she continued as she chewed through her words. "Did Scot make any alterations to the eyes that night before you crossed over?"

Marnie had recalled being there but was far enough away that she hadn't seen the entire scope of Scot's finishing touches. The piece was buffed before anyone who would take notice had taken a picture, leaving her with no means of confirming her theory.

"Come to think of it, I think he did," David replied, straining to recall." I think he added a circular accent right here." He pointed to the location of the missing moon on the picture of the Mooch version of the piece.

"That must be it," Marnie exclaimed.

"So what are we waiting for?" David responded.

Marnie gave a knowing look toward the windows before uttering, "Dark."

"Oh yeah," David said as he bit into his own slice of pizza.

***

After dinner, David began filling up his pack with spray cans and protein bars. Marnie took note that he was packing much more spray than they would need for the touch-up. She could tell that there was much he was holding back. Each time Marnie tried to pry further information from David, he would only promise to tell her more once he had returned with Scot.

They waited until a little after midnight then headed over to the wall. The 'Oak Man Redux' as Marnie had taken to calling it was still intact. Marnie had surmised that her mother wasn't yet aware of it, lest it already be covered.

"Well I guess this is good luck," Marnie said, as she went in for a hug.

"I'll bring him home. I promise," David replied through his already welling eyes.

"Don't make promises you can't keep," Marnie responded.

"I promise," David said, his words lingering as he turned and raised the can of silver spray paint to the Green Man's eye socket.

***

"Well that was anticlimactic," Marnie mused after they had waited a minute without any movement from the wall.

David shook up the can in a way that said he was thinking, "must be broken," before hitting the wall with another shot.

"So...uh...why did you think that was going to work?" Marnie questioned when it was clear the second attempt had also been unsuccessful.

"Maybe it's the colors?" David pondered, going back to his earlier hypothesis.

"I don't think so, these are sigils, they would have been created similar to a petroglyph, etched into stone. Color should be irrelevant," Marnie said, further exhibiting her newfound expertise. "I was so sure the extra moon was it."

***

It was getting close to two o'clock and they hadn't made any progress. Marnie tried her hand at redoing the sigil, wondering if it needed to be fresh paint even though this line of thought didn't make any kind of logical sense. She then considered the context that they were trying to open a doorway to another realm and that trying to frame their actions in logic was ridiculous. She might as well try to get Dobry involved, as he was there that night, for what she had now just metaphorically thrown at this physical wall.

"I don't get it. This makes no sense. We're never going to get this to work," she sputtered as she shook her clenched fists by the sides of her head. "We've failed...Scot is lost...he's not coming back," Marnie continued, throwing her back against the wall as she started to sob quietly, sinking to the ground.

David crouched down beside her, "We'll figure this out. We know it's possible. It's already happened once before. All we need is one good idea and the rest will take care of itself." This was his attempt to mimic Scot's style of encouragement, he had already plagiarized his art, so why not one of his motivational speeches as well?

Marnie appreciated the sentiment. She was working on her reply just as her vintage Casio watch beeped indicating the new hour. She looked at the time and was ready to call it quits just as a guttural tone started to emanate from the piece. It was a tone that she hadn't heard in five years but she was already anticipating what would happen next. The sound started to grow and the ground beneath them started to shake.

They both stood up and faced the Green Man, withdrawing from the wall. The tone and vibration ceased. "The witching hours," Marnie whispered as one does when saying 'the witching hours'.

"The what?" replied David.

"The witching hours," Marnie repeated, this time louder. "I thought it was just Scot having a bit of fun. He used to go on and on about how it was the best time to work. Something about the barriers allowing the good ideas through being thinner. He once told me that the church had banned activities this late at night because that's when the devil works his magic."

"He used to say something similar to me," David recalled.

"Touch the wall," she beckoned to David.

David touched the wall and nothing happened.

"Hmm," Marnie murmured before hesitantly placing her hand on the wall. The tone started to build again, followed shortly by the vibration. The sigil began to glow with blue luminescence, a detail she had missed five years prior, possibly owing to the lights on Dobry's cruiser. She removed her hand once more causing the sigil to deactivate.

"Marnie, are you a witch?" David questioned, smirking. He was actively masking his current knowledge advantage, hoping Marnie wouldn't pick up on the deception.

"I'm not sure what this means," she said, pondering her next words. "It doesn't look like you have a choice now. I have to go with you."

"It's too dangerous. We have to find another way," David pleaded.

Before David realized what was happening Marnie had grabbed hold of him and was attempting to activate the sigil. He wrestled with her in an attempt to get her outside of the wall's reach but she was steadfast. The tendrils had begun to emerge, wrapping themselves around him. Marnie was still struggling with him, trying to force her way into the entanglement. David kept pushing against her and with his last bit of his strength, gave her a final shove.

Marnie fell backward onto the pavement as David was sucked into the wall, not understanding why he had fought so hard if she could just reactivate the doorway and follow him. She stood up, went back to the wall, and laid her hands upon it. The sigil eyes started to illuminate once more, then flickered out. She stood there for a second and tried again, this time the light hadn't come back. It seemed as if the markings had been drained of their power or perhaps it had been her that had been drained.

Marnie reasoned it could take five hours, five days, or five years to recharge. She was no expert in these matters and would be hard-pressed to find anyone who was. She was once again lost. One thing was certain, David had known more than he was letting on.

Marnie took a few minutes to stare at the wall in defeat before deciding to head back to the loft.

***

On her way back to the apartment Marnie pondered the nature of what she had just experienced. It was in these moments that she thought on the possibility that the Dying may be connected to the dangerous realm from which David had returned and subsequently reentered. There was the distinct possibility that she may, on a personal level, be inexorably linked to both. She now had far more questions than answers and wasn't willing to wait for the sigils to recharge to find the solutions she craved. Marnie needed to find a way over immediately. She felt she couldn't afford to let David get too much of a head start.

***

Upon returning to the gallery building, Marnie entered the studio and rounded up her stash of extra spray cans. She had taken to keeping them there to hide them from her mother. After securing the paint, she reentered the loft and started work on her own means of crossing. Marnie had to work quickly as there was only an hour left before the witching hours would come to a close, at least as far as she understood them. She knew what she needed to do.

She started by clearing all of the furniture away from the brick wall that once served as the backdrop to movie nights with Scot. Marnie then looked through the stack of stencils that David had left behind when he was making room for spray cans and energy bars in his bag. She chose the stencil Scot had created for the 'Ivy Woman'.

Working with a vibrant green, she started to spray in the outline, paying no attention to over-spray drips. She needed to work quickly and deliberately. Marnie then started to rotate through the complimentary shades of green she had chosen as she worked her way inward on the piece, leaving hollows for the eyes and forming other facial features as she went. She didn't know how accurate she needed to be but erred on the side of caution. She added ears and hair then started to free-hand accents with silver to give the piece a little depth.

Marnie took a quick second to survey the work, thinking to herself that it was better than David's but still lacked the flourish of Scot's. She free-handed the sigil that had been used on the two 'Oak Men' and tested the creation.

The sigil started to glow and Marnie started to feel a small semblance of relief but it, like the other, flickered and went dark. She looked at her watch. It was quarter to four. Witching hours may be coming to a close. It was at this moment that Marnie made what she knew could very well be a very reckless decision. She opened up Declan's sketchbook and chose the next most similar sigil.

Marnie blackened the eyes and started to freehand the freshly chosen symbol. This one also featured a quarter moon on its side but the three other full moons were stacked on top of each other as if they were three different-sized coins.

Once she finished with the eyes, she touched the piece again. She was again greeted by a low register tone and a familiar vibration. The sigil had also started to glow, this time with a purple luminescence and devoid of the previous flickering.

Marnie pulled her hand away and took a glance at her watch...five minutes to spare. She knew if she wanted to cross this day, this would be the moment she would have to decide. She had a quick thought of her mother.

"What would it do to her if I too went missing?" she uttered in the darkness of the room before pausing for a moment to consider another thought. "What would it mean to her if I brought him home?"

Marnie scribbled out a quick note and left it on the butcher block work table. She then proceeded to cram as many spray cans as possible into the oversized messenger bag she used on bombing runs. She also packed three sketchbooks: Declan's sigil book, Scot's planning book, and her sketchbook from the night Scot went missing. Marnie approached the 'Ivy Woman', turned her back to it, and stepped backward with her arms at her sides, offering herself to the tendrils as they began to envelop her. She took a deep breath. As she began to exhale, her world faded into darkness.

Chapter Five

"...the crag of Scylla and dire Charybdis' vortex..."

"Martin,

Tell Mom I'm not missing. Going with David to find Scot. Be back soon.

Love,

Marnie"

Underneath the note, Marnie had drawn the new sigil she used to cross over.

Marnie's note was short and cryptic. It was all she could manage to get out if she wanted to get through to the other side in time. She didn't know if there was a hard limit on the end of the witching hours but wasn't willing to take the risk.

***

Martin found the note the next afternoon while letting the mover in to box up the items destined for storage. On top of the note, Marnie had left a key to the apartment. It wasn't immediately obvious why she had done this or why she had addressed the note to him. After a few minutes, it dawned on him that he had to use the deadbolt to get in. Marnie only had one key to the loft.

Martin searched around the apartment in case Marnie was playing a trick on him. His search came up empty. He also checked the windows, which he found to be locked. Martin was dumbfounded but wasn't sure if there was a lack of explanation or if the Dying was affecting his ability to come up with one. He had noticed the smell of fresh spray paint upon entering the loft and had taken a moment to inspect Marnie's 'Ivy Woman' but took an additional moment to gaze upon it further. He took note of the eyes and how they matched the symbol she scrawled on the note.

He thought back to the prior day and his conversation with Marnie regarding the 'Oak Man' sigils and the eyes of Declan's old works. Martin thought to himself for a moment. He had a fleeting idea that the sigils had an unexplainable power, that there was something in his memory linked to the notion. He eventually shrugged it off as nonsense.

His heart sank when he realized he was going to have to tell Diane that the last remaining member of her family had disappeared. This would be no small feat as he was having a hard enough time rationalizing to himself that there was now another lost Murphy; another Murphy who had once again vanished under extremely mysterious circumstances.

Chapter Six
"...straight on till morning."

Marnie was unable to move. She was still tightly wrapped in the tendrils that had emanated from her painting and could feel herself being continuously pulled backward and re-enveloped in pitch-blackness. She wasn't frightened at first. Marnie had the overwhelming feeling that what was happening was being done with a sense of purpose. She was being carefully passed down a long corridor of sorts.

It was only when Marnie had been moving around for what felt like ten minutes that she started to get nervous. What if all the portal held was a bunch of vines that passed you around forever? What if this was the horror to which David alluded? What if this is what happened to her father all those years ago?

Marnie's heart started to race and she began to hyperventilate. The coping mechanisms her therapist had given her were useless here. Marnie couldn't comprehend how to 'just lean into the anxiety' when she was surrounded by the physical manifestation of the panic she had experienced so many times before. Marnie's heart was pounding with an intensity that was painful and her breathing felt hollow; like she was breathing but couldn't feel the air filling her lungs. Her face was starting to tingle and her throat was getting tight. It was as if she was mainlining raw existential terror.

Just when she thought she couldn't take anymore, when she was ready to let her mind slip into madness, Marnie was disgorged from a large stone doorway.

***

Marnie laid on her back with her eyes closed for a few minutes catching her breath and waiting for her heart to slow. The air was crisp and clean, having a light odor of lavender, rosemary, and thyme which would come and go on soft warm breezes.

The aromatics provided a calming effect that eased her back from the brink of mental collapse.

When she finally opened her eyes, she found herself to be staring up at the night sky. She immediately began to take stock of this brave new world she had been thrust into. There were stars but they didn't appear familiar. This was a world that had constellations all its own. These heavenly bodies didn't glow with white fire alone. Instead, there were hues of blue, green, red, and purple. Marnie had a passing bout of wonderment, pondering if they were planets like back home or perhaps something else.

Some of the objects began to move. Many of them weren't stars at all. The little lights above her started to swirl and flock together before making their way down to her. Marnie was able to make her way to her feet as they started to reach her. There were thousands of the tiny orbs making slow circular passes around her. It was as if she were stuck in the eye of a small hurricane. She didn't feel fear at that moment. There was something about the lights that made them feel welcoming, almost warm.

A handful of the orbs came closer to Marnie as if they were performing their own inspection. She could see that they looked like fireflies. However, these creatures didn't glow the familiar greenish yellow of the ones she had remembered catching with Scot on the camping trips of her youth. They were the same mix of the blues, greens, reds, and purples that she had seen in the sky above. After a few moments, the lights began to settle down into the tall grass that they had become unsettled from upon her arrival.

Marnie gazed upward and was pleased to see that the stars were indeed the same colors that she had thought they had been before. She continued to scan the sky in an attempt to get some semblance of a bearing. She was overwhelmed when her eyes happened upon the three moons floating in the sky just above the horizon. The largest of the celestial bodies glowed purple. Marnie thought it must have been six, maybe seven times the size of the moon back home. There was a small red moon that appeared closer in size to the one she was accustomed to. The third moon appeared to be just behind the larger of the two moons. This moon was the most interesting. It glowed green with little patches of blue and had what appeared to be clouds. She had the passing thought that perhaps this moon sustained life. The size of the third moon appeared to be somewhere between the other two.

If someone were to gaze at the green moon long enough they would observe it grow and shrink. Marnie would eventually come to realize that this moon was, in actuality, orbiting the larger purple moon and not the planet on which she found herself standing. It was a moon of a moon. Lower on the horizon Marnie thought she detected the intimation of dawn's first light.

Scanning her immediate surroundings, Marnie could see she was in a small clearing surrounded by forest. She found herself in the smaller of two concentric circles. The smaller circle consisted of twenty large cuboid stones. They had the appearance of being the tops to a henge but there was no detectable evidence of previous uprights. The larger circle was the tree-lined border of the surrounding forest.

To her back was the focal point of the smaller circle, a large monolithic pillar made of green onyx. The pillar was three times as tall as she was with a width that would eclipse her wingspan. Carved into the stone was the visage of a disgorging Green Man.

In the eye sockets, Marnie could see the stacked coin moon sigil that she had used in the graffiti that brought her here. The sigil looked to be composed of quicksilver and appeared to be undulating. The vines that spewed forth from the face's mouth wrapped around the pillar's back side. They had formed what Marnie had recognized as a knot pattern resembling the ones seen in Celtic crosses.

Marnie attempted to activate the monolith by touching it as she did with the Green Men of her world. The eyes started to light up in the familiar glowing purple luminescence of the 'Ivy Woman'. Just as she had observed with the redux versions of David's 'Oak Man' and her 'Ivy Woman', the lights started to flicker then slowly faded. She was stuck here, not knowing for how long or even if she would be able to make it back. She tried to remind herself that she knew this would happen when she chose to embark on this particular endeavor.

Marnie looked at her watch and found it to be a quarter after four. She did some quick mental math and realized that she was in the portal for less than five minutes, much less than what she had originally thought. The witching hour had come to a close and regardless of whether there was any actual bearing on her ability to harness novelty, Marnie's ability to think was being depleted with every passing second.

She was exhausted, currently without food, and didn't have a working plan in this unfamiliar place. This was one of those look-before-you-leap situations that her mother had often cautioned her against. Marnie was only now considering that there may be some wisdom in that particular line of thinking. One thing that gave her a small bit of comfort was knowing that Scot and David were able to survive here. "There must be a way that I can too," she thought. Marnie curled up by one of the stones in an attempt to keep herself hidden in case any of the local fauna came out of the woods and started to poke around. She set the alarm on her vintage Casio for six hours, hoping that would give her enough time to recover, and that David wouldn't gain too much of a lead.

Marnie had a hard time falling asleep but eventually succumbed to her exhaustion, passing out rather than drifting off.

***

David was ejected into a place he was all too familiar with. It was the place he and Scot had first camped after their previous crossing to this strange world.

He was standing in the middle of a forgotten underground cistern. The cistern was encapsulated by a dome-shaped ceiling which was covered in a type of climbing ivy. This was a species of vegetation that would have been unfamiliar to the mind of an outsider. When Scot and he had previously arrived, the vines possessed a vibrant bioluminescent glow. The leaves on the vines were colored in hues of blue and green, while the stems were of a brilliant purple. To David's eyes, these appeared as similar shades of blue and yellow. Most living things in this world possessed a similar glow. It was a glow that had greatly faded in the last five years.

Under David's feet was a large cobblestone disk that was centered in the middle of the cistern. It measured a little over five meters across. On one end of the disk was a long floating walkway joining it to an archway exit. On the opposite end was a monolith similar to the one Marnie had encountered. The eyes on this disgorging Green Man contained a familiar sigil. It was the sigil that had caused David's initial emergence into this world and now his subsequent re-emergence. As he gazed at the face, he was stuck with the thought of how simplistic the answer he was looking for had been, even if he wouldn't have had the ability to harness its power. The usage of the mysterious sigils was something that should have been easily guessed.

David set down the bag he was carrying and removed one of the cans of spray paint contained within. He painted a small sword on the ground before setting down the can and reaching for the drawing with intention. From the ground David lifted a glowing scimitar, leaving behind no trace of the paint. He picked his bag back up and walked toward the archway exit. The sword decayed with each step he took away from its origin point. By the time he had reached the door, the sword had become nothing more than tightly packed dust. David cast it aside. The sword was dashed into a cloud of glowing smoke which quickly dissipated into nothingness. "Well at least some things are constant," David muttered to himself

He wound his way through the all too familiar catacombs which were being lit by the various patches of mold growths and the occasional crop of ivy that had intruded through cracks in the brick wall. David looked down at his hands. His veins had already started to glow a familiar blue. This was a known byproduct of existing in this world's environment. The effect had been much more drastic in Scot, to the point that even his skin exhibited a pale blue glow. He could also pick up on his clarity of thought returning; the lack of which being something he hadn't been prepared for when crossing over to Earth.

David eventually came to an exit covered by a heavy top-hinged grate. He set down his pack and used all of his strength to push against it and was just barely able to slide down through the bottom edge. He then fed his bag through the bars and turned on his heel while slinging it over his shoulder before striding off.

To his back was the great walled-in city of Ærratum. He had thought it unwise to reenter the city due to the circumstances that surrounded his previous exit. The constabulary would surely arrest him on the spot. David knew his next stop would be the Cloister. There he would find some much-needed rest and consultation on his next move.

David checked his surroundings for prying eyes that may be gazing upon him with unknown intent. His keen sense of awareness had rarely betrayed him. Perhaps it had on the night of Scot and his crossing but it wouldn't betray him this night.

***

Traveling by foot had become much more dangerous since the light started to diminish. Highwaymen were thought to have become a forgotten relic of a past age but under the cover of darkness, the likelihood of running into a resurgence of murderous thieves had become much more likely. David crossed a small creek bed where the overflow from the cisterns had drained. He then made his way across a small field making sure to crouch, hoping the contrast between his dark robes and the luminous grasses wouldn't betray his position to any onlooker he may have missed.

He made it to the tree line undetected and located a familiar footpath, deciding it would be his safest option. David dared not take his chances on the Geddes road if he could help it. The dark road was fraught with danger beyond the threat of thieves; half-light messengers, constabulary, and even the occasional mega trompf roamed the route.

The mega trompf was a moose-like animal; being twice the size and having a giant four-foot-long horn on its snout in addition to its dagger-like antlers. The animals were typically harmless but could, when startled, become very aggressive. Before the recent darkness, it had been said that more people had been killed inadvertently than through malicious attacks. In the nights since the darkness began, the creatures had become much more antagonistic, there had even been some reports of the beasts stalking wandering children.

David followed the path he was on for a little over two hours without incident. He was five minutes from the Cloister when a shadowy figure caught his eye as it darted across the trail in front of him. He stopped cold in his tracks, heart racing. He could hear rustling in the leaves behind him as the apparition shot across the trail again. He looked around, unable to detect the source. The sound of rabid snarling started soon after.

David quickly took a can of paint out from his bag and hastily drew what looked like a cricket paddle on the ground before lifting it to brandish against the mysterious foe. Just then he heard a crashing sound in front of him to the left as it broke onto the trail. The pitch-black figure paused for a moment, staring David down as it started sprinting straight toward him. Before David could wind back for a swing, it had closed the gap and had leaped into the air pouncing on him and knocking him off his feet. The creature then disappeared into the woods to circle again.

As David fell back, terror started to overtake him. He hit the ground with a thud, the back of his head bouncing off the hard-packed dirt behind him. He lay there dazed as fear started to overcome him.

Satisfied that his prey had been incapacitated, the creature leaped out onto the trail and slowly approached from the front. It lurched over the top of David, its putrid breath lingering in the air over his face. He closed his eyes in anticipation of the fatal blow and waited. The moment felt like an eternity but the blow never came.

David managed to pry his eyes open and just as he did he felt hot breath and a slimy tongue licking up one side of his face and down the other. An instant later, the creature's longish hair burst with light, its tail trying to wag itself off its body. The light was that of brilliant gold. David, relieved, started to laugh uncontrollably. A golden retriever here was the same as anywhere.

He walked with Brutus the rest of the way to the Cloister. The dog peeled off for the kitchen as soon as they entered the grounds. David made his way to the great hall in hopes that the Forgotten Master was already awake.

He entered the hall and spied the hooded Master already in a trance as part of his daily meditations. David took a seat on a mat beside him and assumed a cross-legged pose. After a few moments the Master spoke, "Did she take the bait?"

David's head sank. "Yes Master, she couldn't have been very far behind."

"Good...Good."

Chapter Seven

"...six impossible things before breakfast."

Marnie's watch alarm had already been going off for forty minutes. Her mind was finally rested enough that it could no longer ignore the rousing effect. She looked at the time thinking, "This can't be right, it's still night out."

Continuing to look at her wrist she noted that her hands had started to glow. Marnie pushed up her sleeves to find that this new development wasn't relegated to her hands alone. She then checked her ankles and abdomen finding the same results.

She paid particular attention to her veins, which had started to shimmer an electric blue. This was in stark contrast to the soft yellowish-green glow of her skin. Marnie was vexed by this new development. The kindling of panic had started to once again well up in her chest. The only thing keeping it at bay was the mantra that had been slowly developing in her brain since her arrival, "If Scot and David could survive here, so can I."

Marnie was able to push the worries aside and set about getting her bearings. She looked up at the moons. They had traversed the sky and were sitting on the opposite horizon from where she left them before falling asleep. The blue and green moon was now in front of the purple moon and appeared twice as large as it had eight hours prior. The red moon was just about to disappear. She checked the horizon for signs of dawn's first light. The glow she had detected earlier remained exactly where it had been.

Marnie had a decision to make. Would she stay where she was and hope for the sun to make an appearance or would she traverse the forest in the middle of the night? She didn't know how long the darkness would last or if it would even be safer to go out in the light of day. Marnie was no stranger to working under the cover of darkness, making her decision an easy one. She decided she wouldn't waste any more time sitting around.

Owing to the existence of the monolith, accompanying stones, and the path leading to the forest, Marnie surmised that there must be intelligent life in this world. She became intent on finding some as she started down the path into the woods.

She marveled at the luminous canopy above and would occasionally catch a glimpse of the fireflies that she had encountered earlier buzzing through the air. There were occasional patches of glowing moss covering the road. As Marnie stepped on them, she observed her shoe prints leaving behind a void of darkness that would illuminate again moments later.

There were other curiosities to marvel at. The squirrels and chipmunks of this world also glowed. Their fur appeared to be translucent, providing a fiber optic-like effect, similar to that of a polar bear. The hairs glowed in red, brown, and gray hues which matched the skin underneath. There was also the occasional owl, colloquially known as glowls, whose body displayed a similar effect. The hollows of the feathers channeled light from its body. Their eyes were mesmerizing, almost piercing the soul, possessing a reddish glow with little flecks of yellow.

***

Marnie walked for a little over forty minutes before reaching a crossroads at the edge of the forest. The crossroads featured a signpost of the type that was rarely seen as anything more than a novelty at a tourist attraction. Arrow markers were pointing in several directions and featured the names and distances to various locations.

To her surprise, she saw that the markers were emblazoned with what appeared to be characters from a Latin alphabet; even more remarkable was the fact that the characters formed words she could pronounce. The sign also used familiar Arabic numerals used to mark distances. The included unit of measure, however, was one she wasn't familiar with. The sign pointing toward the direction from which she came, read, 'Umphraidh Menhir 2 Sm'. She judged that by the rate of her walking, it was roughly equivalent to a little over two and a half miles back home.

The crossroads had three possible branches excluding the one she had traveled to get to this point. Marnie headed into the open field that bordered the forest to take stock of her surroundings. To her right were two of the three moons she had become acquainted with. Directly in front of her, off in the distance, Marnie could make out what she believed to be a modern roadway; the first sign of possible civilization. On the horizon to her left, she could see the glow she had previously detected.

Knowing how cagey David had been about this world and the dangers that lived in it, Marnie opted to avoid the roadway and take the path that bordered the forest to the left, hoping it was indeed the correct path. After making her decision, she went back to check the sign, reading 'Ærratum 55 Sm'. She turned her back to the moons and began her long march toward the light, hoping to find the answers she sought.

***

While Marnie had been taking stock of the new world, the new world had started to take stock of her. In the forest that Marnie had just left, a curious beast, known locally as the Razor-Sìth, had started to stalk her.

The Razor-Sìth was a black lynx-like creature that measured nearly two meters from the tip of its nose to the end of its tail. It stood just under a meter high at its shoulder blades and weighed a little over one hundred and fifty pounds.

The term razor, as one would have been mistaken to think, wasn't indicative of its long claws or its sharp teeth but of the fur on its spine. The hair in this area grew in a direction opposing the rest of its coat, a feature typical of the Earthen dog breed the Rhodesian Ridgeback. When startled or posturing, the creature's hair would stick up and forward like the teeth of a saw blade.

The beast's fur didn't glow like the other creatures in this world. Its thick dark fur served to hide the creature's skin which glowed with ultraviolet fluorescence. This feature went mostly unnoticed unless it was frightened or as was more likely the case, doing the frightening. In these situations, its fur would stand up, allowing its luminescence to escape, causing the surrounding area to be bathed in a purple light. In a world with so much naturally occurring fluorescence, this was a sight to behold. The amplification that the ultraviolet light cast over the surrounding forest was nearly blinding. It disoriented the beast's prey and in most cases was the last thing a hapless creature would see.

When not posturing, the creature's presence could only be betrayed by the white glow of the long hair on the tips of its ears and its long whiskers. If a victim was close enough to see these features, it was already too late. Unlike many stalking predators, the creature was relentless and wasn't known to stop a hunt until its prey had met its end. It had now caught the scent of Marnie.

***

Marnie had been walking on her chosen path for thirty minutes when she detected that there was something amiss. The forest directly to her right had lost its voice. Previously she had heard the chirping sounds of various birds and the buzzing of insects but now there was nothing. It was as if a storm was coming, bringing along a shift in pressure, pushing everything back into their holes. The feeling was unnerving. Marnie felt like she was being watched.

In the forest, the Razor-Sìth was climbing over hill and branch, continuing to silently stalk its prey. Its heartbeat had slowed with its considered movements and its eyes had dilated to allow for better tracking.

Marnie attempted to shrug off the feeling, thinking the muted forest was her mind playing tricks on her. It was just the feeling of being so exposed, she thought. It wasn't much different than the exposed feeling she had doing a late-night bombing run back home.

She cautiously continued for a few hundred paces before reaching another divergence of path. This split lacked the signpost of the previous intersection. The right-hand branch would allow her to continue her journey out into a field and allow her to keep heading straight to Ærratum. The path to the left led back into the woods. She surveyed the situation for a moment. Her first thought was to take the straight path. It seemed like the logical one as it was more direct. Marnie considered that the path to the left may take her to some form of civilization sooner, something she wasn't able to detect on the straight path. Marnie's hunger had started to grow and would soon need sating. She stood still for a moment, weighing her options.

The Razor-Sìth had taken this opportunity to stealthily move back into the field and circle to Marnie's right. It continued through the open grass until it was a hundred lengths ahead. The creature then let out a blood-curdling yowl, a yowl it would typically use when defending territory from a rival predator. The creature was toying with her.

The scream took Marnie off guard. Her heart rate spiked dramatically. She was now convinced she hadn't been imagining things earlier. The sound was a sharp reminder that perhaps instincts are to be trusted and made her directional decision much easier. Marnie started to slowly move up the path into the forest, careful to keep her vision focused in the direction of the sound.

When she was confident that the immediate danger had subsided, Marnie moved her focus forward as much as she could. She picked up her pace in an attempt to gain distance from the creature, assuming it might still have her scent. She was mindful not to move so quickly that the spray cans she was carrying would bang together and rattle; a sound that, she was worried, would betray her position.

The creature continued to stalk, content for the moment in forcing its victim down the intended path. It slowly started to recover some of the ground it had lost, still being careful to be as silent as possible.

Marnie kept moving forward with her eyes constantly scanning her surroundings and her ears keenly attuned to the sounds of the forest. She listened for any rustle or branch snap that may indicate she was no longer alone.

She wasn't on the new trail for long before her nose started to detect the faint smell of burning lumber. Continuing for a couple hundred more paces, she was able to hear the distinct popping and crackling of a small fire. A few more paces and she had started to pick up on the light murmurings of conversation. Before long she was able to detect an orange glow a short way off in the distance. She became cautiously excited and started to make her way toward the fire, intent on surveying the situation but also waiting to engage for the sake of safety. Marnie had barely made it another ten paces when the Razor-Sìth chose to make its presence known.

Marnie's ears, still attuned to the sounds of the forest, heard the crashing of branches behind her. She swung around only to catch the fleeting glimpse of a shadow darting across the trail. Marnie once more picked up her pace. Moments later she heard the creature crash across the trail again. Marnie was now in a full-on sprint. She yelled out, hoping for benevolence from the fire's owner, "Help me! Help! Something is after me!"

It wasn't long before she could hear the pounding of the creature's massive pads on the forest floor behind her. Marnie looked back. She still had no idea what was after her, only being able to detect the occasional displacement of the soft glow of the forest's grasses and mosses as a dark shadow passed in front of them.

She didn't have much sprint left in her. It was only a matter of time before Marnie's form started to break. Her lungs felt like they were on fire. Her quads were burning, causing her stride to become wobbly. She checked over her shoulder again and could see the approaching darkness no more than thirty lengths back.

Consumed with trying to catch a glimpse of her pursuer, Marnie hadn't seen the root growing over the side of the trail. Her left foot caught the growth and kicked out behind her as her right foot attempted a quick stutter-step to compensate. Marnie's forward momentum proved to be too much and she went crashing to the ground in a slide.

She started to scramble forward, managing to claw her way up to her feet, before spinning around to face the beast. The creature had closed to fifteen lengths and slowed its pace but continued to lurch its way forward. It had approached close enough that she could now make out the glowing white tufts of hair on its ears as well as its white whiskers.

Marnie did the only thing she could think of at this moment and reached into her bag, grabbing one of the cans. The creature sensed her intention and started to posture, raising the fur on its back into forward-facing spike formations. UV light leached from its skin and out through its hair, amplifying the light of the nearby plant life. Enough luminosity had been produced to give the forest surroundings the sudden appearance of daylight, leaving Marnie temporarily blinded.

Her body's overactive fight or flight response had kicked in, with her brain selecting the former. She raised the can in anticipation of the charge. As she did, the glow in her right arm drained down and pooled into her hand; the concentrated light seemed to forecast her intention.

"If you want to live, drop the weapon lass!" a voice to her left shouted.

Panicked, Marnie did as the disembodied voice suggested. Mere moments later, the Razor-Sìth decreased its posture and the light show started to die down. The concentrated glow in Marnie's hand then started to creep back up her arm.

"Now set the bag down and lower your head, keeping your eyes on the beast," the voice continued.

Marnie complied.

"Now start blinking, slowly."

Marnie followed the final instruction which seemed to calm the creature, causing it to slink back into the shadows of the forest. She could hear the rustling of leaves and snapping of branches. The creature was no longer trying to hide its presence. "What...what was that thing?" Marnie asked, only then realizing that the person she was talking to had been speaking English.

"That wee lass was the Razor-Sìth. Noble creature...cunning too. Don't much care for human meat. Hunt us for sport, truth be told," a second voice had chimed in with what Marnie recognized as an almost Scottish brogue. The figures that stepped out of the forest, however, didn't look much like any Scottish person whom Marnie was familiar with. The glowing light in their veins also didn't make them look very human for that matter. Had she been facing a mirror at that moment, she would say she didn't look very human either.

Marnie was boxed in on the trail with one of her rescuers to the front and the other behind. She surveyed them both and found them to not be very threatening. The advice alone should have been enough assurance but her doubts were further assuaged by their possession of what Marnie considered to be kind faces.

The person in front of her had been the one to give her the life-saving instruction. He was on the tall side standing half a head above Marnie's average height. His long blood-red hair had been combed back over the top of his head and sat between two braids that ran back from his temples and down the back side of his ears before meeting in a single braid at his neck. The hair glowed in contrast to his similarly glowing light green veins. His face appeared very angular, featuring an almost elf-like quality. The clothes he was wearing were very chic. His teal pants were embroidered with a silver brocade, which coordinated well with his silver collared shirt and purple overcoat. This was Marnie's first encounter with anyone from the strange new world but had correctly assumed that the man before her had a bit of a dandy flair.

The person behind her sported shorter electric blue hair, which complemented the glow of their purple veins. They had similar angular features and were a bit smaller, standing a whole head shorter than the man to the front. The fashion they had chosen was a bit more reserved. They wore simple gray jeans and a black shirt with a logo Marnie didn't recognize. For their outer layer, they wore a form-fitting black zip-up hoodie. Neither of the pair wore shoes.

"Name's Chauncey and the one behind you is Trig," the man in front said, continuing the dialog.

"Marnie," Marnie responded. "Nice to meet you and thanks for the help."

"Don't mention it," replied Chauncey, as Trig slowly bowed their head, echoing the sentiment. "Truth be told, I wasn't sure it would work."

"Wait, what?" Marnie said, alarmed that Chauncey may have been a little cavalier with his suggestions.

"Listen Marnie las, listen, that beast has been following us for the last night or so now. We kenned that it had not considered us worthy prey and decided to let us alone." Chauncey continued, "You should take it as a compliment, looking at you now, you do appear to be much more worthy."

"I'm not sure what you mean," Marnie puzzled.

"It means we have much to discuss," Trig chimed in before beckoning, "Please, please, join us by the fire. Share a meal and tell us your tale."

Chapter Eight
"...let the theory go."

"**I** still don't understand why she couldn't cross with me," said David, questioning the Forgotten Master's instructions.

"Because it wasn't part of the plan," replied the Master. "Your face is everywhere. We couldn't risk her being seen with you."

"But she is stuck out there all alone," David protested.

"Do not underestimate her cunning. She was able to find you passage back to this place, was she not?" the Forgotten Master pointed out. "Better that she be stuck out there all alone than in some cell in the city, or worse. Who knows what Imperium would be able to do if they managed to get their hands on the likes of her? You yourself took a big risk making your ingress point the city."

"It's not like I planned it that way. I don't know how the portals work and you haven't exactly been forthcoming with that bit of information," David replied, half suspecting the Master may have been as ignorant on the topic as he. "She could be anywhere. She doesn't even know what she is yet."

"And I would pray that information remain undiscovered until you find her," the Master replied.

"I don't understand," David responded. "You know as well as I do of the darkness that exists beyond the city limits. She would at least be able to defend herself."

"Without proper training? She would be doing no more than turning herself into a beacon. She would be hunted by this world. If the darkness finds her she may end up dead...If Imperium finds her, she may well end up wishing she was." The Forgotten Master stared longingly toward the window, as if drawing on a lost history before continuing, "This young David, is why your next mission is of paramount importance and must be conducted with haste."

"When you put it that way," David relented, knowing his role would be critical.

"You must go into the city and find a tavern called The Violet Huntress," the Master commanded. "A tracker named Luci will be waiting. She will not be expecting you but sure enough, she will be there. She is the one that will help you find the girl."

"What makes this Luci so special?" David asked. "Why can't we use one of our own?"

"It is as you said...She could be anywhere," replied the Master. "Our trackers are good but they aren't magicians. They need a lead. A point of origin. A sighting...Something. Luci comes from a line of Masters that managed to hold on to a bit of their Muse after the Flood."

"But I thought everyone like that was snatched up by Imperium," David responded.

"Well, you see the curious thing about rangers," the Master replied using a supercilious tone, "...is that they can not only do more than find that which wants to remain hidden but can also become hidden...Her more than most."

"Point taken," David replied. "How will I know who she is?"

"Her appearance is, let's say, ever-evolving to suit the situation. No description I can give would be accurate. Take Brutus with you. He's always been able to sniff out her kind," the Master said.

"And we can trust her?" David questioned.

"We can't...But I trust that our mutual distrust in Imperium may very well be all the trust we require...She also owes me a debt," the Master responded. "...One she should be eager to repay."

"I think I already know the answer, but what will you be doing while I'm off on this errand?" David replied. He had learned not to press the Forgotten Master for certain details. Either for the sake of safety, a selfish need to appear mysterious, or the vain need to not seem weak by admitting he doesn't have everything figured out, the Master kept a great number of details close to the vest.

"Searching..." the Forgotten Master cryptically replied. "Now make haste. Time is of the essence."

David did as instructed and set out on his mission back into the city to find the mysterious Luci. He hoped that the Forgotten Master was correct and that this tracker could help him find Marnie. Marnie who had become his last best hope of rescuing Scot.

***

The Forgotten Master returned to his meditations. He had made a large gambit in having the girl brought over. He was convinced there would be no stopping Imperium if they managed to get their hands on her but he was equally convinced there would be no stopping them without the power he suspected she possessed.

The Master used his meditations to search his mind for lost history, solutions for the strife affecting Eternal Dawn.

The Flood had removed dominion over the Muse from the hands of the Master lineages who had controlled it. It had been redistributed with equity among all of the sentient beings in the land, creating a balance that had remained undisturbed for over a decade.

Muse was the primary means by which ideas were actualized into corporeal existence. It flowed through everything possessing life in Eternal Dawn like a finely woven tapestry and was the source of the glowing light that all of this life exhibited. Gifted craftspeople known as Musers were able to harness the Muse to produce any manner of product. Children would marvel as toys and trinkets slowly took form out of nowhere in the palms of one so gifted at channeling this mysterious energy. In the decade immediately after the Flood, the only true currency was in that of the ideas provided for production and the Musers saw it as a duty to bring to light any idea valid enough for said production; to share the fruits with anyone who was in need. For a short time, the denizens of the world were content in their ability to harness the Muse and provide for themselves.

After the Flood, the world would see other positive effects outside of the redistribution of Muse. The pockets of darkness created when a Master drew power toward them no longer existed, further serving the balance. This allowed the creatures of the now undarkened forests to become less feral. There were also fewer dark alleyways in towns and cities, leading to less crime. It was supposed to be the start of a new age of prosperity.

It was in the days just prior to this Flood-born peace that the Master was now attempting to search. These were the final days of the Last War, a war fought, like so many wars, to hold onto ill-gotten power.

The Geddes lineage had created Muse orbs in service of their last great Master-work, the Geddes Road. The apple-sized glowing orbs of pure concentrated Muse allowed for a shortcut to creation which also meant a shortcut to progress on the

Masterwork. Rather than sending all of the gifted Musers to the far reaches of the road and having them sit idle as they waited for their spent energy to regenerate, the Geddes could harvest Muse elsewhere and ship it there, greatly speeding up their efforts. With an accurate enough schematic, even the layest of Muse users could produce a structure in short order.

The Geddes Road had promised prosperity but that ultimately proved to be a lie. The road's completion did provide a short-term boon with its ability to easily move ideas to far away cities and less populated rural areas. It created a global network that was intended to allow the free flow of ideas, allowing for much quicker advancement and better quality of life for all those who partook.

Prosperity, however, didn't come without cost. Problems had arisen due to the road's orb-driven means of production and these problems were twofold. Once concentrated, the Muse couldn't return to nature until used. This again created pockets of darkness where Muse couldn't diffuse as fast as it was being concentrated. The second issue was that this power only rested with a small set of lineages, specifically the Geddes and the handful of families they chose to share the Muse aggregation process with. The scarcity of natural resources had effectively changed Eternal Dawn's economy to revolve around the orbs. Their value was such that, rather than use the orbs for creation, most were forced to use them in trade as a form of currency. The marketplace of ideas that had served the land well for thousands of years was almost dead.

The level of oligarchic power that the Geddes had amassed was unprecedented in modern Eternal Dawn, leading to the inevitability of the Last War.

Entire towns and villages had been leveled in service of this war. The rival Coimín Master lineage had been completely wiped out. The remaining unaligned lineages banded together under the lost lineage's banner in an attempt to fight back but even with their combined power, they were no match for the Geddes war machine.

The Flood had been the final Masterwork of the legendary Vagabond Master. When the dust settled, the event had almost completely redistributed the Muse across the land. The ability to concentrate the power was extricated from the Master lineages and the methods of orb production were lost, now only discussed as matters of speculation. The Flood took the Vagabond Master and with him the method of its execution.

The Flood had become the focus of the Forgotten Master's search as a new concentration of Muse had now reached a point where a war against it may not be possible. It was a concentration that was no longer supposed to be possible. A concentration the Forgotten Master was convinced he could end. A concentration that had created the 'Dying of the Light'.

And so he searched.

***

David had to be careful making his way back to Ærratum. The disruption to Muse flow from his and what he assumed was Marnie's inevitable crossing, was sure to have put Imperium on alert. With Brutus by his side, he took a different path away from the Cloister. He wasn't about to use the same path twice and risk inadvertently betraying the order.

After she had helped him to get back, David half hoped that his search would come up empty, that Marnie would leave the crossing well enough alone. He felt terrible getting her involved and even worse that he had tricked her into doing it. The temptation of forbidden fruit, he knew, would have been more than Marnie could ignore.

He felt, however, that if the Forgotten Master were correct, she could be Eternal Dawn's only hope to escape the darkness. Marnie, at that moment, may have been the only hope for Earth as well. He may not have been as well reasoned as either of the Murphy siblings but it was plain for him to see that the problems facing the two worlds were inextricably linked.

David decided his best option would be to take the eastern entrance to the city. The Geddes road attached itself to the city on the western side. Ærratum had evolved to accept the new roadway. Fresh construction had tended to favor the western side, causing it to become trendy and desirable, leaving the east side to languish. In more recent years, with the latest Muse concentration and the darkness that followed, the disparity had become much more pronounced. It had become a place where respectable people didn't want to be and the constabulary didn't want to go.

While David could remain relatively undetected from the prying eyes of Imperium, this side of the city presented its own set of dangers. Some of the Geddes allied lineages had gone underground after the Flood but in recent years had started to reemerge. While not able to wield power over the Muse as they once had, they still were able to wield the power of muscle.

David's concerns also extended to the matter of identification. His first action upon taking his initial flight from the city was to burn his papers. With the events that had taken place immediately before his departure, they would only serve as a liability. He was, after all, a wanted criminal.

Despite his concerns, identification wouldn't end up being required. The guards stationed at this gate possessed considerably fewer scruples than those found at the western gate. They weren't the type to shy away from a good bribe. Despite Muse being in short supply and Imperium's cuff technology, ideas were still seen as valid currency in some pockets of the city. Luckily for David, much of his and Scot's wasted youth was spent watching late-night infomercials. This night would count the third time he had traded a guard the idea for an ultra-absorbent cloth that could clean up any kitchen spill for entry to the city. He was always very careful to not provide any ideas that were actually useful for fear that they could fall into the wrong hands.

He had neglected to tell the Forgotten but David was well aware of where the Violet Huntress was located. Before the rise of Imperium, he and Scot would frequent the location, often able to trade a night of fun for a simple cocktail recipe from back home. The tavern was only a few blocks away from the east gate and he was able to cover the distance with Brutus without so much as a second glance.

As David entered, he mused to himself, "What a perfect place to start a new adventure," recalling the fantasy books he had read in his younger years. The tavern he found himself in was quite rustic. The room was dimly lit. Its vaulted ceilings were propped up by branches of purpleheart. The living branches had been carved into, wounded to expose the light flowing beneath the bark.

On one of the walls, there was a large cobblestone fireplace, of which the mantle sat chest high to David. A majority of the light in the room, however, was supplied by a giant chandelier made of trompf antlers. Even detached, the antlers retained a Muse reactive fluorescent property, providing an automatic self-adjusting ambiance. The more lively the discussion and the more ideas flowed in the tavern the brighter they would glow. As evenings dragged on and a great number of libations were imbibed, the chandelier would dim, providing cover for idiotic and nefarious activity alike.

The focal point for the tavern was the eight-foot-tall full-body portrait painting of the eponymous Violet Huntress which was perched above the fireplace. It was a hunting portrait of the lady in a purple safari suit. Her braided violet hair complemented her mauve skin tone but stood in contrast to the green-stocked, brass-barreled thunderbuss she was holding.

David had entered the tavern with caution, the hood of his dark robe raised in an effort to conceal his face. In the times since the Flood, it had become a haven for miscreants and grifters alike. While there had been a sort of honor amongst thieves when he and Scot had occasion to frequent the establishment, the sort that sojourned themselves there as of late could no longer be trusted. Aside from the possibility of Imperium spies, there was also the possibility of former acquaintances ratting him out for even a small orb of Muse or an extra charge to their cuff. He was lucky on this occasion, the patrons paid no mind to him or the dog Brutus.

David surveyed the room, half expecting Brutus to immediately pick out who the mysterious Luci was. He should have known it wasn't going to be so easy. There were a little less than two dozen patrons in the tavern, any of whom could have made David, spelling disaster for his mission. He immediately ruled out the ten largest patrons. It was exceedingly rare to find a tracker taller than six feet and they were rarely bulky. The need to blend into crowds and get into tight spaces was very much a requisite of the profession. David was unaware of having met a chameleon before but as far as knew, they lacked the ability to alter their mass and bone structure.

He was also able to rule out the five slightest patrons, perhaps with a small bit of prejudice. A bit of muscle and stored fat was, in David's estimation, also a prerequisite to the job. Depending on where a job took you, a tracker needed muscle to be able to navigate rough terrain. There was no guarantee that one would be able to light a fire for warmth or cooking lest their position be revealed. A little bit of insulation would prove useful in these situations.

This left David with six possible candidates, which he couldn't narrow down further. It would be useless to divide the pool by gender as chameleons could slightly shift fat deposits and skin features allowing them to pass for whichever gender they choose. He didn't dare approach any of the suspects to inquire directly. For all he knew, they might be Imperium spies.

David walked a lap of the room with Brutus but the dog made no hint that he had detected the tracker. Aware that he might be raising suspicion with his activities, he pressed up to the bar and ordered a negroni, one of the drink recipes he had traded to cover a previous tab. He then took up residence at an empty table, continuing to survey the crowd in an attempt to further eliminate potential suspects.

The candidates were in odd groupings. Two of them were sitting amongst a party of five engaged in lively conversation. Another two were seated at a table with four others playing cards. Yet another was sitting in an alcove booth reading a book. The final one was posted up at the bar trying to mind their own business. After some deliberation, he considered it unwise to discount anyone. His hunch told him it was the loner in the booth but there was no hard rule that a tracker had to be alone, even if the rangers of the fantasy books he had read in his youth had been portrayed as such.

David took a moment to consider what the Forgotten Master had said about Brutus being able to detect 'their kind'. It had struck David at that moment that perhaps what Brutus was picking up on were the moments when a chameleon was in the process of a shift. The shift he suspected required a rapid generation and consumption of Muse. Brutus as with all golden retrievers in Eternal Dawn had a keen enough sense of smell to pick up on changes in the essence. David's thoughts had begun to focus on how he could force a chameleon shift.

He had a recollection that both Eternal Dawn's and Earth's chameleons would undergo rapid changes as a response to stress, often darkening in color. David didn't know if it was the same in humanoids but reasoned it may be worth a shot. He needed a way to create a sudden disturbance that wouldn't bring too much attention to himself or the dog.

With Brutus lying dutifully under the table, David studied the room for a little over an hour. In that time he watched the comings and goings of the patrons, the bartender, and the barback. The potential suspect sitting at the bar made their exit and hadn't returned, a strike against suspecting a loner. He had taken note that the barback went through and cleared the tables of empty glasses every ten to fifteen minutes. David had a sudden flash of realization that this barback was the key to accomplishing his goal.

At this moment he was grateful to still be wearing his Cloister robes, primarily due to the flared sleeves providing concealment for his next act and secondarily for the hood covering his face. His small epiphanous moment had caused the chandelier above him to emit a quick flash, causing a few heads to turn and Brutus's ears to perk up. The moment also caused David to feel a quick and pleasant rush as the Muse pulsed out of his brain and started to emanate through his body. It felt like a warm hug. The veins in his face and body were sure to have been glowing with neon intensity. If not for the robes, this would have surely drawn unneeded attention.

Brutus hadn't become any more engaged, causing David to surmise that the chandelier flash hadn't been enough to rouse his target. That or she had been the one to leave.

David proceeded with his plan. He started by removing a spray can from his pack, not paying attention to the color. Luckily for him, color wouldn't be an issue in his plan. With the can hidden in his large sleeve, he leaned over, positioning the nozzle an inch off the floor. David started spraying the floor with what he was hoping were solid circles no bigger than grapes. After he had fifteen of them in a tight cluster, he secured the can back in his bag and waited a few minutes for his opening.

It wasn't long before the barback started to make another round. His routine for the evening had been to go to each of the nine tables in the bar, wipe down any of the vacant ones, check on the patrons, and ask to collect any empty glasses. Two minutes would pass before the barback would reach the area that surrounded David's table.

He waited until the barback was halfway through his latest round before acting. David started by focusing his intentions. He could feel the Muse drain from most of his appendages and pass through his chest before collecting in his left hand. As his hand hovered over the paint, the trompf antlers overhead gradually started to dim. This caused Brutus's attention to shoot to David's hand.

Moments later David scooped up his creations. He proceeded to roll his newly minted marbles across the floor and into the path of the barback. Then just as the barback started to lose his balance, David stood up and began to move swiftly across the tavern.

He had no sooner reached the other side of the bar when he heard the shattering of half a dozen glasses, which was followed by the thud of the barback hitting the floor. In the moment that followed the disturbance, the chandelier flashed a bright white light. David checked the floor surrounding his victim and as intended, he watched the marbles dissolve into nothingness. He had put enough distance between himself and his creations.

David hoped the flash of light was the result of a forced stress response from his target and not by his disappearing marbles releasing their expended Muse. He surveyed the room for Brutus who had left the safe confines of his under-table vantage point. He glanced over at the poker table and then to the party of five, seeing nothing. His eyes then shot to the alcove booth with the loner who had been reading. This is where David had found Brutus, with a shimmering golden glow and a viciously wagging tail. The stranger was attempting to comfort what she assumed to be a very startled dog.

David made his way back across the room to the alcove booth mere paces from where he had been sitting.

"Luci I presume?" David said as he reached down to pat the dog's rump for a job well done.

"Dude, you could have saved all of the effort and just come up to me. I've been sitting here doing the international, 'I'm a ranger sitting alone in a dark alcove thing...' It's not that hard," Luci replied, amused by the effort David had put in to find her.

"I'm with the Cloister," David responded. "We need your help."

Chapter Nine

"...eddying darkness seemed to swim round me..."

Marnie was seated cross-legged by a fire that either Trig or Chauncey had built. She thought that the smart money was on Trig but the question wasn't important enough to pursue. She was debating how much of her story she should share. Where she was from, a person would be committed for attempting to explain what she had been through. She had been prone to having insane-sounding esoteric conversations with Martin but he was an artist and understood her need to 'get weird' as part of the creative process. She wasn't very well going to have a conversation akin to the Dying with her mother. She decided she would need to probe her rescuers to find out if they were 'cool'.

"What did you mean when you said I was a much more worthy opponent?" Marnie asked.

"He said worthy prey, not worthy opponent, lass," Trig responded. "There's a big difference. In all likelihood, that thing would have shredded you to bits."

"Now now now, now now, now now," Chauncey chimed in. "I think you are splitting hairs here my dear Trig. Had I known who she was when we approached I would have let her alone to handle herself."

Trig scoffed, "Oh, do enlighten me as to who you think she is." The emphasis on 'do' was exaggerated, the implication being that they were about to hear yet another tale of fancy.

Marnie perked up with interest. Perhaps he was alluding to other Earthlings existing in this world. Perhaps he was referring to Scot. "Yes do enlighten," she chimed in, unconsciously adopting a bit of Trig's manner of speech.

"Look at her skin. Look at her veins. Just look at how much Muse is flowing through her. I ken she's a Master of course!" Chauncey exclaimed.

"A Master...A Master? Here we go again. With brilliant ideas like these, it's a wonder Imperium hasn't snatched you up yet. Real wonder the Sìth didn't try to attack you instead," Trig responded mockingly. "There hasn't been a Master worth a damn in over fifteen years."

"Tell them," Chauncey begged, looking over at Marnie, expecting an affirmative response.

"I...I don't know what you're talking about," Marnie stammered.

"Oh, right," Chauncey winked at Marnie. "We don't work for Imperium. See," he said, showing his empty wrists before proceeding to grab at Trig's as well. "See, they don't have them either! You can trust us."

"Stop that," Trig ordered, slapping Chauncey's hands away.

"I don't understand. What don't you have and what is this Imperium you keep talking about?" Marnie responded, hoping that something in this world would soon start to make sense.

"Why the cuffs of course. You're funny. You know Imperium. Imperium, the evil organization hell-bent in their dragon-like hoarding of Muse. Imperium. Evil-sounding name. Imperium," Chauncey kept insisting in a tone that indicated he thought Marnie was having a laugh at his expense.

"Can't you see she doesn't know what you're talking about?" Trig chimed in. "Marnie, you're not from around here are you?"

Marnie, not exactly sure if the pair were 'cool', had gathered enough to know that they may be 'cool enough'. "I'm sorry, I'm not," she responded.

"No need to be sorry Miss Marnie," Chauncey stated, now even more intrigued. "You must be one of the Masters from Arthur, the moon of the moon Uthyr. Sure enough, you are. I've heard tell that that's where they went. Went up there to watch over us they did. Finally decided things were bad enough down here to intervene huh?"

"Here we go again. For the last time, they didn't go to the moon. They gave up their power or were stripped of it by the Vagabond Master during the Flood," Trig jumped in, knowing this would in fact, not be the last time. "Quit trying to turn it into another conspiracy theory. The Masters are gone. It doesn't have to be more interesting than that."

"But..." Chauncey attempted to start in again before being cut off by Marnie.

"I'm not from this world or that 'moon of the moon'," Marnie said, hesitating slightly on the moon description. "I came through a Green Man from my world," she continued, only realizing after the words had left her mouth, how acutely insane they sounded.

"Wait wait wait, wait wait, wait wait," Chauncey chimed in again excitedly. "Are you the new Vagabond Master? I can't believe it. Sitting at my fire. The Vagabond Master. Rumor is, he was the only one who could use the Green Doors. I thought he was dead. You must be his successor, right?... Right?"

"I'm never going to hear the end of this," Trig uttered under their breath, hoping that Marnie would answer in the negative. The realization that Chauncey had made a rare point wouldn't be something that was quickly lived down. The Vagabond Master had been the only known person capable of using the doors.

"I don't even know what a Vagabond Master is, let alone any other Master of which you speak.," Marnie said with confusion, each interaction leading to more questions than answers

Trig took this opportunity to shush down Chauncey and provide Marnie with an abbreviated although coherent narrative history concerning the Masters of Eternal Dawn. They started with the nature of the Muse, continued through the 'Last War,' and closed with the Flood which had caused the war's end.

***

With the bored affect of a history professor teaching a 'one-o-one' course, Trig concluded, "...And so it was almost fifteen years ago that the Vagabond Master made the ultimate sacrifice, thereby removing dominion over the Muse from the Masters and giving it to the people."

Chauncey added, "That wizard-looking gentleman was the greatest citizen Eternal Dawn has ever known. We sure could use him now."

"Wait, the Masters aren't wizards?" Marnie questioned, again realizing how deranged her words sounded after they had already been uttered. With what she had already seen of the world, she was ready to believe anything.

"Oh, no no no, no no," Chauncey answered. "Magic is for fairy tales. The Masters are, or were...well...hopefully still are, scientists and artists, sometimes both. When I said the Vagabond looked like a wizard, I meant he had long hair and a long bushy beard. He also had an amazing sense of style and I should know. I mean...look at me."

The surrounding trees, mosses, and fireflies began to illuminate with greater intensity. Trig had been the only one to take note but hadn't said anything, almost anticipating what was to come next.

"What...what kind of art did you say the Vagabond Master did again?" Marnie asked.

"Oh I didn't lass...but he was a sculptor, a really good one too. Real shame he's dead," Chauncey said as he continued to drone on, singing the Vagabond Master's praises.

Marnie sat in stunned silence not hearing the words Chauncey had continued to speak. "Could it have been him?" she thought.

"Little known fact," Marnie heard Chauncey's voice creep through the fog. "Those that knew him best called him Declan. Hush-hush on that though. Commoners aren't supposed to know these things..."

Chauncey continued to drone on as Marnie once more tuned him out. After a few moments there was a blinding flash, followed by an immediate darkness, then tears.

***

Marnie was unsure why the revelation of her father's demise hit her as hard as it had. He disappeared when she was barely four and was only in a handful of her memories. Perhaps it was the final closing of a chapter in her life that had remained open for far too long. Perhaps it was because she had lived in the shadow of his legacy for fifteen years. Fifteen years of looking at his unfinished art. Fifteen years of theories surrounding his disappearance. Fifteen years of her mother's refusal to mourn him. Perhaps she wasn't weeping for the man but weeping for the unresolved legacy that had helped to mold her. Marnie sat alone with her feelings, waiting for the moment to fade.

***

Trig and Chauncey left Marnie's side to survey the sudden shift in their situation. Their main concern had become the epiphanous flash which left them in nearly total darkness. The Muse fluctuation stemming from the revelation Marnie had just endured was sure to have caused the forest to take notice. If they were lucky, that would be the only attention they would attract.

Trig had learned not to rely on luck and immediately took point, trying to determine the extent of the blowout. Without being able to detect light in any direction, they sent Chauncey up the nearest tree before checking their inventory of Muse orbs, hoping the stash in their bag had been insulated from destruction. To their surprise, the orbs were still intact.

Chauncey returned from the tree after a few moments, having investigated the event's reach. For well over five miles in every direction, the light had completely washed out of every living being, both flora and fauna. This made the immediate surroundings particularly dangerous. Trig had never experienced a blowout of this magnitude but was sure it would be at least a few hours before the light would leach back to their current position.

To make matters worse, the moonset for Arthur and Uthyr was about to begin. The red moon, 'Lonely Sister', wouldn't make her appearance in the sky for another four hours, leaving only the stars for light, light that was only sporadically creeping through the forest canopy above.

"I've never heard of a Master being able to do this, at least not at this magnitude," Chauncey uttered.

"I should think not," Trig replied.

"Did you see her glow? I mean, while we were talking to her. It's like she's not affected by the Dying at all," Chauncey said with an excited fascination.

"You mentioned the glow already," Trig responded with mild annoyance.

"What do you think she is then?" Chauncey demanded, trying to force Trig into indulging his earlier theory.

"At this point...I would have to concede...that she is of Master lineage if, of course, the Vagabond was indeed her father. What else...I cannae say," Trig responded, qualifying their statement but knowing what they said would rightfully be heard as an admission of earlier ignorance.

"So she is the Vagabond Master. I knew it. I knew it. I told you," Chauncey said, the smile on his face made no attempt to mask his gloating. He paid no mind to the fact that Trig had simply been working with the facts at hand, while he had been working with theory and conjecture. It was simple luck that on this one occasion, he happened to be proven correct.

"In time she may be. But for now, I ken she is just a sad, scared girl. A girl that doesn't need any more of your probing questions. A girl that is going to need our help. A girl that we need to get out of this darkness with haste," Trig replied as a woeful feeling started to overcome them, a feeling that they had just become entangled in events that might not alter their life for the better.

***

Trig approached Marnie, attempting to speak with a reserved and compassionate tone, "Marnie deary, I know you are going through some pretty heavy shite right now. A lot of things aren't making sense and I'm sorry but now isn't going to be the best time for answers. We are really...really going to need to get the hell out of here."

"I'm sorry, I'm sorry, I'm sorry, I'm sorry," Marnie repeated almost under her breath, not knowing what else to say. She could feel the danger creeping in as she started to hyperventilate again. She couldn't help but feel responsible. "Maybe this could have been prevented," she thought, had she been better at controlling her panic.

Trig crouched down and looked Marnie in her face. "It's alright...it's alright. Just focus on my voice and breath. Know that this feeling will pass, and breathe," they said quietly, elongating the word breathe in a further attempt to provide consolation. As Trig was monitoring Marnie's breathing, they were struck with another observation. An observation that was novel but not exactly ideal in the face of the trio's current predicament. With each passing breath, Marnie's glow was regenerating. This was in contrast to their glow which had blown out with the rest of the forest and wouldn't likely return until they had removed themselves from the darkness. Marnie was quickly becoming a beacon.

"Marnie, are you okay to get moving yet? I understand what you are going through and I don't want to put undue pressure on you but it's not exactly safe here," Trig asked with a muted tone, attempting to avoid intensifying the feelings that she was enduring.

"I think I'm good," she whispered as she hesitantly rose to her feet, still feeling uneasy.

"Here, I got this for you," Chauncey said quietly, as he helped to steady the girl before handing her a dark robe. "It's to help hide your...well your glow."

Marnie looked down at her arms then at both Trig and Chauncey, continuing their hushed conversation, "Why aren't you..."

"We'll need to explain walking," Trig responded, as Marnie began to cover herself with the new garment. They continued, "Now to pick a heading."

"I was heading toward Err-err-rratum," Marnie said, offering a suggestion, not exactly sure of her pronunciation.

"Ahh the belly of the beast," Chauncey replied. "A woman in search of adventure I see. Let's do it. Oh, and it's Air-rratum."

"On second thought, maybe we should avoid that for now if we can," Marnie said, trying to temper Chauncey's zealousness in the wake of his statement. 'Belly of the beast', were words that had given her pause. "It was just what was closest on the sign when I got here and I thought I could see light pollution from a city on the horizon," she finished.

Chauncey was quick to reply, "What's light pollution?"

Marnie responded, curious if it was called something more eloquent here, "It's like when a city is too bright and its light blocks out the stars. Do you not have that?"

"Nay Miss Marnie, you must be very lucky to come from a place with so much Muse that it washes out the stars," Chauncey responded with wonderment.

"Oh no, we don't have Muse where I come from, we have light bulbs, powered by electricity," Marnie clarified, mildly amused that Chauncey was now the confused one.

"I'd hate to break up this discussion but like I said, we need to tell it walking. The blowout was bound to attract attention," Trig interjected, reiterating their concerns. "I'm not willing to head into the lion's den just yet either. At least not until we have a few more answers about what you are and the nature of your quest. The way I see it, we will be in danger no matter the direction. I also hesitate to head east as that would take us closer to the road. Only the constabulary and Imperium are still using it at this point. Either or both of them may be heading this way now."

"We still need to complete the delivery," Chauncey replied, reminding Trig of their original purpose for being out in the forest. "We could keep going south to Drumlocke. I've got it from a source...that got it from a source...that it's rumored...that a former Master works in the library there. Wordsmith, I believe they're called. May be able to provide some insight." He knew acutely that it was Wordsmith but didn't want to come across as too eager.

"'Fraid to admit it, that's kind of what I was thinking, at least about the delivery. Not sure we should be talking to anyone about Marnie just yet, least of all a former Master," Trig responded. They placed no trust in the former Masters, having become orphaned in the Last War, a Master's war.

"It's settled then. Marnie, any objections?" Chauncey replied, querying Marnie to make sure she at least felt like she had a choice.

"Good with me," she said, not knowing what else she could do. She was still feeling numbness from the adrenal depletion of her panic attack.

"With any luck, the darkwash has dampened that Sìth's senses," Trig mentioned as they started down the southern path with Marnie and Chauncey in tow. It was a thought they should have probably kept to themselves but with Marnie being the only being with Muse for at least a couple of miles, it had become a valid concern.

***

Once the moons had completely set, Trig produced three small Muse orbs from their inventory. The orbs would provide a source of light in the pitch-black forest. In their unused state, a small orb generated enough light to illuminate an average-sized room, which, in the forest they found themselves in, was enough light to illuminate the path just ahead.

Marnie's eyes took a few moments to adjust to the new light source and it wasn't long before she started to catch glimpses of the random twinkling of eyes. The rightfully startled fauna in the area had begun to stir. Some creatures were just lost, wandering aimlessly in the darkness, while others had come to investigate. Marnie couldn't help but feel bad for the disruption her presence had caused but also feared for what may be lingering in the darkness.

Trig was busy keeping their ears open for unexpected sounds. The level of noise in the forest had been tempered by the blowout but there was still the expected chirping of crickets, the scurrying of rodents in the fallen leaves, and the babbling of a nearby brook. As of yet, there had been no indication that the Razor-Sìth had returned or that of any other nearby creature that may be intent on doing them harm.

"So what are we hauling?" Marnie asked, referring to the delivery run she now found herself to be a part of.

"The very Muse orbs we are holding," Chauncey replied, much to Trig's chagrin.

The devices weren't, strictly speaking, legal. In the time since the Flood, Muse concentration had been outlawed in Eternal Dawn. This prohibition extended to all existing orbs and birthed a black market of sorts for any device that hadn't already been confiscated and destroyed. They were the perfect product for this kind of enterprise. On top of their infinite utility, they were highly portable and untraceable. In the far reaches of Ærratum, the Dying had also generated seemingly endless demand. This was a black market in which Trig and Chauncey were active contributors.

"Must be similar to your 'light bulbs'," Chauncey whispered, his pivot serving to reignite an earlier conversation. "...powered by electricity? You must have very clever Musers to be able to harness lightning."

"It's not like that," Marnie responded, trying to think of a parallel that would make sense. "Well, I guess it sort of is...It would take too long to explain all of it. But we call our Musers, artists, inventors, and engineers and they didn't exactly harness it...but in a roundabout way I guess it did all start with lightning."

"Aye Marnie lass, those words are not foreign to me. They all fall into the Muser bucket. Hell, once upon a time there was a Master called The Engineer," Chauncey gleefully replied, happy to be creating a shorthand with Marnie. "I would be more than happy to discuss further. Under safer circumstances of course," he continued with genuine intrigue, steering away from the topic as it would require a focus that he currently needed to monitor for immediate dangers.

"If the light on the horizon isn't a city, what is it?" Marnie questioned, trying to get closure on her outstanding query.

"That's the sun," Trig offered, joining in the conversation.

"Ooooh...I thought there must be one here. How long are the days?" she continued to probe.

"Tidal locked. There are no days here...only nights," Trig stated.

"So the sun never rises?" Marnie asked before answering on her own, "...Eternal Dawn."

"Yeah...Eternal Dawn," Trig confirmed, hoping her small epiphany wasn't enough to trigger another event of some kind. Then out of nervousness, they appended, "Can we keep the revelating questions to a minimum for the time being?"

Chauncey and Marnie obliged, understanding the request as they continued to hike through the forest. They had walked for another ten minutes before Trig whispered at them to stop. They started to swivel their head, keeping an ear pointed toward the darkness. They listened closely, thinking they had heard the murmured sounds of a garbled conversation, eventually chalking it up to the babbling brook, before signaling to move on.

A few moments passed before Trig thought they saw small orbs of light darting back and forth across the trail just ahead. They motioned to the others to stop once again as they scanned the outer edge of their circle of light, trying to focus their eyes and peer into the darkness. As Trig's vision started to become clear, they started to notice a few of the things they had been hoping to avoid. At roughly waist height, Trig could detect the slight glow of nine and a half sets of amber-colored eyes. Eyes that were reflecting the orb's light back at them.

"What is it?" Marnie whispered.

"Moblins, don't make any sudden movements," Trig said as they slowly collected the two orbs from Chauncey and Marnie.

"Moblins?" Marnie questioned, thinking she had misheard but knowing she should try to avoid being surprised at any of the creatures she had encountered in this strange world.

"Goblins in a mob," Chauncey chimed in.

"Is that bad?" she asked, surprised at the casualness with which Chauncey had replied but already anticipating the answer that followed.

"Very," Trig quietly answered. "On my cue, we are going to need to run." After taking a moment to collect their thoughts, they then barked out, "You can come out, we know you're there."

On the trail directly ahead, the creature belonging to the half set of eyes stepped out of the shadows. Marnie began to take stock. It was indeed a goblin of legend. There was a leather eye patch over one of its eye sockets. Very obvious scars crept out from under the patch's borders. Its ears were much smaller than the ones she had seen in books, possessing an almost elven quality about them. Its nose was stubby and flat. The creature's mouth was full of jagged pointed teeth. It wore crude hide sandals which only appeared to cover the top portion of its feet, leaving its unkempt claw-like toes exposed to the elements. Its legs were covered in a type of leather Marnie couldn't identify. On its pants, she was horrified to see what appeared to be the tattoo of a sigil or ward similar to the ones found in her father's sketchbook. On one side of the creature's waist, there was a sheathed dagger. On the opposing side, there was a metal ring that had small spherical vials tied to it. The vials contained what appeared to be a dark liquid, the color of which wasn't easily identified in the pale yellow-green light of the Muse orbs. The creature wore a patchwork vest made up of assorted textiles with varying colors. On top of its head, it wore a cloth cap that appeared to have an air of dampness; its sheen reflected the light of the orbs. The creature's face was covered with dried dark drips which looked to have run off of the moist cap.

Shortly after the creature had made its presence visibly known, the other goblins crept out from the shadows. They had a similar appearance but lacked the cap, vials, and ocular mutilation of their leader.

"Muse!" the leader's shrill gravelly voice demanded.

Trig, in an attempt at a diplomatic solution, stepped toward the goblin with one of the Muse orbs in their outstretched hand.

"No! Muuuse," the goblin leader barked in response to Trig's advance. It had taken its dagger out and was pointing it toward the glowing Marnie. "She reeks of it."

The other goblins mirrored this action, pulling out their various blades and clubs. The leader then advanced a step and the others followed suit, shrinking the radius of the circle surrounding the trio.

"That is not going to happen," Trig said, responding to the demand.

"It wasn't a request, human," the leader's shrill voice responded. The goblin took another step closer, causing his compatriots to respond in kind. It then snatched one of the vials from its belt and smashed it into the cap at the top of its head. This caused the others to respond with roars in a type of war cry as they raised and pumped their weapons in the air.

Marnie watched in horror. The viscosity of the liquid dripping down the goblin's face made clear that the vial had been filled with blood of unknown origin. She thought if Trig was going to act, now would be the time, otherwise, this could be her end.

It was at this moment that Trig did act. They ordered Chauncey and Marnie to cover their ears before forcefully throwing one of the Muse orbs toward the ground, causing it to fracture and explode. The broken orb produced a luminescent vapor that lingered around Trig's feet. In a matter of seconds, the Muse vapors had been pulled into their lower legs, shooting through their veins. The purple glow of Trig's body had become restored and amplified as the Muse completed working its way through their extremities. The shock of electric blue hair on their head was illuminated with a vibrancy that hadn't been there in years. Then as quickly as their body had flushed itself with the powerful substance, it was pulled back out, pooling into their right hand. Trig threw a second orb at the ground, screaming, "Run!" They covered their ears while still holding the final orb as best they could as a source of light for their escape.

Moments later the sound of an air raid siren started to blare. It was deafening, able to pierce through the hands that muffled the trio's ears. Light started to strobe with various colors and intensity as bolts of Muse lightning shot out of the device Trig had created.

The machine had the desired effect. The goblins tried to cover their ears and eyes to escape the sudden assault on their senses, leaving them in anguish. One of them had forgotten to sheath their blade, running it into their ear as they attempted to quash the noise. Another ran up to the device to destroy it but was hit with one of the Muse bolts. This miscalculation left the goblin as a pile of ash and a pool of metal which had once been their blade.

***

The trio of humans were running as fast as they could down the trail, keeping their eyes focused on the dimly lit ground in front of them as they searched for hazards. They had gained a thousand meters before their chests started to burn with an intensity that beckoned them to slow down. The device Trig had devised started to fall silent as it used up its infused Muse fuel source.

"The moblins will no doubt be giving chase," Trig said. "We have to keep going."

"I'm not sure how much more I've got," Marnie managed to eke out between labored breaths.

"Well, you're going to have to dig a bit deeper, lass," Chauncey managed to get out between his own breaths. "What dear Trig did may have given us a bit of a head start but it was sure to have done not much more than piss them off. They may be short but they're quick. The devils will catch us up 'fore too long."

Chauncey was correct in his assessment. The trio had only been able to run another five hundred meters when they started hearing the shrill hollers of the creatures behind them. Trig could just barely make out the border of the dark-wash in the far-off distance. If they could make it there before the moblins caught up to them, the trio might have some potential to hide in the woods where the leaves still glowed with Muse. Perhaps this would allow Marnie's 'scent' to blend in with the surroundings. The trio kept pushing forward, their pace slowing with each passing step despite the sound of the moblins continuing to grow.

"Why can't we just set another trap with the orbs?" Marnie barely managed to say with her lungs on fire the way they were.

"It was only because of the blowout that I was able to do it the first time," Trig responded through their labored breaths. "If there is so much as a small amount of Muse left in my body, the cycle charging would more than likely blow my veins apart...Vasoimpedance...I'd like to try and avoid that if you please."

"And Chauncey?" Marnie questioned.

"Aye Miss Marnie, nonstarter I'm 'fraid," Chauncey spoke for himself, gasping through his words. "Aside from the fact that I wouldn't know how to begin absorbin' from an orb, I'm nay a gifted Muser. Barely be able to muster a kazoo and a sparkler compared to dear Trig here. Be a waste of an orb."

The longer the three ran, the more obvious it had become that they wouldn't be able to reach the potential safety of the illuminated forest ahead. Without a plan, they had no choice but to carry on while hoping for some manner of 'deus ex machina' to save them from their immediate peril.

Marnie had slowed to a speed that necessitated Trig grabbing her by the arm in an attempt to push her forward to keep the pace. It was at this moment that the group realized that the moblins had quieted down.

Trig knew better than to think they had given up their chase. They thought in all likelihood the moblins had started to stalk through the surrounding woods, getting poised for a second ambush. Goblins only had so many tricks up their ratty sleeves.

Trig's premonition proved correct. In short measure, they had run up on a group of three goblins blocking the path ahead. This caused the trio to stop cold in their tracks. Glancing toward their back, Trig detected another four goblins blocking a rear escape. They knew that their small group would be nowhere near as nimble as a goblin, negating the possibility of a sideways exit through the forest.

Trig then realized the leader was missing from the ambush and wondered if he had been killed in the last encounter. This could give them the fighting chance they needed to escape the situation. A leaderless group of moblins was disorganized and chaotic. If they were to savage one of them brutally enough, it may shock the others into giving up.

Trig had no sooner finished the thought when, out of the corner of their eye, they caught a glimpse of the capped goblin in the middle of a flying leap. The goblin leader was coming directly at them. Trig was barely able to maintain their balance as the goblin's clawed feet dug into either side of their body.

Chauncey and Marnie stood watching, paralyzed with fear. The four rear goblins used the inaction to their advantage and moved between them and the engaged Trig. The goblins pulled out their daggers to keep Chauncey and Marnie at bay while their boss exacted his revenge.

The goblin leader grabbed hold of the hand Trig was using to hold the lighted orb and latched its gnarled teeth into the fleshy part of their forearm. Trig screamed in agony, dropping the orb, which rolled off to the side of the path. The goblin paid no mind as it rolled away, the initial attack serving the purpose of avoiding the creation of another disorienting device. The creature then started clawing at Trig's chest, grabbing hold and locking their right arm against the side of their torso. The goblin was now actively trying to bite at Trig's throat.

With their left fist, Trig was able to catch the goblin's own throat with a quick punch. This jarred the beast, causing it to grasp at its neck and lean back as it gasped for air. Trig then ripped the goblin off the side of their body and with both arms forcefully slammed it into the ground. The subordinate goblins started to encroach as the leader rolled away, scrambling to get back up to his feet.

"No! Mine," the goblin shrieked, causing the others to back off a step. The goblin then pulled out its dagger and ran up on Trig again, stabbing them in the left calf as he passed by. Trig screamed and immediately grasped at their leg before falling over in pain. The leader took a few breaths to admire his work. With menace, he approached Trig and grabbed a fistful of their electric blue hair, using it to manipulate their head.

Trig knew they had reached their end. They continued trying to flail against their captor but it proved no use as he effortlessly swatted away their hands.

The goblin moved in closer, breathing its rotten breath in Trig's face, adding further indignity to their anguish. The creature raised its rusty blade in anticipation of cutting at the human's throat. "Think you were smart human? That big brain mean nothin' now does it? Gon' be tasty. Gon' wear your skull as a hat," the goblin shrieked with glee, savoring the moment before its victory.

The shriek was immediately echoed by the darkness of the forest. The red-capped goblin leader's head turned, searching in the direction of the noise with bewilderment on its face. Having not observed anything, the goblin shrugged off the sound and turned his attention back to his victim.

As the rusty blade moved closer to Trig's neck, a shadow leaped from the darkness and tackled the creature to the ground, pinning it there. The goblin leader screamed in terror as the shadow slowly crawled up his short body. Audible snaps could be heard accompanying the compression of the creature's chest. The goblin desperately tried to slice at the shadow, continuing its panicked screams. A moment later the screams were silenced as the shadow from the darkness ripped the vile creature's throat out with its razor-sharp fangs. With the light of the Muse orb projecting a tableau of brutality onto the nearby trees, it became clear that the stalking Razor-Sith had finally found worthy prey.

Chapter Ten

"A warrior will sooner die than live a life of shame."

After leading Brutus outside, David took a moment to bid adieu to his furry friend. The next part of the adventure would pose too much danger for a beast as friendly as he. He gave the dog an ear scratch and a quick belly rub for a job well done, before commanding, "Home!" as he pointed in the direction of the cloister. Brutus produced a long guttural yowl of acknowledgment and turned his back. The dog gamboled into the darkness, his light fading with each bounding step. David caught the final visible wag of his friend's tail before heading back into the tavern.

***

"You know, I used to have a dog just like him," Luci started. "So, the lookout, huh? I thought you'd have been shorter." She jumped into conversation upon returning from the bar, having taken the opportunity to fetch another round during David's goodbye.

"I seem to be at a disadvantage," David responded with mild unease. Scot had usually been the one to curry recognition. "How did you know?"

"Simple, there are two people in this world that can do what you just did with the paint...If you were the other one the marbles wouldn't have disappeared," Luci replied. "Oh, and your face is on half the wanted posters in town. Also, I happen to know where the other one is. "

"Yeah, you and everyone else," David responded. The irony hadn't been lost on him. Even with all of his rumination on the ephemeral nature of street art, it had been Scot's creations that stuck around. "But you are wrong on one point. There are now three."

"We've only just met and already the plot thickens. Do go on," Luci beckoned as her neutral greenish glow heightened slightly in intensity at the revelation.

"Wait. First, can you provide some proof that you are who I think you are," David asked, realizing he may have already given up more information than he should've without first taking proper precautions.

Moments later he was in awe as the face of the woman contorted into a form that was as if he was looking into a mirror. This visage had hair, reminding him of his younger self.

"Satisfied?" Luci replied.

David was indeed satisfied, "Yes, but can you change back? It's kind of freaking me out."

"That better?" Luci asked rhetorically, as David nodded. "Now, why have you darkened my alcove this evening? Is it about this mysterious third?"

"It is about this third person, yes. I need help finding them," David answered.

"This third person have a name? Who are they to you?" Luci continued to probe.

"There are some things I'd like to keep close to the vest...for the time being," David replied. "We can discuss that once we have a plan to find her...if...and only if, it becomes relevant."

"So 'they' is a she," Luci intuited, observing the small grimace of flagellation on David's face at once again giving up more than he had intended. Luci continued, "What are the stakes here? I want to know what to charge."

"Helping to end the Dying. I imagine that should be enough payment on its own," David replied. "Besides, the Forgotten says you owe him."

Luci's eyes looked down, fixing themselves to the table. David could tell she was in deep thought, as if recalling a past she would have liked to forget. Thirty seconds had elapsed before she responded, "I should have figured he wouldn't come calling with a lost dog or missing wedding ring. You had to come in here with what could be the highest stakes shit of my very illustrious career. Then you try to guilt me into doing it for free."

"If I had any other option, trust me, I would not have brought it to an outsider," David replied. "And I didn't ask you to specifically end the Dying. I just need you to get me to the girl. Your obligation is done after that."

"If you think that's how that weirdo wizard operates, you haven't worked with him long enough," Luci retorted, knowing that once she started, she would likely be on the hook until the bitter end.

"If you don't want to do it just say so. I'm sure we can find another way," David tried to bluff, knowing she had a point. He knew there was something about a request from the Forgotten Master that made a person feel duty-bound to the larger mission.

"I didn't say that. I'll do it. I just want you to understand that it is with great reticence. You should feel guilty for getting me involved in this," Luci replied, sarcasm coating her voice. "As for payment, I guess if we succeed, the black market will be dead. Not going to be much call for orbs anymore. Better I be the one to kill it than be the chump who didn't see it coming. If we succeed," she paused for a moment. "If we succeed...I want a fresh start."

"If we succeed, I'm sure you'll be seen as a hero. Isn't that fresh start enough?" David asked. The reason she owed the Master a favor had entered his mind as he thought, "What happened between them that only world-altering adventure could fulfill the debt?"

"I mean a real fresh start," she replied. "Under the remote circumstance that we actually succeed, I want you to take me back with you...to your other 'where'."

"I don't know what you mean," David replied, trying to evade. "You mean the Cloister? It's common knowledge that we accept anyone with enough talent. If you're as good as the Forgotten has led me to believe, it shouldn't be any problem."

"Don't bullshit me," Luci responded. "You know what I mean. You know as well as I do, your friend, son of the Vagabond..."

"That is not going to happen. You've seen what happens when people from another world come over here," David said. "You see how they've used my friend. We have no idea what would happen if someone from here went over there. Best case scenario you end up getting dissected on a government table. Worse case...well worse case...just look around!"

"I guess it's like you said. You can find another way. I guess we're done here. Tell the old man I'm sorry will ya...hope you find the girl," she replied, calling his bluff.

David thought for a moment. He was considering his next words, knowing he was being outplayed. "Fine, fine. If we succeed...and if we can make it back across…and right now those are very big 'ifs'… then you can come with us. But you have to see this through to the end," he stated, cementing their deal.

"Well I guess that settles it," she said as she spit into her hand and reached out toward David for a shake.

David hesitantly spit in his hand and reached forward.

"Gross!" Luci said as she pulled her hand back, slicking it through her hair.

"Okay, I guess it's settled. How do we start?" David asked, trying to hold back a smile, anxious to begin the search.

"With a good night's sleep," Luci replied, much to David's chagrin.

David protested but his words fell on deaf ears. Luci was eventually able to convince him that sleep was needed. He had to admit that he had leaked information he otherwise wouldn't have in his tired state. David hadn't had an opportunity to rest for more than an hour since arriving back in Eternal Dawn.

***

Luci agreed to let David crash on her couch and they made the three-block walk back to her apartment building. The building she lived in was ten stories tall and had the appearance of having grown out of the ground.

In the time prior to the Dying of the Light, the best of the architect and engineer Musers were responsible for creating and augmenting buildings in the city. When such things were still feasible, the Musers would start by planting a single hearty tree or multiple smaller trees. Then using focused Muse they would speed up the growth process.

The buildings could be seen growing as a tree would when sprouting branches. The Musers would guide the growth of the various trunks and branches, using them to form individual floors, walls, and ceilings.

Light was provided by the still-growing leaves on limbs that ran through all areas of the building. Before the Dying, the leaves were much brighter. They functioned by picking up on the mental energies of the building's inhabitants similar to the trompf horns in the Violet Huntress. When the occupant's minds were less active, as with sleeping, the leaves would automatically dim. When active, as with reading, the leaves would brighten to produce sufficient light.

Plumbing was a simple matter. The roots of each of the buildings fed into the ancient cisterns beneath the city. Water would then be carried through the vascular system of the building and could be withdrawn with a spile, as one would tap a maple tree.

Luci and David finished walking up the eight flights of stairs, a feat which would have been easier had there been adequate Muse to keep the stairwells lit. David surveyed the apartment. It had a south-facing balcony that overlooked the slums of Ærratum. The glitzy west side could be seen by craning one's head past the railing and looking to the right. There was a bedroom with a bunch of hanging vines serving as a door much like a beaded curtain. The kitchen area flowed into a living room similar to Scot's loft.

The living room area featured a series of bookcases containing volumes with which David was mostly unfamiliar. He hadn't had much occasion to take in the word of the land. When he did read, his intake generally focused more on research than leisure. Luci's library did contain a reference section, having a couple of books with which David had a passing familiarity. 'Piper Piccolo's Poisonous Plants' was one that he found especially useful when his adventures started to take him further into unknown wilds.

Luci informed David where to find the bathroom and let him know that he was welcome to anything in her fridge, knowing there were only a few beers and some condiments. She then retired to her bedroom to pack for adventure and fell asleep.

David was left alone in the living room. He took a few minutes to sit on the balcony and look out over the land. He observed the fading gradient of Muse as his eyes started to drift past the city walls. He could almost see veins spreading out in all directions from Imperium Spire at the city's center, drawing Muse in but not sending it back with the same concentration. David again pondered if he would have been better off abandoning his friend and staying on Earth. A feeling of shame washed over him for even considering it. He didn't know that his sense of loyalty wouldn't have allowed him to desert Scot even if he'd tried.

Upon reentering the apartment David selected a book from the small library, 'The Life and Times of the Malevolent Masters: A Study of the Geddes'. He sat on the couch and started reading, only managing to skim through a page and a half before sleep took him.

***

David had been sleeping for four hours when Luci crashed through the living room on her way to the balcony.

"David...David! Wake up, wake up!" she demanded.

"What...What's going on?" David questioned through his groggy mind as he tried to rouse himself.

"I'm not sure. But something is going on with the Muse...Get up!" she responded.

Luci was able to get out onto the balcony just as a compression wave of luminescence passed through the building and everything in it. This caused a fleeting flash of light in the apartment, possessing a much greater intensity than the one David had caused in the bar earlier. She watched as the wave kept moving in an east by northeastward direction, continuing past the city walls.

"What is it? What's happening?" David yelled as Luci ran back into the apartment searching for something.

"I'm not sure yet. Hold on, let me think!" She responded, continuing to search for a few moments before finding what she was looking for on one of her library shelves.

"Aha!" she exclaimed as she came back with a pair of high-powered field glasses. Luci looked through them in the direction of the wave and watched as it faded into nothingness. She then turned her attention to the opposite direction, searching for an origination point. "There...there it is!" she said.

"What is it!" David demanded, becoming more flustered.

"There," Luci replied, shoving the binoculars into his face and pointing in the direction of what she had seen.

"I don't see anything," he responded. "What am I looking at?"

"Nothing...that is to say, you are looking at a blowout," Luci said in excitement. "I'm going to take a guess and say that we should probably start our search there."

"Shit," David muttered, knowing that, with the current state of Eternal Dawn, only Marnie could be responsible for such an event. "Well, Marnie and Scot," he amended, but he knew exactly where Scot was.

He had feared that Marnie would start to discover who she was before he could get to her. He wasn't there to provide guidance. He should have disclosed what could happen when they were still in Rochester. For all he knew, she was all alone, having just created a dangerous situation for herself. It was a situation that could very well lead to Marnie's demise and the downfall of Eternal Dawn along with her.

"Well this is going to complicate things," Luci stated, knowing they wouldn't have been the only ones to detect the disturbance.

"Yeah, we need to move," David replied. "Is there anything I can do to make this go faster?"

"No," Luci responded bluntly, heading to her closet.

She threw the double doors open. To David's surprise, though he wasn't immediately sure why, there was a small armory. David, to this point in his life, hadn't been in a situation where he was part of what he deemed to be a cliché action sequence. "For good reason," he thought. "This kind of thing really only happens in the movies." David was struck with the memory of a movie night conversation he had had with Scot so many years ago.

***

"Tropes aren't clichés, they're tools," Scot would argue. "Take the bad-ass hero stocking up in their armory. It's a shorthand that tells you so much. One, this person has been at this for a while. Two, they are very skilled at what they do. This helps fill out their often nebulous backstory. Three, some serious shit is about to go down. And four...well four, it just looks cool."

David had hoped Scot was wrong about point three. At the same time, observing the cliché, it was starting to dawn on him that perhaps Eternal Dawn and Earth were more connected than he had originally thought.

***

Luci surveyed her curated collection of arms. She grabbed a bandoleer containing pockets for multiple Muse orbs and slung it across her chest. She handed another one to David.

"I can't use these," David stated. "Never been able. I don't have direct access to the Muse, hence the paint."

"I know...they're for me. You're going to need to mule some of this stuff for me," she replied, as she started to shove additional orbs into every available pocket.

Luci put on a belt containing sheath holsters. She then grabbed a pair of daggers off the walls and spun them around in her hands before sliding them into their proper place. David stared at the display, shaking his head.

She donned her dark robe by throwing it up into the air, seamlessly sliding her arms into each sleeve as the garment fell around her body. Luci then slung a go bag over her shoulder, and in a singular fluid motion, took her collapsible bow and clipped its attached carabiner to one of her belt rings.

Luci looked at David's stunned face and asked, "What?"

David replied, "How often do you practice this shit?"

***

The pair walked back down the eight floors to the building's entrance and then another into an underground garage. The garage was ceilinged by the roots that supported the building above. They spread out from the central trunk and dropped into the ground below at random intervals.

With David in tow, Luci produced a Muse orb for light and then proceeded to walk to the darkest corner of the garage. In the darkness, there was a canvas-covered mass. She grabbed a corner of the dusty canvas and with one swift motion, pulled it away, exposing the vehicle underneath.

With the haze of dust in the air, David stared at the vehicle with awe. "Is that a cyclocycle?!" he asked, with the acute knowledge that it was.

The vehicle she unveiled was the Eternal Dawn version of a sport bike. It had a tubular black metal frame, deep purple ironwood fenders, and an electric blue leather seat. In the place of a traditional headlight, there was a carved Green Man head, whose eyes would shoot light at the road. The fork was made up of skeletal wooden arms, which gripped the hub on either side of the front wheel.

The bike lacked a traditional combustion motor and fuel tank. The motor resembled a translucent particle accelerator. It consisted of a ring of glass tubing which was wrapped with copper coils at five junction points. The device was surrounded by a shroud which was used to hide less attractive components underneath. In place of the fuel tank, there was a slot where one would deposit a Muse orb.

Luci dropped an orb into the fuel slot and David watched as it cycled through the motor's glass tube. It accelerated to a rate where it could no longer be tracked with the naked eye, instead producing a ring of glowing blue light. In truth, it glowed purple but with his color blindness, David couldn't tell. He had also taken note that the motor was dead silent. He had expected there would be at the very least a small hum or mechanical whir but there was nothing.

"I thought they all were destroyed," David stated, "...or ended up in museums." He had been mostly correct in his line of thinking. After the Flood, most in Eternal Dawn divested themselves of any object that ran on the orbs or had said objects converted to run on straight Muse.

The conversion of cyclers was something that the Musers couldn't quite figure out. They were small enough that the achievable Muse collection would only allow them to reach speeds of four or five miles per hour, greatly reducing their utility. This was before the Dying reduced the available Muse even further. Owing to its fuel source, being seen with a cyclocycle was an open admission that the user was involved in the black market.

The cyclocycles were an early collaboration between the Vagabond Master and the Road Masters, the temporary name given to the Geddes during their final Masterwork.

"Get on," Luci ordered as she threw her leg over the side of the bike in a smooth motion, the tail of her robe fluttered in the air; a light woosh sound that accompanied it.

"Well that's the final piece of the cliché I suppose," David said, not realizing he was thinking out loud.

"What's that?" she asked.

"Nothing, nothing," David responded, biting his tongue a bit too late as he climbed onto the bike behind her.

"Hold on," Luci commanded. When she felt David lightly put his hands on the side of her hips, she forcefully grabbed hold of them and firmly wrapped his arms around her waist. "Like this," she scolded.

"I suppose that's the epilogue," David thought to himself. He could feel a dull pain as the Muse orbs in his bandoleer started to dig into his chest.

***

The cycle exploded out of the garage and onto the street in front of Luci's apartment building. She had decided on a direct route, assuming there was going to be a race to the blowout's epicenter.

"What are you doing?!" David questioned loudly over the sound of the wind rushing by his ears. He was sure that the current course of action was going to draw too much attention. "I thought you were a ranger. Why aren't we keeping a low profile?"

"Do you want to get there before Imperium or not? I can slow down and do this cautiously," Luci replied, decelerating the bike to a slow crawl.

"Alright, alright, point taken," he responded, signaling her to pick up the pace once more.

Luci drove aggressively through the side streets of Ærratum, ducking and weaving the bike between horse-drawn carriages and small automobiles alike. She was pushing the cyclocycle to speeds well above what vehicles running straight Muse were capable of. Onlookers turned their heads to catch a glimpse of the spectacle. It was clear to them that this was no legal machine.

As the pair drew closer to the city's center traffic on the roadway became more dense. Much to David's displeasure, the additional maneuvering required didn't serve to slow Luci down. His terror was compounded by the low visibility of other vehicles in this land of eternal twilight. His distinct lack of head protection didn't help matters. When the Vagabond Master brought the concept of a motorcycle from Earth, he neglected to bring along the concept of a helmet.

It wasn't until they reached the fifty-story Imperium Spire at the city's center that the duo started to attract the wrong kind of attention. For David and Luci it had become apparent that a mobilization was currently in progress. There were a dozen employees dressed in tactical gear but none of them were openly brandishing weapons. David was sure the security forces wouldn't hesitate to break out arms as soon as they were past city limits.

Imperium had many loyal employees and cuff users in the city and preferred to keep a clean-cut image when public and government eyes were watching. They had only gained enough power and influence to skirt the law, not outright break it. With their current trajectory, it wouldn't be long before Imperium and the government were one and the same.

The posse of Imperium soldiers was in the middle of pairing off and climbing into a series of identical vehicles. They referred to the vehicles, which possessed the appearance of an Earthen dune buggy, as scramblers. The only hot deserts on the planet were in the uninhabitable zone facing the sun, precluding any recreational activity involving a dune.

"Those are new," Luci remarked. She had been used to seeing Imperium riding around in slow-moving vehicles similar to parking trams.

The speed with which Luci and David traveled prevented the use of the hoods on their robes, leaving their faces exposed. While none of the members of the posse were able to make Luci, one of them recognized David as the pair passed by. He was still a wanted fugitive after all.

One would be hard-pressed to find someone inside Imperium who didn't know what he looked like. David had been charged with assault against their leader two years prior. It was a crime he had never answered for.

Upon spying David, an Imperium soldier radioed the constabulary to let them know to be on the lookout for 'the lookout'. It was a move that was sure to slow the pair down and keep Imperium's hands clean inside city limits.

Seeing the posse caused Luci's renewed interest in the bike's accelerator and the pair jolted forward. They were able to cover a mile and a quarter before the telltale signs of flashing lights appeared on the road ahead. "This soon?" she exclaimed loudly over the wind. "We must be in the nice part of town."

They were in fact driving down the main road of the city. The road to which all other roads in Eternal Dawn lead. The Geddes may have been gone but this part of their legacy remained.

"What are we going to do?" David shouted, concerned their mission would end just as it was getting started.

"We..." Luci emphasized, "...are going to drive this bike as fast as we can toward those lights and hope they don't have a dampener."

Luci twisted the accelerator until it would no longer turn. There was a slight wobble on this latest lurch which had caused David further trepidation. Before long they had reached top speed and the bike evened out. They were traveling in excess of one hundred fifty miles per hour. It was the fastest speed that David had ever traveled. In all likelihood, it was faster than almost everyone in Eternal Dawn had ever traveled.

"A what now?" David questioned loudly just as they were approaching the impromptu barricade ahead.

"A damp...awww shit!" Luci exclaimed just as they had narrowly passed through the constabulary's attempted blockade. She had glimpsed the feared device mounted to the top of one of their vehicles.

Within seconds the cyclocycle started to slow down. Luci had released and cranked on the throttle but the bike wasn't responding. The constables were able to get off a disruptor pulse just as they had passed by; a considerable feat considering how fast they were going. Luci attempted to throw another orb into the fuel slot but it was sucked into nothingness.

"What do we do? What do we do?" David asked in rapid succession.

"Stay cool. Let me think," She replied as they continued to slow down, their speed dropping to less than one hundred miles per hour.

"Can you think quicker? They've already started to move," David stated, putting further pressure on Luci.

"You're not helping!" she exclaimed.

"What do the dampeners do?" he shouted, over the wind that was still passing by his ears.

"As far as I know, they're just giant Muse-powered magnets. They stop Muse flow in orb-powered devices for some reason. I don't know why," she responded.

"Stop the bike!" David commanded.

"Why?" Luci questioned

"I don't have time to explain, just stop," he answered. "I know what to do."

Luci did as requested and abruptly stopped the cyclocycle, which caused the rear wheel to kick out, almost throwing David to the ground. They dismounted the bike and with Luci taking David's lead, laid it on its side.

"You better know what you're doing or it's our ass," Luci half shouted.

"Just hold them off while I work," David ordered.

They had been able to coast for two and a half miles before stopping. In the far-off distance, Luci could see the constabulary approaching in their small chase vehicles. The term chase had been used loosely by the constables to describe them. With the current low level of Muse in the world, the vehicles could barely manage thirty miles per hour. They were no match for Luci's cycle and barely enough to chase down a horse rider on a good night.

"We might have three minutes. Probably less," she said, as she pressed David to move quicker.

"You're not helping," David responded, echoing her earlier words back at her. He had pulled a can of spray from his bag and proceeded to paint a series of outlines onto the roadway.

Luci then watched as David's Muse concentrated and pooled into his left hand. Focusing his mind, he pulled a two-foot-long metal spike up from the ground. David took a pause and waited for his Muse to regenerate to allow him to work on the next object. He knew it would be half a minute before he could continue.

"They're getting closer…Two minutes tops and they're on us," Luci shouted over her shoulder. She could see the vehicles growing larger in the distance, now only a mile away.

Luci retrieved one of the orbs from her bandoleer and threw it at the ground. A standing quiver of arrows appeared at her side as she proceeded to pull the collapsible bow from her belt. She pulled hard at both ends of the foot-long mass forged from nondescript woods, hinges, and pulleys, causing everything to snap into place. Luci had produced a hybrid compound recurve bow as tall as she was. She then knocked an arrow as she readied herself to stall the pursuers.

David, ignoring Luci's previous statement, proceeded to pull the second object out of the ground. The object was a fifteen-pound sledgehammer. He used the hammer to start pounding the spike through the top layer of the road and immediately became thankful that it hadn't been constructed of concrete or cement.

David had only knocked the spike down five inches before he heard Luci shout out, "One minute." He continued hammering, making slow but steady progress as he attempted to ignore the anaerobic shock that had started to attack his system. He knew he would be all the more sore the following night for pushing through the pain.

The constabulary forces continued their approach and were now upon them. Luci worked to keep their pursuers at bay by clout-shooting arrows in their direction. The explosions of light the arrows made as they hit the ground proved to be more than enough to serve the purpose.

While she was working at distracting the cops, Luci observed the Imperium scramblers drive past in the other lane, the occupants of which gawked at the pair with a sense of victory as they did. Luci was able to clock the vehicles as having speeds faster than what the approaching chase vehicles had been capable of.

David, thankful this world wasn't dumb enough to create gunpowder, precluding a bullet to the back, continued his work. He drove the spike eighteen inches into the ground, hoping it would be enough. He then turned his attention to the final outlined tool and by once more focusing his energies, pulled up a three-foot-long copper rod.

He hesitated as he approached the bike. "This is going to suck," he said to himself as he leaned down. David bunched up the end of his robe under his feet and took a deep breath. Holding the copper rod in his left hand, he touched it to the metal rod that had been driven into the ground. He took one more breath and touched the other end to one of the coils on the bike's motor.

The results were immediate and expected. A jolt of pain shot up the nerves in David's left arm as electricity discharged from the engine's capacitors and traversed the rod before traveling down the spike into the ground.

"What happened? What did you do?" Luci questioned as she shot another volley of arrows in the law's direction.

With David's left hand still trembling, he worked to stand the bike back up before grunting through his pain, "Science. Muse and electricity don't mix."

He had correctly surmised that the magnet created an induction charge in the cyclocycle's engine coils, causing the bike's capacitors to load up with electricity. This condition blocked Muse from being consumed by the bike and dissipated it into the ether instead.

David didn't have time to consider that the dampeners were also a contribution from the Vagabond Master. They had been used to immobilize the Geddes' war machines in the Last War. The dampeners experienced continued popularity with the constabulary and were used after the Flood as part of their fight against the black market orb economy.

David popped an orb into the fuel slot, causing the engine to spin up and reach capacity within a few seconds. "Okay, we should be good," he shouted over to Luci who was still peppering the area between them and the constables with exploding arrows.

"Not a moment too soon," she spoke, as she grabbed the cloth quiver from its stand. She slung it across her back before backing toward David's position. "You're going to have to drive," she ordered, knowing she needed to keep the arrows flying. She didn't want to risk giving the constabulary a chance to use the dampener again.

David, having not so much as ridden a dirt bike, hesitantly mounted the cycle. Luci took up a reverse mount, pressing her back against his to allow her to keep shooting. David cranked on the throttle and the duo sped toward the city gates with Luci still loosing arrows toward the approaching law enforcers.

David, surprised at his ability to handle the machine, sped down the road and passed through the western gates before the constabulary could provide further impedance. The pair was on the heels of Imperium, intending to overtake them as they sped toward Ærratum's southern reaches.

Chapter Eleven

"It isn't what we say or think that defines us..."

After witnessing the brutal death of their leader by the jaws of the Razor-Sìth, the moblins scattered and crawled back into the dark holes from which they spawned. In time the most cutthroat of the vile creatures would murder half the mob for the right to dawn the red cap.

The Razor-Sìth, appearing to finally be satisfied, disappeared back into the darkness. While they weren't sure they could count on the beast to be their protector, Marnie, Trig, and Chauncey were of the mind that it meant them no further harm. This knowledge would help to ease their exit from the forest.

Chauncey tended to his friend's injuries by taking an extra shirt from Trig's pack and tearing it into strips. Due to the bespoke nature of his garments, he wasn't willing to sacrifice one of his own. He tightly wrapped the makeshift bandages around the bite on Trig's arm and the stab wound on their calf. He wasn't able to stem all of the flow but was fairly certain Trig wouldn't bleed out before the trio reached their destination.

Trig inspected the patch job and was satisfied, in so much as Chauncey hadn't made anything worse. The goblin's blade had pierced into Trig's muscle, which made walking difficult but not impossible. Their concern hadn't been focused on the tissue trauma but instead on the consumption of a course of antibiotics as soon as possible. They could almost feel the bacteria from the red cap's mouth coursing through their veins. There was no telling what manner of damage was being inflicted on their body.

The trio left the site of the brutal attack and continued on their previous heading. Within ten minutes they had exited the blowout's darkwash and entered the safer harbor of the lighted forest. Marnie, Chauncey, and Trig would encounter no further obstacle on the remaining three-mile hike to Drumlocke.

***

Drumlocke, of late, was under-served by the government and the Muse alike. This was a common problem for towns in the rural areas of Eternal Dawn. In the years before the Dying, when Muse wasn't being sucked away, Drumlocke had served as a major trade and tourist stop between the capitol and the southern cities. Save for a trinket vendor and a fruit stand, which still held out hope for a return to the way things were, the market stalls lining the main street now sat vacant. As with many small towns, the government had lost sight of the village being a valuable resource. There hadn't been so much as a magistrate visit in over a year.

Being a traveler's rest, Drumlocke still had many features that towns located further off the road didn't possess. It contained multiple tavern inns, a library, and a staffed clinic. There was also a general store that contained all of the odds and ends a weary traveler might require.

Drumlocke was a town known for its artists and artisans. The local gaffers in particular had been responsible for the production of the glass orbs which were used to hold concentrated Muse in the time of the Geddes influence. In the nights before the flood, many of the gaffers saw crafting the orbs as a great honor. The sand used in their creation was procured at great risk from the deserts beyond the horizon. The material was special in that it contained a higher silica content and lacked the impurities of the lake bed sands which were more commonplace. This ultimately allowed for the creation of finer products; products that fate, it seems, had dictated be returned to their source by the hands of Trig and Chauncey.

***

The trio started by visiting the clinic just off the main market street. Without disclosing too many details, the doctor on duty was convinced to provide a strong course of antibiotics. Trig wasn't entirely pleased about the havoc the pills would wreak on their digestive system but figured it would be better than dying from some form of goblin sepsis. The doctor was able to close the wound on Trig's leg and ply it with a fresh bandage. They had also supplied an analgesic which served to dull the pain.

The next point of concern, at least for Trig and Chauncey, was the delivery of their black-market wares. It was a delivery for which they were already three nights late. This was owed to Chauncey's insistence on taking charge of navigation in the nights before their encounter with Marnie. One would be thankful to spare their ears the torrent of profanity that spewed forth from Trig's mouth when Chauncey was discovered to be holding their one and only map of the realm upside down. Had Marnie been aware of the incident it would have been a mistake to be thankful for on account of their new companionship.

***

The trio made their way to the City Hall Inn. In recent times the location had become a meeting house of sorts for those looking to conduct less than legal deeds. It also happened to be owned and operated by the current mayor of Drumlocke, an old friend of Trig and Chauncey's whom they were now seeking to meet with.

"'Bout time ye darkened my door," the barrel-chested man behind the bar bellowed as he saw Trig and Chauncey enter through the establishment's saloon doors.

"Apologies Pherson, we had...complications," Trig replied, glaring at Chauncey.

"Say no more, say no more," Pherson replied with an air of understanding. This hadn't been the first time that the pair had been late due to one of Chauncey's 'diversions'. Pherson was much more interested in the mysterious cloaked figure that had accompanied his usual pair of black-market peddlers. "So what do you have for me today?" he stated with acute knowledge of what the pair had in their possession.

"Let's not do this out in the open," Trig requested.

"Nobody's here, let's just get it done," Pherson responded, knowing he represented the closest thing to government that existed in Drumlocke. It wasn't like he was going to be locking himself up. Pherson had become used to conducting his 'less than legal' business out in the open.

"I'd rather do it in private this time," Trig countered, thinking the half a dozen people scattered around the bar didn't exactly count as nobody. They had been on high alert since meeting Marnie. The subsequent incidents with the Sith and the moblins hadn't served to dampen their wariness. There may have been a lack of government oversight but oversight wasn't what Trig was concerned with. Imperium had enough resources to have eyes and ears in even the farthest reaches of the land.

"Fine, fine. Follow me," Pherson replied, sensing there were additional layers to the current deal. He beckoned to one of the less inebriated patrons, "Roy, can you mind the bar while I see to some business?"

Pherson led the group down a hallway containing the privies and his office. The room wasn't exactly what Marnie had expected out of the Mayor's office. It was a small room, barely large enough to house the oversized desk that filled it. She had correctly deduced that the desk was the product of a Muse orb. It was either that or the inn had been built around this large piece of furniture which had the appearance of being carved from a single chunk of lumber. Trig took one of the two visitor chairs and gestured to Marnie to take the other. Chauncey took up a lean against the back wall between the seated pair.

Mayor Pherson surveyed the trio before he spoke, "I don't suppose the need for secrecy has anything to do with the wave of Muse that passed through here a couple of hours ago?" He made the statement while staring at the cloaked figure to Trig's left.

The question had been an attempt to elicit a response from Marnie. She had remained quiet and covered since entering the town. The air of mysteriousness drew a bit of unwanted attention but not as much as if they'd walked down Main Street with someone possessing the glow of a pre-Flood Master.

"Our business is our own," Trig responded. "Now let's discuss 'our' business." They gestured their hand between Pherson and themselves. They then brought out a large pouch containing the stash of Muse orbs before commenting, "Thirty orbs minus two."

"Alright, alright. Have your secrets," Pherson responded, snapping his suspenders. "What happened to the other two?"

"Car trouble," Chauncey chimed in, feeling the conversation required more levity.

"What's the ask?" Pherson questioned, knowing he wouldn't be getting a straight answer to his previous query.

"Same as always, just a safe room to rest our heads, a good meal, and the assurance that those orbs get into the hands of those that need them most," Trig answered.

The bioluminescence of the room immediately flickered with Marnie's realization that the pair she had found herself aligned with appeared to have a streak of benevolence. They had saved her life twice already but this was the final proof she needed that the pair were in fact 'cool'.

"Same as always then," Pherson said smiling, taking note of the flickering. If Pherson was nothing else, he was a man of his word. The pair of Trig and Chauncey had been able to provide a much-needed service to his village in the times since the beginning of the Dying. He then asked, "Anyone going to come calling on these?"

"Anyone ever come calling?" Chauncey responded rhetorically.

The mayor had posed a fair question. There were no longer any legal means for obtaining the orbs. In truth, the pair's operation involved sneaking into destruction depots and stealing orbs that had been seized but not yet processed. On occasion, in the reaches of the city, an anonymous tip or two may have been filed if supplies were running low and the pair suspected someone of hoarding the illegal substance. At that point, it was only a matter of waiting for a depot deposit to be made.

"You've got me there. You two really are the best," Pherson stated. "Is it too early to plan a date for the next delivery?"

"That's going to be a hard one to answer?" replied Trig. "Orbs are coming harder and harder to come by. They've shuttered three more depots in the last month to lack of need."

"I don't know how we are going to keep this town going when it all dries up. We're edging closer and closer to unsustainability," Pherson lamented. "People are getting desperate. We were supposed to be the last bastion holding out against Imperium's influence. I've seen nary a cuff or pair of void eyes since we declared ourselves a sanctuary. Hate to let down those who don't want to take part in the vileness."

Marnie's head tilted at the mention of the cuffs she had now heard mention of again. "What is the significance?" she thought to herself, marking the query for future conversation.

"They are sad times indeed," Chauncey replied.

"Let's hope that someone does something about Imperium soon," Pherson added.

"Let's," responded Trig. The group sat in silence for a few awkward moments before Trig continued, "Well it's about time we made our leave," concluding their conversation with the Mayor of Drumlocke.

***

"Even with my ideas, I know it's a bad one to stick around here tonight in light of the blowout," Chauncey commented during the group's dinner conversation. They were eating in a private room in one of Drumlocke's finer establishments, The Free-Blower.

"We aren't sticking around," Trig replied. "The way I figure, with the vehicles Imperium has, we have minimum five, maybe six hours before the Imperium thugs will have descended upon this place. That will give me enough time to enjoy this much-needed dinner, grab a shower, and a few quick winks in a soft bed. Then we will be off."

"You don't have to go through all the trouble," Marnie chimed in. "I can figure it out from here. There's no reason you should take more risk because..."

"Aye, Marnie deary, let me cut you off there. We wouldn't hear of it. Would we Trig?" Chauncey interjected after letting a slurp of trompf soup fall out of his mouth and back into the bowl in front of him.

"He's right. We couldn't possibly leave you out there alone. Especially after what we've already been through," Trig said, mirroring Chauncey's sentiments. "You're a trouble magnet. We couldn't let you on your own in good conscience."

"Thanks. Honestly, I was hoping you'd say something like that. I'm lost and losing more of it by the second," Marnie spoke, relieved as she bit into a slice of the pizza-like flatbread she had ordered. "There are a few things I'd like to discuss since we have a little bit of time. Though some of it may sound stupid."

"I'm the king of stupid. Query away Marnie miss," Chauncey responded.

"Can we try to avoid anything that is overly epiphanous or emotional?" Trig interjected in an attempt to avoid further incidents with Marnie's newly discovered condition. "Or at least build up to any 'aha' answers so we can gauge if there will be a repeat of our evening's earlier event. We still don't know the cause."

"I think that's fair," Marnie answered, agreeing to the terms, knowing that there may be some risk.

"For starters...and I know it's not that important but it just struck me. When you say earlier in the evening...well, isn't everything earlier in the evening?" Marnie said, asking her first question. She was trying to build a vocabulary for this new world.

"Right you are, right you are...technically," Chauncey answered. "We do mark every rise of Lonely Sister as a new night though, if that helps."

"Ahh got it. Thought it might be something like that. Okay, next question. How is it that you speak English? Or have pizza here? Or anything from my world?" Marnie said, peppering this set of questions.

"That...that we cannae answer Miss Marnie," Trig chimed in. "Not for lack of wanting. It is as strange to us that you speak the common tongue, and know of our foods, and some of our customs. I suspect our worlds may be entangled in more ways than one. I also suspect there are few if any that would know the answer to your query."

"The Vagabond probably would've," Chauncey chimed in, immediately biting his lip and waiting for the lights to flicker. "Sorry, sorry. I almost forgot," he said, glancing over at Trig who was now staring daggers at him. After waiting a few seconds the lights hadn't flickered.

"It's okay, it's okay really," Marnie responded, once more feeling horrible for complicating the situation of her new friends. She was still building up to the harder questions concerning the nature of her being and her quest to find her brother.

She soldiered on, "I've heard mention of cuffs a couple of times since we met. I get they are somehow linked to the Imperium. What's the significance? I take it that they're not just jewelry."

"Hate to split hairs but it's just 'Imperium', no 'the'," Chauncey stated as Trig rolled their eyes upon hearing superfluous correction. "The cuffs..." he continued.

"The cuffs are a vile means of control. Imperium..." Trig said, cutting Chauncey off, "...Imperium uses them to mine Muse directly from any person dumb enough to get caught in their web...That...that's not fair. You don't have to be dumb, just easily led. Which most seem to be."

"Why would people want to do that? What do they get in return?" Marnie questioned.

"It's twofold," Trig answered. "Wearers get a jolt of pleasure if they hit a daily quota for 'donation'. Epiphany they call it. Not sure you would have noticed it during the blowout with everything going on but at times of great realization and sometimes not-so-great realization, you can achieve the same effect. Do you have that on this 'Earth' of yours?"

"Not to a degree that anyone really talks about," Marnie responded, "...Well except maybe for Scot."

"Not sure you would have felt it when you figured out why Eternal Dawn is named the way it is either. Probably still too fried from the blowout," Trig said, continuing the explanation. "I think you may have had one in the Mayor's office. Anyway, the cuffs shortcut the need to actually think of an idea or have any kind of 'aha' moment. They just let you feel like you have."

Marnie nodded. She had felt something was tempering her emotions in the moments after the blowout but had definitely felt a warmth in the mayor's office. She had chalked it up to her new-found trust in the pair. She then replied, "Yeah I felt something in the office now that you mention it. It was when I found out that you were 'Robin Hood' criminals and not 'criminal' criminals."

"Robin Hood?" Chauncey questioned, "...You know what, never mind. I think I understand."

"And the second thing?" Marnie asked.

"The second thing?" Trig responded, "Oh yeah the cuffs. The second thing is that you can store a charge of Muse in them and use it similar to the orbs. Create a quick device like I did in the forest or put a meal on the table. The thing is, you don't have to have any talent to do it."

"That doesn't sound so bad," Marnie said, seeing the utility of the device in question.

"But the skill is not earned. At best, the items most create are shoddy...At worst they're dangerous," Trig said, their passion nearly breaking their voice as they spoke. "At least with the orbs you still need to be somewhat of a Muser," they continued. "On top of that, the Muse doesn't get returned when it's spent. Some does, but not anywhere near a replacement rate, hence the Dying of the Light."

"And the thing is," Chauncey chimed in, "nobody knows precisely where that extra Muse goes. I mean we have to assume it's the city, but even Imperium doesn't have a big enough building to store all the light missing from the world. There aren't any Masterworks going on either...as far as we know."

"I get that Muse is your power source. The building blocks for this beautiful world of yours. It's truly magnificent. I get that it also used to be a lot brighter everywhere. When did this Dying of the Light of yours start?" asked Marnie, on the verge of connecting dots she had hoped wouldn't black out Drumlocke.

"Aye, it started a little over two years ago," Chauncey replied. "Our years... I suspect your years may not be exactly the same."

"I think they're pretty close. At least according to the history lesson Trig provided as it relates to my father," Marnie said. "It does give some credence to the theory that our worlds are linked in more ways than one."

"How so?" Trig questioned. They were now thoroughly intrigued which was no small feat.

"I think your Dying of the Light may be the same as my Dying of the Art, and I think Scot may be what connects the two," responded Marnie. The room suddenly brightened and then briefly extinguished before its blue and green lights returned to normal. Marnie felt the warm feeling of pleasure Trig had described. At once she understood the appeal and the dangers involved in the cuffs.

"What is the nature of this Dying of yours?" Trig said, probing further into this discovery. They were now content that the conversation they were having didn't present the same dangers that accompanied the one they had had back in the forest.

"In a manner of speaking, I think it is almost the opposite of what is happening here," Marnie responded. "We have the will, material, and desire to produce but lack ideas. It's like my city is the epicenter. Nobody knows why."

"I suspect your suspicions may be valid. Can be no mere coincidence," Trig replied.

"I beg your pardon...but who's Scot?" Chauncey chimed in, having heard the name a few times now.

"Oh shit," Marnie exclaimed as the room's lights dimmed slightly. "I forgot...I was keeping that under my hat until I figured out if you two could be trusted. He's my brother. He's why I'm here. I'm trying to find him."

"Aye, the plot thickens. It seems we have all the makings of a grand adventure," replied Chauncey, deeply excited at the prospect of a quest. "But I think we would have known if a Vagabond of your power had shown up before now."

"He may not possess the power that Miss Marnie here has," Trig said, before cutting at Chauncey. "We do live in a world where someone of my talents has to exist next to someone of yours."

"In a world where ideas are currency, even the bad ones will buy you something," responded Chauncey. "I'll take that as a compliment." He was parroting words of wisdom that only a mother could have given him.

"I think with his talent, he may be more powerful than me in a place like this. He was...is an artist with much more skill than me," Marnie interjected. Only once the words had left her mouth, she wondered what Martin would say hearing her latest deprecation. "You really haven't heard of him? There would have been someone else with him, our friend David. Tallish, bald, bearded man, with a scar on the side of his head." She took another bite of pizza after miming David's height and scar location.

"I haven't heard tale of anyone similar to either. It's possible that Imperium has them as prisoners," Trig said, withholding their thoughts of another possible fate, a much worse fate. They had seen David's wanted poster before but Marnie's description didn't match up. David had earned the scar in the two years after its picture had been produced.

"Not David," Marnie cut in before Trig had time to finish their thought. "He came back to my world and I helped him get back here. He's the one that let me know Scot was still alive. Said Scot was in trouble and was going back to get him. If what you say of this Imperium is true..."

"We'll cross that bridge when we come to it," Trig said, cutting Marnie off. "But at this point, and I hate to say it, at this point, we need to talk to Wordsmith...assuming the rumors are true."

Chauncey perked up in excitement at the prospect of meeting a former Master, "Wait, we do? Yes, yes, yes...why?"

"We need information. Information only a former Master could possess," Trig responded, once more annoyed that one of Chauncey's ideas had come to pass. "I hope the rumors are true. I hope we don't regret it."

The trio finished their dinner and left The Free-Blower, heading for the library.

Chapter Twelve
"...that dare not speak its name."

His searching had so far not yielded more than fragments. The Forgotten Master knew he needed to call in the girl but for what, he was not yet sure.

"Prophecy...the sun rises...only once all is lost...what was lost will be found...in deepest darkness...watcher watches...twins unite...adept ascends...at heretic falls...dawn's first light...a fool forgets...the morning flight," the Forgotten Master mumbled as he came out of his trance, repeating words that had been delivered to him by a soft feminine voice.

He crossed the courtyard of the Cloister upon completion of his nightly meditations. "Prophecy, there was something about a prophecy," he said.

The images the Forgotten Master had seen were like memories, somehow from another life, as if he was watching the past through someone else's eyes. "What does it all mean?" he mumbled. "Did what I see already come to pass...Will it?... Am I just grasping at straws? I need more answers. But what?... Where?"

"Where? Is the correct question indeed," the Forgotten Master pondered as his words became internal. He already knew where he must go but out of dread, his mind was fighting him to think it.

"Oraculum," he finally managed to speak. As soon as the word left his lips, the Master felt a soft pull in his chest toward the place of which he spoke. He wasn't sure if the feeling was real or imagined but knew it wasn't a signal to be discarded. He had felt an immediate sense of conviction when the idea of bringing the girl over had arrived. He was now experiencing the same convicted feelings about venturing to the Oraculum.

To the outside world, the Oraculum existed only in myth and legend. Proof of its existence was a secret to all but a handful of Masters. For those chosen few, it was a place even they feared to tread. In legend, the Oraculum was described as a room within which no Muse could reach, located at the center of a labyrinth under a near-endless maze of catacombs.

A year prior to the Flood, the Vagabond Master had made the perilous journey in his attempt to dispel the creeping darkness. The Forgotten Master now wished he had had the good fortune of meeting the room's previous occupant. The counsel they could have provided would have been invaluable on the journey that he knew he need now embark.

***

David and Luci sped out of the city heading west on the Geddes road. They had driven ten miles before Luci had David stop the bike to switch positions. He was being much too cautious for her liking.

It was another ten miles before the pair would overtake the Imperium convoy. The bike was able to pass by the scramblers as if they were standing still. One of the scramblers had veered toward the cyclocycle causing it to wobble as Luci took corrective action. It was a maneuver that put David even more on edge but they were able to continue without further confrontation. The speed advantage gave the pair a much-needed head start in their search for Marnie.

They had traveled another fifty minutes before arriving at a crossroads on the edge of the forest. It was the crossroads Marnie had reached after arriving by way of the Umphraidh Menhir. Luci made an attempt to drive the bike on the trail but as they went deeper into the forest it had become clear that the machine was becoming a hindrance.

The pair rolled the bike ten meters off the side of the trail. Luci purged the fuel cell, expending the rest of the orb to prevent possible theft. They then camouflaged it with gathered leaves and branches, hoping it would remain hidden in the event that it was once again needed.

From Luci's pack, she produced a set of goggles and affixed them to her face. They had the appearance of antique welding goggles.

"What do those do?" David questioned.

"They help show me the things that should not be," Luci replied cryptically. In truth, the goggles contained, among other features, an ultraviolet filter in one eye and a polarization filter in the other. The contrast between the two filters gave an almost three-dimensional effect to disturbances in Muse light. The effect put a sharper edge on anything that was either too dark or too light to match its surroundings.

Luci took the lead as they ventured further into the forest. She kept her ears keenly attuned to the surroundings in an attempt to detect anything amiss. She was also keeping an ear out for the Imperium forces that would no doubt be crashing through the woods behind them before too long.

It was in these moments that David was finally able to detect the ranger in the person who had been co-opted into his mission. The pair soldiered on at a brisk pace, getting closer to the blowout with each step. Luci occasionally stopped to check the surroundings, making a show of looking under a random leaf or investigating a broken branch. David was unsure if this was part of her process or something she was doing for his benefit.

It had been twenty minutes before they arrived at the border of the blowout. Luci again stopped to point out the beautiful blue, purple, and green lights that were creeping back toward the epicenter of the event. To David, they all appeared to be shades of blue, a fact Luci would have pitied him for had she known. She pushed her goggles up to perch on her forehead and pulled out two orbs from her bandoleer. She handed one to David to use as a light source as they headed into the darkness.

"So who is this girl that we are trying to find?" Luci said, once more trying to solicit information from David.

"I'll let you know if, and when, that information becomes relevant," David responded, thinking that despite the proverb, a common enemy doesn't necessarily make one a friend.

"It would have to take someone with pretty immense power to do this. I've only known one other person with the ability to do something like this and he paid the ultimate price for it," Luci replied, attempting to goad David into revealing more information.

"Hopefully for your sake, the same fate has not befallen her. That would bring a pretty quick end to our relationship. She's probably the only one able to grant you what you want," David said, sniping back at her prying.

Luci had brought up a point he had considered but had tried to keep locked in the back of his mind, "What if Marnie had perished in the blowout?" The Forgotten Master had told him the story of the Vagabond's sacrifice. With the current state of Eternal Dawn, David hadn't thought it possible that any one person would be able to possess this much power. Not even Scot had shown himself capable.

"How is it you know of the Vagabond?" David questioned. "You would have been a little young to be involved in that mess, wouldn't you?"

"You have your secrets, I have mine," she responded. In truth, David hadn't considered that her abilities as a chameleon may allow Luci to present a more youthful appearance.

The pair had reached an impasse and were content to leave both of their queries unanswered for the time being. Luci was more or less sure the information she desired would present itself before long. With what David had gathered of Luci thus far, he wasn't sure if he would ever have answers to his questions or if she would ever be someone who could be fully trusted.

***

David and Luci continued hiking on the trail until they reached a fork. Luci picked up on the faint footsteps of a single traveler moving in an east-by-northeast direction.

"What is it?" David questioned, noticing a change in Luci's disposition.

"Footsteps," she stated. "They're heading toward the epicenter. The feet are small like a small woman or large child." She took note of the odd tread pattern of the footprints. They weren't patterns she recognized and appeared to contain words in the more pronounced steps. She knew the owner wouldn't be local as nobody in Eternal Dawn wore footwear unless it was a formal occasion, doing so would disrupt Muse absorption.

They continued to head in the direction of the footprints. Luci was careful to step on top of them in an attempt to obfuscate their origin from their pursuers. This was a tact that she was taking out of habit rather than need as it wouldn't likely be useful for their current situation. The pair didn't have the time needed to make tracks on the other branch of the trail as she normally would. "With any luck, Imperium won't have a gifted tracker," she said.

It wasn't long before David and Luci reached what she assumed to be the epicenter of the blowout. What Luci found concerned her greatly. On the ground, she detected the movements of a large feline, possibly a high country cougar or even the mighty Razor-Sith. She also found the footprints of two more beings. She was sure one of the sets belonged to a lightweight man but wasn't confident about the other.

"It looks like there was a confrontation with a big cat over here," Luci said, gesturing toward the spot on the path where Marnie had had her encounter.

"Oh no," replied David, this was the exact kind of situation he had hoped to spare Marnie from.

"It looks like the cat ran off. I don't see any blood. That's a good sign," Luci said in an attempt to ease David's mind. "Then the girl joined the two others by the fire over here. The footprints get a little chaotic at this point. I'm thinking this is where it happened."

"You can tell all that by looking at footprints?" David asked, now realizing why the Master had sent him to her.

"Yeah, this is why you hired me isn't it," she responded nonchalantly, detecting the respect that had peppered David's comment. "It looks like there was a little confusion. Then it looks like they all went this way," she continued, pointing down the southern path. "I bet they headed toward Drumlocke. It's the only thing around."

***

The pair headed in a southern direction until they reached the site of the first moblin ambush. David became nervous at the sight of the dead goblins and his eyes started to shoot around nervously hoping they wouldn't encounter Marnie's body. "What happened here?" he asked with concern, now fully trusting Luci's abilities.

Luci surveyed the two goblin corpses and the device that Trig had created. She replied, "Looks like a moblin ambush. Hopefully, the person who created this device is friendly. This is one of the more sophisticated devices I've encountered. They took a big risk making it."

"How so?" David questioned.

"With the blowout's darkwash, they would have had to cycle-charge Muse with an orb. Then spend another to make this. It takes a lot of guts. More than I'd have. If they had even the smallest amount of Muse left in their body...well, they'd be lying here beside it I suppose," Luci answered. "It does look like they ran away from here...fast."

"We should probably pick up the pace as well. We may be able to put a few more minutes between us and Imperium if we do," David responded, concerned the situation for Marnie had become direr after a moblin encounter.

Neither of the pair had yet been able to detect the Imperium mercenaries behind them. Luci had concluded that the darkness likely slowed the posse down. They wouldn't have had the ability to use orbs if they had cuffs equipped. It would also not have been good for Imperium's image if any of their members were caught with them. The blowout, she thought, may have also been a blackout area for the cuffs. Luci agreed with David's assessment and after secreting the unknown Muser's diversion device into the woods, they picked their pace up to a jog.

The pair continued to travel down the trail until they reached the site of the second moblin ambush. The light had already crept back far enough for Luci's goggles to be useful. The leader's exsanguinated body was still on the trailway. Luci could see that it had been stripped of a cap, eye patch, and foot coverings. Unknown to her it had also been stripped of its belt.

There was a second goblin body three meters off to the side of the trail, still clutching one of the blood vials. The body had obvious signs of blunt force trauma to its head. To Luci, it was an obvious sign of a power struggle. "The leader's body has just started to cool and they're already fighting for control...shame," she stated.

"The people with Marnie did this?" David said, looking at the former leader's mutilated body.

"So she has a name," Luci commented, noting the slightly dejected look on David's face. "No this was a big cat. A manner of Sìth judging by the bite pattern. Probably the one from the blowout."

"And Marnie?" David asked, the concern in his voice was obvious.

"Marnie...Marnie appears to be fine," she responded, emphasizing the name to rub in David's slip-up once more. "Her traveling companion, the one who created the device, not so much. Looks like they were the focus of this one's ire," Luci continued, gesturing toward the goblin leader. "Looks like the cat may have saved 'em. They have an injured leg and appear to be losing blood. Bad for them, good for us."

"How's that?" David replied.

"Blood shows up in especially high contrast with these," she replied, tapping at her goggles. "It loses Muse real quick outside the body. We should be able to track them even as they get close to town and start walking on more heavily trafficked paths."

"Oh shit," David declared.

"What? What is it?" Luci asked.

"Look behind you," David responded, his set of lookout skills now on display.

Luci looked back to see light rays peeking around tree trunks of the still blacked-out forest in the far-off distance. Imperium had started to catch up. "That's not good," she said before taking a moment to think. "I've got an idea."

She produced two orbs from her bandoleer and immediately threw one at the ground. Then before both their eyes, a contraption sprouted from the ground. Luci picked up a small cubic box that had an attached tripwire. She placed the contraption on one side of the trail and then ran the wire to a tree on the other side of the trail.

"Is that what I think it is?" asked David.

"Sure is," replied Luci as she placed the second orb inside the box. She then directed her focus into the box as she shook it to crack open the orb. Then with David's help, she set about scrubbing out the detectable Razor-Sìth prints before finally flipping the trigger switch to activate the box.

"What did you put in it?" David responded. He had heard tales of the device but had never actually seen one, not sure they existed until this moment.

"There are some things in this world which have names I dare not speak," Luci replied; a dourness coated her words. She wasn't naturally a superstitious person but there were some lines even she wouldn't cross.

This explanation was one David knew would have to suffice. Eternal Dawn was a world in which it was hard to distinguish folklore from factuality. It was a world he knew contained genuine horror for one who was willing to look.

With their distraction firmly in place, the pair turned and picked up their pace into a run. Before long they had reached another fork in the road. The fork contained a crossroads sign which pointed toward the direction of Drumlocke.

With David's help, Luci was able to rotate the sign to point down the wrong path. The move was a long shot but one that may buy them more time. They stopped for a moment to catch their breath and listen for any indication that their trap had been sprung. Neither David nor Luci was able to detect the telltale signs that it had and they continued on.

It was another five minutes before they hit the forest's border and another five before they could just barely make out screams of horror emanating from the direction they had come. This put Imperium twenty minutes behind them. They could see Drumlocke a short way in the distance and set their heading.

***

The designated Imperium tracker hadn't possessed the same skill set as Luci. The Imperium posse was also at an informational disadvantage. To them, this was simply a large-scale Muse event; one which warranted investigation. Their main concern was determining if there was a force in the world that could threaten the rapidly growing monopoly the company had been building.

The tracker possessed enough skill to determine that there was a party of two in pursuit of a party of three and correctly assessed that their boss's assaulter was in the pursuing party; granted, everyone in the posse had assessed that. It would have been a hard fact to miss, having been passed twice by the assailant at breakneck speed.

At the site of the blowout, the tracker had only been able to determine the epicenter of the event but not how it had been created. He was of the mind that it may have been a combination of the group of three possibly making a major mistake with orbs. Had he participated in advanced study surrounding the nature of orbs, he would have realized the physical laws regarding the conservation of energy wouldn't have permitted such an event. It would have taken much more energy than all the unaccounted-for orbs left in existence had the potential to release.

At the site of the first moblin ambush, the tracker hadn't detected Trig's confusion device which had been hidden by Luci. He had incorrectly assumed that the group of three had gotten the better of the two felled goblins.

At the second moblin ambush, he had missed the body of the second goblin in the woods and was unable to find the cause of the red cap's demise. The tracker was able to determine the direction in which the two groups had headed and beckoned his fellow Imperium soldiers to start down the trail. They had only walked ten paces before they triggered the device that had been left behind by Luci.

The tracker hadn't seen the wispy wire that broke with their tenth step. The group had also not immediately noticed the proliferation of black fog that started to gather below their knees. They made ten more paces before the device started to emit a loud ghostly shriek. In the moments that followed, the security forces started to hear the plodding clop of horse hooves from the darkness further up the path.

The tracker was the first among them to catch a glimpse of the two glowing red eyes belonging to a beastly animal. The eyes were bobbing up and down, growing in size as the creature continued its approach. Moments later, a second set of eyes belonging to its rider appeared above the first.

It was at this point the tracker used his cuff's Muse charge to produce a torch. It would provide a brighter light than the soft glow of the cuff's built-in flashlight. It was a decision that the tracker instantly regretted. The apparition that had appeared before them was no mere horse and rider. The tracker knew at once it was a horror of old.

The creature that charged at them was only vaguely horse-like in appearance. It may have possessed an equine form but didn't possess any skin to speak of, leaving its layers of glowing red muscle, bone, and sinew exposed. It had a slick appearance, caused by the thin layer of blood which coated it. The rider on its back wasn't a rider at all but an integrated part of the beast. A demon without legs, possessing an elongated ichthyic face, was conjoined at its waist to the horse, sitting at the base of its oily black mane. The demon's arms were exaggerated in length, its knuckles dragged on the ground even at full stand.

"Nuckelavee!" the tracker screamed out. It was the name Luci had fear to speak. It was a name that brought terror to the seaside towns of Eternal Dawn, a fact that Luci had hoped the Imperium security force would overlook. The closest sea to Ærratum was well over three hundred miles away. Even in those parts, there hadn't been so much as a sighting of the Nuckelavee in many years. Most in Eternal Dawn doubted that it ever existed at all, chalking up its accountings as nothing more than the ramblings of drunken old sailors making attempts to frighten children. Whether it existed or not, its visage was too frightful to rationalize.

"Run!" the tracker managed to yell out between panicked breaths.

It was a command that scattered the force. Half of them had run in the opposite direction of the beast. The others scattered into the woods on either side of the trail. It was at this moment that the tracker tripped over the body of the second goblin coming face to face with the would-be moblin leader, prompting another terrified screech. Another discordant shriek emanated from the Nuckelavee, further heightening the tracker's feelings of dread.

Looking back, the tracker saw that the creature's gaze now appeared to be fixed upon him. The horse snorted in anticipation. The gangling hands of the attached rider reached out toward him, causing him to once more scream in terror as he attempted to scramble in the opposite direction. His heart was racing as the creature clawed at him, not quite being able to grab hold. Its incorporeal hands were unknowingly passing through his frightened form.

Moments later the Nuckelavee appeared to respond to the noise that the abandoning soldiers were making on their retreat and shifted focus before giving chase. It wasn't long before the tracker started to hear their terrified screams off in the distance.

The tracker and the team members who had laid low in the bushes waited a few minutes until it was clear the creature was unlikely to return. Upon reentering the trail, the tracker tripped over the nightmare box that Luci had set up, kicking it into the open dirt of the path. In that moment he realized that the creature had been nothing more than an illusion. He shouted to his team leader, "Hey Sara! Look at this. We've been had."

"Shit Richard! Isn't this the exact reason you're on this team? To watch out for shit like this?" Sara admonished. "We're half a team down. I don't expect we'll be seeing those cowardly fools again. Not after the sight of that...that thing," she finished, not daring to speak its name lest the real one make an appearance.

***

It would be five minutes until the screaming behind David and Luci ceased. It was another fifteen before they reached the main road entering Drumlocke.

Their first stop after losing the trail of blood was the City Hall Inn. It was a venue that David had a more than passing familiarity with. He and Scot had cause to visit Drumlocke on multiple occasions and made a habit of wasting their evenings away at the establishment. The city's library was what had drawn them to the small town as it was well enough equipped to handle the nature of the questions that Scot had had upon their arrival in Eternal Dawn. It was also where they sought answers in their subsequent attempts to leave.

During the Last War, there had been a knowledge purge; an unfortunate custom for fascist regimes. In the years after the war, the rotating roster of librarians made it their mission to collect the lost works of Eternal Dawn. It was an attempt to preserve that which should not be forgotten. This was what made the library such a valuable resource.

"David! How long's it been? A year? Two?" Mayor Pherson exclaimed as the pair entered the Inn, "Can I get you something? It's on the house."

"It's been a little while. Thanks for the offer Mayor but we're just looking for some information. We're kind of in a rush," David responded.

"Seems like everyone is today," Pherson replied.

"What's that mean? Who's in a rush today?" Luci chimed in, latching onto the notion that someone else had come in with a sense of urgency in a town that was, as far as she could tell, void of any need for it.

"Hey! I don't know you. Perhaps using a little tact when addressing a public official would behoove you," Pherson said, playfully scolding Luci. "Now if you would like to do this all proper like, my name is Mayor Pherson Pierson...and you are?"

"Luci," Luci responded bluntly, unwilling to entertain the Mayor's playfulness.

"That moniker come with a last name?" Pherson prodded once more.

"Not if you want to keep your teeth," Luci responded.

"Be nice," David interjected in an attempt to break the forming tension.

"Well, well, well, rough customer," Pherson responded. "Now what was it I could help you with?"

"We are looking for a young woman. May have passed through here in the last few hours," David started. "Little shorter than me. Doesn't look like she's from around here. May be traveling with two others."

"Oh, I don't know. I get so many people passing through these days and none of them look like they're from around here," Pherson said, evading the question. "Hell, I know everyone who is."

"Don't get smart with us," Luci responded, obviously agitated with the mayor's sidestepping the question.

"If I was smart, I wouldn't be mayorin' in this jerk water town, would I?" Pherson responded.

Just then Luci grabbed hold of his arm and stabbed a dagger down through his jacket sleeve and into the bar. The mayor winced in expectation of a pain that didn't come. He had fully expected Luci to stab through his arm.

"Luci! Stop it! A simple bribe would have sufficed," David commanded, pulling the blade out of the bar top before handing Pherson two of the orbs from his bandoleer. He was familiar with the double-speak the mayor would use when he had information for sale.

"Yeah, I'm a public official, a simple bribe would have sufficed," Pherson responded, pulling his arm back across the bar. "She was with a couple of orb mongers. Didn't get a good look at her on account of the robe but she had some power. That, I can tell you. Likely responsible for the wave that passed through here a couple hours ago if you ask me. Went to The Free-Blower for dinner. Haven't seen 'em since."

"And the mongers," Luci questioned, "...Anyone to worry about?"

"Obviously not for you," Pherson responded. "The small one is the more clever of the two, injured though...Not that it matters to you but they're friends. Please try not to hurt them."

"Some friend you are, selling them out like this," Luci responded.

"I'm not selling them out. I'm trying to remove a potential danger from this town. Jerk water though it may be, it is mine," Pherson replied, attempting to rationalize his betrayal.

Chapter Thirteen
"Ships that pass in the night..."

On their way to the library, Marnie, Trig, and Chauncey passed by a park containing a graffiti-covered wall. The styles that graced the bricks were similar to the throw-ups and stencils Marnie had been used to seeing in Rochester. There was an added muralistic quality to the wall's art. While it contained the unsigned signatures of multiple artists, the individual pieces blended together in a way that hearkened to a tattoo artist attempting to combine multiple disjointed works into one cohesive sleeve. Another detail that struck Marnie was that there was no evidence of any of the pieces being buffed or bombed over. Some of the works had the weather-worn appearance of years-long run times.

Marnie admired the art for a few moments before noticing a familiar image in the bottom right corner of the wall. It was the image of a Green Man done with a stencil, one that was worked top to bottom to minimize drips through the piece. A Green Man that used the same flourishes she had seen Scot use so many years ago. Marnie made note of an empty space on the wall big enough for a piece of her own, hoping she would have the opportunity to return.

***

"Can I help you?" the tall lanky woman behind the counter asked as the trio walked through the door into the Drumlocke City Library.

"We're here to see the librarian," Trig stated.

"Do you have an appointment?" the woman replied.

Trig, looking around and not seeing any other people, asked, "Do we need one?"

The woman twirled a strand of long black hair around her finger and replied, "It's procedure."

"O..kay. I'd like to make an appointment then," Trig responded.

The woman opened up and flipped through a planner to the page representing the day's activities. "Oh. It looks like there is an availability in four hours, then another in six, and let me see...one right now. Which would you prefer?" the woman questioned with a matter-of-fact tone.

"Put us down for the one right now," Trig responded, baffled.

"Can I get a name?" the woman replied.

"Is that really necessary?" Trig queried.

"Procedure," the woman repeated.

"Fine, it's Noble...Alex Noble," Trig answered, using the alias to which they were accustomed.

"Thank you. Please have a seat over there and I'll let you know when it is time for the appointment," the woman said.

Trig, Chauncey, and Marnie walked over to a row of chairs and sat down. At the exact moment their backsides settled, the woman called out to the room, "Alex Noble, it is time for your appointment. I repeat, Alex Noble, it is time for your appointment."

Trig glanced over at Chauncey and Marnie, giving them a quick eye roll before heading back to the counter.

"Oh, you're here," said the woman. "Follow me back to the office."

The woman guided them down a hallway to a secluded room. There was lettering on the door that simply read, 'Librarian'.

"Go in and have a seat. The librarian will be with you shortly," the woman beckoned, before heading back down the hallway to the front desk area.

The office had much the same setup as Mayor Pherson's, though the desk wasn't nearly as large and one of the walls was lined with bookcases containing large leather and canvas-bound tomes. The books had a certain pristine quality about them as if they weren't available for circulation. There were once more only two guest chairs and the trio took up the same postures that they had at the City Hall Inn, with Marnie and Trig sitting while Chauncey took a lean between them. It didn't matter to Chauncey. He was giddy at the possibility of being able to meet a bona fide, dyed in the wool, Master. He wouldn't have been able to sit regardless.

Five minutes later a cloaked figure walked into the room and sat down behind the desk. They collected up some scattered papers and tapped them to flush their edges before setting them aside. The figure then lowered the hood of its cloak.

"You have got to be kidding me," Trig muttered as the librarian was revealed to be the woman they had dealt with upon entering the library.

"Ser Noble I presume," the woman said as she looked at Trig. "I am Wordsmith. A pleasure to make your acquaintance."

"So the rumors are true. Pleasure," said Trig, still baffled by the stranger's odd behavior. They were now holding on to a thread of hope that the visit wouldn't be a waste of time.

"And whom may thee unaccounted members of your party be, pray tell?" Wordsmith continued.

"I don't see how that's important," responded Trig, trying to obfuscate as many details as possible from this person they couldn't possibly trust.

"I was forthright with who I am. Decorum would oblige your party to behave with the same courtesy," Wordsmith replied with no hint of irony.

"Hark, I am Sir Fauntleroy," Chauncey interjected before Trig could offer a further argument. In his attempt to sound official, he hadn't bothered to mask the surname he no longer had need of; it had almost been lost to time in his years on the road. "The pleasure is all on this side of the desk," he added.

"Lady Lexington," Marnie replied, as she nodded her head in an almost bow, hoping she had used the correct honorific. She had been thoroughly amused by the proceedings, having started work on the alias after hearing Trig use theirs.

"Now that we are properly introduced, if nobody has an objection, I motion we dispense with any further attempts at high speech and procedure," Wordsmith said, inquiring to the group.

"Aye, Master Wordsmith we have no problem dropping it," Chauncey responded. "And must I say, it really is an honor to meet you."

Trig and Marnie nodded in the affirmative, not sure why the pretense was needed in the first place.

"Motion carried then," Wordsmith said before continuing. "Aye laddie not much need for the 'Master' these days, simply Wordsmith will do. Now what is it I can help you lot with?"

"Well," Trig started, noticing their host's immediate shift in demeanor, "We require some information that may have been lost during the Last War and I need you to be straight with us."

"I am nothing if not honest," Wordsmith responded.

"Which side were you on?" Trig pushed, as Chauncey looked on stunned. He would have been unable to be so blunt with a Master, former though they may be.

Wordsmith eyed Trig. "Does my previous affiliation hold bearing on the information that you seek?" she said, trying to hold onto a small vestige of the formality she had previously been cloaked in.

"I just want to know how little you can be trusted," Trig rudely pressed on. "You Masters were all the same. Always speaking doubly. Always crossing doubly."

"I wonder...Would it help your opinion of me if I told you?" Wordsmith pondered as she stared into Trig's violet eyes. "...In the interest of honesty, I was aligned with the Vagabond. Flawed though his plan now appears in the hind's sight of Eternal Dawn's current lightlessness; he was the finest among us. I still hold that he did what was needed for the time...I do wish we had had accounting for the eventual rise of an entity such as Imperium. It hadn't occurred to us that there would be so many looking to give up so much for such a meager reward."

Trig sat for a moment in silence. They hadn't expected such introspection from a former Master, having previously decided that the Masters were too full of hubris to be capable of admitting a mistake. While their position on the Masters as a whole hadn't shifted, they were willing to soften slightly in the presence of this former one.

Marnie was warmed by the reverence that Wordsmith had shown for her father, thankful that the hood of her robe was there to mask the tears that were welling in her eyes.

Chauncey was still in wonderment at being in the presence of a former Master.

"My apologies for the impertinence," said Trig, offering the mildest of mea culpa.

Wordsmith spoke once more, "Think nothing of it. You are not the first and I suspect you will not be the last. Your opinions are well earned and you'd do well to remember that. Now, once more, what was it I could help you with?"

"We need some information that I suspect was largely lost in the war," Trig replied.

Chauncey couldn't resist the opportunity to jump in, "Is it true that the Geddes worshiped the Mórrigan exclusively?"

"We don't have time for your nonsense," Trig chided.

"Apologies Ser Noble. Please, do go on," Chauncey uttered with the slightest tinge of sarcasm.

"If one needed to locate a pre-Flood Master, how would one go about it?" Trig questioned.

"I fail to see how your query would hold any more relevance than your partners," Wordsmith replied. "They both speak to a bygone age."

"Humor me," Trig responded.

"I suppose you would need an attuner. It was a device used to identify Master lineages," said Wordsmith, as she rose from her desk, heading toward a bookcase. Her fingers brushed over its many volumes with intention before landing on one of the leather-bound tomes. She brought the book back to the desk. To the group's mild wonder, she forewent skimming through the pages and opened directly to the one desired, before turning the book around. "Here's one."

An exploded diagram of the device was staring at the trio from the page. It had the appearance of a large compass, extending across the bottom edge of a palm to the first finger joint of an average user. There were all manner of gears and levers hiding behind a clock-like face. The face was inscribed with sigils of a similar style to the ones Marnie had used to cross over.

"What do the sigils represent?" asked Marnie.

"Oo, oo, oo, I know this one," replied Chauncey. "They represent one of the fifteen disciplines that a Master may possess."

"Very good," Wordsmith complimented, causing Chauncey to beam as if he had just answered a question correctly in front of the whole class.

"Where can we find one of these attuners?" Trig questioned.

"The simple answer is, you cannot," Wordsmith responded before continuing, "They were all destroyed in the war. The keepers thought it much too dangerous for a device of its nature to exist. I was the one who oversaw their destruction. This tome may very well be the last reminder of their existence."

"Let's just go get one of those orbs and create one," Marnie offered.

"Aye lass, not as simple as that," responded Wordsmith. "These devices lived outside of the Muse, forged in darkness by an unknown author. Attempts to reproduce them with conventional methods yield a useless device. In this rare case, the Muse actually taints them."

"Is there nothing else like them?" Trig asked.

"Well, now that you mention it. As I understand it, those wicked Imperium cuffs have a much less sophisticated version of an attuner inside them. It can't discern disciplines and doesn't have nearly the range. Might be good for thirty meters. It's used to find areas with higher concentrations of Muse to amplify its reward function. I suppose, in theory, it could be used to find this theoretical Master of old," Wordsmith replied before pondering, "I would like to know how they got around the Muse tainting problem."

"This leads to my next theoretical question," Trig continued. "If I were Imperium and needed to imprison one of these theoretical Masters in Ærratum, where would I do it? Due to government oversight, I couldn't very well build a private prison in the spire."

"That one's easy," responded Wordsmith. "The spire is built on the foundation of the old Geddes citadel. Was thought to be a place of great power. Lonely Sister hits its apex directly over it every night exactly halfway through the witching hours. Anyway, there were dungeons under the citadel, so you wouldn't need to build anything. Figured it was common knowledge at this point. Spent some of the worst times of my life there. I haven't talked about it. Guess the others would want to forget too. Had a good view of the Ebony Wellspring though."

"Ebony Wellspring?" Marnie questioned.

"Do they teach nothing in schools these days," Wordsmith replied. "It is a font which no light can penetrate. The old tales tell that it is where bad ideas go to die. It was heralded as a sacred place of rebirth by acolytes of the old magics."

"I thought magic didn't exist," Marnie stated.

"In days of old, magic and science were thought to be one and the same," Wordsmith responded.

"Is it comforting to know from where you were birthed, Sir Fauntleroy?" Trig quipped, teasing Chauncey before continuing the inquiry, "One final question. If one needed to break into this prison to rescue this hypothetical Master, how would one do so?"

"That...that would be an easier proposition to speak than to perform," commented Wordsmith, as she pondered the question. "I suppose the old cisterns may be an option. You would have to be an extraordinary swimmer though." Wordsmith continued to contemplate the question before adding, "Follow me."

***

The trio followed the librarian to a nearby room featuring a large central worktable. The table appeared to have been constructed out of a large tree trunk. Upon further inspection, Marnie realized the feature had roots that penetrated the floor.

The room was surrounded by various flat files and hanging maps. Light was radiating from amber-colored fruit hanging off the branches that supported the ceiling above. The room had an ambiance akin to that of the captain's quarters on an old pirate ship.

Wordsmith walked over to one of the flat files and rummaged through the many layers of maps in one of its drawers, before selecting a cartograph and laying it out on the central worktable. The exposed wood of the stump lit up, causing parts of the map to glow in contrast to others. Certain features appeared to rise off the page in an almost holographic manner. What they were looking at was an underground map of Ærratum. It included the cisterns, the foundations of prewar structures, an old cave network, and various tunnels.

"This map represents the topmost layer of subterranea for Ærratum. You can see the connection I was discussing here," Wordsmith said as she pointed at the map. "This one is the private cistern of the citadel and you can see the underwater tunnel to one of the public cisterns here."

"Are you kidding me? That would be impossible. You said, strong swimmer. You'd have to be one of the mer to make that distance," Trig responded with an almost exasperated tone.

"I am starting to get the sense that this is not strictly academic," Wordsmith replied, having already made the deduction by the second query. "But that would mean..."

"What are those?" Marnie interrupted, pointing at various sigils that were shown in holographic relief, pulling her father's sketchbook out of her pack to compare the images. She had found several to match the ones in the book including the one David had used to cross.

"Those are the locations of menhirs...Grendoors...useless to all but the Vagabond Master and those in his immediate presence," Wordsmith replied, unaware of the redundancy in the knowledge she was providing.

The light of the table increased slightly with the revelation of a possible better way to acquire access to the citadel. Marnie bit her lip so as not to speak anything further, remembering what Trig had said about trusting Masters.

"This is a pre-war map though," Wordsmith continued, "The Geddes destroyed a number of the doors in an attempt to hinder the Vagabond and his passengers."

"What would happen if the Vagabond tried to use a door that no longer existed?" Marnie asked, considering the passive disclosure before deciding it was worth the risk.

"Depends," Wordsmith replied. "If it was completely destroyed, probably nothing. However if the eyes of the Green Man exist without a mouth to disgorge the traveler, they could be lost in darkness, forever being wrapped in the vines that connect the doors. That is all speculative of course. We dared not risk using them once we received word they were being tampered with."

The light in the room waned slightly as Marnie came to the realization of how risky her crossing had been. She was thankful she had not possessed this knowledge before.

"Is there any way we can get a copy of this map?" Trig questioned, after realizing what Marnie was getting at.

"Of course," Wordsmith replied as she retrieved a blank sheet of parchment from a separate flat file, laying it on top of the map. She laid her hands on the table, "Do you have a novel idea for trade? I'll need to charge the table."

Chauncey saw this as his opportunity to shine, "How about Salmon Sorbet? It's like having ice cream for dinner."

"I...I don't think that is going to be enough," Wordsmith replied, keeping her response politic so as not to insult Chauncey.

"Hmm...erm...more in trade you say...How about reverse suspenders? They go between your legs and help keep your shirt from riding up?" he once more attempted.

"I think it's going to take a little more," Wordsmith replied, glancing from Trig to Marnie hoping they would step in shortly.

Marnie glanced over at Trig only to catch them glancing at her. Marnie could see that Trig was about to jump in and shook her head as if to say, "Not yet." She rested her hand on the worktable and waited.

"Okay..okay..buuuut I've been saving this one for a special occasion. Don't go telling it around. I'll know it was you," Chauncey demanded.

Wordsmith looked at Chauncey giving him a nod of acknowledgment while continuing to reserve her true thoughts.

"How about a pickle pocket? It would be a waterproof pocket in your pants to store briny treats," he said, expecting a level of awe for one of his finer inventions..

She was once more about to open her mouth to refute the idea but something peculiar happened. Unbeknownst to Wordsmith, Marnie had focused her intention into the table much the way she had done when activating the Green Doors.

There was a quick flash from the surface. It was as if a picture had been taken. Marnie's eyes took a moment to readjust from the bombardment of light. She stared at the table with a tiny bit of wonderment. The map had been duplicated onto the top sheet, creating a fresh cartograph.

Wordsmith stood confused, knowing the ideas Chauncey provided were sure to be destined for the Ebony Wellspring.

Trig took the moment of confusion to act. "Well, that should about wrap it up," they said, rolling up the map before Wordsmith could comment further.

"But..." Wordsmith started to protest, still trying to figure out what had just happened. She was keen to launch into an inquiry regarding the true nature of the meeting. The wave from the blowout had already put her on alert, she couldn't help but wonder if the odd trio was somehow connected.

"We've really taken up too much of your time," Marnie jumped in. "Thank you so much for the information, it was quite enlightening. Really helps with my school project."

The trio rushed out of the library doors, attempting to avoid further analysis of their actions by the former Master who had been so forthright with the requested information.

***

David and Luci walked the three blocks from the City Hall Inn down to The Free-Blower in search of Marnie and her traveling companions. The wait staff were much less reserved with information than Pherson. They had confirmed the trio's visit but were unable to provide a heading. The pair went back out to the street to contemplate their next move.

***

"Did anyone else think it was odd how forward Wordsmith was with all that information?" Marnie asked.

"I wouldn't read too much into it deary," Trig responded. "Just a Master without her power trying to bolster their hubris by showing the size of their brain I should think."

Trig looked into the sky, assessing the position of the moons. Between dinner and their visit with the former Master, they had been in town for an hour and a half. They considered the timing and calculated that they would have a few more hours before Imperium was sure to arrive. They thought for a moment weighing their next moves.

"I'll have to forgo the nap but I'll be damned if I'm not going to grab a rinse," Trig stated. The putrid stench of the red-capped goblin had followed them from the forest and they were anxious to be rid of it. "After this small bit of respite, my mind should be clearer to contemplate our next moves."

"I'd like to stay down here and have a look around the park if you think that would be okay," Marnie replied. She wasn't looking for permission. She was verifying the safety of taking such an action.

Trig picked up on the tone, "Probably not a problem. This city is pretty removed from Imperium influence. We should have at least four hours before they start poking around, three if they have a good tracker. We should plan to leave in one. Chauncey, stick with Marnie…And for once, try to do what I would do. I'll come find you when I'm done."

***

Luci's tracking skills always served her better outside of towns and cities. She had initially lost the trio outside of the clinic where Trig's blood trail ended. It was only at David's suggestion that they headed to the City Hall Inn. The dining establishment had left them without further direction.

She was working with three facts: Marnie had entered the city, she was in a traveling party of three, and she would probably be the only one in town wearing shoes. Shoes, while not an entirely foreign concept, were rarely seen outside of formal occasions. Most would be remiss to obstruct the body's main point of Muse absorption.

"What would they need next?" Luci asked herself.

"My assumption is...that she would go straight for Scot," David replied, not realizing that the question hadn't been intended for him.

"That would be a very dangerous proposition," Luci responded. This time she was intentionally inviting further discourse.

"We can't assume she is still with the people who helped her in the woods. Anybody with sense would avoid this quest like a plague," David said, correcting one of her assumptions while insulting their own involvement in said quest.

"In any case, she or they are going to need some information. This town have a bookstore or library?" Luci replied, knowing they only had a few moves left before Imperium would arrive to complicate the situation.

"This way," David said, pointing in the direction of the building in question.

"You want to put your hood on? They can't be far behind now," Luci replied, before changing her face to match a passerby who was headed toward the City Hall Inn.

***

Trig made their way back to the City Hall Inn to take the coveted shower, leaving Marnie and Chauncey to roam the park. Marnie's intention hadn't been to roam the park but to put up a piece of her own next to her brother's on the art wall.

"I don't think this is a good idea," Chauncey stated, before immediately rebutting, "That must mean it is then. Although it was my idea to see the Master...and pickle pocket, that was mine too. Do I have good ideas now? I'm confused."

"Why do you let Trig tease you like that?" Marnie said, asking a question that had bothered her since she had first observed the chiding behavior hours before.

"Aye, it's not like that. They don't mean anything by it," Chauncey replied. "Besides they're right. My ideas are usually bad ones. Way of the world. It keeps the balance and helps the gifted stars shine brighter."

"That's no way to talk about yourself," Marnie responded, drawing on her inner Martin.

"Miss Marnie, I don't think you quite catch my meaning," Chauncey replied. "It's an actual physical law of the world. Someone who can harness the Muse like Trig can only exist in opposition to someone with my distinct lack of ability. It's part of a balance. Besides it's not like I don't get my own jabs in…and occasional wins. I'm going to be dining out on the pickle pocket for years, it's a real winner."

"Maybe my presence is throwing things into limbo," Marnie stated, not knowing how close to the truth she was. She had pulled a respirator out of her bag, getting ready to put a piece on the wall.

"I hadn't thought of it until this moment but you're probably right," Chauncey said, taking a moment to consider the thought before finishing his own, "At the end of the day Trig is my best friend. Under threat of torture, they'd have to admit the same of me."

In light of the discussion, Marnie started to freehand her first piece in this strange new world. Utilizing her usual motifs, she started by spraying the side profile of an SLR camera body. She then sprayed in a telephoto lens. The camera was pointed toward Scot's green man as if it were taking a picture. She then added silver accents to mimic buttons, logos, and trim.

Keeping the silver in hand she started to work her way down the piece, roughing out the torso of a robot body. The body possessed telescopic arms that reached forward toward Scot's work. She then picked the black back up and used it to outline and accent the robot's body parts.

Continuing to use the can, Marnie sprayed what looked like a single tire a short distance under the torso. Using the silver once more, she sprayed in a hubcap and what appeared to be the strut of a motorcycle.

She then rummaged through her bag once more and selected two other colors. She didn't have teal but did have aquamarine which would be close enough for her purpose. Marnie drew what looked like pants between the strut and the robot's body. Taking the other color she drew Chauncey's red hairstyle on top of the camera. For the finishing touches, Marnie picked up black in one hand and silver in the other, adding accent and detail where she deemed appropriate. She then took a step back to stand by Chauncey and admire the work.

A tear started to form in Chauncey's eye. He was touched. Nobody had ever seen fit to use him as a reference for a piece of artwork.

"Is that..." Chauncey started, staring at the pants.

"It is," Marnie replied. "Do you want one?" she joked as she mimed reaching toward the robot's pants, not prepared for what happened next.

It took her a second to realize that when she pulled her hand back she was holding a pickle. Her eyes drew wide as she stared at her hand, unable to rationalize what had happened. Marnie looked from her hand back to the painting. Her jaw fell open at what she was now witnessing. The robot was in the process of peeling itself off the wall, using its telescopic arms to birth its way into three-dimensional existence.

Marnie backed away as the robot completed its emergence. Once it was on the ground it retracted its arm before gyrating its camera head to face Marnie. The robot gave her a quick nod as if to say, "Thank you," before turning its head forward and taking off down the road.

"You gonna eat that?" Chauncey managed, as the pair stared off into the distance at the departing robot.

***

Luci and David walked out of the library having caught a glimpse of the calendar during their own procedural wrangling. Seeing the words 'Ser Noble and two guests' had been enough to tell them that the trio had already been and gone. The library, David knew, wasn't heavily trafficked. It would be lucky to have three visitors in a day, let alone for a single meeting.

"What the hell was all that about with the procedure?" Luci asked rhetorically. "No wait, what the hell is that?" No sooner had she completed the thought when the red-headed mono-wheeled robot that had been barreling at them cut between her and David.

The pair looked at each other, then behind them at the robot, then back at each other.

"Marnie!" David exclaimed as he began to run toward its point of origin with Luci following closely behind.

Chapter Fourteen
"...barefoot from distant travel..."

"N**ot that you've given me much to go on but I haven't seen anyone matching that description," Pherson said to the two Imperium agents that were questioning him. He continued speaking in defiance of their presence, "And if I had, I sure as shite wouldn't tell the likes of you."

"Richard, I think we have the makings for a hero here. Are you a hero, sir?" The sarcasm that coated Sara's voice was tainted with malice.

"Come on Sara, not again," Richard pleaded.

At this moment Trig was making their way down from the room they had used to shower. They had heard the commotion and had paused just out of sight in the hallway leading to the back office.

"I don't want any trouble," Pherson replied. "If you leave now all can be forgotten."

"It isn't forgetting that I want you to do, now is it?" With these words, Sara reached over and grabbed Pherson by his lapels, dragging him over the bar top. She threw the mayor to the ground and commanded, "Tell me what I want to know!"

As Pherson was pleading for Sara to stop, Trig snuck into the inn's back office to reclaim the Muse orbs that had been part of their earlier transaction. After finding the orbs, they returned to their previous vantage point within earshot of the commotion.

Pherson was lying on the floor clutching his stomach after Sara had stomped on it with her calloused foot. "Tell me what I want to know and this can all stop," she ordered before once more before bringing her foot down onto his stomach.

"Ugh..un..uh," was all Pherson could manage. He had acted out of a need to preserve Drumlocke in selling out the first set of outsiders to the second but he wasn't about to betray anyone to Imperium.

"Is this really necessary? He doesn't know anything," Richard pleaded, uncomfortable with the inquisition.

"How can you be so sure that he doesn't? These outsteaders are not very forthright with information that can help our cause," Sara replied. "They're selfish." She was acting out of the sick pleasure she received when torturing one she thought to be a zealot. The irony in Sara applying the term zealot would remain beyond her reach. She thought on Richard's words for another moment before deciding that he had had a point. Her brutality should have knocked something loose but the thought wouldn't deny her one more kick to the man's stomach.

"Stop it!" Trig commanded, popping out from around the corner.

"And who are you to stop me?" Sara replied with an almost palpable level of disdain for the disruption.

"I'm the reason you're here and if you want to get out of town with your heads, it would behoove you to leave now," Trig responded, attempting to draw attention away from their friend.

"Behoove me...behoove me. Richard, I think we have ourselves a hero here. You a hero?" Sara asked Trig rhetorically.

It wasn't lost on Richard that this was the second time he had heard this line of questioning in the last ten minutes. Sara hadn't been recruited for her ability to harness Muse. In Imperium, matters of creative thinking were left to specialists, not team leaders.

"Suit yourself," Trig replied. Using orbs they had secreted up the sleeves of their dark robe, they closed their eyes and in one swift motion, stretched their arms wide before bringing their palms to bear, smashing the orbs together with as much force as they could manage. Trig performed the act with the intention of having no intention.

The energy expulsion from the event created the desired effect. Trig had created a mini blowout, covering the area of a single block. It wouldn't give them much time to act but with any luck, it would be enough. They had just enough time to hide another orb up their sleeve to act as a light source in the now pitch-black room.

Trig started by closing the gap between them and the shocked Imperium aggressor. They flashed the orb just long enough to allow them to stomp on the team leader's ankle, causing her to scream out in pain. Their next move was to help drag Pherson up to his feet, allowing him to stumble-run half doubled over, toward the door.

Trig and Pherson managed to make their way up the street and around the corner before the Imperium soldiers collected enough of their wits to give chase. For the moment they were safe.

"Mayor, sorry to bring this trouble your way. We had hoped to be clear of this town before they arrived," Trig said. "Had I known what they would do..."

"It's no matter. Truth be told, even without the big blackout, they would have gotten around to us eventually. At least you were here to stop it. I'd..I'd likely be dead," Pherson replied, the pain in his stomach still sharp.

"I had to take the orbs," Trig said, continuing their apologetic tone.

"I sus' you'll need them more than us," the mayor reasoned. "While we're 'pologizing...Imperium...they're not the only ones after you. Man and woman pair were looking for you too. 'shamed to admit I was weakened to a bribe and gave them a heading. Watch out for the lass. She was mean like the Imperium stooge. Smart though. Could pro'ly be reasoned with."

"We all have our weaknesses. I'd be a hypocrite if I faulted you yours," Trig responded, sensing Pherson was just trying to do right by his town.

Pherson nodded in acknowledgment, "Must be getting off to the clinic then...make sure all my guts are intact."

Trig lamented, "Hope this isn't last goodbyes but...well it's been real."

"Hope to see you," Pherson responded after a moment of contemplation, finally understanding the gravity of the evening's events. Pherson continued his labored pace in the direction of the clinic, disappearing into the darkness of the alley.

All at once, the feeling of peril that accompanied the path ahead hit Trig. They only had a few moments to process the events of the evening. There was a feeling that a wheel of fate had been put into motion, setting them on an inexorable path toward an unknown destiny.

Trig shook off the feeling and collected themselves, refocusing on their current objective. They had to reach Chauncey and Marnie and they had to do it before Imperium.

***

"What...what just happened?" Marnie said flummoxed, staring in the direction of the robot's travel, still trying to piece together the events that had just transpired. The thought of one of her works birthing itself into reality should be putting her on edge. She had a moment to consider that her fight or flight system must be fried. At her normal baseline, an event like this would have been more than enough to trigger an attack.

She was struck by another thought. Perhaps between the Green Door, the Razor-Sìth, the revelation about her father, and the moblins, the panic center of her brain had started doing what it was supposed to do. "Time will tell," she thought. She resolved to try and enjoy the reprieve as long as it lasted.

"You...You're a Master Marnie," Chauncey responded. "Though I've never heard of anyone creating something with sentience before. That's a new one on me." He had read numerous books of dubious authorship on the subject and none of them had ever mentioned a Master actualizing a new being into existence. There were of course the stories of golems but they weren't creatures so much as they were humanoid Muse vessels able to respond to their creator's intentions.

"Wait, are you saying that I...I created that?" Marnie asked. She had considered herself to be secular but even with that, the thought of creating a creature with a mind of its own seemed somehow sacrilegious.

"That's what I'm sayin'. But grain of salt if you will," Chauncey replied. "Bad ideas and all." He could see the revelation had put Marnie on edge and was attempting to temper it.

"Marnie!...Marnie!" a voice from the distance called.

Chauncey and Marnie turned to look at who was using her name out in the open.

"David?...David!" Marnie shouted, breaking into a run towards the voice with Chauncey in tow.

***

"Trig? You know you could have said something when Marnie mentioned David," said Chauncey as he gazed upon David's traveling companion. "How do you know each other? Did you get taller?"

"Well uh...I uh," Luci started to stammer.

"Run! We need to Run! Imperium...They're behind me," another voice started to yell from a distance, gaining ground with each step.

The other voice caused Chauncey to do a double-take. He looked at the Trig in front of him then to the Trig off in the distance and back to the one in front of him before again looking back to the one in the distance. "What's going on?" he demanded.

"Shit," David muttered. "I thought we had a few more minutes, no time to explain, we need to get moving."

The words had barely managed to exit David's lips when the two Imperium agents following the real Trig appeared at the top of the knoll. The group turned in the other direction and started to run. The two Trigs were scanning the road, looking for a dark alleyway that could be used for escape, a task made all the worse by the need to negotiate the cobblestone roadway underfoot.

The group was able to put distance between the two Imperium agents. Trig realized the blow they had delivered at the Inn had been enough to give the woman a limp. They would have been content with this knowledge had it not been for the approaching vehicles in the other direction.

Three of the Imperium scramblers were working to box the group in. The sight of the vehicles was enough to explain how Trig had been so wrong in their time estimation. They knew Imperium was innovating faster by the day but hadn't expected this much advancement.

"Marnie you wouldn't happen to have another blowout up your sleeve would you," Chauncey asked.

"I didn't mean to make the first one. It's not like I can have a panic attack when it's convenient," Marnie replied.

"Worth a shot I guess," Chauncey rebutted. "Anyone else have any bright ideas?"

Trig, annoyed at the suggestion, started, "One, it wasn't a good idea, and two..."

"I don't think we have time for this right now," Marnie chided, knowing that their bickering wouldn't serve their escape.

Luci used an orb to create a quiver of arrows. After nocking one, she yelled at the Imperium leader as they lurched forward, "Stay back! I'll shoot."

Sara, testing the command, advanced a few more paces. Seeing this as an act of aggression, Luci loosed an arrow, dropping Trig's face for her previous one as she did, seeing no need for further artifice.

The leader felt the arrow whiz by her ear before hearing Luci shout, "The next one will be your head."

Sara stopped in her tracks replying, "Is this what it's come to? I don't want a fight." She looked past Luci as she continued, "David, tell your friend to take it easy...I just want answers!"

"You know this psycho?" Trig yelled over to David as they threw their own orbs at the ground, bringing up a pair of revolving hand crossbows. They then turned to face the soldiers in the scramblers.

"She's not the type to look for answers without first having a fight," David replied.

"Yeah, I got that impression laddie," Trig responded.

"We can talk about who knows who after," Luci shouted. "If you don't mind I'd rather focus on getting out of here in one piece!"

"I have an idea. I'm not sure it will work," Marnie said in a voice she had hoped would be muffled by the time it reached the soldiers. "We'll need to get back to the wall, the one in the park."

The three soldiers that had accompanied the remaining scramblers exited their vehicles. Using the charges in their cuffs they had each produced a full-length transparent riot shield. They also produced long swords. Then, in a move that appeared to have been drilled into them, the soldiers stood side by side in a shield wall.

In lockstep, the wall started advancing toward the group. Trig fixed their aim at it, waiting for it to get close enough to make a penetrating shot. Luci's aim remained pointed at Sara who she suspected, even with the limp, would be the most capable fighter among the aggressors.

"David, I hope you're working on an idea," Luci called out. "We're outnumbered for fighters right now. You need to do something."

Marnie and Chauncey knew not to take offense. Luci had been correct. Marnie didn't yet have a grasp on what she was capable of and didn't know how much Muse it would take to do the one thing she knew she could. Chauncey knew his dapper duds didn't scream out fighter. He was used to Trig being the heavy in these situations.

"I've got this," David said nonchalantly, dropping his bag to the ground before removing his bandoleer and letting it and his robes fall off his body. His well-toned arms were now exposed, revealing a patchwork of tattoos that completely sleeved both arms. The tattoos had a soft glow that appeared to be pulsing. He reached down into his bag, pulling out a can of silver paint.

Marnie looked at him in surprise. "The David I knew back in the day would have never gotten a tattoo," she thought.

"Let them get closer," David said as he squatted over the ground, spraying one narrow two-meter-long line.

Luci, seeing what David was doing, criticized, "What the hell do you plan on doing with that?"

David, paying no mind to the derision, held his hand over the line. Light rays shot up from the ground to the height of his arm. They moved from one end of the shape to the other, almost mirroring the aerosol from the spray can. In a matter of moments, David was holding a two-meter-long silver bō. The bō was tapered at both ends giving it the appearance of a javelin.

David allowed the shielded soldiers to advance within the Muse tether range of his painting. He took a focused breath before sprinting directly at them. In one swift motion, David planted one end of the staff into the ground and used his momentum to vault over the top of the soldiers.

He landed in a crouch, using his continued momentum and lowered position to take his first strike. The staff swung around as an extension of David's arm, making contact with the side of the knee belonging to the soldier to his right. The action produced the unmistakable crunch of snapping bone. The soldier cried out with an agonized scream before falling to his side, grasping at the injury.

David then twisted his body to the right as he stood up to face the other aggressors. The soldier on the left had abandoned his shield and was in the process of bringing his blade down in a cleaving motion toward David's skull. David brought the staff up, holding it with two hands in a block before giving the blade cushion and letting go of the left side. This caused the soldier's sword to follow the bō's path to the ground. With the soldier bent over, David was able to spin his body anticlockwise, cracking the soldier in the lower back. The soldier took a stumbled step before turning in an attempt to take another swing. David brought the staff down hard onto the man's wrist, forcing him to drop his weapon. He then whipped around once more, cracking the soldier in the shin. The soldier fell to the ground and immediately attempted to stand, not realizing the extent of his injury. Marnie retched as she saw the leg fold upon itself, causing the soldier to topple once more. The soldiers' wailing added to the growing chorus of torment.

David then walked over to this second attacker and picked up the sword that had been dropped. He turned toward the remaining soldier, sword in one hand, staff in the other, and started to advance. The soldier stood with his shield facing David, ready to glance an incoming blow. David reached back with his sword and brought it down on top of the shield, embedding it in the defensive instrument. His strike caused a shock to run up the attacker's arm. The soldier quickly abandoned his shield and took up a two-handed stance with their sword. David swung his staff at the soldier but they were able to parry before returning an attack in kind. With one end of the staff, David made a quick windmill motion at the attacker's wrists. This caused the sword to rotate past the orbital point of the soldier's hand, wrenching the blade from his grip. The soldier then grabbed hold of the end of the bō in an attempt to thwart David's advance. At this, David abandoned the staff, dropping it as he closed the gap between him and the aggressor. He balled up his fist and sent it upward into the attacker's jaw. The soldier's head shot backward, followed immediately by the rest of his body. If he wasn't asleep before hitting the ground, he would have been knocked out when his head bounced off one of the cobbled stones.

Sound-tracked by the pained groans of the once-shielded soldiers, David collected the staff and one of the swords before walking back through the group on his way to confront Sara. As he passed by Trig, he uttered, "Shoot out the tires." Chauncey and Marnie stared on, their mouths agape.

"But couldn't we could use those?" Chauncey protested once he gained his wits. Trig was already in the process of loosing bolts at the scramblers from their hand crossbows.

"Not if we don't want to be tracked," Trig replied in agreement with David's request.

"You were saying?" David asked Luci before moving his attention to Sara.

"You've been practicing," Sara called out to David.

David stood there as stone, staring Sara down without uttering a word.

"Why don't you come closer, maybe I can give you another scar. Add some symmetry to that pretty face of yours," Sara continued to taunt.

In response, David launched the bō turned javelin at Sara. Its destination was her head but she made no effort to move, not even a flinch. Two meters before hitting its intended target, the staff disintegrated into a Muse vapor as if it were glass shattering against a wall. She had known enough to stand just outside of the limits of David's particular brand of magic.

Luci, whose aim never waned from the Imperium agent, followed up by loosing another arrow which whizzed past the leader's ear. "You'd do best to stay right there until we're gone," she suggested, before adding, "The next one won't miss."

Richard, the tracker, was nowhere to be found. He had slunk into the shadows behind Sara in an attempt to remove himself from the situation entirely, making no attempt to back up his team leader.

Luci and Trig kept their weapons trained on Sara as the group moved back up the hill. David kept the sword at the ready but it was already starting to decay in his hands. His touch had an adverse effect on constructs that had been actualized from the Imperium cuffs. He suspected the reason was related to his inability to use orbs or access Muse directly.

"Be seeing you," Sara said, once more jeering David as he passed by. She then pursed her lips into an air kiss.

This time David ignored the taunt as the group headed up the street toward the wall, leaving the Imperium leader to inspect their wounded and the damage that had been inflicted on the scramblers.

***

"We know of two safe portals," Marnie said as she pointed at the map. "This is the one I came through and this would be the one David came through."

Luci who had already picked up on his tells, looked over to David and could see he was biting his lip to prevent another slip. She opted to keep her mouth shut rather than force an interjection, thinking he was holding back information that could prove to be detrimental if revealed. After seeing his battle prowess, she had gained a modicum of respect for the man.

"Wait, are you saying what I think you're saying?" Chauncey giddily butted in, "Do we get to travel like the Vagabond?"

"If you're asking which we should take, lass," Trig interjected. "It would behoove us to travel to the first one at Umphraidh Menhir. Best not be jumpin' right into the fire. Still have a lot of unanswered questions." Trig looked ponderously at the woman who had worn their face not twenty minutes prior.

"I would have to agree with your new friend here," said David. "We can discuss our next moves on the other side but we need to get out of here before Sara and her cronies regroup. That couldn't have been all of them."

With that, Marnie looked at Scot's mural and pulled out a can of silver spray. She laid in the sigil containing the quarter moon with three nested half moons that had originally brought her to Eternal Dawn. Marnie then checked the sky to see that the Lonely Sister was still perched to mark the witching hour. She hadn't yet realized that, for the doorways on this side, it was always the witching hour.

Marnie laid her palm on the Green Man. Light started radiating out from under her hand, illuminating the visage as it crept through the branches and vines like blood seeping out from an exposed vein.

When Scot had painted the piece, he laid in some flower buds as detail. Under the power of Marnie's touch, the buds on the wall started to bloom. She recognized the flowers as that of a night-blooming cereus. The meaning wasn't lost on Marnie. They were the botanical equivalent of Scot's view on street art. A flower that blooms but once a year with the runtime of a single night. Ephemera in its purest form.

Marnie guided each of her travel companions through the Green Door. She took a final look at the beautiful flowers as she let the vines envelop her. The flower petals wilted and fell to the ground before dashing into nothingness. Marnie vanished into the Green Man.

***

Unbeknownst to the adventurers, an uninvited guest cloaked in darkness had taken up purchase across the street. They had witnessed what appeared to be the return of the Vagabond.

Chapter Fifteen
"...making the darkness conscious."

The Forgotten Master approached the old Druidic temple henge just south of Ærratum with caution. There was no dearth of traveler's tale concerning the strange happenings surrounding these particular burial grounds.

The Master had prepared as best he could for any possible trials that may lay ahead. Aside from the Cloister's customary black robes, he carried with him a pack containing water, a couple of small rations, a flint lighter, and most importantly, an old iron sword.

For the mission the Master was on, cold iron would be prized most amongst all smithing materials that Eternal Dawn had to offer. It was alleged to have a warding effect against fae and spirit alike, an allegation he hoped wouldn't require testing. The length of the sword's three-foot-long blade was inlaid with sigil coins depicting the moon phases of Ærratum. This kind of inlay was said to amplify the warding effects of the iron. They also served the more tangible purpose of providing light in the darkness. The coins served as small Muse concentrators. The Forgotten Master hoped, in his depleted state, that he still retained enough Muse in his body's stores to fuel the sword's light through the labyrinth.

The final two items he carried with him were a small leather-bound notebook and a piece of lead that could be used to scribe notes. If he was lucky these would be the most useful pieces of his kit.

The Master surveyed the three concentric rings of the temple, representing the three moons that orbited the planet. Between the outside ring and the middle ring, he could see and smell the lavender flowers that flooded the space. As he walked past the first ring his presence roused a handful of fae light bugs which began to stir in the air. Continuing between the second and third ring, he took in the sights and scents of the flowering rosemary, his footsteps causing even more of the creatures to stir. The Master approached the end of the stone path at the third ring, encountering the central altar field which was covered in red creeping thyme. The aromatics produced as the Master stepped on the plants completed a bouquet of smells that helped soothe his mind as he approached the entrance to the catacomb. The aromas were said to help ease a soul's passing into the beyond. In truth, as some believed, they were there to mask the acrid smell emanating from the crypts below.

As the Forgotten Master approached the center of the field, he had amassed a swarm of curious fae bugs. They were spiraling around him, putting him in a peaceful hypnotic state as he traversed the earthen ramp into Ærratum's undercroft.

The smell of decay invaded the Master's nostrils only moments after he crossed the catacombs' threshold, snapping him out of his trance-like state. The glowing mosses, lichen, and fungus that spread across the walls of the catacombs provided ample illumination to navigate. He ventured forth knowing the entrance to the labyrinth would be well hidden.

The Forgotten had surmised that the entryway would be located in or near the oldest parts of the crypt. Typically in catacombs, these would be the areas closest to the entrance as new paths would radiate out from an origin point. This wasn't the case for the Ærratum catacombs. In the time of the Old Masters, the period within which catacomb construction began, even the best Musers of the day hadn't anticipated a city growing beyond a few thousand inhabitants. The Druidic Temple had been relocated at least three times according to Masterwork records. The Forgotten knew that the number could be easily doubled. Historically a Master's ego was a fragile thing. If a Masterwork failed, they would do whatever was possible to have its existence excised from public record. This included any changes which may have precluded the failure. The unneeded relocation of sacred ground wasn't something a Master wanted to see attached to their legacy.

The thought of record destruction had been especially disturbing to the Forgotten. His mission since the Flood, not unlike Wordsmith's, had been the preservation of that which should not be lost. It was a mission that served to strengthen his knowledge of Ærratum history and that of the surrounding area. His expertise advantaged him in knowing that the oldest foundations to have been discovered were in Ærratum's east-side slums. To the Master, this was self-explanatory. It was the part of the city that was left behind as expansion advanced westward and he knew it would be the best place to start. The soft pull in his chest that brought him to this point agreed.

The Forgotten Master hadn't had occasion to visit the catacombs since just after the Flood. That visit hadn't provided him with the knowledge he would now require. This last occasion was part of one of his first acts as the Master Prime. He was tasked to lay the Vagabond Master's honored friends, Gilbert and George Coimín, to rest after the end of the Last War. The Coimíns had been interred in one of the newer tunnels which had been excavated to the west of the entrance, a far distance from the ossuaries that were the catacomb's origination point.

Navigation of the catacombs, the Forgotten Master hoped, would be the most treacherous part of the journey. There was no lack of stories concerning young people exploring the catacombs and getting lost, never to be seen again. As with most tales concerning the crypts, their veracity was subject to speculation. The Master possessed the wisdom to not outright discard them and proceeded down tunnels with the respect the catacombs deserved.

***

He had walked for an hour before the acrid stench started to fade. The deeper he walked and the more twists and turns he made, the further back in time the Master found himself. He had reached a locus where the surrounding residents were desiccated to the point of no longer being viable hosts to the agents of decay, preventing the smells that accompanied them.

Up to this point, the various tunnels of the catacombs had been marked with street names, of which the Master was quick to take note. This was done in an effort to aid with his return trip. As he ventured further, the markings started to appear much more sporadically. It was another hour's walk before all navigational markers had disappeared completely. This was something the Master had anticipated, choosing instead to note an arrow for any direction he turned, hoping it would be enough to help him navigate in reverse on his return trip. The draw in the Master's chest was now the only thing serving to guide his way.

By his estimation, he had reached the halfway point of his journey, if the entrance to the labyrinth was where he thought it would be. The Master was starting to get travel-weary. He had made the impulsive decision to strike out shortly after the revelation brought on by his meditation, not giving thought to rest. He knew he would eventually have to stop for a few hours but figured he could hold out until he reached the entrance to the labyrinth.

***

When the Forgotten Master first heard the skittering of feet in the corridor ahead of him he chalked it up to the scurrying of rats; they were no strangers to the catacombs. It was only when the sound of children's laughter started that he started to feel unnerved. It was a sound he typically didn't mind hearing but being more than three miles into a maze of corridors, surrounded by the bones of the long deceased with only the pale glow of the mosses, fungi, and lichens to light his way, 'unnerved' was the quaintest of words.

A few moments later the Master heard the scurrying of feet off to his right. Then there was another round of giggling directly behind him. He took a quick peek behind him and then advanced up to the end of the current row. He looked down the shafts that ran parallel to the one he was in. His eyes strained to search the darkness but they couldn't glimpse the creature or specter that was producing the strange noises. The laughter once again moved around him and started to bombard him from multiple directions. The disorientation the Forgotten Master experienced moved him from unnerved, skipped over frightened, and jumped directly into terrified. The sound of a hundred pitter-pattering feet started to approach him from behind.

Out of instinct, the Master took off on a run, ducking and weaving through the cryptic corridors. In his rush to escape the terror behind him, he hadn't taken so much as a mental note of which paths he had selected. By the time he stopped running fifteen minutes later, he was well and truly lost. To make matters worse, he had hit a dead end when he entered a large ossuary. This would have been good news, he thought, had it not been for his pursuers. Ossuaries had long since fallen out of use and would have been located in the oldest sections of the catacombs, the very sections he had been seeking.

"Well at least if I'm going to die, I'll die spectacular with an audience of thousands...an adventurer's end," the Master muttered, referencing the almost uncountable number of skulls that lined the bone room he found himself in.

The Forgotten Master turned to face the entryway of the room, preparing to make a final stand. The footsteps that were following him had grown silent during the chase but were once again growing with intensity. He wasn't able to put a number to his stalkers. He thought there may have been five or six when the chase began but it now sounded like the count may number a hundred.

When the Master caught a glimpse of the first creature he thought to himself, "Shite, I should have known." What he observed was a naked figure with slender elf-like features no taller than his knee. Its entire body intermittently pulsed a phosphorus green. Shortly after, nearly seventy others poured into the room, all with various heights and builds but none rising much more above the original. The creatures stared at the Forgotten Master in wonderment. It was clear to him that this band of pixies had likely not seen a humanoid of his stature before.

No sooner had the Master thought, "Perhaps these ones will be able to help me," when they began to giggle again. The creatures started to dance, some pointing at the Master as they laughed. He realized they had lived up to their reputation for mischief by helping him to lose his bearings in the underground maze. In the face of this indignity, the Master unsheathed the iron sword, hellbent on testing its fae-warding abilities.

He thrust the sword toward one group of pixies, taunting them to touch it. One took the bait and immediately recoiled, its hand in a burning pain. The being looked at his hand back and back to the sword with hesitation, once more touching it before recoiling again. The small fae looked up at the Forgotten Master and bared its teeth while starting to growl. The Master couldn't help but smirk at what sounded like a tiny angry dog. The other pixies took notice of what was going on and stopped dancing to watch for the giant's next move. The Master took a false lunge at the group he had been taunting, causing them to scatter. Seeing that this worked to disperse the vexatious horde, he started to run in circles, waving the sword above his head in an antagonistic manner but not actually attacking, all the while producing somewhat of throaty a battle cry. It wasn't long before he cleared the room, causing the pixies to vanish. They dispersed through the attached tunnels and back into the darkest recesses of the catacombs from which they had originated. Their mission was complete.

The Forgotten Master took a moment to collect himself. It had been far too long since he had the opportunity to experience the mixture of fear and excitement that accompanied true adventure. He then thought out loud, "The years appear to be catching up with me."

***

Marnie exited the portal last, finding herself back at the Menhir where she had started. She found the experience to be less traumatic than her earlier passage. Time passed as if she had through a normal doorway. The sensation was far removed from the panic-inducing strangulation she endured the first time, being closer to a warm hug. She suspected any return trip to Earth would remain difficult and that she would have to endure the torture once more.

"Well I guess proper introductions are in order," Chauncey began once the group had taken a moment to catch their collective breaths. "I'm Chauncey, Chauncey Fauntleroy and this here is my partner and trusted confidant Trig, Trig..."

"Just Trig," Trig said, halting Chauncey in his speech. They were guarded in the information they were willing to dispense to unknown entities.

Marnie glanced over at Chauncey, realizing that he hadn't used a pseudonym back at the library. "That tracks," she thought, even though she had only known the man for a short time.

David had no reason to obfuscate his surname. "Well met. Name's David Almánzar," he offered as he performed a rotation of his open palm toward his body before bringing it to rest, palm up. His fingers were joined as they pointed at Chauncey in acknowledgment, bowing his head in sync with the movement. This was Eternal Dawn's customary greeting but one would hazard to find many who used it so far removed from the capital city.

"Marnie...but I think everyone already knows that," Marnie chimed in, slightly embarrassed to be the focus of everyone's current problems.

Luci spoke, nodding to each as she said their names, "Well met. Marnie, Chauncey, Just Trig, I'm..."

"Deirdre..." Trig cut in sharply, "Deirdre Lucille Geddes." The scorn that tinged their voice was palpable.

"Wait...what?" David croaked in disbelief. He was shocked by the accusation that had just been lobbed.

"You should really think about vetting your companions better lad," Trig continued, an obvious jab at his apparent connection with their previous combatant, Sara. "I mean this one should have been easy. Deirdre Lucille Geddes may very well be the last person in all of Eternal Dawn to possess the Morrígan's Favor. This one is literally two-faced...and then some."

"Is it...is it true?" David asked, pointing his question toward Luci.

"It's not what you think..." Luci started.

"What, you're not a Geddes?" Trig attacked, cutting her off again. "Funny, the stories say you met the same fate as your treacherous parents. Shame it's not true. There were rumblings saying you made it out. If I'd have known."

"Wait, wait, this doesn't make sense," David said, trying to apply reason to the revelation that was still unfolding. "Why would the Forgotten Master send me off on a mission with a Geddes?"

"I..I can explain..." Luci tried once more to jump in and defend herself but was again cut off by Trig.

"Because laddie, you can't trust a Master," Trig replied, their voice teeming with anger. "And judging by the company he keeps, you *really* can't trust that one."

Marnie and Chauncey stood by watching. Marnie couldn't help but feel bad for Luci at this moment. She hadn't witnessed an attack like this since her mother's last murder trial. Diane liked to make a show of going after defendants and arguing with lawyers as if she was on 'Law and Order'. The behavior Trig was displaying was all too familiar.

"I mean, in the past hundred fifty years, there's been nary a war or manner of pestilence that a Geddes hasn't had a hand in," Trig continued with no sign of letting up. "Surprised she isn't up in Imperium spire calling the shots for this current Dying of the Light. I had just assumed she was the 'face' behind it. What game are you playing Deirdre?"

Luci had become visibly agitated with the rudeness she was being shown but knew the remarks weren't without merit. "I don't think you're being fair..." she started, trying to defend herself.

"Fair?...Fair?" Trig retorted in the rhetoric. "Was it 'fair' when your parents sent their war machines to Kilstag for the 'crime' of...what? Not wanting anything to do with their Masterwork? Was it fair when those machines leveled my city? Was it fair that I had to help my parents pull the lifeless bodies of my brothers and sister from the rubble? Was it fair that your father had my parents killed for daring to have a problem with this? All...all for what? A stupid fucking road and a miserable quest for power."

Marnie, David, and Chauncey continued to watch, unsure of what to say or do next. They had taken note of a blackness spreading out from where Trig was standing. Trig, sensing that all eyes had been drawn to them, took a few labored breaths before producing a hollow noise from the back of their throat and running off behind the menhir. It was unclear whether the noise was an attempt at a scream or an exasperated sigh. In truth, Trig wouldn't have been able to say either.

The light that had drained from the area where they were standing had started to creep back in. The four that remained stared awkwardly at each other. Seeing that no one else was going to make a move, Marnie made an attempt to follow but Chauncey was quick to stop her, "Best to leave 'em be lass. Can't not but help but not to be comforted in times like these."

Marnie took half a moment to try and reason out what Chauncey was trying to convey but opted to rely on context for meaning. The floodgates had been opened, pouring forth fifteen years of repressed memories and anger. Marnie more than anyone could understand what Trig was going through and, at Chauncey's suggestion, opted to provide the same space that had been afforded to her in the wake of her recent calamitous realization.

David looked over at Luci whose eyes were welling up with their own tears. A moment had passed before a single glistening drop rolled down her cheek, rested for a moment, then evaporated into vapor. The image stood in stark contrast to the steely no bullshit projection she had been presenting to this point. David had seen a crack form in the veneer. At once he was able to understand the reason she had taken the job, as well as the reason for her terms.

Chauncey was in the middle of processing his own set of feelings about the revelations. Eternal Dawn was full of people holding an active distrust of the Masters but he hadn't met many who would routinely discuss the topic with the same level of scorn as Trig. In this conversation, he had found their reason. For Chauncey, this revelation opened so many avenues of question. Why hadn't they told him before? Was this why Trig approached life with an abnormal level of cynicism? What else didn't he know about his best friend?

He had thought it odd that Trig was able to warm up to Marnie so quickly in the moments after she found out about her father's demise. He had half expected Trig to say good riddance to the memory of the dead Master but now realized they shared a common pain.

The four of them stood staring at each other for a few moments before Chauncey decided it would be best to break the tension, "Is...is it true?"

Marnie looked at the ground, embarrassed for Chauncey in this moment of questioning the obvious. The others stared at him in disbelief.

Another moment passed before he spoke up again in an attempt to earn a reprieve, "What?... I'm just trying to open a dialog here."

Marnie was undecided if Chauncey was still confused as to whether Luci was who Trig said she was.

"They speak the truth. I am the daughter of the authors of the Last War," Luci finally offered before hanging her head. "I was barely old enough to understand what was going on but that didn't stop me from spending fifteen years atoning for sins I have no ownership in. Fifteen years of wondering if I was going to wake up on the wrong end of a blade or not wake up at all. Fifteen years as an outcast...a pariah...a...a heretic."

Marnie listened to her words and couldn't help but feel a small amount of kinship with the stranger. For better or worse, she had also spent the better part of her life living in the shadow of her own father. It only struck her at that moment how long a shadow he must have cast in the world within which she was now trying to find footing.

Picking up on the understanding in Marnie's eyes, Luci continued, "The only thing that saved me was this family curse and the Forgotten. I just want one day where I can walk out the door without the pain that comes as the cost of wearing another's face."

Luci went on to explain that, in the aftermath of the Flood, it had been the Forgotten Master who had secreted the young Geddes out of Ærratum. The populace hadn't yet come to understand the true effect of the Vagabond Master's work. In the upheaval, there had been an active hunt for members of the lineage; part of a short-sighted attempt to prevent a resurgence of power. Even without full insight into the long-term effects of the Flood, the Forgotten Master saw no reason for a child of fifteen to suffer the fate of her parents.

In the years after the Flood, the Forgotten Master had hidden Luci in the Cloister and helped her to obtain proficiency with her gifts. She possessed an innate ability to perceive changes in Muse which helped guide her into her current profession. It was however the Mórrigan's Favor that took the greatest effort to master and the one that made her the most safe. It was this ability that allowed her to change appearance. However, the universe had demanded a trade for the use of this ability. The trade came in the form of a gnawing pain under the skin in the areas of change. It was a pain that wasn't easily ignored and one she had to endure in her efforts to stay safe. This physical pain coupled itself with the emotional pain of not being able to have attachments or just be herself. It was this pain that had taken its toll on Luci, making her willing to give anything for a shot at some semblance of normalcy.

"Aye lass, why didn't you let yourself be recruited by Imperium?" Chauncey asked. "They would literally kill to have someone of your talents."

Marnie had quickly judged Chauncey's query to be more offhanded than it would have been coming out of her mouth or David's. To Chauncey, it served the purpose of complimenting the skill of a potential Master while also preventing a lull in the conversation. To Marnie and David, the question would have been that of motives. It would have come off as rude if served with the same bluntness Chauncey had applied.

"My family has done enough damage," she said bitterly. It was a short answer but it was clear to Marnie that she spoke out of truth. This was a person who just wanted to get out of the shadows.

There was a moment of contemplation that was meant to linger a little longer than was allowed. Chauncey was quick to barrel over it with another round of questions, "So...the Mórrigan. Do you still worship her? One being or three? What's the deal with that? I have to know."

Luci started to open her mouth to provide an answer when Trig reappeared from behind the monolithic stone where they had retreated. "We need to move. It can't be long before Imperium figures out where we went. We aren't as far from Drumlocke as we should be," Trig spoke, trying to act as if the uncomfortable encounter with Luci hadn't occurred.

Marnie, Chauncey, and David exchanged glances and nods in the unspoken agreement that they wouldn't press the subject, while Luci uneasily glanced at the ground.

Trig's keen hearing had picked up some of the finer points of the conversation. What they heard wasn't enough to allay their suspicion but did serve to quiet their anger. They resolved to keep a watchful eye on the Geddes until they reached their final objective.

***

After his pixie encounter, the Forgotten Master spent a few moments recovering his wits before beginning his search. He tried to secret the feeling of being lost to the recesses of his brain, desperately hoping that the pull in his chest would also be there for the return trip...that it would still be there once he found the answers he was looking for...if he found the answers he was looking for.

The Master started his search for the labyrinth entrance within the bone room he had been chased into. He scanned the perimeter for additional doorways, an arch, a small alcove, anything to indicate the presence of an entryway in the dead end of a chamber. Coming up empty, he mused that it would take an incredible stroke of luck to find what he was looking for in the first place he just happened to be scared into. The Master took a moment to consider that there could be twenty to thirty of these rooms, as he looked grimly in the direction he had come.

He left this ossuary in search of the next, wandering the alcoves of the catacombs for fifteen minutes before encountering another. The many arches that adorned the room were filled from top to bottom with the stacked bones of Ærratum's previous inhabitants. This room looked nearly identical to the first, so much so that he wasn't convinced that he hadn't traveled in a circle. As he gazed into the empty sockets of the thousands of skulls that lined the room, he couldn't help but feel that they were gazing back. He again searched among the bones for the hidden doorway that would take him into the labyrinth below but once again came up empty. He decided to withdraw back into the tunnels in search of the next room.

Another twenty minutes of searching had passed before the master stumbled upon a third ossuary. To his increasing discomfort, he observed that it also appeared to be identical to the first two. He still had the sneaking suspicion that he had simply performed another loop and ended up in the same room.

The Forgotten Master took a few moments to consider his options. He attempted to sense if the pull within his chest would allow him to divine a path forward but couldn't detect its presence. It was only at this moment that he realized the concentration of lichens, fungi, and mosses that had been providing light for his path, had been slowly diminishing to an even softer glow. His eyes were strained by the unconscious need to correct for the darkness and a migraine had started to form in his head.

The Master decided it would be best to activate the sword as an additional light source. He was cognizant of the fact that this action would start a timer, one that would ultimately expire when his body's reserves had been depleted. He knew he wouldn't be able to pull much Muse from the dimming surroundings. He hoped to the gods, both old and new, that he had enough to help him find the entryway.

With sword in hand, he ignited the blade's runes by channeling his Muse. The sword was now glowing a brilliant neon orange. He immediately felt reprieve from his ocular ailment and the headache and disorientation that had accompanied the pending migraine. This led to a heightened clarity of thought that the Master was unaware he had been missing.

The Master considered the issue at hand. There was likely to be a great number of these rooms and the first point of order was to verify that he was indeed finding a unique room with each attempt. The second issue he thought, would be the race against time he was now engaged in. The race wasn't just against the depletion of his Muse but also to find the answers that he was confident would be needed before the girl would be able to attempt her rescue. This race was something he tried to push to the back of his mind if only to set his thoughts fully upon the first challenge.

The solution the Forgotten Master devised for the immediate problem was an inelegant one. He would use the blade of the sword to notch a hash mark onto the floor underneath the threshold of the ossuaries. Taking the blade, he drew it against the floor and proceeded to write with it, marking a number three even though he was unsure if this had indeed been the third room. The blade hadn't so much scratched the floor but instead, acted like a pen using the Muse as ink.

The Master took a quick moment to observe his handiwork, a glowing orange numeral on the ground. What occurred next was unexpected. The glowing three rose from the stone leaving no trace of its existence on the floor. The luminous molecules that composed the numeral then merged into a single small orb. Without close inspection, it could have easily been mistaken for a fae light bug. The orb then took off down one of the tunnels almost beckoning the Master to follow.

Impatiently, the Master snatched up the nearest skull from one of the room's arches and smashed it onto the room's threshold, creating a more corporeal marker. He hoped that he wouldn't have to answer for this desecration. The soft pull in his chest had returned and appeared to be keyed in on the orb. He gave chase, hoping he wasn't being led further astray.

He followed the orb for what felt like thirty minutes as it slowly faded into nothingness. The Master once again made a mark on the floor which immediately formed another floating orb allowing him to continue. He opted against extinguishing the blade as the orbs were leading him further and further into deeper darkness.

The Forgotten Master repeated the orb creation twice more before reaching the threshold of a room that was dissimilar from the others. The size of this ossuary was easily big enough to contain the previous three and then some. Its scope was perplexing to the Master. He was convinced that the combined deceased population of all of Ærratum wouldn't have been enough to fill the room. What he was beholding shouldn't have been possible.

Save for its grander scale, the room was engineered in very much the same manner as the others. There were of course the archways that were filled with the stacked skeletons of the long-since deceased, the most prominent feature being the skulls. "Always with the skulls," he thought, "Always watching."

The room did feature two major details that weren't common to the other rooms. The first divergence was that of a giant thirty-foot-wide chandelier consisting of the long bones and rib cages of Eternal Dawn's ancient inhabitants. To the Master's surprise, the chandelier possessed a soft pallorous glow, one that he was sure would have been much more vibrant in the days preceding the Dying of the Light. At the sight of the fixture, he extinguished the light of the sword, pulling the remaining Muse back into his body. While there was some errant Muse in the room, the Master was sure that even with the additional light in the room, none of it would serve to recharge his body's stores.

The second feature was much more imposing and much more ominous. In the center of the room directly under the giant chandelier stood a pyramid of skulls. Many of them were from creatures of higher sentience but the carefully stacked pile wasn't limited to the bones of intelligent creatures alone. The lower levels of the pyramid featured mostly mega-fauna, consisting of the skulls of trompfs, horses, and various other beasts of burden, some of which the Master recognized as creatures of legend. Scanning his eyes up through the desiccated relics, the Forgotten Master could spot the skulls of larger felidae, canidae, and trollfae. Further up the stack, he was able to detect those of the humanoids, mostly humans but there was also a smattering of skulls once belonging to reclusive elves. Capstoning the pyramid, he could see the skulls of the smaller creatures, including smaller felidae, canidae, goblins, and pixies. Had his vision been better or the light brighter, he would have been able to detect the skulls of the even smaller rodentia, pixies, and faeries at the very top.

The Forgotten Master had stumbled into what was potentially the largest bone room in all of Eternal Dawn. This chamber appeared to be more modern than the other ossuaries but advanced building practices which would have developed in the intermeaning years weren't, alone, enough to explain its size. The Master sensed that this space was significant. The mass of skulls in the center had been his biggest clue. It wasn't traditional practice to bury the skulls of those deemed unintelligent. Very few would deign to bury the skulls of even the smartest troll or goblin amongst those of even the dumbest of human or elven origin.

He pondered for a moment, searching his mind for an explanation. "It couldn't be," he said, whispering his thoughts.

What the Master had correctly deduced was that this burial chamber represented the result of the First War, an event most claimed never actually happened. Even before the Flood, the Last War, and the many knowledge purges that preceded it, the First War was viewed as something akin to the Earth realm's Arthurian legend. A hodgepodge of stories passed along the ages until they were spun into a singular common narrative thread, containing spectacle and a reliable set of archetypal heroes.

To most historians, the First War was likely no more than a small-scale battle becoming more and more grand in each generation of its retelling. To the Forgotten Master, the massive three-story tall pyramid, made up of a nigh uncountable number of skulls, indicated anything but. The makeup of the monument was an indicator that perhaps the stories had been wrong, not only on its scale but on many other accounts, the primary among which was the victor.

The stories told that the First War was how the Druids of Eternal Dawn had met their demise. The monument's inclusion of creatures of lower sentience like the mice, domestic cats, and lesser trolls had, however, stood in direct contradiction. The Druids were the ruling class of the time and ascribed value to all living creatures. They worked to protect those who couldn't protect themselves. To their adversaries, more often than not, the protection the Druids offered was detrimental to those that were considered higher life forms. Detriment was a harsh word for actions the Druids had taken, inconvenient would have been the more appropriate term. Rather than the devastating clear-cutting of forests for building production and warmth generation, the Druids advocated for Muse-assisted construction. Rather than diverting waterways, they advocated for the use of ivies and bamboo to absorb moisture out of the air. The problem with methods like these was that, as with most good things, they came with the cost of time. The concept of Muse concentration was over a millennium away. Rapid progress in the days before the First War arrived at the expense of lesser life forms.

The Forgotten Master now realized that the pyramid possibly represented a Druidic victory. Their opposition wouldn't have taken care to honor 'lesser beings' and according to legend, there shouldn't have been enough of them left to construct such a monument. In any case, the Master thought if he had the good fortune to survive the trials ahead, he would bookmark the topic for in-depth research. Perhaps, with his newfound perspective, the archives in Drumlocke would possess answers to his questions.

Having taken a few moments to come down from his epiphanous realization, the Master set about the task of searching the room for clues that may lead to the labyrinth's entrance. Aside from its size and the two additional features, the room was constructed much in the same manner as the other three, or one, he was still not convinced he hadn't traveled in circles.

He couldn't detect an entrance. The Master searched the room for any manner of hidden passage or crack in the wall, something that would shed some light. He walked around the pyramid in hopes that the entrance may be on the opposing side. He tried once more to ignite and scrape the sword on the floor. He could see the Muse rise into the air but then saw it rapidly dissipate into the ether. His waypoint had abandoned him.

There was something about his current mission that seemed familiar. He couldn't quite put his finger on it but the Master felt as though he was treading on familiar ground, as though a voice from the past was still there to guide the way.

The Forgotten Master took this moment to sit cross-legged in his meditation pose, his searching pose. He made an effort to blank out the thoughts in his mind as he surveyed the room with only his eyes. He searched the room starting with the threshold he had crossed upon entry, performing a slow scan of the room's horizon. The Master was hoping his unconscious mind would hone in on a manner of keyhole that his conscious mind had missed.

Unable to justify the reason to himself, the Master felt compelled to approach the pyramid with the intention of picking up a skull. He hoped the action wouldn't be considered a desecration by an unknown entity that may be spying on the evening's events. His attempts were met with failure. The mass of bone had been affixed to the skulls behind it or was otherwise held in place by an unknown force.

To the Master, this was a good sign. It indicated that the structure may serve a purpose beyond honoring the sacred departed. He tested a few more skulls and found them to be equally as steadfast in their placement. He theorized he might be able to climb the structure but would leave the supposition untested. Even in his half-meditative state, he knew he had already tempted fate enough for one evening and was none too keen on pressing his luck further. He suspected he would require whatever reserve of divine fortuity remained in his possession. The trials to come may not be mastered by skill and cunning alone.

In his haze, he had the feeling that there was some manner of spirit guiding his movements, perhaps someone from the past, perhaps someone who had tread the ground before, perhaps the Vagabond Master. He once more felt the soft pull in his chest beckoning for him to retreat to the position antipodal to the room's threshold.

The Forgotten Master glimpsed the pyramid from his new vantage point but couldn't detect much variance from the side he saw as he entered the room. In his initial investigation, he hadn't performed an examination beyond checking for passageways constructed on the back side of the monument.

The more he stared, the more he started to detect features in the stacking of the skulls. He moved closer to investigate but the features seemed to dissipate. As he stepped back the features started to once more take shape. There was an almost anamorphic quality to what he was seeing. No matter how much he squinted or widened his eyes, he was unable to make sense of what was being produced by the skulls acting as tesserae for the macabre mosaic.

In a move that he thought he may very well come to regret, the master opted to add additional illumination to the room. He once again brandished the iron sword. Approaching the monument he took the blade into both hands and pointed it upwards toward the chandelier high above. Unsure if he was needlessly wasting the reverses in his body, the Forgotten Master focused his remaining Muse into the sword. The weapon glowed with the appearance of what educated people on Earth would call St. Elmo's fire. He started to feel the essence in his body dwindling. The Master also started to sense the chandelier reaching out for the light source in his hand. It was a few more moments before he could feel the chandelier, not so much yanking at the weapon, but trying to suck the Muse through it. He tried to resist but was quickly overpowered. The sword acted as a conduit for his Muse to be pulled from his body into the light fixture above. He watched in amazement as the essence was atomized above him, the chandelier absorbing all of the energy and illuminating the room with a brilliance his eyes hadn't feasted on in the two years since the Dying of the Light began.

Not knowing how much time he would have, he scurried back to the location where he had previously been standing and once more looked upon the monument, this time in astonishment. The Master's eyes were now gazing upon the illuminated visage of a giant oaken Green Man.

He watched the face as the fluctuation of the light above affected the skulls below, causing their shadows to dance and give movement to the three-dimensional face before him. He moved forward once again but the illusion quickly dissipated. The Master moved back into position and waited, pondering his next move, hoping he would figure out what to do before the Muse above depleted.

Muse depletion was something he need not worry about. As he was waiting, the chandelier had cast its net, performing its own search for additional Muse to devour. It was three minutes before it had sucked the energies out of the plant life that still managed to survive this deep in the crypts. It took a further two minutes until it had depleted the pixies that had caused the Master so much trouble earlier in the evening.

As the Master gazed on, he observed the room get brighter and the face become more and more defined until it finally disgorged from its mouth a set of vines that reached out toward him. In this moment he felt a sense of deja vu, as if whatever had been leading him to this point was trying to comfort him. The Forgotten

Master sheathed the depleted sword and let himself be taken into the darkness, hoping that he would find himself in the labyrinth below.

Chapter Sixteen

"...awoke one morning from uneasy dreams..."

Marnie and her traveling companions had been walking for the better part of four hours before true exhaustion started to set in. The cloud of the day's activities hung heavy in the air. The blowout had fried her ability to experience anxiety and panic as she was commonly prone to do. Instead of constantly being worried about a flare-up, she was perceiving everything with a tinge of numbness, almost viewing every action as a third-party observer.

Her therapist had been advocating exposure therapy as a means of developing a tolerance to the stimuli that normally provoked her fight or flight systems. It had been something she was dabbling with on smaller-scale issues of public speaking and traveling. It wasn't, however, a tactic she could employ in this realm with every experience being rife with novelty. Perhaps, she hoped once more, that this was her fight or flight systems realigning to deal with the situations they were evolved for. She could only be so lucky. She passed out near the campfire that evening, hoping the night's rest wouldn't lead to a recharge of those centers of her brain; the centers that had caused so much trouble for her newfound friends Trig and Chauncey and everyone else who had been inconvenienced by the blowout.

***

Chauncey, Trig, David, and Luci stayed awake discussing next moves while Marnie slept. They all knew their journey would eventually take them to the very center of Ærratum but were unsure of what the path would look like.

"It's going to be too dangerous taking Marnie into the heart of the city," Trig said, continuing the conversation. "We've seen what she can do firsthand. What if Imperium gets hold of that power? What if she blows out again and takes out a hospital?"

"Which is exactly why we need to take her to the Cloister to see the Forgotten," David replied. "He said she would be needed. He'll know what to do next."

"If he was so sure about what to do next, why didn't he just tell you?" Trig responded.

"They've got a point," Luci agreed. Trig's eyes shot over to her.

Trig interpreted this to be an attempt to garner undeserved goodwill. "Never trust a Master," Trig continued, an obvious jab at Luci which also served the purpose of casting doubt on David's proposed plan.

"Why don't we just march up to the tower, sneak in, and get her brother back?" Chauncey interjected. "We've got the map, surely there is a way to locate this lad Scot and secret him out."

"It's not that easy," David replied before Trig could work in a derisive comment about the foolhardy nature of what Chauncey had just suggested. "The security in that place is better than Fort Knox."

The others stared at David, not catching the reference.

"Sorry, better than...better than," David stumbled trying to find a reference that they would understand.

"The Antiquarium," Luci offered, catching the meaning he was trying to convey. It was a building that housed what were deemed to be the most priceless art and artifacts that Eternal Dawn had to offer. Many of the items possessed large amounts of concentrated Muse but were protected due to their perceived historical significance.

"Yeah, like that," David replied.

"And how would you know about the security of the spire?" Trig asked with suspicion.

"It's common knowledge," David replied. "That and I was trapped in there for a time."

Trig thought they detected an air of evasiveness in the offered answer but couldn't be sure. They had been on edge since the Geddes was invited into the party and was in a mood to question motives.

"Besides we wouldn't have a way to find Scot once we got inside," David said, still entertaining Chauncey's suggestion, not yet realizing that his ideas didn't merit following.

"Would these work?" Chauncey said producing three Imperium cuffs.

"Where did you get those?" David replied.

"I lifted one of them from the goons you took out. Light fingers are part of the business mate," Chauncey replied before also pulling out Luci's collapsible bow and tossing it over to her.

Luci instinctively reached down to her belt, dumbfounded that she hadn't noticed the disappearance. "What if I needed that?" she demanded.

"Relax, I was just taking a peak...Interesting mechanism. Surely not Muse created," Chauncey replied, content in the knowledge that there was a level of cunning in the skill he had displayed. He interpreted the reactions he received as respect.

"No...It's handcrafted," Luci responded, still mildly bewildered at the violation.

"The other two I lifted from some randoms when they first came out. Never had the nerve to try one. Didn't feel right," Chauncey offered. "Anyway, the librarian said they could be used to locate Muse. Thought they might come in handy in the search for the boy."

"She also said it had a very limited range, making the damn things useless," Trig jumped in, trying to prevent David and Luci from entertaining Chauncey's idea.

"Well, there are only so many places Scot could be. Wouldn't rule it out quite yet. Hang on to them. They may come in handy," David responded.

Chauncey shot Trig a knowing grin of, 'Who looks dumb now?'

Trig barely noticed, too focused on the man who possessed an inordinate amount of knowledge concerning Imperium's inner workings.

"So the cloister it is?" David once more offered.

"Until we have a better idea. But that shouldn't take much more than a good night's sleep," Trig replied caustically, hoping that some rest would improve clarity of thought. "We should also get her thoughts on the matter," Trig continued, pointing at Marnie who had been so drained that even the evening's bickerings couldn't wake her. "'Tis rudeness to make these decisions without her consult. As much her journey as it is ours...More so even."

After further argument, it was decided that David and Chauncey would take turns keeping watch. Trig didn't feel comfortable enough to allow Luci to serve as a lookout while they slept and David didn't feel comfortable enough with the pair sharing a watch without incident.

***

The Forgotten Master felt a halt in acceleration. He wasn't sure if he had reached top speed and was still moving or if he had reached the opposing doorway at his destination. While he no longer felt the otherworldly tendrils of the darkness, his body still felt constricted. After taking a few breaths to gather composure, he tried peering wide into the darkness but could see only an unyielding blackness in all directions. A few more moments passed before he realized the tightness he was feeling was his blood flowing back into the parts of his body where the doorway's appendages had had their most constrictive effect. "To be ten years younger," he thought, feeling his advancing years working against him.

The Master made an attempt to take a step and found his footing; it was the necessary proof he needed that he was out of the ether. Try as he might, he couldn't force his eyes to adjust to the darkness. There were no traces of light anywhere, Museborne or otherwise. Knowing that further attempts to see anything would be in vain, he attempted to attune his other senses to the new environment.

He opted next to test his hearing. There was an unnerving silence. He tried to focus on ambient noise but was only able to detect the sound of his own heartbeat and the gurgling in his digestive tract. He stomped his foot a few times to test acoustics but was only able to hear the soft thud of the non-soled appendage. The Master then started to clap his hands together, first softly but he increased intensity with each strike of his palms. Again, the only thing he could hear was the thud of his hands. There were no echoes. There was no resonance. It was as if the surrounding area was absorbing all excess noise.

He tested what he considered to be his lesser sense, smell, and by association taste. This attempt also proved fruitless. The air was noticeably dry, stripped of all humidity. There wasn't a scent to be detected. If it wasn't for the feeling of the ground beneath his feet, The Forgotten Master would have presumed himself dead.

After he finished taking stock of his senses, the Master deduced he was most likely alone in the darkness and it would be safe to try more invasive methods to find his bearings. He brandished the iron sword in an attempt to produce sigil light. He tried focusing his intentions into the blade but couldn't produce the telltale glow. As he suspected, opening the doorway had cost him the entirety of his Muse reserve. His veins had gone dark but he had hoped there was some sub-dermal area of his body where a small modicum of the essence may still be hiding.

The Master then thought back to his initial preparations and recalled the flint lighter he had packed. With the help of the sword, he cut off a small section of his robes and wrapped them around the tip of the blade, producing a makeshift torch. The Master worked on producing a flame and after five strenuous minutes, achieved success. Knowing this solution would be unsustainable, he immediately set upon scanning his surroundings.

Underfoot he found the surface black and incapable of reflecting the light he was carrying. Further scanning his environment, he found a ceiling overhead, barely above arm's reach. Toward his back, he found the other end of the Green Door, a mirror image of the oaken Green Man that had brought him to this point. Blackened tendrils spewed forth from its mouth. Its eyes were hollowed, reminiscent of the skulls that formed its sibling door. On either side of the doorway was a wall.

The Master found himself at the very start of the passageway he had to hope would lead him to the Oraculum and clarity on his fragmented prophecy. He reached out toward one of the walls to feel its surface, finding it to be smooth, almost slippery. As he pulled back his hand, he could feel the wall pulling back as well, as if it were attempting to suck more Museborne essence directly from him. The wall's thirst would have to remain unquenched, for the Master was depleted.

The torch's flame started to diminish and eventually faded into darkness. The Forgotten Master opted not to make a new one, knowing there weren't enough robes in all of Ærratum to last the length of the path ahead. He sheathed the sword, placed his right hand against the right wall, and took his first plodding step forward into the nothing.

***

The Forgotten Master walked for what felt like hours. In truth, with the darkness, it could have been minutes or it could have been days. He had resorted to counting. First, it was the beating of his heart. Then it was the steps of his feet. Then it was just counting to count. He did this in an attempt to stave off the madness he was sure would eventually try to leach into his mind. The count had numbered just over ten thousand before his body had succumbed to the trials of the day.

He set the sword down with its point facing in his direction of travel. The Master didn't want to risk backtracking and thought this modest solution would keep his trail true. He then took up a meditative posture and considered his current predicament. Was he indeed under the maze of catacombs? For all he knew the doorway could have carried him thousands of miles away.

He was able to take one small comfort in that he had found himself in a true labyrinth, at least as far as he could determine. He hadn't encountered a single branch in the passageway up to his current position. The Master was careful to probe with the sword at the outside corners he had encountered up to this point, checking for the existence of T or X intersections, or a larger chamber which could contain any number of additional passages. He had so far just scraped the wall on the opposite side of the hallway. It was a small comfort but a comfort nonetheless. As long as he didn't lose his mind, he himself wouldn't be lost.

After performing a quick inventory of his remaining supplies, he took a sip of water and a small bite of a ration, not knowing how long he would need to make them last. The ration was supposed to be a small bit of jerky and a mouthful of bread. As with everything else in this miserable blackness, the very essence of the food had been sucked away. He could barely taste the salt in the cured meat and the bread had similarly become dull and flavorless, leaving only its texture to define it.

The Master then set about his meditations, hoping his proximity to the objective may force some new revelation into his mind. The attempt proved fruitless. Normally he would have something to focus on, an object in the room or the singing of a sparrow...something to distract himself from the actual effort of meditation.

In the darkness he had naught but the sounds of his own breath, the digestion in his stomach, and the beating of his heart. They were all things that drew his focus inward. "Is there enough air in here? Do I have enough food and water to last the journey? Should my heart be beating this fast?" They were thoughts that gave him anxiety and drew attention to the fact that he may have left the crypts behind if only to enter his tomb.

There was another factor that required his consideration. He was without the Muse. The very thing that turned his thought into action...his ideas into reality.

It was the force that connected him to everything else. Without it, he had only the darkness ahead. Without it, he was truly alone.

***

Marnie awoke to find herself sitting behind the counter in the gallery, waiting for Martin to come and relieve her for her afternoon class. He was later than usual, a quality he wasn't known for. She thought she had mentioned her midterm but was slowly growing less sure. "I'll give him another ten minutes before I just close the shop and go," she thought before popping open a sketchbook to work on her less-than-legal extracurriculars.

She turned to the page she had been working on. It was a mechanical dog with camera lenses for eyes. The oversized lenses gave an almost Margret Keane 'Big Eyes' aesthetic to the work, an aesthetic Marnie was sure would translate to the wall she had chosen just off Pearl Street.

The area of the piece that had given her the most trouble was the tongue. She wasn't quite sure how to approach it. The decision was whether to go robotic or organic. In this moment she opted to go with an organic tongue, feeling it would be a nice juxtaposition to the cold steel face and needle-like fur that fringed it.

Marnie proceeded to draw in a soft pink tongue. As she was adding texture to represent the papillae, a curious thing happened. The tongue started to crawl up off the page and reach out to her like a constrictor snake going after its prey. She stared in awe as it began to lick at her face with a perceived joy. She reached up her hand to fend off the attack, only to be met with a loud air horn-like snort.

The sound startled her awake and she was greeted with a deer-like face withdrawing its tongue back into its mouth. A shout of fear had escaped her mouth before she could catch herself, rousing the four sleeping members of her traveling party, and causing at least a dozen other deer-like heads to pop up from the long grass they had used as camp.

The purple and blue-hued lumendeer stared at Marnie for a moment before deciding they were equally as startled and crashed off into the surrounding forest.

Marnie looked at the others to catch their reaction and immediately saw Chauncey's guilty gaze. His eyes were already starting to tell the story of the hell he was about to catch.

"When we gave you the duty of watch," Trig started in, "you said you were wide awake. You said it would be no problem. You said..."

"What's done is done," Luci spoke brusquely, cutting Trig off, hoping to spare Chauncey the ear beating.

Trig, slighted by the rebuke, shifted some of their derision to Luci, "Hey lassie, if you could be trusted we wouldn't be in this mess in the first place, now would we? Could've had a competent person on watch!"

"If it wasn't for me, you'd be dead right now and the girl would be in Imperium hands!" Luci responded, trying to remind Trig that they wouldn't have been on equal footing with the soldiers.

"How do we know you didn't lead them to us?" Trig shot back, knowing that the argument held little water but still feeling gripped by the need to press the attack.

"Enough!" Marnie bellowed at the two adversaries. In shouting them both down, she created a contained version of the previous night's blowout, barely escaping the group's radius. All four of her companions snapped their heads in her direction, giving her their full attention. They were unsure if the blowout had been intended or was just a side effect of her aggravation.

"This is not going to solve anything," Marnie firmly stated. "I am fine, you are fine. If this is how it is going to be all the way to Ærratum, I would just as soon leave you all here and go save Scot myself. I do not want to have to deal with the fighting." There was a moment of stunned silence. As Marnie continued, her tone didn't waver in her attempt to drive home the point, "Now if you are quite finished, we should really talk about our next move because I would prefer to have your help."

Feeling as though they had been scolded by one of their mentors, a flash of guilt crossed the faces of Trig and Luci. David and Chauncey looked on, content in not having been on the receiving end. They had both been privy to the, "I'm not mad, I'm just disappointed," rebukes that accompanied youthful rebellion. The shame they experienced by proxy was more than enough to give them each flashbacks to a greater version of the feeling.

"David, I think we should visit this Forgotten Master of yours," Marnie said, unknowingly agreeing with the consensus of the group. "I think he knows more to the story than he has led you to believe." In truth, Marnie thought David himself knew more of the story than he was letting on. She supposed he was just saving her from the harsher realities of what had befallen her brother. She figured the answers would come in due time.

"Well, we best get goin' then. It's two and a half day's walk...three if we're careful," Chauncey said, trying to rouse the group, thankful for the reprieve that Marnie's words had offered.

"Not quite yet," Marnie responded. "There is still the matter of that Imperium leader that we need to address. Sara was it?" she said, looking at David.

David's face dropped, he had half hoped that Marnie would ignore the issue as unimportant and not press further.

"Who was she to you?" Marnie questioned with a compassionate tone, sensing that she may be wading into something more personal than she was originally led to believe.

"Yeah, I've been wondering that myself," Trig said, echoing Marnie.

David, knowing he wouldn't be able to dodge the uncomfortable question, stammered into his explanation, "Well I...ah...I uh...used to work for Imperium." He took a breath before continuing, "We were about a year in, so a little over four years ago, and it was starting to look like we may never make it back. There was only so much partying and exploring we could do on the ideas we could remember from infomercials. It was Scot who insisted that we not use any ideas of real substance. Nothing that had potential to destabilize the Muse flow. Nothing that would draw too much attention to us."

"Wow you must have gotten in on the ground floor then," Chauncey interrupted. "They've only been around for what four maybe five years."

"Yeah, that was the thing, Imperium allowed Scot a cover to experiment with bigger ideas in this world. In turn, this allowed for its rapid rise...Marnie, you know how Scot was, always liked having an idea better than executing an idea. I'm sure you've already figured out what having an idea feels like here."

"Wait...was?" Marnie's face had grown sullen as she braced for bad news.

"Is...sorry is, is," David corrected his tense, causing Marnie's face to relax slightly. "Anyway, that's how they got their hooks in him, by getting him hooked on that feeling."

"So what? He's some kind of addict?" Marnie questioned.

"In a manner of speaking, yes," David replied.

"What manner of speech is that," Trig interrupted. "Sounds exactly like what he is laddie."

"You're...I guess you're right. Epiphany...Epiphany is a drug and he can get a hit of it whenever he wants. He barely has to think of an idea anymore," David responded.

"So the cuffs, the Dyings, that's all him?" Marnie continued to press David. To her surprise, she remained relatively calm during the interrogation. She was unsure if it was her earlier blowout that had tempered her reaction to the revelations or if she was starting to gain some semblance of control over her body's discharge of Muse.

"It...it's not like that. He's insulated from the effect he is having on the world. I don't think he knows what he has wrought. Not quite a prisoner but with the addiction he might as well be," David said, half mourning Scot's plight and half mourning Eternal Dawn's.

"Wouldn't be so sure of that," Luci interjected, "Sounds like he may be the lynchpin to the whole operation. Not likely to let him walk out the door. Sounds like a prisoner to me."

David nodded in agreement.

"And Sara?" Marnie questioned, steering the conversation back to the original query.

"So...as you can imagine, my usefulness as a Muser was short-lived. I never had the creative prowess...not like Scot. Anyway, rumors of a new Master had started to get out into the world. Imperium needed to set up a paramilitary wing of sorts. There was and still is a lot of anti-Master sentiment floating around from the Last War and the Flood. Imperium wanted to protect the golden goose."

On hearing the phrase anti-Master sentiment, Chauncey attempted to deliver a pointed glance to Trig but they were too enthralled with the conversation to take notice.

David continued, "I was shunted off to help run this wing. I had hoped it would help me keep an eye on Scot. That's when Sara came into the picture. She was brought in to help run this new wing. I was to handle strategy and she was to handle training and operations. Her tactics were brutal. She had sociopathic tendencies which weren't being addressed. As you saw last night, they still haven't. I tried taking my concerns to the upper floors but nobody would hear me out. It wasn't long before my position had been usurped and I found myself subordinate to her, all the while becoming more and more removed from Scot. She...she used her position to abuse, even using it to force herself on me."

Tears had started to well up in the sides of David's eyes. "I...I tried to stay as long as I could for Scot's sake. But...but it became too much. I tried to get him out. I tried so hard," his voice had broken apart by the time he reached the end of the sentence. There was a conflicting mixture of fear, sadness, and anger washing over him as he tried to press on, "That...that was two years ago. I've been trying to get him out ever since."

Marnie had one lingering question remaining, the question of how David had found himself back on Earth but after his story, she didn't want to press him further. In light of the revelation, she assumed that Imperium had somehow used Scot to force him back and prevent further meddling.

***

The group gave David some space to compose himself before setting about the discussion of their next move. They had already decided on the Cloister as their destination but the manner of travel was still up for debate. Marnie once more pulled out the map they had attained from Wordsmith for the group to study.

"Can we use the green door to the cisterns?" Marnie questioned, debating the idea with a fresh mind.

"It's still too dangerous," replied David. "They saw my face. They know Scot's and my history. My bet is they have a platoon camped there now."

"And there's no other door we can use?" Marnie responded, hoping David had missed a possible avenue in the wake of the fight.

"I'm afraid I can't say," David replied.

"Can't say or won't say," Trig interjected.

"Can't, as in I don't know. Scot and I searched long and hard for a way to get back. We knew about the menhir in the cistern and the one we went through last night. There was also the one by the Wellspring here," David said, pointing at the map in the area of the old citadel foundations under Imperium's spire.

Marnie looked where he was pointing, seeing no markings to indicate its existence.

"But that one I could never get close enough to to check out," David continued. "Wouldn't have mattered though, we couldn't get the other ones working, even just to help us move around here. Hell, I didn't even know about the eye socket sigils until you figured it out."

"Scot must have figured it out eventually. I mean they used him to force you back to Earth didn't they?" Marnie responded, finally seeking closure on the last part of David's story that didn't make sense.

David took a deep breath, "I tried to get us both back...I tried so hard."

Marnie accepted this as an affirmative response to her question. She took a few beats to think before decisively speaking, "Okay we take the long way to the Cloister."

David, Luci, Trig, and Chauncey nodded in agreement. They packed up the small vestiges of the camp which remained and set out once more.

Chapter Seventeen
"I defy you, stars!"

It took a minute for the Forgotten Master to decide if he was actually awake, having opened his eyes he was half panicked at the nothingness before him. His mind was still conditioned to expect the soft glow of his room's light fixtures and the sounds of chirping frogs and crickets outside his window.

He hadn't had a restful sleep, having become acutely aware of the sound his blood makes when traversing the vessels of his body. It was an experience he found to be deeply unsettling, creating another system to monitor, again drawing his thoughts inward. The sound was something he had never had cause to notice but contrasted with the unrelenting silence, it had become deafening...almost maddening.

To his dismay, he had found his thoughts to be as clouded as they were before he decided to rest. He had no indication of how long his respite had lasted. Was it the seven hours he was used to? Was it seven minutes? Perhaps it was a couple of days. The Master instinctively looked toward the sky to garner a rough time of day, only realizing the futility once his eyes had reached the expected apex. There was no moon or stars to be seen.

The only saving grace was that his body's energy was somewhat restored. Restored enough at least to carry on with his journey. The Master searched around on the ground for any errant articles that may have exited his pack during the night. He checked for the point of the iron sword and aligned himself to face its direction before sheathing it. Once more he started to trudge into the darkness, counting, trying desperately to keep the madness from creeping in.

The Forgotten Master had nothing but time to consider his role in the events that he had set in motion. He second-guessed his every decision. "Was it wise to send David to fetch the girl? Was she even necessary? Should I have had her brought right to the Cloister instead of having them separate? Why did I do that? It sounded like a good idea at the time...lessen the risk...lessen the danger to Eternal Dawn. Should I have involved the outcast Geddes? Why did I come here? Did I really hear a prophecy? Do I even believe in prophecy? Am I going to die down here? Is this my tomb, never to be found, doomed to truly become forgotten?"

***

The questions the Forgotten Master had would cycle on repeat, remaining unanswered in the darkness. He was starting to hope another voice, perhaps the one that had set him on his current path, would come to provide the answers or at the very least provide him company. But there was no one to answer his questions and he only had his inner monologue to keep him company. The Master had never felt so alone, so helpless, so useless.

His knees had started to ache. He was becoming acutely aware of the patina his advancing years imbued on his body, seemingly coating his joints, causing them to bind and grind with each subsequent step. His lower back had developed a dull ache which would occasionally be accompanied by a shooting pain that came on and departed for unknown reasons and at unpredictable intervals. Under most circumstances, the Master would curse these aches and pains. On this journey he welcomed them, if only to be a reminder that he was still alive, still capable of feeling something in the darkness which had stripped so much from him. And so he trudged on, hoping to reach the eventual end of darkness.

***

It had been hours since the five companions set out from the Umphraidh Menhir. Up to that point, there had been a distinct lack of excitement, as if the creatures of the realm were keeping a wide berth. It seemed that word had gotten out about the immense power concentrated in a new Vagabond.

Trig managed to keep their sniping comments to a minimum. Their distrust of the Geddes child had started to wane the more time they spent in her company, realizing Deirdre nay Luci may have been as much a victim of the Last War as everyone else and had perhaps, even been saved from following in her father's odious footsteps. The perspective they had gained, however, hadn't been enough to offer an apology. They would continue to keep a watchful eye on the would-be Master waiting for any misstep that could dispel the sliver of trust that had burrowed under their skin.

Marnie spent some time watching David as he was spending his time watching their surroundings, keeping a keen eye out for danger. She was once more struck with the thought that she was seeing less and less of the boy who went missing five years prior and more and more of the man he had become. Gone were the days when he was always on edge, sheepishly hoping to avoid getting caught for the slightest of trespass. She was now looking at a man who was still seeking to avoid danger but was more than willing to confront it when the need arose. It was an enviable trait, even if it meant having to mourn the days when she could make him nervous by sneaking penny candy into his pockets. He never appreciated being made an accessory to her childish crimes but was much too loyal to turn her in. It was a trait that carried through to his watching out for Scot on their nighttime bombing runs.

Chauncey was busy counting his luck. He wasn't sure what he would have done with himself in the weeks prior had he known that he would be finding himself on an adventure with not one but two Masters on a quest to save a third…a third Master and possibly the realm as he knew it. He had a thousand questions he wanted to ask the heretic Master but didn't want to badger her, reasoning that Trig had stirred up enough of the past that further discourse would rest in the area of bad taste.

Luci had taken point and, like David, was also keeping an eye out for dangers. She wasn't harboring resentment toward Trig or their words. She had become heated in the moment but her anger quickly faded. She learned a long time ago that prejudices, no matter how poorly earned they seemed, were rarely subject to change by word alone, especially words of scorn. For those that were capable of change, actions and familiarity were much better catalysts. In this instance, she hadn't made it a quest to change Trig's mind. Given the short time they would be together, she didn't see the point. In a few days' time, she hoped, she would be in a world where her past no longer mattered. That wasn't to say she wasn't intrigued by the figure that had shown her so much disdain. There was something she found enviable about them, whether it was their cunning with the creation of the moblin ambush device or their unabashed candor, she couldn't say.

"Are we worried about the Razor-Sìth that has been following us for the last couple of miles?" Luci posited matter of factly, having refocused her wandering thoughts. The reason for the lack of forest activity was becoming apparent to the rest of the group. She had expected that this news would put everyone on alert but David was the only one that had become visibly agitated.

"Where?" David demanded, scanning the tree line. His mind was conflicted as to whether to feel shame or fear. Shame for not noticing as part of his role as a lookout or fear of the legendary beast which had only tales of its furiosity to precede it. He couldn't be faulted though, Luci was wearing her ranging goggles, giving her a distinct advantage over his defective eyes.

"Not unless you mean us harm," Chauncey replied. "We have what you would call...something of an understanding," he continued, before telling the story of their encounters with the creature. The stories only served to mildly calm David's nerves but they were more than enough to ease Luci's.

"Why didn't you mention it sooner?" David asked.

"Wasn't sure it was following us at first, wanted to make sure," she replied. "He's right though," Luci continued as she gestured toward Chauncey. "If it wanted to do us harm, you'd already be minus a throat...I'm actually comforted."

"That makes one of us," David responded.

***

The group kept their pace as they traveled up the trail, continuing until they reached the border where the woods met the plains. It was here that Marnie was able to catch her first glimpse of the city of Ærratum, still miles off in the distance, a glowing beacon in a sea of darkness. The scourge that Imperium had wrought was now on full display. The gradients of luminosity in the fields surrounding the city moved in waves. One could almost see the Muse flows being drawn toward the city. Given enough time one would.

The Geddes Road carved a swath from the city through the fields before seemingly coming to an end at the top of a hill to the west. The section of road they could see remained largely unused. It was an artery of light stretching west from the city. Marnie couldn't help but consider the Muse that was wasted in giving it light.

She also observed a smaller road crossing the field in the distance ahead of them. She was certain that this was the same road she encountered at the crossroads shortly after her birth into this new world.

"We should camp here," Luci suggested. "We are going to need our wits about us for the last big push."

"How close is this Cloister of yours, David?" Marnie questioned, hoping she could convince the group to keep pushing through their fatigue in an effort to draw that much closer to their objective.

"Now is not the time to push our advance," Trig chimed in. "The Geddes is right. The nearer we draw to the city, the more dangerous it is going to become. Besides, distances can be deceiving this far out. Looking at the city we probably have fifteen maybe sixteen more miles to go. A full day's travel if we do it smartly."

David looked around the group, considering the strangers Marnie had drawn to her. The location of the Cloister was a guarded secret. He had half hoped that Trig and Chauncey would abandon their quest once they realized the young woman was in much more capable hands. But there they remained, steadfast in seeing the mission play out for better or worse...as if they were called to it. They did appear to be nothing if not loyal. Marnie had put her trust in them. To David that was about as good a judgment on their character as he was going to get. He did not worry about Luci, her existing relationship with the Forgotten meant that she already knew the location.

David hesitated but offered, "Cloister is an extra three miles north of the city. In the Cursed Forest."

"Cursed Forest?" Marnie questioned, the ominous-sounding name was cause for concern.

"So named to discourage visitors," David replied. "Or so I've been told. The true curse lies over the city."

"The real problem is going to be the road," Luci said, ignoring the eponymous portion of its true name. 'The Geddes Road', never felt right coming out of her mouth.

"Right," Trig chimed in. "By now Imperium is going to know something's up. It's going to be under a watchful eye."

"Can't we just go around it the other way?" Chauncey suggested. "Around the back side of the city."

"Right...Are we just going to cut across the plains the whole way...out in the open?" Trig replied. "Or are we going to stick to the southern borders of the forest and add at least a week to the journey? Do you even stop to think about what you are saying or is it just one continuous stream from your brain to your mouth? Is there even a brain up there?"

"Hey, that's enough!" Marnie cut in before Trig could keep on with their own cutting words. "We have a saying where I'm from. If you don't have something nice to say, then don't say it. You'd do good to remember that. You may be adept in many matters and want people to know it...but darkening someone else's star doesn't make yours shine any brighter...There is nothing wrong with sharing an idea, sometimes it's the bad ideas that inspire the great ones," Marnie finished, echoing Martin's maxim, watching Trig's face to see if her words had made an impact.

"I...I suppose you're right Miss Marnie," replied Trig after taking some time to consider the words, the shame that tinged their voice was almost palpable. They hadn't been called out like this before, instead, opting to keep anyone that would past arms reach. It hadn't hit Trig before but in many ways, Chauncey was a muse, even if they had to start their ideas from the exact opposite perspective of what was normally being suggested. "I'm sorry."

"It's not me you should be directing the apology to," Marnie replied.

Trig then did something they hadn't known they were capable of. They turned to Chauncey and offered a sincere apology, "I'm so...so sorry."

Chauncey's jaw dropped. The four words that had been uttered, while simple, spoke volumes. Trig wasn't just apologizing for this latest transgression but for all of their transgressions. "I...I don't know what to say," Chauncey replied. For once he was speechless.

***

The group set up camp on the edge of the forest with a plan to strike out across the plains in the morning. Trig and Luci took the first watch while David and Chauncey took the second. David had still been nervous with the prowling Razor-Sith around and suggested that he and Luci split watch, being the two most skilled in the art of violence.

197

Trig, still not fully trusting the Geddes child, parlayed their newly mended fence with Chauncey to convince the others that there wouldn't be a problem with sharing a watch with Luci. Marnie and the others hoped they could use it as an opportunity to mend another fence.

Only once, before the start of watch, would they hear the grotesque scream of a dying creature off in the distance. Marnie would come to think it was a creature that meant them harm in this forest of waning light. She took the moment of calm to open her sketchbook and document an image of their Razor-Sìth protector, working on it until she had become too tired to continue.

Marnie fell asleep, thankful for the watchful eyes of both David and Luci as well as the watching eyes of the beast in the shadows.

***

The count would reach north of fifty thousand before the Forgotten Master once more had to stop and recover. Along the way, he had encountered so many twists and turns that he couldn't keep them all straight. This prevented him from forming a mental map of his prison's geometry. The Master didn't know if he was halfway through, almost done, or just getting started. Pushing forward may have been a struggle but he knew that it was his best option...his only option.

The Master once again set his iron sword way-point and took stock of his supplies. He had used up much more of the water than he had anticipated. That or the walls which had such a hunger for Muse were attempting to pull in other life-affirming substances in its stead. He checked his rations; those too were starting to dwindle at an alarming rate. "Perhaps there are other creatures in the labyrinth. Perhaps one of the pixies I had chance to encounter in the bone rooms had followed me and is stealing my food," he thought.

In truth, he was so focused on keeping his count, his effort to stave off madness, that he hadn't realized how often he was going into his bag to grab a bite to eat or take a sip of water. Thinking back, he could only remember four distinct times when he had reached a ten thousand-count milestone that he decided to reward himself with some nourishment. His recollection had been betraying him as he missed counting his reward at seven thousand two hundred forty-eight, another at thirteen thousand eight hundred sixty-three, and at least two others.

He knew he was already under-fueled but this revelation of dwindling supplies truly alarmed him and thoughts of an impending doom started to creep in. He knew it would be another night where sleep wouldn't fully take him. The Forgotten Master had once more become aware of the sound of his pulsing blood as he shut his eyes, unsure of why he had bothered to open them in the first place.

***

"Warm winds tonight...Will keep the spirits at bay," Luci said in an attempt to keep the conversation light as she tried to pass the watch with Trig without incident.

"Superstitions are for the weak of mind," Trig responded, almost unaware of the comment's abrasiveness as it passed through their lips.

"How's that working out for you?" Luci replied. She agreed with the sentiment but not with the tone.

"How's what working for me?" Trig questioned with the same pointed inflection.

Luci took a second to ponder if she was 'baiting the bear' before commenting, "Being so cynical all the time. It almost seems like you don't know you're doing it."

"We all have our charms. You act as if it's not a virtue," Trig responded. "Saves a lot of time spent on conversational drudgery."

"Not much for small talk then?" Luci replied.

"Abhor it," Trig said, hoping that the Geddes child would take the hint.

Luci thought for a moment about letting the fledgling conversation die before commenting, "Must be a real riot at parties."

Trig glanced over at Luci almost as if they were looking over the top of invisible glasses. "What are we doing here?" they responded, exasperated, sensing that their attempt to quell the conversation was failing.

"What? I'm just trying to pass the time, maybe get to know you a little," Luci replied.

"If I wanted you to know me, you'd know me," Trig said before continuing, "Look...we may have allowed you to stay in the group but that doesn't mean I trust you or want to get to know you. In a manner of speaking, it's not me...it's you."

Luci had started to sense that she was getting under her watch partner's skin but this last comment cemented the notion. At this moment, despite her better judgment, she adopted a mission to prolong the conversation as long as she could. With Trig's last abrasive comment, their continued annoyance had become a recreational endeavor. "Fine, fine...I'll leave it lay," she said, seemingly ending the discourse.

"Thank you," Trig responded, relieved.

Luci waited just enough time to allow Trig's false sense of victory to reach its crescendo. She picked her next query carefully, hoping it wasn't a step too far, "So are you and Chauncey...like...a thing?"

Trig's face grimaced at the thought that had been forced into their head. "We were going to leave things lay," they demanded.

"What? I'm just curious. You seem like you'd make a good pair," Luci pressed further, seeing how far she could take it.

"I know what you are trying to do," Trig replied. "It was this kind of willful provocation that sealed your parent's eventual fate," they continued, unaware of their hypocrisy in not leaving things lay.

"Pot meet kettle, shit. You want to talk about willful provocation," Luci responded. "It's a real wonder you only have the one friend. He'd have to be a bad idea guy to hang with the likes of you."

"Oh yeah, 'cause I'm sure you've got plenty of people lining up to be your friend. Do you tell them who you are right away or is that a second date kind of thing?" Trig rebutted, their hushed voice didn't hide their apparent disdain.

"That's it," Luci said as she stood up from her seat by the fire and marched over to Trig, hoping that by the time she reached them, she would have a properly-cutting comeback.

Nothing of proper substance had come to mind as she marched the eight steps. She was staring at the seated target, exasperated while at the same time being more than aware that she was complicit in her own state of agitation.

Trig stood up in an attempt to meet Luci's eyes. They were half a head shorter and had to crane their neck but they did meet them. They were angrily huffing as they braced for the verbal or physical assault that they had earned.

Luci stared into Trig's eyes for a beat longer than that of a standard moment.

Trig stared back, not knowing what to do, hoping that something would happen soon to break the tension that had been building.

Suddenly, Luci reached her hands around Trig's body and up to their head, grabbing a fist full of hair. She didn't yank on it, instead, she used it to hold their head still as she continued to stare into their eyes. Luci slowly leaned down allowing her lips to meet Trig's.

After a heartbeat, Trig recoiled, pushing her back a step. They stared at Luci for a second before echoing a previous query, "What are we doing here?"

The question lingered in the air for a moment before Trig was overcome. The soft warm feeling of epiphany flooded their brain as they returned the gesture in kind, wrapping their arms around Luci's back and grabbing hold of her shoulders to lower her body and allow their lips to once more meet.

At the moment just before they touched, Luci denied the advance, spinning Trig around, allowing her to caress their body from behind. She blew softly into Trig's ear causing their knees to buckle as a pleasant shiver crept up their spine. Luci gently guided Trig's body down to the ground on top of the blanket Trig had been sitting on.

A new battle had begun between the two. It was a fight to see who could get more of their body to touch the other, attempting to merge into one as their lips softly caressed the exposed areas of each other's skin.

The two eventually settled into a spooned cuddle with their legs entwined. The glows of their Muse had started to pulse. As they lay there enjoying each other's warmth for what they hoped could be forever, it wasn't long before their frequencies met. Luci's once neutral green glow shifted to match Trig's violet as they fell into a rhythm, still tightly entangled, hearts and bodies pulsing as one.

Chapter Eighteen
"Unfortunately the cave contained a lion."

The Forgotten Master awoke once more, opening his eyes, half forgetting they would be greeted by the infinite blackness of the labyrinth. He checked on his sword, verifying it was where he left it and that it was keeping his trail true. Then he once more shouldered his pack, sheathed his sword, and continued to trudge into the abyssal darkness.

The count would reach just north of twenty thousand before the Master would encounter a diversion on course. In his endless plodding, he had become much less conscious of his steps, sacrificing safety for speed. It would be this complacency that led to him crashing into the ground. He could barely hear the noise of his sword scraping against the floor as he slid face-first down the hallway, the echo-less sound being absorbed into the walls as quickly as it was generated.

The Master rose to his feet and checked his body to make sure he hadn't received gashes from the blade that dangled at his hip. He counted himself lucky in that he hadn't shed his own blood. He had received what he assumed would be a substantial bruise on his upper leg just below his pelvis where the cross guard connected to his body during the fall. He judged the injury to be mostly superficial, only bringing mild discomfort to his already labored gait.

Once satisfied that he hadn't earned serious injury, the Master checked his immediate surroundings for the cause of his stumbled crash. He swept the ground with his foot, working his way backward through the corridor. He had only regressed six small steps before encountering the reason. Probing the object with his bare foot he assessed the mass to be a little over four feet in length and a little over a foot tall. The form didn't appear to be solid as it moved slightly with each push of his foot, not reacting in any manner to indicate it was alive.

Satisfied that a more in-depth tactile investigation wouldn't lead to the possible sacrifice of one of his more important appendages, the Master leaned down next to the object and started to observe it with his hands.

As he moved from one end of the mass to the other, an unseen pallor started to grow on the Forgotten Master's face. The object had a rough leathery texture as that of a horse saddle left out to rot, thirsting for oil that hadn't been applied in years. It wasn't until the Master's fingers reached the end of his obstacle that it struck him what he was touching. The object was that of a mummified human body. The head possessed a long beard which partially disintegrated with touch. The body was in a fetal position with a pack resting under its head as a makeshift pillow. Searching the ground near the body, the Master detected an iron sword much the same as his own. He could feel the embossing of the runic designs that adorned the blade and made note that it was pointing in the opposite direction of his travel.

The Forgotten Master immediately surmised that the body belonging to the labyrinth's former occupant was also that of a Master.

"But which one?" he thought, investigating the body further. The Master gently wrested the pack from under the mummy's head, detecting the muted sound of skin being peeled away from the skull, skin which had merged with the bag after many years of rest. Searching the tattered pack, the Master found near-identical contents to his own, being that of a flint lighter, a piece of lead, a tarnished notebook, and an old canteen for water, the contents of which had long since been exhausted. As the Master explored the pack further, he heard the sound of a small rip and felt it quickly decrease in weight as the sound of two soft echoless thuds emanated from the floor beneath him. He reached down to the ground, searching for the two items, quickly finding them. What he found gave him the answer he was looking for. There was a small hammer and accompanying chisel. The Forgotten had found the body of the lost Vagabond.

Although this was a man he had never met, the Forgotten Master felt compelled to provide as proper a burial as he could. He moved the body to the side of the corridor to prevent further desecration in the unlikely event someone else was ordained to take a similar trip into the heart of darkness.

He put the pack back under the Vagabond Master's head and carefully laid his sword beside his body in the direction of his return path. The Master then took up the chisel in one hand and hammer in the other to inscribe a V on the wall above the fallen. He knew it was a marker no one would ever see but he felt compelled just the same.

The Master prepared himself to take his first strike then followed through. There was a quick flash of light that seemed to illuminate the corridor as it diffused unnaturally slowly. In this moment the Master acquired his first look at the savior of Eternal Dawn. As he gazed on the face he found a set of undecayed eyes staring back at him. "How could this be?" he thought before observing them quickly blink. The Master could feel his heart skip as the light faded back into blackness.

The Master sat for a moment knowing it was either his mind or the labyrinth playing tricks on him. He once more took a swing of the hammer to complete the makeshift memorial. What he saw next caused sheer terror. The corpse of the Vagabond was reaching out for him, their eyes locked on his own. More unsettling, the eyes he was staring into were that of his own. The hands had almost reached their perch at his neck when darkness once more took the corridor.

The Master waited for a moment in panic, expecting the decaying hands to encircle his neck in an attempt to make him their bedfellow but nothing happened. He reached up to take another ill-advised strike on the improvised headstone but found his hands to be empty.

The only thing he felt was his foot falling into step as he unconsciously took another, only realizing at his third that he had been dreaming. His pack felt heavier and he started to hear the soft clink of metal on metal being produced with each incrementing number of his count. He chalked up the notion as the onset of madness as he continued his considered plodding into the void.

***

"We're never going to get close enough with that cat running around," Richard said, eyeing Sara's face, being careful to not draw further ire in her agitated state.

"Well, we can't very well leave the girl alone to do what she pleases. Can we, Richard?" Sara replied coldly. After her own visit with the ex-master Wordsmith, the objectives of Marnie's traveling party started to take shape.

The encounter with the false Nuckelavee had scattered the posse of Imperium soldiers. Five of the missing seven had rejoined the fold, knowing that dire consequences would befall them if they had just gone back to base. The other two wouldn't be seen again, opting to start new lives in the far-flung reaches of

Eternal Dawn, desperately trying to hold onto their sanity after witnessing the horror that was the beast.

"We'll need to bait it," Sara continued. "One of us is going to need to get close enough to be considered a threat." She looked at Richard, the implication being that the bait would be him.

Richard looked behind him to see if she might be looking past him. "M...Me?" he stammered sheepishly, pointing at himself.

Sara guffawed before adding, "I said threat you milquetoast coward."

Sara looked around the group of assembled soldiers, shaking her head disdainfully as she glanced at the three that had been savagely beaten by her former boss-turned-peon. They were still nursing their wounds. She then surveyed the five that were before her, weighing the cowardice they showed in abandonment against the courage they showed in returning, ultimately deciding it was a wash.

"It's going to be me," she uttered, observing the sighs of relief, further lowering her opinion of the troops in her charge.

A cloaked figure observed the one-sided discussion, hoping their decision to join the Imperium posse was as pragmatic as they had thought.

***

"Remember, throw the harpoon where it's going, not where it is," Sara snapped before adding, "And don't kill it or it's your ass. We need it to draw out the watchers."

She turned her back to the two soldiers who'd volunteered and started her march toward the forest where Marnie's party had made camp. She used a charge from her cuff to create a sword five meters ahead, smoothly snatching it out of the ground as she walked by. Her limp had become nonexistent as she willed herself to ignore the pain that had been inflicted the previous evening.

She walked only a few hundred yards before the faelight bugs stopped rising around her. The chirping of crickets had also died down. It was at this moment that she knew the void cat was upon her. She scanned her perimeter to make sure her attendants were still flanking her. Using one of the extra Muse charges she was afforded due to her station, Sara added a glow to the sword, becoming a beacon in the sea of tall grass. Now at a standstill, she listened for the stalking predator.

It was only moments before she heard the wishing of a creature cutting through the vegetation behind her. Sara took a forward roll, watching the Razor-Sìth leap over her and charge back into the grass as she tumbled out of the way.

The flanking soldiers, still clouded in darkness, hadn't had fast enough reactions to make a move. Sara could now see the grass ahead of her parting as the beast readied to make another approach.

She settled into a defensive stance, waiting to deliver her riposte should the Sìth attack again. Once more the beast started a charge. The action was followed quickly by the whizzing sound of a harpoon taking flight.

There was a thunk as the weapon buried itself in the ground. Sara, still in her guarded stance, observed as the Razor-Sìth changed direction, heading toward the thrower, who at that moment, was paralyzed with fear.

There was no time for the air to escape his lungs and allow a scream as the cat dragged the soldier to the ground, liberating him of his larynx. An arterial spray of blood cascaded across the seed heads of the surrounding glow-wheat. The soldier grabbed at his throat trying to keep his life essence from escaping the wound.

The Razor-Sìth made a slow circle around the soldier, admiring its work. It waited for the soldier to bleed out before turning its attention back to Sara.

Sara's eyes remained fixed on the beast holding its ground not forty meters away. She barely flinched seeing the level of brutality that the large cat was capable of. The previously slicked hair of the beast stood up on a razor-sharp edge as it started to posture. Ultraviolet light escaped its fur and served to highlight the blood that had been shed, turning it black as the Muse dissipated from the dying platelets, giving a living abstract impressionistic quality to the field that had been made into the cat's canvas.

Sara, still en garde, glanced at the remaining soldier. To her surprise he had crept in closer, coming to a distance within fifteen meters. After the incident with the gruesome horse beast horror, she had expected him to once more turn tail.

The soldier had reasoned that the only way he was getting out with his life was to stop the Razor-Sìth. He was much too slow to outpace the creature, precluding running as an option. He also knew that if his boss somehow came out on top after once more being abandoned, he would have been better off trying to go up against the cat.

Sara turned her attention back to the posturing beast. It had remained in place, clearly opting to force Sara into making the first move. She stood steadfast for a moment, waiting and weighing her options.

After taking a breath and deciding on a course of action, Sara took a feinted lunge toward the Sìth. The provocation caused the creature to respond in kind and it leapt forward.

Sara sprinted to a point twenty degrees off of the remaining soldier's right side. She could hear the heavy pounding of paws closing the gap behind her as she drew nearer to her destination. When she no longer detected the sound of approaching footsteps, she cast her sword aside and went into a crouching roll, knowing the creature had once more launched into a pounce.

The next sound she heard was the wailing banshee-like cries of the fallen cat. The soldier had taken his shot, harpooning the Razor-Sìth through its left thigh.

Sara and the soldier stood above the cat as it screamed and writhed trying to escape the pain. After savoring the victory for a moment, Sara once more took up her swords. She then proceeded to whack the creature on the back of the skull with her weapon's pommel, knocking it unconscious in preparation for the next phase of her plan.

***

The Forgotten Master continued on his pace for a length of time he was unable to determine. His rations had run out hours before, maybe it was days; he no longer had the strength of mind to know. The counting had long since become a distant memory. He could have been at forty thousand or for all he knew, he could have imagined the last couple days or weeks and was now only ten meters from the entrance.

The Master knew nothing but the forward motion of his steps and the beating of his heart, unsure now if there was a difference between the two. In the time since his encounter with the fallen Vagabond, his reason for embarking on the journey had gradually escaped him. Had it all been a dream? Was that moment the start of his decline or just the beginning of its end? Had he met his demise by the incorporeal hands of a Master turned wraith? In this, the deepest darkest reaches of the labyrinth he had finally lost everything, or had it all been stolen?

The Forgotten Master was in no shape to answer these questions. He was in no shape to continue and was actively trying to quit. Trying to stop and curl into a ball in the middle of the hallway, ready to give up, ready to be forgotten.

It was by sheer force of an unattached will that he kept going, pulled along by the tug on his heart that he had felt back at the Cloister, a tug he no longer knew the meaning for. Madness...madness had taken root.

***

It would be another hour before the voices would start. The company the Master so desperately desired in the days prior had shown up to ridicule him. He could pick out three distinct intonations in the chatter but was only able to absorb small snippets of this new bombardment.

"You're helpless you know..."

"...you are not ready..."

"...this is your life now..."

"...brought her here to die..."

"...a failure..."

"...you'll never be ready..."

"...going to die down here..."

He couldn't be sure if the voices were coming from within or being produced by an unknown entity in the labyrinth. Based on the behavior of sound in the corridors, the occasional presence of an echo on the voices would suggest that they were imagined. The Master was in no state of mind to consider this thought much less debate it. His internal monologue had become lost in the chatter.

It was another fifteen minutes before the bombardment would become too much. The Master slunk to the floor, resting into a seated fetal position, wrapping his arms around his knees, rocking back and forth in an attempt to self-soothe...trying to block out the litany of accusations.

"...you're a failure..."

"...why did you think you could do this?..."

"...that's right, sit there and die..."

"...you are not ready..."

The Master tried to fight it...tried to bring order to the chaos. Plugging his ears served no purpose. Screaming on the inside wouldn't drown out the voices as they carried on mocking him...taunting him.

***

The voices repeated for hours as the Forgotten Master sat in the darkness, no longer knowing who he was or the nature of his purpose. The only thing he knew was the fight to retain whatever fragments of his sanity remained.

His heart rate became erratic as the taunts carried on, continuing to repeat the same themes and motifs over and over. A sense of impending doom had overcome him.

"...you are not ready..." a voice said again.

"I'm not ready," the Master agreed, the other voices had given his thoughts of self-doubt room to be heard.

"That's right you're not ready," the voice repeated.

"...only once all is lost..." a new voice chimed in. It had a soft feminine tone that echoed in contrast to the shrill goblinesque ones that had been lobbing their abuses.

"...will what is lost be found..." the Master vocalized, not knowing why. The prophecy that had brought him here was a distant memory.

"...you're useless..."

"...just give up..."

"...brought her here to die..."

"...you are not ready..."

The shrill voices continued. The Master's mind continued to fight them off, putting up a wall between him and the final void. Protecting himself from their torment.

"Giving in is not giving up...surrender," the soft voice suggested.

The Master took a moment to think on this proposition, as much as his mind would allow.

The other voices continued to taunt him.

"...you are not ready..."

"...you're irresponsible..."

"...your hubris will kill you..."

"...you are not ready..."

"Let the darkness in," the soft voice beckoned.

Out of instinct, the Master continued to fight off the bombardment, somehow he knew he could hold up against them to his dying breath.

"Don't be afraid," the soft voice once more chimed in.

In his mind the Master was starting to come to the conclusion that the shrill ramblings were there to prevent him from giving up, giving him something to fight against. He didn't know if the soft voice could be trusted.

"I don't know how," The Master said, trying to speak to the soft voice alone.

"Just lean in," the soft voice said. "Stop fighting."

"...you are not ready..."

"...you are not read..."

"...you are not..."

"...you are..."

"I am," the Forgotten Master once more spoke out loud, giving up fighting, giving in to the voices, allowing them to take over.

The Master could almost feel the crisscrossing of the synapses in his mind as the voices collapsed into themselves, creating a unified piercing shriek that reached an ultimate peak. The Master felt as if his head were about to explode. The shriek sustained itself at this level for a duration beyond what the Master thought his body to be capable. The noise once more fractured into unintelligible gibberish which shifted its pitch down to a lower bass resonance. The voices came and went in waves before once more merging into one. The tides of sound came and went, bouncing from one ear to the other, causing the Master's eyes to shift left to right and back again. He was being hypnotized.

The speed of the waves picked up until his eyes could no longer keep up, leaving them vibrating in a state of nystagmus. The sound was now that of a constant hum; its volume increasing with each passing second until it had once more become intolerable. The intensity grew to a level beyond the previous shriek, causing the Master's body to vibrate at a point just short of full convulsion.

The Forgotten Master wasn't experiencing pain but raw sensory input. The shaking continued to grow, shortly reaching an intensity that rivaled the hum inside his head. It was at this moment that the Master fully surrendered, resigning himself to whatever came next, even if it meant his death.

Then all at once there was a flash of light followed by the immediate ceasing of the sound and sensation. The Master was once more deprived of his senses, this time not even feeling the ground beneath him. He was floating in blackness, not sure if he was alive or dead, no longer caring either way as he yielded fully to the void.

***

An abundance of thoughts had been rolling around in Marnie's head, preventing sleep from fully taking her. Thoughts drifted to the pending reunion with her brother. Would she hug him or speak to him first? What would she say? Would he even recognize her anymore?

These were all pertinent questions but the one that caused her the most trouble was, "What happens if I have another blowout upon seeing him? What would that do in a city the size of Ærratum?" The notion of another blowout gave her pause and increased her anxiety. She could feel her panic grow as she watched the Muse around her being sucked into her body causing her skin to glow with a brighter intensity. It wasn't uncommon for the worry about having a panic attack, to cause an attack. It was a vicious cycle she was all too familiar with. She knew this wouldn't be a bad one and remembered her counselor's advice, "Sometimes, the only way out is through. Instead of fighting it…lean into it. Become acquainted. Look at panic as less of an affliction and more as your friend. They're in our body for a reason."

And so Marnie sat up and leaned in, taking this low-stakes moment to test the panic's interaction with the Muse, forcing herself to explore all outcomes of having a blowout in the city.

She thought, "I would darken all lights in the entire city. Hospitals may not be able to give care. People may trip down some stairs or get stuck in elevators or whatever conveyance is used there. It would be all my fault." She sat in the moment, knowing that she was drawing in more Muse light than before. "…but at the end of the day, I don't know that any of that will happen…and if it does, life goes on," she thought out loud, taking in and expelling air slowly. She watched as the excess Muse flushed out of her in waves with each passing breath before her body finally reached a state of stasis.

The visual representation was the proof she needed that her shrink's advice actually worked. This revelation was like taking the final steps on the first leg of a journey. For the first time since the attacks started, she finally felt like she may have some semblance of control over them. She approached the revelation with caution, knowing it was going to be some time before she could claim lasting dominion over her affliction-turned-buddy.

"This new development warrants being shared," Marnie thought, as she stood up and made her way out of the sound-dampening tent within which she had been resting. Trig had created a pair of tents with the Muse orbs. It was an attempt to maximize the potential for sleep but also served the greater purpose of preventing Trig from having to listen to Chauncey as he would inevitably start to prattle in his sleep. That privilege, they thought, could be shared with his bunkmate David.

Marnie made her way over to the fire with the intention of letting Trig and Luci know of her breakthrough. When she arrived, she was more than surprised to find that the watch partners were in a state that could only be described as less than vigilant. Luci's arm was still wrapped tightly around Trig as they lay side by side on the ground, sleeping, clothing and hair disheveled.

Marnie wanted to spare the pair the immediate embarrassment of attempting to explain their current situation. She also wanted to spare them the potential for embarrassment that would accompany Chauncey stumbling upon them in the unlikely event that he woke himself up for watch relief. She didn't know what would be worse, Trig having to admit they were wrong about Luci or Trig being caught neglecting guard duty in a manner similar to the one that led to the lumendeer encounter.

She devised a quick strategy of surreptitiously waking the pair, allowing them to retain their guarded dignity. Marnie proceeded to gather a handful of small rocks before heading to the doorway of her tent.

She lobbed the first stone in the pair's general direction hoping that they would become startled. The sound hadn't been loud enough. She then lobbed two more stones at once, aiming closer to the pair. The effort was still to no avail and they continued to sleep soundly. At this, Marnie was thankful that there hadn't been any commotion up to this point in the evening, assuming the Razor-Sith was serving to be the better lookout.

Marnie looked around for a slightly heavier stone and threw it once more in their direction. To her horror, she could see the rock make a high arc before connecting directly with Luci's skull. A moment had passed before she heard, "Ahh shite, get up...get up, we're sleeping through watch." Marnie quietly snuck back to the tent to watch from behind a flap.

Luci immediately sat up and leaned her back against a large log perched next to the fire. Marnie could see Trig sit up as well, moving closer to nuzzle up next to Luci. She continued to watch as Luci extended her arm, wrapping it around Trig. She let the moment linger for a few minutes, mired in thoughts of how quickly the party's dynamics had shifted. She was lightly patting herself on the back, thinking some of it may be due to her admonishment of Trig concerning their treatment of Chauncey.

Marnie then made a bit of a production out of exiting her tent, stretching and running her hand through her hair, yawning audibly, giving ample time to allow Luci and Trig to put on whatever artifice they deemed necessary. She made her way over to the fire, taking up a seat across from the pair. Trig had moved a meter away from Luci by the time she arrived. It was clear they were in the process of trying to figure out how to act naturally.

"Hey Marnie, good news Trig and I aren't enemies anymore," Luci opened bluntly to Marnie's surprise. "In fact, now you could say we're 'friends'."

Trig, annoyed that they weren't consulted in the matter of information sharing, tried to backpedal, "I...I wouldn't say that. Where do you come off?"

"Don't you mean 'get off'?" Luci replied.

Marnie smirked at the twist of phrase, knowing that Trig would be dying inside.

"What...I thought this was good news. You can't tell me you didn't feel something while we were..." Luci continued.

"While we were...uh...talking...Yeah, I have to admit I misjudged you," Trig said, cutting her off, trying to dam up the words that were spilling out of Luci's mouth with such casualness.

"No, I meant before, when..." Luci started, before catching Trig's eyes. She stared at them for a few seconds before realizing that Trig was trying to keep their activities private. "...yeah talking," she continued. "We were just talking. We have a lot in common."

"So what keeps you up?" Trig interjected. It was a clear plea to change the subject.

Marnie thought for a moment about disclosing her most recent discovery but opted to spare Trig further embarrassment by revealing the one that was antecedent, "So...I'm not one hundred percent sure yet but...I think...I may be able to control the blowouts."

Trig and Luci stared at Marnie with anticipation of a revelation that could potentially make the extrication of Imperium's prisoner that much easier.

"It's probably easier if I show you," Marnie said, rising to her feet. She moved to an area a few more meters from the fire to better display the contrast in the feat she was about to perform. She tried to drift her thoughts back toward the 'what ifs?' in regards to getting a panic attack in the city. This train of thought was to no avail. She had already 'leaned in' and was comfortable with the notion. She tried other lanes of thinking, her departed father, 'What if the Razor-Sìth decided to attack?', 'What if they weren't able to rescue Scot?' None of it seemed to heighten her anxiety. Marnie then proceeded to purposely hyperventilate but even that didn't avail her in the endeavor.

Trig and Luci continued to stare at the awkward show.

Marnie was getting agitated but she had never made an attempt to purposely trigger an attack. "Why would I?" she thought. "I thought I had something. I'm sorry," she voiced.

Noticing the heightened state of aggravation, Trig started to open their mouth to offer condolences in the wake of the failed attempt. They were instead cut off by a shrill cry being made by a creature that was clearly in agony.

"What was that?" Marnie questioned, her focus immediately leaving here failed panic attempt. "Did the big cat catch more prey?"

"I'm not sure," Luci replied, dropping her goggles over her eyes to scan the immediate surroundings.

The pained cries continued, seemingly without end.

"That cannae be any Sìth prey. Much too quick and deliberate with the murderin' that one is. Ken it helps it to keep a low profile," Trig said, offering their reasoned opinion on the matter.

Marnie looked over at them, "Do you think we should check it out?" Her empathy started to grow for whatever creature may be producing the tortured noise.

"It would be against my better judgment," Luci said, offering her opinion on the matter. "'Tis the nature of life. Suffering also exists without observation. Who are we to interfere?" She looked at the other two who stared back in disbelief. She instantly felt regret for her comment and the callousness that coated it. As much as she tried to leave the past behind, echoes of her father still had a habit of bleeding through.

Another sustained yowl of pain echoed across the field bordering the woods. "On second thought..." Luci continued, rolling back her previous statement, "...we should go check it out. At the very least we can ease the creature's suffering."

Marnie was satisfied, although she wasn't sure what Luci had meant by 'ease the creature's suffering'. She opted to save her judgment and any necessary scolding until its need arose.

"We'll go check it out. You stay behind and wake the others if we don't return," Trig said, imploring Marnie to stay back.

"No, I think I'll go along," Marnie replied, protesting the request.

"Trig's right. It could be dangerous," Luci jumped in, trying to implore Marnie to stay behind. She would be lying to herself if she didn't consider that the errand would also provide more time to probe if her earlier activities with Trig were discretions or indiscretions. It had all happened so quickly but she had to admit that there was a feeling of connection with her previous antagonist. Her continued existence as a Geddes in Eternal Dawn precluded connections. Some would kill her if they found out the truth but equally as dangerous were those that would fetishize her for who her family was. How could she possibly trust anyone?

Trig's inner monologue served as an echo of Luci's. They had felt more connected to Luci in the words they hadn't shared than the ones that had. It may have been one act but they had never been able to let their guard down like they had in those moments...not with Chauncey...not with anyone. Trig was a jumble of emotions, "How could it have been with a Geddes of all people?" It was a notion that had them questioning the entire basis for their long-held beliefs. They knew that they were going to have to discuss what happened and what it meant if nothing else.

"You're going to stay here. It's settled. We can't risk your safety," Trig commanded. They had come to count the girl as a friend and genuinely didn't want to see harm come to her but there was also the notion growing in the back of their mind that she was going to play a major role in breaking the proverbial spell that Imperium had over the land.

"You want me to let Chauncey know what I saw when I just left my tent?" Marnie questioned, playing a card she hoped she wouldn't have to. It was a bluff. She wasn't one to betray another's confidence.

Luci could see Trig thinking hard about the position, knowing now that Marnie had seen more than she initially let on. "Oh just let her tell him," she said. "You're right. It's too risky to bring her."

Trig thought on the matter for another moment debating on whether to call Marnie's bluff, "You would probably just follow us anyway wouldn't you?"

A Cheshire grin crept across Marnie's face.

It was the only affirmation that Trig required, "Okay...but stick close. Leg is still sore. May not be able to react fast enough if something happens." This also served as a warning for Luci to be more alert.

***

The trio left camp, leaving Chauncey and David to continue sleeping in their sound-dampened tent. They headed out across the field of grass and glow wheat. The stalks shaded with greens, blues, and purples, swayed in the warm breezes of the eternal evening's air. They were a compliment to the auroras that crept over the horizon to the east. If it wasn't for the tree line in the far-off distance, one would be hard-pressed to tell where the field ended and the sky began. The majesty of the night sky was lessened by the sporadic yowls of the suffering creature off in the distance.

The cries grew louder with each passing step of the ten-minute walk. As they approached, the sound the creature was making seemed almost human, fostering a heightened sense of empathy among the travelers. Upon glimpsing the noise's source, it had become clear that the wounded creature's agonized wailing belonged to that of the Razor-Sith.

Marnie's eyes met the beast's as it lay writhing in the grass. It let out another yell but this one sounded markedly different. It sounded guttural, almost word-like as if it were trying to say, "Run!"

The words, "Oh no," dropped out of Luci's mouth as her eyes scanned the creature's body. With her goggles, she was much quicker to pick up on the Sìth's bound body being staked to the ground with a harpoon through its thigh. She immediately reached for her bow.

At the same time, Trig started to reach into their pocket for an orb, immediately picking up on the sense of danger contained within the two little words Luci had uttered.

"Hands in the air," a voice from behind them commanded.

Trig ignored the order, continuing to reach into their pack. The unmistakable sound of a crossbow bolt could be heard whizzing by their ear. Their reaction was immediate compliance, hand freezing halfway into the pocket holding their orbs. Marnie and Luci already had their arms raised.

Moments later, the trio were approached by Imperium soldiers who relieved them of their bags and weapons. Sara closed in on a disarmed Luci and took the goggles that were perched upon her head. The Imperium leader donned them and peered around the field. She then took them off, giving them a final inspection before shrugging and tossing them aside.

"But how?" Trig was able to muster in their defeat.

A cloaked figure then emerged from the shadows behind Sara. The person was holding a device that was no longer supposed to exist. It was a compass-shaped mechanism that contained sigils trimming a clock face. The darkened individual was holding an attuner. The figure dropped the hood of their cloak revealing her identity. Wordsmith then spoke, "You really shouldn't trust a Master, Ser Noble." She then looked down at her device, "Or should I say Master Coimín."

***

The soldiers were quick to bind the trio's hands into versions of the Imperium cuffs that had been modified into manacles. Marnie could feel Muse being sucked out of her body at the wrists. She watched as light slowly depleted from Trig and Luci's bodies.

"You do know this is criminal don't you," Trig said, speaking directly to Sara.

"Who's going to stop us?" Sara replied. "You really think anybody's going to miss an orb monger, the last Geddes, or the unknown descendant of the Vagabond Master?"

"With this one," she continued, pointing at Marnie, "even the government constabulary will be powerless to stop us."

"You can't do this," Luci pleaded.

"Gag them and put them in the scramblers," Sara commanded.

"What of the cat, the watcher, and the fool?" Richard asked.

"Leave 'em. We got what we came for. There is nothing any of them can do now," she replied.

The Imperium troopers did as instructed, loading the three into separate scramblers sound-tracked by the writhing yowls of the Razor-Sith.

Marnie, try as she might, was unable to trigger a blowout, something to help them escape their situation. Due either to the manacles on her wrists or lack of command over the Muse, she didn't have it in her.

Having claimed their prize, the Imperium scramblers sped off toward the city.

***

As the Forgotten Master floated in the darkness for an unknowable amount of time, the passing of which had lost all meaning, a light had started to grow around him. The light was accompanied by a warmth he could feel in his chest that radiated out from its origin to all of his extremities. Pulses could be felt as the light traced its way through each of his nerve endings before resting on top of his skin. The sensation he experienced was that of being hugged by an unknowable endless love.

The feeling continued to grow to a level where the Master no longer knew how much more he could take. He experienced a few moments in this state of near nirvana before all at once the light was pulled into his body. The sensations then tapered off, diminishing to a more tolerable level with each beat of his heart.

The Master looked down at his hands, seeing them softly glow in contrast to the darkness of the surrounding corridor. He could once more feel the floor under his feet. He felt restored. The clarity of his thought was once more intact.

He unsheathed his runic sword and it glowed with a light that the walls of the labyrinth were unable to steal.

The Forgotten Master raised the sword above his head, using it to scan his surroundings, hoping he could find the correct waypoint in the wake of his previous trial. He scanned the hallway directly ahead of him before turning around.

Feelings of surprise and excitement welled up inside his body as he was greeted by the giant face of the corridor's final guardian. The Master approached the face, laying his now luminous hand upon its nose.

A red glow radiated out from the Forgotten Master's palm, tracing each individual feather that made up the basis for the door's figurehead. The face that was taking shape wasn't of the Green Men he had been familiar with. He had never seen one that wasn't composed almost entirely of some manner of vegetation. The face was a feminine one, possessing a regal almost godlike beauty. The visage possessed a crown composed of vines and antlers which intertwined with the face to the point that it wasn't clear if the features were one and the same.

The red glow reached the tip of the antlers before the hallmark vibration began and tendrils started to appear from the mouth. The door may not have looked like a typical Green Door but it had these features of one. The Master, thankful to leave the labyrinth, let the vines take him.

***

The Forgotten Master instantly found himself on the other side of the door. He was no longer in the cold unfeeling reality that was the seemingly endless corridor. In the Oraculum, he was greeted by candlelight, emanating from a nearly uncountable number of candles that circled the cavernous room. The chamber was reminiscent of the catacomb bone rooms he had left an unknown number of days prior.

Scanning the room, he could see a library's worth of bookcases, a large table in the center, and a bed to one side. The bookcases and table appeared to be constructed with an ebony wood of unknown origin. The head and footboards for the bed were constructed with the antlers of the various megafauna found in Eternal Dawn. The trompf horns that topped each of the four posts had long since lost their glow.

The most striking feature of the room, however, was that of the giant fireplace off to the left. It measured more than two meters tall and was at least one and a half times as wide. There were two large throne-like leather chairs angled to face it. The one whose angle faced toward him was vacant. Glancing at the one that had its back turned toward him, he could see a delicate arm, clad in a down-lined leather bracer. From the armband dangled various adornments composed of feathers and bone. They appeared to be reliquaries and hung from delicate chains that wrapped around the bracer. They moved hypnotically as he watched the arm they belonged to move upward. The long fingers of the exposed hand moved in a wave suggesting a come hither motion. The soft feminine voice to which the hand belonged beckoned, "Please come...Have a seat...It's been a long time Declan."

Chapter Nineteen
"What hath night to do with sleep?"

David woke up feeling remarkably refreshed. Too refreshed for the four hours that had been allotted to sleep before his turn on watch. He stepped out of the tent and immediately gazed at the sky. "Lonely Sister shouldn't make an appearance for at least another two hours," he thought. But low on the horizon, he could see it starting to cross the path of the large purple moon. The green and blue moon Arthur was peeking out just behind the left side of its primary, Uther.

"Weird, it looks like there will be a convergence in the next day or so," David thought. It was a development he would be excited to see if there weren't more pressing matters needing to be addressed. A lunar alignment hadn't occurred during his past five years in Eternal Dawn.

David, knowing at this point that he had indeed overslept, gazed over to the fire expecting to see Luci and Trig passed out beside it. He had assumed that they had neglected their watch in much the same way Chauncey had. However, he wasn't able to detect the pair. He moved in closer, thinking it may be due to the now-smoldering fire not giving off enough light. Still nothing.

David walked over to the tent Marnie had been sleeping in, hoping that for some unknown reason, the pair had simply forgotten to wake Chauncey and him for watch. He was further alarmed to find the tent empty save for Marnie's pack, which had been left behind.

He scrambled back over to his tent. David grabbed Chauncey by the shoulders and shook him violently to try and awaken him. Chauncey was for all intents and purposes, dead to the world. He shouted at him, "Chauncey...Chauncey! Wake up!" There was still no response save an unconscious murmur of seeming indifference.

David was becoming more frantic and upset. He dragged Chauncey off of his Muse-created cot. Chauncey fell in almost slow motion as David watched his head hit the ground and bounce before settling into the dirt underneath it. This had the rousing effect that David was looking for.

"What...what's happening?" Chauncey asked blearily, feeling a dull pain on the back of his head that would soon blossom into a bruise, one that he would constantly be touching in an attempt to make sure it hadn't disappeared.

"It's Marnie...she's gone!" David replied.

"Did Trig and Luci see where she went?" Chauncey asked, knowing they wouldn't just let her run off alone.

"They're gone too!" David responded.

Chauncey leaped to his feet and exited the tent as if he had been shot out of a cannon. He went over to the tent Marnie had been sleeping in to inspect. He then peered over at the near-dead fire and exclaimed, "Yep, they're gone alright."

"No shit, that's what I just said," David replied, looking at Chauncey in disbelief.

As they stared at each other in a moment of silence, daring the other to speak the next word, a sound echoed across the field that next to their forest camp. They both looked in the direction of the noise and then looked back at each other. Without uttering a word, they agreed on a course of action and darted toward it.

***

David and Chauncey crossed from the forest to the plain, heading in the direction of the pained cries.

They arrived at the location of the sound within minutes, not exhibiting anything close to the same level of caution that Marnie, Trig, and Luci had shown hours before. The pair didn't see signs of their missing party members but did locate the agonized Razor-Sith still writhing on the ground. It was obviously exhausted but still trying to free itself.

"We have to help it," Chauncey said, his empathetic eyes staring at the beast.

"I'm not going anywhere near that thing," David responded. He was only aware of tales of the creature's brutality, causing him to be more than concerned with his own well-being. "I like having a throat, thank you very much."

"Come on, I'll need you to keep it stable while I pull the skewer from the ground," Chauncey replied.

222

"I...I don't know. You're supposed to be some kind of bad idea-guy. How do I know this isn't one of them?" David questioned.

"There is rarely a bad idea in the service of empathy," Chauncey responded.

David stood for a moment considering the words and debating his next course of action. He stared down at the creature who was staring back up at him. Its eyes were locked on him, pleading for his assistance.

The Razor-Sìth yowled once more. Chauncey was convinced that he heard the word 'help' in one of the creature's layers of vocalization.

David could have sworn he heard it too. "Alright," he relented. "What do you need me to do?"

"Just hold it still while I yank on this," Chauncey replied, pointing at the harpoon.

"Hold it still? This thing must weigh at least fourteen stone," David said.

"Just do your best," Chauncey responded. "We need to try and keep the muscle damage to a minimum."

David looked once more at the creature. He could swear it nodded at him as if to say, 'Go ahead'. He then straddled the creature's abdomen facing its hindquarters and grabbed hold of the creature's thigh just below the harpoon, feeling the body writhing beneath him as he did. David then placed his other hand on the other side of the piercing. He gave a glance up to Chauncey and said, "Okay, ready as I'll ever be."

"Okay, one...two-oo...three." Chauncey yanked the shaft in an upward motion as hard and fast as he could. The hold gave free easier than expected causing him to lose balance and fall backward into the surrounding grass.

With raised fur, the Razor-Sìth spewed forth a blood-curdling cry before producing a bright flash of ultraviolet light. The wild glow-wheat that surrounded them illuminated in brilliant colors as a light compression wave cascaded through it, radiating outward from the beast in the center. The light faded out fifty meters away returning the wheat to its diminished post-Dying glow.

The next thing David saw was Chauncey's arm shooting into the air, victoriously holding the harpoon over the grass.

Chauncey moved up onto his knees and worked to remove the bindings on the creature's front and rear paws, allowing it to stand.

The Razor-Sìth took a moment to circle the pair, testing out its damaged leg before coming to a stop in front of them and resting on its hind legs.

"What do you think it wants now?" David asked Chauncey, hoping the answer wouldn't be his throat.

"Excuse me! I have a name," an offended voice said.

David looked at Chauncey who was equally astonished before uttering, "Holy shit, this thing talks?"

"I would thank you to use it," the decidedly male-sounding voice chimed in. "It's Wishbone."

"I..have..so many questions," Chauncey managed to eke out.

"No time for that lad. Imperium took your friends and headed for the city...You best make haste," Wishbone said cutting him off. "I thank you for your assistance but I'm afraid I need to take my leave as well..Important people to see. Important things to do...Best of luck to you. Don't mess this up."

With that, the talking cat started its hobbled walk away. It picked up speed with each step, gradually working into a sprint. The Razor-Sìth's front paws moved as one to pull the mass of its body forward. It drew its injured leg up toward its rear, using only its undamaged hind leg to keep balance as it disappeared back into the darkness.

"Thank you Wishbone!" Chauncey yelled into the darkness, still in astonishment, not sure if the creature could hear him.

There was a flash of light from an ultraviolet ejection. Chauncey took this as acknowledgment as he and David gazed on.

"Oh shit, Marnie!" David said, shamed that he had taken a moment to revel in wonder, momentarily forgetting his cause.

David turned to head back to camp and noticed Luci's goggles on the ground. He picked them up and perched them on his head before returning to the tents with Chauncey.

***

The pair packed up their bags in short order, combining the equipment that Marnie, Trig, and Luci had left behind into a single pack.

"We need to head south," David stated before asking Chauncey, "How fast can you run?"

"You do realize that Ærratum is east right? I mean...I know I'm supposed to be the 'bad idea guy' here but..." Chauncey spoke before being cut off.

"How fast can you run?" David repeated

"I'm fast enough but I don't know what you're getting at," Chauncey replied.

"There is a cyclocycle a little over two hours south of here..if we run," David responded. "It's going to make getting into the city a lot easier."

"Go backward to go forward. Makes sense to me," Chauncey said, not quite sure if the plan made sense but he wanted to seem agreeable. The prospect of riding a cycle appealed to him, precluding the need to argue the point further.

The pair started their labored run down the edge of the tree line, heading for the location where David and Luci had ditched the bike.

***

"I think you have me confused with someone else," the Forgotten Master said as he approached the woman seated by the warm fire. The light from the hearth was straining his eyes, almost blinding him. It wasn't unexpected, having spent so much time in the labyrinth's dark oblivion. He hesitantly took a seat.

"You are the one who travels, are you not?" the woman spoke, her voice having a harmonic resonance, almost as if three voices were speaking in concert. "Surely you have come to finalize your debt. I see you are prepared to deliver."

The Master's eyes strained to focus as they adjusted to the light, allowing him to gaze upon the voice's owner. Before him sat a beautiful young woman. Her left arm had a bracer to match the one that adorned her right. She wore a flowing black dress featuring a metallic bodice. The bodice was, in fact, a blackened steel breastplate, ornately embossed with the feathers of a raven. The skin around her eyes was darkened by a smoky kohl color. The Master was unsure if this was makeup or a facial feature. On top of her long black hair, she wore a headdress featuring the wings of a raven, flanking the sides of a wolf's head. The wings pointed backward, giving her head the appearance of forward motion.

"I traveled to get here if that's what you mean," the Master responded.

"I'm afraid that's not what we mean Declan. Not what we mean at all," she responded.

"Wait, are you referring to Declan Mhurchaidh...the Vagabond?" the Master responded. "I'm sorry to tell you this but he's been dead going on fifteen years."

"Curious," the woman responded.

"You are the oracle, are you not? This is the Oraculum, is it not? This seems like information you would have surely divined," he responded, hoping at this moment that his journey had been worth the pain endured.

"That we are...of sorts. That is to say that we bear witness to the things that have not yet come to pass," she replied. "We have yet to witness the demise of the one you call Vagabond. As for this place, you call it Oraculum?"

"Yes," said the Master, almost asking a question with his response. He could feel himself being led in the conversation.

"We call it prison," the woman's voices responded, their harmonic inflection bordering on scornful. "Did the trials you endured not give you pause to ponder this certainty?"

"Are the trials not the price for knowledge sought?" the Master replied, his unease was building. He hadn't considered the possibility that the labyrinth had served more than the purpose of keeping people out.

"Funny, you said something similar to us on the occasion of our previous encounter," the voices replied.

The Forgotten Master looked around the room for other occupants, only then realizing the woman was speaking in majestic plurals. "Us...we...," he muttered softly.

"Oh don't be so thick Declan. Did you hit your head or something?" the voices once more spoke.

The Master stared at the woman with deep concentration, searching. Pieces had started to connect in his mind. He could feel he was on the verge of revelation.

He remembered the raven feathers that adorned the Green Door through which he had just passed. He looked at the women. The wolf's head, the raven wings, the eye black, the reliquaries, the voices, the prophecy.

The woman met his gaze, watching the gears in his head shift and turn. Seeing that he was on the precipice of realization she whispered, "Go on...Say it."

"The Mórrigan," he whispered to himself. In that moment he felt the rush of epiphany course through him, hugging him, warming him. The dark revelation stood in cold contrast to the warm feelings, tempering the sensation. "It cannot be. She..they rather..are, are a myth."

"Yet here I sit before you," the Mórrigan replied. "You, Declan, were so quick to believe in the possibility of divination. Did you not stop to consider who may be performing the divining?"

The Forgotten Master sat in silence, studying the visage before him. "Could it be? Is she? Am I?" he thought to himself.

The Mórrigan stared back at the Master, performing her own assessment. She spoke once more, "My dear Declan, it is clear that you require further substantiation. Call it intuition but rest assured that your dubiety will be properly sated once we have had occurrence to settle our accord."

The Master continued to stare at his host, unsure how to continue. He hadn't been prepared to meet a god or someone pretending to be.

"Out with it!" she commanded. "I may not receive many visitors...but you are starting to bore me."

"I..I have received fragments of a prophecy in my meditations. I have come to see if the remainder can be retrieved," the Master spoke.

"Meditation...pffff...You have a lot to learn about prophecy," the Mórrigan responded, her tone awash with disdain. "Go on. Tell me of this 'prophecy'."

"Okay, but I preface this by saying it's a bit fuzzy..." the Master spoke before getting cut off.

"Declan! Just spit it out already!" the Mórrigan's voices bellowed. She reveled in the nervousness of the man who sat before her.

The Forgotten Master started, hoping he was remembering everything that had come to him, "A sun rises...once all is lost...the lost will be found...the dark watcher watches...twins unite...an Adept ascends...at heretic falls...dawn's light...it is a fool who forgets...the morning flight."

The Mórrigan looked at the Master, almost mournfully, as she spoke, "Declan. Declan. Declan. What have you done to yourself?"

The Master had been growing increasingly agitated with each use of the fallen Master's name until he finally demanded, "Stop calling me Declan! The Vagabond is dead!"

"Oh, well, you are a Master of note, are you not? Did you go to his funeral? Have you seen his body?" the Mórrigan replied, challenging his assertion.

The Forgotten Master thought on the questions for a moment, considering his answers. "I had never had occasion to meet the Vagabond, it would not have been proper. As for the body..." he responded, cutting himself off as he considered his next line. Had he actually encountered the Vagabond's remains in the corridor or was it a trick of the mind?

It was common belief that the Vagabond Master, Declan Mhurchaidh, had been obliterated and consumed by the Muse, resulting in the Flood; a self-sacrifice in his attempt to force Eternal Dawn's escape from impending darkness.

The Master thought for a moment longer before producing a well-reasoned argument, "If I was the Vagabond, someone would have surely recognized me. He was the most famous of all of us."

"What did this Vagabond Master look like?" the Mórrigan responded, taunting and teasing with each new question.

"Well he uh, he looked like...well most say he looked like a wizard of lore but specifically he looked like...uh..." the Forgotten Master started to speak but the words weren't coming.

"If you are not Declan then what is your true name?" the Mórrigan cut in once more.

"It's uh...my name is..." he continued, trying to grasp at answers that should flow easily but were dammed up in his mind, lost somewhere out of reach.

"Let me tell you a tale," the Mórrigan said, once more interjecting into the lull left by the Master's hesitancy. Her chorus of voices had diminished to one, the warmest of the three becoming the dominant as it started to speak. "It concerns this so-called prophecy for which you have quested so perilously. It is a story of your so-called 'Vagabond'."

"...Declan came to me some time ago, I no longer know when. As you may have experienced, it is a trying feat to track time in this prison...The sculptor came to me seeking a solution to a great peril affecting the world above...or is it below?... So hard to say...But I digress...He wanted to exact a balance, claiming that the world was becoming wicked at the hands of your so-called Masters, specifically those that claim to be acolyte. Curious thing...their so-called tributes and tithes never seem to reach me..." the Mórrigan took a beat to ponder her words.

"...Balance...a way to dilute the Muse from those driven by hubris. But was it not hubris that brought him to me...a man believing himself worthy of parlay with a god..."

"He had an outsized impression of what my capabilities would be to help him in these matters. Like you, he was unaware that this room is no more than a prison. Designed to keep me blind to the world above..."

"...but then how would my prophecy..." the Forgotten Master interjected.

"In due time Declan...in due time..." the Mórrigan replied, watching the Master's face contort as she once more referred to him by his deceased predecessor's name.

"A solution was offered, one that would allow for my sight to reach into the never. For a small taste of Muse, we would gaze into the abyss, unspooling two threads of Fate. Two threads of my choosing, representing two paths to effectuate the ends that he had sought. You may call this prophecy...a vulgar term implying a lack of free will. We offered a choice, it was his to make, let us taste of the Muse and take one of the two paths or leave and find the way on his own."

"...There is something enticing about Fate, it offers a covenant with the future...a guarantee..."

"...And so a covenant was forged. A taste of Muse for a glimpse at that which had not yet come to pass...We watched as the infinite stretched out before us...It was a simple thing to find the threads to which we would offer for pulling...It would be perfidious of me to say that the threads we put on offer weren't self-serving...but they did also serve his purpose....the purpose of balance."

"The first was one of war...a continued war...When your enemies have no more lands to conquer...and the raven has taken flight...call upon the horrors...dampen the ground with the blood of friend, foe, and fiend alike. The acolytes will fall. The count of the dead shall number three of the quick. It is only in total darkness that new light will be born. Kill the old so that the new may live."

"It would be disingenuous of us to say that our interest was not piqued at the prospect of war. You may argue it is unfair to present such a dour option but we ask of you, what are the lives of the millions when measured against history? We offered a chance to start over, to make the world anew, balanced in all things."

"The second thread was not as straightforward...The good ones so rarely are...It would seem that your broken mind has forgotten much of it...But it did hold some meaning for you once upon a time."

"Take the black way to the Fonte of the Inane...Flood the world with its ebony dark...wash away the profane...let the sacred breath without hindrance...allow the son to rise and the cycle to repeat as he is consumed...soon the girl of two worlds will find fellowship...only once all is lost in the deepest of dark will what was forgotten be remembered...a watcher will watch as the lonely twins unite...a heretic will fall at dawn's first light...the Adept will ascend as the fool forgets...a traveler will mourn the prisoner's flight."

"Not as straightforward as the former, indeed," the Forgotten Master said in response. "I am at a loss for what it all means. Perhaps you could shed some light."

"Oh, Declan. Declan. Declan...you misunderstand what you call 'prophecy'. Some of it is not meant to be known until it has come to pass," the Mórrigan responded, continuing to enjoy the furrowing of his brow with each mention of his supposed predecessor's name. "They are all so personal to the one that receives. It is not for us to find the meaning in what is meant for you. In our imprisonment, we are only capable of finding meaning in that which has reference to us. Judging by your presence, there is one thing of which we can be certain...your 'Vagabond' chose the second path."

"Why then, would you send me prophecy destined for another?" the Forgotten Master queried, now ignoring or perhaps no longer hearing the Mórrigan's insistence that he was the fallen Master. His eyes had started to drift toward the fire.

The Mórrigan had become vexed, "Declan...look at me! Have you not listened to a word that has been spoken? This..." she gestured with her arm. "This is a prison! Our sight comes in fragment and our word cannot escape the confines of these walls. The messages you have 'heard' have come from within."

"But...how?" the Master replied.

"Perhaps...for a taste of the Muse...we may show you," the Mórrigan replied, her voice once more becoming soft.

The myths, which for all that he had seen may as well be history, had made it clear that one would be unwise to bargain with the gods, the one that sat to his side foremost of all. It was also clear to the Master that his options had reached their limit. The fate of Eternal Dawn's light may very well rest in what he decided to do next.

The Forgotten Master relented, "What is required of me?"

"Grab our hand and focus your essence as you would when creating a quill pen," she replied.

"Quill pen? You really have been down here a while," he quipped.

"Funny, it seems you have a predilection for repetition. You said this same thing on our last occasion of meeting," the Mórrigan once more taunted.

The Master stood up from his seat and crossed the five steps it took to reach the raven-crowned woman. She reached her hand up toward him as if to offer a regal handshake and he took it into his own. As instructed he focused a portion of his Muse into her hand with the intent of generating the requested quilled pen.

The Master watched as light passed from him to the god seated before him. The pen appeared to be working from the inside, drawing a line up her forearm toward her head and into what he assumed was her brain. "Do gods have brains in the conventional sense?" he pondered for a moment.

"We do indeed Declan," the Mórrigan said, replying to his unspoken words.

The Forgotten Master could feel her rooting around inside his mind. In an effort to sever the link, he tried to withdraw his hand.

The Mórrigan held fast, not allowing the disconnect. "Declan...you have done a number on yourself...Quite foolish...What is this wall?...No matter...Let us see what secrets are held beyond...Oh my...Did you try to outsmart Fate?"

"We see shades of insight. It would appear you saw things you wished you hadn't on our first encounter...A son...A daughter...Forced to weigh their safety against the lives of the millions. You thought you could have the best of both...This is rich..."

"You thought you could stop at the Flood. That the Flood would be all the balance required...You made yourself forget. Forget your son...your daughter...Made them half orphan to protect them..."

"Forget and remove your temptation...Forget your other world...Forget your earthly wife...Forget your Earthly life...Forget everything that made you the 'Vagabond'..."

"You made Eternal Dawn forget. Forget who you were. Forget the method of the Flood...Forget quite a number of other things over the years it would appear..."

"Walled it all up in your mind where even you could not reach...You shouldered that...Created a new lineage...A sixteenth Mastery...One to house the information so dangerous it should remain forgotten...Such hubris Declan...I'd be impressed if it wasn't so stupid...Forgotten Master...what a joke."

The Forgotten Master continued to fix his gaze on the eyes of the Mórrigan. All of the fear that he had felt in the corridors had welled up inside his stomach. He tried once more in vain to withdraw his hand.

"Declan, Declan, Declan, we haven't even gotten to the best part," the Mórrigan replied to his efforts.

"I...I brought her here..." the Forgotten Master responded despondently as his head sank.

"The very thing you tried to prevent. You tried to outsmart Fate," the Mórrigan crowed. "There is no offramp on the road to destiny."

"Why...why...would you provide these paths? Why would you show me this?" the Forgotten Master begged.

"We thought that would be obvious," the Mórrigan replied. "Those were the paths that would guarantee our reascension."

The Mórrigan's choral voice returned as she proceeded to quote the prophecy, withdrawing her hand, "Only once all is lost in the deepest of dark, will what was forgotten be remembered."

"...Say their names and break down your wall."

"...Scot...Marnie...What have I wrought?" Declan Murphy finally spoke.

Chapter Twenty
"...this bitter world where vice is king..."

"So we get on this contraption, head to your 'cursed woods', get guidance from the Forgotten Master then go and rescue Marnie, Trig, Luci, and this mysterious Scot?" Chauncey asked as he admired the cyclocycle, the genuine article, likely created by the Vagabond Master himself.

"Cursed Forest...But yeeeaaaah, that was before. In case you hadn't noticed there is a bit more urgency now," David replied.

"So we're just going to ride up to Imperium spire, go through the front door, and..." Chauncey contested, concerned that he was the one acting as the voice of reason.

"We'll figure it out on the way," David responded, not sure if either Chauncey or he would be capable of forming the coherent list of tasks required to aid an escape.

"The 'no plan' plan..." Chauncey pondered. "Wingin' it...I like it...It could work. All of my classic grifts were off the cuff."

Chauncey didn't let David know that what he considered his 'classic grifts' were the ones fraught with the most danger, having a success rate bordering on ten percent. He and Trig, on more than one occasion, had occasion to occupy a jail cell as the result of his 'classic grifts'.

"Reassuring..." David muttered. "Now help me stand this thing up."

With Chauncey's help, David moved the cycle to the spur of the main Geddes road.

David mounted the bike with Chauncey following suit. He removed an orb from his bandoleer and socketed it into the fuel slot. Then with a conviction he hadn't shown on his first attempt at driving, he accelerated the bike to speeds comparable to that of what its more competent pilot had previously commanded of it.

David had hoped he could make it to the city before anything grievous had befallen Marnie. Marnie, whom he had purposely endangered in the Forgotten Master's ill-conceived plan to save Eternal Dawn.

***

"You know I wouldn't have told him right?" Marnie said.

"Wouldn't have told who what," Trig replied, confused as to what Marnie was referring to in the wake of their current circumstance.

"Chauncey...I wouldn't have told him about you two," Marnie responded.

"Oh lass, I know that, but in case you hadn't noticed we have bigger things to worry about," Trig replied as they stared out of the prison cell that housed the three captives.

They were overlooking the Ebony Wellspring, possibly residing in the very cell that the former Master Wordsmith had occupied. Trig looked up. They could see that the spring was located directly under the atrium of the giant Imperium Spire.

"Your parents really knew how to build prison cells," Trig commented as they turned their attention to Luci.

"Great great grandparents actually," Luci replied. "It was my mother and father who finally managed to fill them all. Not exactly a feat I'm proud of."

"You...you wouldn't happen to know of any secret ways out of here would you?" Marnie chimed in, hoping for a sliver of secret family knowledge.

"Oh, I wish. As kids we were rarely allowed down here, being an active prison and all...and even if I did, there's still the problem of these," Luci responded, displaying the linked Imperium cuffs that bound her wrists. "...Not our innovation by the way."

Marnie looked at both Trig and Luci. The light from their veins had diminished greatly since the attachment of the devices. The cuffs were siphoning off extra Muse in an attempt to lower their threat profile. She looked at her arms, not being able to detect a difference in her levels. "Do you think a blowout might remove them?" she wondered out loud, not sure if she would even be able to conjure one should the need arise.

"I should hardly think so," Luci responded. "These things are mechanical for the most part. Best we could hope for would be to overload the leaching circuits. I'm not sure if that would serve the greater good or not. Best to save your energies."

Trig looked over at Luci with admiration. The words chosen were a paraphrased version of the ones floating around in their mind, "I agree. Let's not be too hasty here lass." They shivered as they looked back down to the Wellspring, "Ugh-h-h-h, I can almost feel the bad ideas flowing through my body, getting sucked into that thing." There was a veil of disgust coating the words as they said them.

Luci took up purchase on Trig's left side, wrapping her arm around them as they peered down at the well. She could feel Trig sink into her side as she said, "Curious. There used to be a menhir overlooking the spring. Must have been destroyed after the war."

Marnie sidled up to Trig's other side and looked out at the prison, scanning and searching the other cells that ringed the cavernous room. She was looking for Scot, trying to get a glimpse of her brother for the first time in half a decade. In the faded light of the cavern, she could barely make out the cell bars lining the wall, let alone any inhabitants that may be occupying the cells themself. She had hoped that Scot would be alight like she was, allowing for his visage to be seen. She also considered the possibility that he was in one of the cells directly above or below, or that he hadn't been kept in the prison.

"I wonder where he could be," Marnie finally voiced.

"No telling in a place like this but don't worry..." Trig started.

"Someone's coming," Luci interjected before Trig could finish. "Let's keep our motives to ourselves, yeah?"

Trig and Marnie nodded in agreement. The less Imperium knew the better.

A quiet blanketed the cell as Trig crossed ten feet from the back wall to the door. They pressed the side of their face against the bars in an attempt to get a glimpse of who may be approaching. Due to the curved nature of the cramped room, Trig couldn't see who was coming but was able to determine by the conversation that it was Imperium commander Sara and Wordsmith. They were followed by two additional Imperium soldiers

"Traitor," Trig hissed at the sight of the former Master.

Wordsmith opened the notebook she was holding and seemed to scan what had appeared to be minutes from their previous encounter at the library. "Looks like I missed taking the note where I pledged allegiance to you," Wordsmith said.

"Were you not an ally of the Vagabond? Did you not say that she was a Vagabond?" Trig rebutted, pointing at Marnie.

"I don't know if you've heard but the Vagabond is dead. As for this thing, she has the stink of the traveler on her but I can't say for certain what she is...Still, I don't need the attuner to see that she was the one responsible for the blowout," Wordsmith replied.

"Are you sure?" Sara questioned.

"You are seeing the same thing I am, aren't you? The cuffs have barely bled her," Wordsmith replied.

"I'm not paid to do this science shit," Sara responded. Had Wordsmith been one of her soldiers, she would have punched her in the stomach for the less-than-direct answer. "You are sure? Right?"

"Yes I'm sure," Wordsmith answered.

"Take her upstairs," Sara commanded.

As the soldiers approached the cell, Trig whispered to Marnie, "We'll figure this out. Save your energy if you can and pick your moment."

"We'll come find you," Luci offered, an echo of Trig's reassurance.

The pair watched as the soldiers unlocked the door and led Marnie away. She was visibly anxious but was managing to hold it together.

Sara looked at them with scorn before spitting on the ground at their feet. She then locked the door behind her. "You coming?" she asked Wordsmith.

"I'll be just behind," she replied.

***

Wordsmith watched Sara and her goons abscond with the anomalous girl before once more approaching the cell.

"Curious...A Geddes and a Coimín on the same side?" she questioned.

"We are not our parents," Luci said defiantly.

"My fathers would be very disappointed in you," Trig said.

"Your fathers barely knew me," Wordsmith responded. "Much too busy with politics and appearances to consort with a 'lesser' Master."

"Why did you do it? What did you stand to gain?" Trig questioned, seeing that the shame play was getting them nowhere.

"The Vagabond never asked..." Wordsmith responded "He acted unilaterally without consent. The Flood took everything from me."

"The Flood ended the war," Luci said.

"But is anything really better? Look around. We are in the exact same place we were," Wordsmith replied.

"They are not just going to give your powers back," Trig reasoned.

Wordsmith considered the statement for a moment before responding, "We have not been playing the same game, my friend."

Luci and Trig looked at each other, trying to parse meaning from the cryptic statement. Trig's eyes moved towards the former Master as a reply took form in their head, only to find that she had already taken her leave.

***

Declan Murphy's head was awash with returning thought as he dipped in and out of his state of confusion. Old pathways that hadn't seen fire in well over a decade had started to ignite. He felt the occasional warm ebbs and flows of epiphany as everything he had given up was reintegrated into his consciousness. The pleasant feelings from the re-revelation overload collided with the shame and anxiety he was feeling at the thought of endangering his children. The flood of old thoughts lasted less than a minute. At the end he sat in the throne-like chair across from the goddess with feelings of contempt, feelings pointed at her but also at himself.

The Mórrigan stared, pleased, at the Master for a minute before offering, "It's a curious thing, Fate...Once you take that first step, there are an infinite number of paths to the one immutable eventuality. You really could have saved yourself a lot of agony had you just surrendered to it, to begin with."

"Why are you doing this witch?" the Master said. His words were no longer that of the Forgotten.

"Ahh there's the Declan I know," the Mórrigan replied. "God of witches actually but we'll let it lie. We told you...Ascension...Freedom. As we speak, the world is ripening for our return. Not even we could have foreseen the willful eagerness to give up the light. My acolytes had to steal it the first time around."

Declan was struck with a thought, "But how could you know..."

"We said that we don't get many visitors, not that we don't get any visitors," the Mórrigan responded. "You really should pay more attention."

***

Imperium Commander Sara led Marnie into the Imperium Spire. They started to walk the helix pathway that ringed the building's atrium, ascending toward the upper floors.

Imperium Spire stood in stark contrast to the surrounding city. Its concrete and steel construction, along with its glass facade, caused it to clash with the organic appearance of the neighboring tree-born buildings. Imperium tried to mask the garishness with green spaces on each of its balconies and roofs but they were executed to poor effect.

"You really could have done better than to fall in with that worm," Sara jabbed, referring to David.

"He was more than a match for you," Marnie responded scornfully. She glanced down through the atrium in an attempt to get a glimpse of the cell Trig and Luci were still in. Unfortunately, the base of the atrium featured a parabolic lens that distorted her view of what was underneath.

"He was flanked by three Masters," Sara shot back, the tone of her voice trying to mask her bruised ego. She ignored the fact that David had taken out what had remained of her battalion single-handedly. "If there is a next time he won't be so lucky."

As they circled each of the rings, Marnie tried to glance into each of the open doors she passed, searching for a sign of Scot. She reached the top floor, coming up empty after losing a little bit of hope with each level they climbed.

***

"Wordsmith?" Declan questioned. He had never given that particular Master much credit. "She wouldn't have the fortitude to make the journey...She is the logical choice though. If anyone had the knowledge to reverse engineer the attuners and make those cuffs, it would be her."

"There's my Declan, always choosing who to free and who to blame," the Mórrigan replied.

"Let's not act like we are so familiar shall we," Declan said. This had only been his second visit to the Oraculum, hardly enough time to be on a first-name basis.

"Oh but don't you see..." the Mórrigan responded, "...oh right, of course, you don't. You, Declan, are ever so tightly weaved into the tapestry of our Fate. Quite the enigma. We are more intimately acquainted than you could possibly conceive. It is you who has given us the greatest of tribute. Millennia we have waited to take flight from this, our oubliette. And it is you...you Declan that has given us the final piece we needed. We have seen this to be true."

"Oubliette?" Declan spoke softly. His gaze drifted skyward for the first time. What he had seen was the last thing he was expecting. A pool of blackness undulated above him. Declan Murphy was staring at the underside of the Ebony Wellspring.

***

Sara led Marnie through the door blocking the entrance to the fiftieth floor of the spire. Upon entering the room, Marnie was struck by its architecture. The space was cavernous, containing no dividing walls. There was a large glass dome that enclosed the floor, allowing for a panoramic view of the surrounding city of Ærratum, as well as the forests and plains that surrounded it.

Near the ramped entrance to the room sat a giant desk constructed of purpleheart which had been coated with an earthen patina. Pulsing violet light escaped the finish in places where the patina had worn thin or had been otherwise scratched or dented. On the desk, Marnie could see the bandoleer of Muse orbs that Luci had been wearing, to the side of it sat her collapsible bow. The desk also contained what appeared to be a map charting rings with varying distances from the spire marked with dates. The map looked almost topographical. She correctly surmised that Imperium was charting Muse depletion over time.

On the other side of the room, there appeared to be a lounge area with some couches, rugs, and displays of objects, almost like trophies. There was a bed and kitchen area further behind the lounge area, an odd addition for an office building, Marnie thought.

Marnie continued to survey the room. On the other side of the atrium, there was an array of giant eight-foot-tall bulbs, reminiscent of old vacuum tubes, the type used in radios before the advent of the transistor. Toward the base of many of the tubes, there was a soft glow that looked to act similar to a pilot light in a stove. They glowed with various intensities in hues of blue, violet, red, green, and yellow. The tubes were surrounded by Imperium scientists taking measurements and making notes.

She visually traced the conduit back from the tubes toward the center of the room. Marnie's eyes scanned over the atrium which terminated at the room's floor. There was a glass banister marking its edge. The railing was interrupted at two points around its circumference by short staircases. Each set of stairs led up to a rotational mechanism that had a dark onyx slab suspended between them.

The slab was perched two meters overhead and was polished to a mirror finish. It was roughly the size of the Umphraidh Menhir which Marnie had used to traverse the void to Eternal Dawn. On the underside of the detached monolith, Marnie could detect the appearance of facial features.

"Another Green Door," she muttered to herself.

"What's that girl?" Sara barked, assuming Marnie was speaking to her.

"Nothing," Marnie replied as she continued to study the slab. The face was unlike the others she had seen, in stone, graffiti, and sketch alike. It was that of a man's face possessing long flowing hair and a long beard. The face was cherubic in nature and was making a blowing or sucking expression with its lips.

"Rotate the platform!" a voice echoed across the room, emanating from where the Imperium scientists were studying the tubes.

Marnie watched as a man across the atrium started to turn a giant wheel similar to one that would have been seen on a pirate ship. She watched as the onyx slab started to rotate along what would have been its vertical axis. The Green Man's face seemed to glance at her as it moved upward to face the ceiling.

What Marnie saw next made her heart sink. On the opposing side of the slab was a shirtless figure, lashed to the menhir at various points of his body. The figure appeared frail, almost emaciated, and didn't move. She studied the man, moving closer to the railing to get a better look.

"No, no, no...It can't be," she said as she reached the edge of the atrium. Upside down, the man's hair had obscured many of his facial features but she could still make out her brother's nose and mouth. "Scot...Scot!" she screamed, trying to attract his attention.

***

"It is a curious thing...After your so-called Flood, people received their own share of the Muse that had been so greedily hoarded by your so-called Masters. The power of self-determination...The power of creation. So eager to give it up...So eager to shirk the responsibility. For what?" the Mórrigan once more taunted as she continued to monologue, "...Instant gratification and a small jolt of endorphins...epiphany...Not even we could have foreseen this. Had the world at their fingertips and let it slip. Humans...never cease to amaze. Such a clever inventor, the other visitor."

"Do you have a point godwitch?" Declan replied. He had started to grow weary of the Mórrigan's harpings.

"Are we boring you Declan?" the Mórrigan responded. "Oh, I suppose you can have the floor. You were the architect, this is as much your ceilidh as mine."

***

As Marnie stared up at her brother, who had seemingly not heard her, she could see Muse light creep in through a hole at the top of the dome. To her, it looked like a picture of the aurora borealis. She had had more than one occasion to reference them as part of color studies for her graffiti.

The spire was acting as an antenna for the Imperium cuffs, pulling in the spent Muse and trapping it. Muse light swirled around the area above the atrium, creating a funnel that reached down toward the horizontal menhir.

Marnie watched as the light created a tighter and tighter cone. The light reached a luminosity that momentarily caused her eyes to squint, forcing them to adjust.

In less than a minute, the funnel kissed the lips of the skyward-facing Green Man. With the Muse connection made, the door activated, pouring light out from previously unseen cracks. It sprouted the telltale tentacle-like vines as it sucked Muse in through its mouth. The tentacles reached around the back of the slab toward Scot, reaching but unable to grab him. The whirring hum of the door had grown to an almost deafening roar. The menhir's vibrations were cushioned by shock absorbers in the rotational mechanisms.

As the door activated, the vacuum tubes attached to the stone started to glow with a bright intensity. Marnie reached up to her ears in an attempt to block out some of the sound but it stopped as soon as her hands reached them.

From her perspective everything appeared to be frozen in time, the funnel, the doorway, the tubes, the scientists, Scot. She glanced over to Sara to see her transfixed by the procedure. Marnie then glanced back to her brother just as all of the Muse was pulled from the tubes and transferred into his body.

Scot let out a yell of agony as the light in his body grew to a level that Marnie hadn't seen since just before she caused the blowout. Then just when she thought her brother couldn't get any brighter, the Muse light shot out of his body forming a singular beam, flowing into the Ebony Wellspring more than fifty stories below.

***

"What is that?" Declan questioned, breaking the silence he had earned as a reprieve from the Mórrigan's ruminations. A glow that shouldn't be possible was penetrating the Wellspring oubliette above.

"That, my dear Declan, is the means of our reascension," the Mórrigan replied. "As we speak, your son is channeling concentrated Muse directly into the doorway above. It won't be long now. We must thank you again for setting this into motion. How does it feel to have a front-row seat to your final balance? *Allow the son to rise and the cycle repeat as he is consumed.*"

***

Marnie watched despondently as the beam diminished along with Scot's glow. She expected him to be writhing in anguish but there were no such indications. Instead, his eyes were rolled back in his head and he was smiling and laughing uncontrollably. His body's undulations weren't that of pain. The platform started its rotation to force the Green Man to stare into the dark abyss below.

Sara led Marnie over to the lounge area and beckoned her to have a seat. She made no movement toward removing the cuffs that still bound Marnie's wrists.

Marnie continued watching as Scot was freed from the platform and was cloaked with a robe. She watched as Wordsmith led him over to the kitchen area. Scot grabbed a bottle of what could only be assumed to be an ale or cider and was led over to the lounge area to have a seat.

Scot's eyes hadn't yet had an opportunity to meet his sister's as he was still recovering from his ordeal. He sat hunched over, staring at the floor between his knees.

Marnie took the first opportunity to speak and with a concerned tone asked, "Scot...Scot...what have they done to you?"

Scot took a sip of his beer letting the words sink in. A feeling of recognition cascaded through his brain as his eyes started their long scan upward. For the first time in five years, he spoke to his sister, "Marnie...is it really you? What are you doing here?"

A tingling feeling coursed through his already raw nerves as he was struck with the sudden realization that he was truly staring at his sister, and not just imagining it. "Nothing quite beats the real thing," he thought, as epiphany's warm hug once more surrounded him.

***

"Why my son? Why my daughter?" Declan appealed, already dreading the answer.

"Children of two worlds," the Mórrigan responded. "Conduits able to push and pull Muse across the void. They are not one of your so-called Masters, Declan. You have created something very novel indeed. We would sit in fear if they had any idea of the true power they possess."

"This cannae be happening..." Declan stated, longing to wake up from the new madness he found himself in. He was gladly willing to return to the corridors that had fractured his mind if it would absolve his children of the peril his hubris had wrought.

"Oh but I'm afraid it is Declan," the Mórrigan replied. "This is not an occasion to mourn…This is an occasion to celebrate. You are finally getting what you wanted. True balance. The Vagabond, so intent on avoiding war…ending war. Your true arrogance Declan was in trying to bring order to entropy. Look where your quest has brought you."

"But entropy is not balance," the Vagabond protested.

"Oh Declan, you greatly misunderstand. Entropy is the only balance. Chaos is the natural order by which all things are equal. War is balance, Declan. War is what we offer," she stated.

The Master stared at the Mórrigan. It was clear that she was getting perverse pleasure from her victory, reveling in his self-pity.

"Now you may have intuited that bringing the girl child here was the worst of your woes. But I say this to you again, we have yet to reach the best part. Declan you have one more wall that must fall," the Mórrigan again taunted.

The Vagabond pondered this statement for a moment, "If not Marnie then what?"

***

"Scot…what have they done to you?" Marnie asked once more mournfully, as she watched the epiphany rush wear off.

"Scot, you know this person?" Sara asked, having picked up on the relationship they shared.

"She's his sister," Wordsmith interjected. "Wasn't it obvious?"

Marnie watched as the gears in Sara's head turned. She picked up on the soldier's small rush of epiphany as the connection was made, a feeling that was quickly tempered by the perceived slight in Wordsmith's question.

"Can you give us a moment?" Scot asked of the two women.

To Marnie's surprise, they obliged and wandered off back toward the tubes.

"Marnie, it's been too long. How's mother?" Scot asked as if he were reconnecting with an old friend.

"Scot, it's been five years," she replied as she watched his reaction remain unchanged.

"Still working on your art I hope," he responded, taking another sip of his beer.

"That's not important right now," Marnie said, before once more asking, "What have they done to you?"

"I don't know what you mean," Scot replied, genuinely appearing perplexed by the question.

"I've come to get you out of here....to take you home," Marnie replied.

"Why would I want to leave?" Scot asked, surprised. "I've got everything I want right here. I mean the ideas flow so easily I don't even have to work to think of them."

"Scot...they're not your ideas," Marnie continued, trying to reason with him.

"They sure feel like they are," he replied. "In the end that's really all that matters, isn't it."

"I don't know to what end but they are using you Scot. We have to get out of here. We have to go home. We have to go back to Mom," Marnie insisted.

"Dear sister...look around...I am home," Scot responded.

With that, Marnie once more scanned her surroundings. The couches, the kitchen, the butcher block table, they were all there. Putting the furniture into context started to heighten her anxiety. Marnie and Scot were sitting in a facsimile of Scot's loft. The only things missing were the walls.

"Imperium is evil, Scot. They are going to use you up. Then what will be left?" she once more pleaded with her brother. "Help me get these cuffs off. Let's get out of here."

"Imperium is not evil, dear sister. I've never been happier," Scot said, once more defending the company.

"Just look at what they've done to you. Look at your body. You're a ghost," she replied, still trying to reach him.

"Done to me?" Scot replied rhetorically. He was becoming visibly agitated. "Done to me?... What have they done to me? Marnie, I did this to myself. Look around dear sister. Look at this world. Do you think any of this could have existed before my arrival?"

The anxiety in Marnie's stomach continued to grow as she listened to the man who sat before her. This man barely resembled the brother she had seen get sucked into a wall five years prior. It was the anxiety she had felt in the years since...every time she woke up screaming in the middle of the night having been attacked by the vines...every time she forced herself to work in a dark alley to keep some part of his memory alive...every time she had to find her own way in the world because her brother wasn't there to show her. It was the anxiety she felt upon learning of her father's passing.

Scot then finished his statement, staring at her unnervingly, "Marnie, just look around. I am Imperium."

At the sound of the words Marnie at once felt her body getting ready to produce another blinding flash. She closed her eyes in anticipation and waited for the Muse to jettison her body.

***

Declan could once more feel a pull in his chest, guiding him toward that which he sought. "What could be worse than the realization that I unknowingly put my child in harm's way."

"Declan, you are so close," the Mórrigan replied, seemingly reading his thoughts once more.

At that moment an idea struck him, one that he almost dared not to speak. "I knowingly put my son in harm's way," he said, dropping his head to stare at his upturned palms as if to say, "What have these hands wrought?"

"Yes Declan, very good," the Mórrigan responded. "You couldn't just peel away the Masteries without having a vessel to house that which you had stolen. Hard to imagine all of that power locked safely away on your 'Earth', trapped in a boy with no more than thirteen years behind him."

"You know, we could feel his presence the first time he passed through the never. And why wouldn't we, the power was ours to begin with. The power of a god once divided, brought into the one. Did you know this Declan? Did you know where your powers came from before you consolidated them from the fifteen? Surely not we would guess."

"It is no worry...They will be ours again soon...When we take flight from this prison and consume the son. If it is any consolation we left his wall up. He doesn't know what you did," the Mórrigan concluded.

Declan's eyes flashed with an anger that had been replacing his sorrow as he digested the godwitch's words. "What do you mean you left his wall up? You mean..."

"You didn't think Wormsmith was the other traveler of which we spoke? They have had occasion to visit but we can only tolerate so much groveling. How impotent she is without her full power."

"It is your son, Declan, your son who you have been up against these past years. He is Imperium. He is the architect of Eternal Dawn's plight. But do not fret. You will have your balance...as soon as he breaks through the black door. You have delivered the last piece of the puzzle he was not aware he required. A drop of essence from the lonely sister. Unadulterated essence of the traveler. From one who had not been stripped, one who was spared corruption on their passage through the void."

***

Marnie could detect the bright flash of light through her closed eyelids. Once it had subsided into blackness she hesitantly opened them to see the damage her blowout had created. To her surprise, the light levels in the surrounding area had remained unaffected, if not slightly brighter. She turned her head to peer out the window, noting that Ærratum had also remained unchanged.

"Whoa," Scot said at the sight of the event. He watched as her light grew to a powerful intensity before it diminished. The cuffs served to temper the blowout, leaking out a concentrated stream of Muse which lingered in the air.

Scot stood up and waded through the cloud, experiencing jolts of epiphany as the essence made contact with his skin and the inner parts of his lungs. He was once more astonished by seeing how quickly Marnie's light was regenerating despite the cuffs. She had the benefit of not having her body be continuously overloaded with Muse.

"We could really use someone like you," Scot said after taking in everything that Marnie's body had done.

***

"Oh don't worry Declan," the Mórrigan started. "It wasn't your abandonment causing him to act out. Truth be told we're not sure how much of your son is left at this point...At least on the surface. He was a beacon in the void, allowing darkness to leach in. There isn't a mortal, living or dead, with the capability to defy the rigors our essence would place on a mind when combined with corruption. He is driven solely by a need to return our power, to make us whole. And you get to see it all come to pass. The sister moon should be making its pass any time now, bringing an end to your so-called prophecy."

"What does the moon have to do with it," Declan thought. "...a watcher will watch as the lonely twins unite."

"Nothing Declan," the Mórrigan replied. "It is simply a timestamp for destiny. You are not required to perform three levels of dissection on every little detail."

"I need to get out of here," Declan spoke, figuring it was useless to attempt to hide his thoughts. He wasn't sure if the Mórrigan was actually in his head or was intuiting his thoughts. He knew it didn't matter either way.

***

"Scot we have to get out of here," Marnie implored, her desperation growing.

"You are starting to sound like a broken record dear sister," the husk of Scot replied.

"Sara!" he called across the room. "Can you see Marnie here to the platform? We are going to break through tonight."

At once Marnie thought back to David's skillful avoidance in discussing Scot. "Had he known all along?" she thought. "Did he think I wouldn't find out?"

Chapter Twenty-One
"How did I escape? With difficulty."

David and Chauncey continued their high-speed race toward Ærratum. Chauncey's robes fluttered in the bike's wash as the Green Man figurehead stretched a beam of light onto the road ahead. Both riders were independently struggling to come up with even the most basic of rescue plans. The wind rushing by their ears prevented lengthy discourse.

David was worried they wouldn't be ready when the time came but nonetheless kept the throttle at its limit. It would be ten more minutes before they would catch sight of the gate at the city's limit. He hoped the fate of their rescue effort wouldn't rest solely on one of Chauncey's 'classic grifts'.

Chauncey, while feeling for his friends' lives, still couldn't get over the adventure he was wrapped up in. The high-stakes nature of the mission they were embarking on gave him a thrill that far surpassed anything he had experienced in his nearly thirty years of life. The city lights were just popping back up on the horizon, softened by the glow of the eternal dawn behind them. The thief was excited to see what destiny had in store.

****

"There is no use, Declan. We are in a prison, remember?" the Mórrigan continued her taunting. "Best thing you can do is sit back down and enjoy the anticipation. We are on the verge of your balance. You have won Declan. Enjoy the spoils."

"You call this winning?" the Master retorted, his voice reflecting the state of his tortured mind. He studied the room, hopelessly searching for anything that the godwitch may have overlooked in the eon she had been trapped there.

"Do you not think that if there was a way out we would have happened upon it by now," the Mórrigan stated before imploring, "Just have a seat and wallow in the inevitable."

In truth, the Mórrigan had considered one possible exit that Declan could use. It was one she couldn't. A simple answer, the way in which he entered. In Declan's restored state, she knew it would only be a matter of time before he figured it out. Due to her hubris, she had taken a risk in helping him drop the last wall in his mind, knowing a unified Declan Mhurchaidh would allow her to relish in the victory that much more. She figured if she could distract him long enough it wouldn't matter.

Declan considered the notion that Scot and Wordsmith had to be able to get in and out and started to think that the Mórrigan may be protesting too much. "What's the matter Morgan, worried I may figure out something you have not?" he said, doing his own taunting.

The Mórrigan's fears proved correct. Declan's eyes drew themselves upon the very door that had disgorged him. He crossed back across the room to perform an inspection of the figurehead.

***

David took the ramp onto the main artery of the Geddes road. He had half expected that he and Chauncey would be waylaid by the constabulary or Imperium shock troops but there was no sign of them. "They have what they came for," he thought, slightly insulted that he hadn't been judged to be of a level of risk requiring further mitigation.

"Half 'spected to meet some friction on our entry into the lion's den," Chauncey shouted over the rushing wind, echoing the thoughts in David's mind. "Element of surprise, my stock and trade. Need a place to think."

"I know a place," David replied, thankful that Chauncey had acknowledged the need for a scheme better than the 'no plan' plan.

David continued to race the bike toward the city taking the last exit before its gates to take the southern loop. He thought he caught sight of the city's constables catching sight of him. Nobody gave chase, not that they'd be able to catch up to them if they had.

They dumped the bike in some bushes just south of the eastern gate, donned the hoods of their robes, and made their way through the slums to break into Luci's apartment.

***

"What do you think they want with her?" Luci asked Trig, not expecting an answer.

"Your guess is as good as mine," Trig replied. "But we've seen what they can do with just the one. Now that they have both, there's no telling."

"And David...Chauncey, you think they'll come for us?" Luci continued her questioning.

"'Ken they'll try," stated Trig. "Can't say I'm holding much hope though. Not too sure about David but between you and me, Chauncey's not been much for makin' plans. Probably end up getting himself caught or killed. The heart and will are always where they need to be, even if his behavior is irksome more often than nae."

"You really do care for him don't you?" Luci responded to the rare compliment.

Trig glanced at the floor in contemplation before offering, "He's been there for me through all my faults...Put up with more of my shite than anyone ever should'a. He ne'er deserved any of it and I ne'er deserved him. Tell myself I'm so harsh to protect him...Protect him like I couldn't my own blood kin. Truly a brot'er to me. Ne'er told him...and now...now I don't know if I e'er will." Trig's eyes remained fixed on the stone at their feet. Tears had begun to flow as they mourned all the times they hadn't shown proper deference to their traveling companion.

Luci closed the gap between them and proceeded to wrap her arms around Trig, bringing them in for comfort. Nobody had ever felt comfortable enough to be as vulnerable around her. It was a feeling that was reciprocated in kind. "If anyone were able to keep me in Eternal Dawn, it might have been you," she thought out loud, only realizing she had spoken the words as they passed her lips.

"You still plan on leaving?" Trig questioned, knowing it was too soon to call what was between them a relationship. The strange new feelings they had were, however, something they wished they had more time to explore.

"Assuming we ever get out of here alive and the girl remains intact, yes...," she replied, realizing at that moment, that her mission may have already reached its failed end. "...Still plenty o' people that want to burn the heretic as it were. Can't very well snog them all into submission now can I...You...you could come with me," Luci continued before adding, "...and Chauncey of course."

Trig thought on the prospect of starting over in a new world before speaking, "I'm...I'm not sure if I can...I mean I...I can't...What of Ærratum? What of Eternal Dawn? Someone is going to need to atone for the sins of our fathers and I don't mean that as hyperbole. Literally our fathers. Stay...show them you aren't like them...show them they need not fear you...please."

Luci drew Trig back in and gripped them tight.

***

"They'd like to get their hands on you right?" Chauncey offered. "What if we put these cuffs on you and turn you in? I'd be like a bounty hunter turning you in and when they least expected it, bam boom pow, you attack."

David and Chauncey had forced entry into Luci's apartment and found themselves in her kitchen. They were hovering over the map of Ærratum's subterranea and the few books Luci possessed containing depictions of the old citadel. The books were opened to the page describing its prison and the wellspring at the center.

"Like in 'Returns'?" David asked.

"What's that?" Chauncey quickly replied, not knowing what a 'Returns' was.

"Ohh...right, never mind," David responded. "Not a horrible idea, except we don't know if they actually want me anymore. I mean they just left us there after grabbing the girls and Trig and nobody gave chase when we entered the city."

"Or they knew we'd give them too much of a fight," Chauncey replied.

"What exactly did you do on our last encounter again?" David questioned.

"Point taken," said Chauncey. "Counterpoint...maybe that scares them even more."

David paused for a second, pretending to consider the notion before replying, "Sure...ah...okay...but maybe we table that idea and come back to it."

"How about if we find a big box, postmark it to this Sara, hire a half-light messenger to deliver it, and then we get inside," Chauncey replied. "It gets delivered, then out we pop. Boom pow."

David bit his lip once more, "Maybe I can take a crack at this."

"Right then, Trig never goes for the box plan either. Would we have to do murder? I don't know if I could do murder," Chauncey responded, eager to see what his new cohort had to say.

"If you look here, there's a connection between the city's waterway and the prison's private cistern," David started, ignoring Chauncey's murder comment. "I think I can make the swim."

"Wordsmith brought it up as a possible avenue back in Drumlocke," Chauncey replied, "But Trig shot it down. Said the distance was too far."

"Wait..." A mortified pallor had started to creep across David's face. "You talked to Wordsmith?"

"Yeah at the library. Didn't you talk to her too?" Chauncey responded.

"We didn't get past the receptionist. We saw your aliases in the guest book and took off," David replied.

"Well, then you talked to her. The receptionist was Wordsmith. Odd lass really. Stickler for procedure," Chauncey said.

"Oh no...no no no no," David fretted. He had become visibly flustered, having not been aware that Wordsmith had been operating in Drumlocke.

"What? What's wrong?" Chauncey questioned, not sure what the fuss was about.

"Tell me everything you guys did and said," David insisted. "Leave out nothing."

"Well, we discussed ways to track a Master. There was some palaver about breaking into the citadel. Your underwater entryway was mentioned and shot down. I helped duplicate this very map you see before you," Chauncey responded before being cut off by David.

"The map, how was it duplicated?" David demanded.

"Well...we had the original laid out on the table," Chauncey began, "Then Wordsmith grabbed a sheet of parchment and laid it on top. Then she said and I'm paraphrasing, 'I need a novelty for trade'. That's when I stepped in and gave her some freshies. I said salmon sorbet. She didn't seem to like that one, you know I don't know why. That's really one of my best..."

"Keep going!" David insisted.

"Sheesh okay, you said leave nothing out. Well, my next idea was reverse suspenders. You ever have your shirt ride up when you are out running or..." Chauncey started in again.

"We really don't have time for this," David said.

"Oh okay, well it's a really good idea but if you insist. The one that did the trick may be my masterpiece. Get this, the pickle pocket," Chauncey said, once more sounding like he was going to launch into a protracted explanation.

"What was Marnie doing while all this was happening," David interrupted.

"Well she was just resting her hands on the table," Chauncey replied.

"Oh no, they know," David said.

"Who knows what?" Chauncey responded.

"Don't you see? It was Marnie. Marnie created the copy. Wordsmith would have figured it out. They'd know who she is. What she is," David said as he crossed the room, throwing open the doors to Luci's arsenal.

"Holy shite," Chauncey said at the sight of the weapons cache. He then followed up on David's statements, "I don't get the big deal, so Wordsmith knows that Marnie has command of the Muse. So what?"

"The Cloister has had suspicions that Wordsmith was...is...rather, working with Imperium. Launched an inquiry but couldn't find anything," David replied. He grabbed a set of collapsible batons and clipped them to his belt at the small of his back. "Must have been true. Only explanation about how they found us so quick. After I left Imperium, I still had some contacts on the inside. From what I've been told they usually have a cooling-off protocol for anyone they kidnap. A protection measure so that nothing happens to Scot. I was counting on this to buy us a little time but if they know...well..." David's words sat in the air for a moment before he questioned, "You any good with weapons?"

"Sorry laddio. Mark of a good thief. Don't have much need for violence. 'specially with how fast I can run...Wait, do we have a plan?" Chauncey replied.

"Don't have time to think. We'll have to go with the bounty hunter one," David said.

"We are going to do a 'returns'? Go in through the front door?" Chauncey asked excitedly, hoping he was using the new terminology correctly.

"Yeah we are going to do a 'returns' and you are going to need to look the part," David replied as he threw Chauncey a respirator and goggles to obscure his face, a bandoleer holding a range of throwing knives, and a long staff.

"This stuff really isn't my style," Chauncey said as he inspected the gear. "Anything with a little more class?"

"Are you serious right now?" David replied, watching a level of disappointment creep across Chauncey's face. "You still have those cuffs you stole?"

"You mean these cuffs?" Chauncey replied, producing the bangles.

"Yeah. Give me two of those," David said as he explained their use to the plan. "The handcuff versions of these are the same thing as the consumer versions, just programmed differently. And a little-known secret...They don't work on me."

Chauncey tossed two of the devices over to David who promptly took a knife from the armory and pried their back covers open. David then used a knife to flip a couple of dip switches, making the devices behave as if they were detention models. He removed the bandoleer he had grown accustomed to and put it into the pack containing the items that were left behind in the wake of the kidnapping. He attached the cuffs and tested their Muse magnetism. They snapped together as they would when used on a supposed perpetrator. David tested their hold, easily pulling them apart due to his body's strange Muse behavior. He then had Chauncey put on the third cuff to finalize his look.

Chauncey felt the immediate rush of epiphany as a first-time user being coded into the device. He at once understood the attraction, wondering if the feeling was what Trig had felt every time they came up with one of their great ideas. "This is a dangerous feeling," he said, echoing his thoughts.

"Don't get used to it. If we succeed, it's all going away...for good," David responded.

The duo then exited the apartment with a heading of Imperium Spire.

***

"You are wasting your time Declan," the Mórrigan said as she watched the Vagabond Master inspect the doorway.

"Shut up witch," he replied, as he studied the Green Man's facial features. "Something's missing," he thought to himself, not quite being able to put his finger on it.

"Do you not think that if that door was functional we would have used it eons ago?" the Mórrigan once more spoke.

"With what power, pray tell?" Declan taunted. "All you have left is the sight and you needed me to help you activate it."

He reached for the door in an attempt to bring the Green Man to life. The door remained dormant, without so much as a light rumble. "Worth a shot," he thought as he continued his inspection. "There's something missing...I know it," he mumbled to himself as he stared into the doorway's eyes. "That's it," he thought. "The eyes, they're blank." Upon closer inspection, Declan could see light smudges of blackness in the area surrounding them, presumably from sigils that had been erased either by the Mórrigan or the doorway itself.

Declan then began to hunt around the room for an implement to create new sigils. He grabbed a plume off of the Mórrigan desk but it wouldn't write on the Green Man's stone face. He attempted to snuff out one of the thousands of candles in the room but their lights appeared to be no more than a Muse generated illusion. He didn't have time to go into the obvious question of who created them, knowing the Mórrigan would have lacked the capability.

"Looking for something?" the Mórrigan queried, knowing full well that the room didn't possess implements capable of making delicate and legible marks required to activate the doorway.

"Scared Morgan?" Declan taunted once more.

"Hardly," she replied.

Declan's frantic search of the room continued until he eventually set eyes on his iron sword. Picking it up, he attempted to scratch sigils into pupil-free eyes. This action proved to be unwieldy and served no purpose further than blunting the tip of his blade, a tip he may require if his escape attempt proved fruitless and he needed to turn it on his cell-mate. He hoped it wouldn't come to that. He wasn't convinced the iron would be able to pierce the undying god or what effect, if any, it would have if it did.

"Can't we just sit here and enjoy the moment Declan?" the Mórrigan said, still trying to crawl under the Master's skin.

Declan, not allowing himself to be distracted, didn't answer as his eyes drew toward his traveling bag. He had set it down by the door upon entering the Oraculum. He didn't recall packing anything that could aid him in his endeavor but didn't want to leave a stone unturned. He spilled the contents of the bag out onto the floor and was instantly taken aback by what he saw. The implements he used when he imagined scribing his own grave marker in the labyrinth were laid out before him.

The Master was perplexed. Had he manifested the implements in the corridor or was there some part of the Vagabond that had been trapped in the recesses of the Forgotten's brain causing him to unconsciously pack them? It was a question that time didn't give him the luxury to dwell on. Declan picked up the hammer and chisel and began the task of forging sigils into the blank eyes.

The Mórrigan had been prepared for this turn of events and opted to play her final card. It was a truth she had been saving for Declan to discover in the aftermath of her ascension. "Declan, you do know that all of your stolen memories, everything that you've made everyone forget, will be restored once you leave these walls, do you not?"

"I don't care," Declan said as he took a strike with the hammer.

"Everything. A father who abandons his children. A father who willfully endangers his child. What do you think Scot will think about that? The powers of a god secreted inside the mind of a child. What do you think he will do when he discovers his newfound abilities? It may very well eat him alive. He may very well eat you alive."

***

Security was tight around the citadel as Chauncey and David approached. It was an expected sight. If Imperium did indeed know who Marnie was, they wouldn't risk a compromise from anyone who might also know.

"Keep moving dickhead!" Chauncey shouted at David as he nudged him along with the staff. "You saw what I did to the great rogue Fauntleroy. I will visit that pain doubly on you." He had dropped his wilder brogue in an effort to sound more like a city dweller.

"I've captured the villain Almánzar, last of his name, batterer of the great leader," Chauncey announced as the pair approached the Imperium garrison.

The garrison stepped aside, allowing the pair to pass. David was able to breathe a small sigh of relief heading into what would be their next trial, the security checkpoint.

"Your arm please," the checkpoint officer requested of Chauncey, who gladly raised his arm. "Your other arm, the one with the cuff," the officer replied to the gesture, looking at him quizzically.

"Oh right right right,' Chauncey said as he put forth his other arm.

The officer reached over with a gun-shaped device reminiscent of a checkout scanner. They looked at the device indicator lights and then back at the cuff, giving it a further examination.

David was noticeably sweating but nobody was taking notice.

The officer called over to his apparent supervisor, asking, "Roland, can you take a look at this?"

A gruff-looking man approached the counter and stated, "You nabbed a real piece of shit here you know?" He then picked up the scan gun and looked at the readings before asking, "Can I see the cuff?"

Chauncey obliged, once more displaying his cuffed hand, allowing the superior officer to rescan it as he mirrored the supervisor's speech, "Yeah a real piece of shit."

"It's an older cuff but it checks out," the guard said, waving Chauncey and his captive through the checkpoint.

As they made their way down the hall toward the ramp to processing, Roland shouted to them, "Hey!"

David kept facing forward as Chauncey's still-masked head looked back.

"Make sure they set you up with an upgraded version of that cuff at processing," the man said.

Imperium had started to produce the cuffs three years prior but created new improved models every six months or so. The ones that bounty hunters would use were expected to be replaced with newer models at least every year.

"Sure thing," Chauncey called back as he waved in acknowledgment. He then faced forward and the pair took the ramp downward toward processing.

***

The pair continued to their final stop before entering the prison, the processing desk. It was the station where prisoner custody would be transferred and bounties would be collected. Bounties came in the form of extra charges to the cuffs. This was also the station where, under normal circumstances, a hunter would part from their prey.

"High-value target coming through," Chauncey stated as he approached the two Imperium guards that managed the station. "I have one David Almánzar for immediate processing."

"We can see that," one of the guards said as he pointed back toward an abnormally large wanted poster behind them.

"Old gods," Chauncey declared, his wilder brogue popping out slightly. "One hundred charges?" he said looking over at David, truly impressed with the price his traveling partner commanded.

This lack of professionalism alarmed David. His stomach had already been in knots entering the building and it now appeared as if Chauncey was actively working to blow their cover.

"Out of curiosity," Chauncey began again. "There was another with this one. Name of Chauncey Fauntleroy. Gave him a beating so bad he couldn't walk. How much he worth? Wondering if it's worth my time to go collect him."

The guard he had been conversing with grabbed a clipboard from under the counter. "Fauntleroy...Fauntleroy...no Fauntleroys here I'm 'fraid," the guard replied as he scrolled through the list of names.

Chauncey's face, thankfully obscured by the respirator, sunk into a frown. "That either means I'm the worst thief that ever played the game...or," he thought as his frown turned into a grin, "...the best."

"Cuff please," the guard demanded.

Chauncey handed off the bangle he had been wearing.

"Ugh...a one," the main guard said, looking at it with disdain as he pulled a new model out from under the counter. "Here take this seven. Your old one couldn't hold all the charges anyway. Won't even deduct payment on account of this one's high profile," he finished as he pointed toward David.

"Much obliged," Chauncey replied, as he watched the guard load his charges using a machine that to him appeared to be the height of technology. To David, it looked like an old radio, resplendent with glowing vacuum tubes.

"Well, that wraps up your end. You can take your leave back the way you came," the guard said.

Chauncey started to make his way back up the ramp as the guards led David through the door to the main prison area. Once he was sure that they wouldn't immediately return, he crept back down the ramp.

***

On the other side of the door, David was led to a screening area.

"When we're done here, I want you to go find Sara and let her know that we have the traitor in custody," the main guard said as he ran a rope through the gap between David's arms. It was all David could do to keep up the appearance that the cuff's bond was secure as his arms were raised into the air.

The secondary guard then proceeded to search David starting with his feet. He patted up each side of his legs and eventually reached his waist. The guard felt around to his back, wrapping his arms around either side of David. It was in this position that the guard seized upon the batons that David had secreted underneath his robe.

"I would have thought a hunter adept enough to bring you down would have checked you more thoroughly. No matter, that's what procedure is for," the guard said as he detached the batons.

This was the moment David had been counting on. As the guard was moving to stand up, David broke the weak link that bound his wrists together and brought his hand to bear on either side of the guard's head, boxing his ears.

The guard instinctively brought his hands toward his ears in an attempt to regain orientation. In his hand's course of travel, the guard discarded the batons, letting them fall.

David managed to snatch the batons out of free fall and forced his wrists to continue their momentum in a downward arc, causing the batons to fully extend. He then propelled his knee up into the guard's chest, causing him to double over. David took this opportunity to deliver a heavy blow with a baton to the back of the guard's head, knocking him unconscious.

The supervising guard made a quick motion toward David in an attempt to spear him in the chest. David sidestepped the rush, hitting the guard in his right knee as he passed. The guard's leg gave out and he fell onto his other knee, pivoting as he brought his injury off the ground toward his chest. David used this opening to swing the other baton against the side of the guard's face, cracking him in the jaw. There was an audible snap as he watched awareness drift from his victim's eyes, the body falling face-first to the floor. Faint snoring could be heard from the unconscious guards as David moved to the door to let Chauncey in.

***

"Someone's coming," Luci said, rousing Trig from their contemplation.

"Get ready to strike," they replied, peeling out from under Luci's arm.

The pair had devised the simple plan of attacking the next person to enter through the door. They would then fight their way up the spire in their mission to save Marnie.

"They're getting closer," Luci said. "Sounds like multiples, get ready."

No sooner had she finished the words when there was a loud crash against the cell door. The noise was followed by a momentary silence then another loud crash.

Luci and Trig looked at each other, preparing for a new hell as they feared the worst.

Their fears were allayed by the sliding of the cell's spy hole and a voice saying, "I swear laddie, if you're jerking us around again, I'm going to smash those teeth out!"

"Chauncey?" Trig questioned. An uncommon exuberance shaded the query.

"Had I known all it would take to make you happy to see me, would be rescuing your kidnapped arse, would've turned you in a long time ago," Chauncey replied.

"Get us out of here," Trig responded as they adopted a more reserved tone.

"We're working on it," David said before directing his muted follow-up at Chauncey. "You were too rough with this one, he's out."

"What are we gonna do? Thought you said we needed one to open the doors," Chauncey replied.

"Yeah that's why I said to keep him conscious," David replied.

"Everything all right out there?" Luci asked impatiently, unable to hear the hushed conversation on the other side of the door.

"Yeah just hold on a sec," David responded.

"What are we going to do?" Chauncey whispered, "We've come so far."

"Try the cuff on the lock," David suggested.

"Ahh, right. Good idea," Chauncey replied. He then held the cuff up to the lock hoping it would sense the presence and open the mechanism. "It's not working."

"Try the guard's. His is the Imperium model," David suggested.

Chauncey attempted to remove the cuff but found it to be damaged beyond usefulness.

"They would know something's up by now. We've got to do something," Chauncey said frantically. He took a beat of contemplation, "Hey hey hey, I've got one, why don't you use that fancy paint of yours and just draw a new door?"

"Like Wile E. Coy..." David started to question before realizing the reference would be lost. "It...it's stupid but it could work," he said, "No offense."

"None taken. 'Tis what I'm here for mate," Chauncey replied.

David reached into his pack, grabbing the first can of spray his fingers touched. It was brown. "A fitting choice," he thought as he quickly scrawled a six-panel door onto the wall. He then sprayed a small circular door knob and set the can down.

"Any night now," David heard Trig say through the door as he attempted to focus his intention on opening the door.

The doorway remained as paint on the wall while David stared in disbelief at his rough painting in panic. His Muse wasn't responding the way it should.

"The cuffs mate," Chauncey said motioning toward David's wrists.

"Shit," David replied before removing them and letting them fall to the ground. He then focused his intention into his rudimentary artwork once more, this time being met with success. David opened the door inward into the cell, startling its occupants who weren't prepared to see such a sight.

"Nice job David," Trig said, offering their appreciation for the completion of the first part of a successful jailbreak.

"None of this was my idea," David replied, giving a nod toward Chauncey. "And none of it should have worked."

Chauncey gave a quick bow as he watched genuine gratitude creep up Trig's face. He knew he had finally won true respect.

"Marnie?" David demanded, cutting through the upbeat mood that the reunion inspired.

"They took her," Luci replied as she grabbed one of her knives from the belt Chauncey was wearing, using it to cut away the bands that bound the cuffs to hers and Trig's wrists. "Wordsmith's turned. There is something much larger afoot than we originally thought. Your friends are at the center."

"Why did the Forgotten Master have to keep so much hidden?" David thought as he walked to the back wall of the cell. "Could really use some advice...some answers right about now."

His eyes rose toward the atrium as he spoke, "If anyone wants to back out, now's the time."

"Told ya before," Luci started, "I'm in this to the bitter end."

"And miss all the fun?" Chauncey replied.

"Laddie, this isn't just your mission anymore," Trig replied. "Belongs as much to us as it does to you."

***

The thought of Scot learning about his misdeeds gave Declan pause. He stopped his carving to look at the Mórrigan.

"That's right Declan," the Mórrigan continued her taunts. "The Forgotten Master remembered as the abandoning Vagabond. Will you be able to live with the truth...Will you be able to live with yourself?"

The thought of his exposure tortured his thoughts for no more than a moment before he shook it off. A reckoning with his past would come in time; it was now an inevitability. A more pressing thought had come to his mind, "Why is she trying to keep me here? There must still be a chance."

The world had suffered enough under his desire to keep knowledge sacred, to keep knowledge secret. The Master drew his implements back up to the eyes intent on completing his work.

The Mórrigan attempted to make one final appeal to Declan Mhurchaidh's fear of failure, "Declan, this is your last chance. The Muse you now possess is all that you have left. You cannot thread the needle's eye as you have and not suffer consequences. You sure you want to spend the remainder on this failure-fated quest?"

"I cannot think of a nobler use," Declan replied as he finished the sigils. He placed his hand on the doorway and allowed himself to be consumed into the void.

***

The Master emerged from the darkness, finding himself in the city's cistern. He stared pensively at the doorway, making sure he hadn't been followed. He looked out across the waterway seeing four unconscious, possibly dead, Imperium guards.

"Welcome back, Monsieur Vagabond. It is time to complete your Masterwork," a voice spoke to him from the shadows. A smile crept across his face as a golden light emerged, a golden light accented and contrasted by an aura of violet.

Chapter Twenty-Two

"...then in the following one it should be fired."

"Let me go! Let...me...go!" Marnie screamed as she was strapped to the menhir bridge perched high above the Ebony Wellspring. She was terrified and felt violated.

"Dear sister, do not fret," Scot said as he looked on at Wordsmith and Sara binding his sibling to the obsidian slab. "The feelings you will experience are beyond the highest realms of pleasure that Earth has to offer. Don't fight it. We are forging a new world and you get the honor of being the key that unlocks the door."

"No! You're destroying everything. This world, our world, all of it. You're leading us into darkness," Marnie again tried to reason.

"Don't you see Marnie? Don't you see? That's what it's about. That's what it has always been about. The Green Men, Dad's art, my art. Life...Death...Rebirth. Did you think I didn't know what was happening on Earth? Didn't plan for it? What we are doing tonight offers a reset, a new beginning...or rather, an old beginning. What we do tonight will restore the natural order. Tonight we set her free," Scot said, his mishmash of thoughts barely molding to form a coherent narrative.

"Our worlds cannot be trusted with novelty. With innovation. Look what they do with it. The frameworks of control. The frameworks of complacency. I'm not causing the death of creativity, I'm just rushing it along. Ripening the world for a new renaissance," Scot said, continuing his rambling as his subordinates finished their preparations.

"Scot you're not making any sense. How is your view of our world any different from what you plan on doing? Just let me go and let's go home," Marnie continued to plead as tears streamed down her face. This wasn't her Scot.

"You will see dear sister. You will see. Once she is free, you will see," Scot replied.

Sara finished attaching the last of the bonds and disembarked the platform. She triggered the rotisserie mechanism, allowing the menhir to flip as she turned the wheel.

Had Marnie not been terrified, she would have found the image below striking. The Ebony Wellspring appeared as if it was a pupil in the center of a floor that was reflecting the red light from the Lonely Sister high above.

"Scoooot noooo!" a voice boomed from across the room. David couldn't believe his eyes seeing his friend's sister dangling from the crimson-bathed bridge. He hadn't thought Scot capable of harming her but perhaps there wasn't much of Scot left.

"David, how nice of you to join us," Scot remarked looking at his old companion. "I see you've made some friends. Made short work of my guards no doubt. I suspected their training had gone south after your departure."

A sudden grimace of shame painted itself upon Sara's face. "I should have killed him in his sleep," she thought. Her shame turned to menace as she stared at David.

"Scot this has to end now," David replied. "This isn't you. Stop this and you can go home."

"Home...home. What's all this talk of going home? As I've told Marnie. I! Am! Home!" Scot said before commanding, "Wordsmith flip the switch."

At this command, Luci grabbed one of the orbs from her bandoleer and threw it against the ground, creating a quiver of arrows. She grabbed five and sprinted toward her bow which was still resting on Scot's large desk. Upon reaching the weapon and causing it to take shape, she quickly took aim, drew back, and loosed one in Wordsmith's direction, causing her to stop in her tracks.

"Don't just stand there. Do something!" Sara snapped, attempting to command the Imperium scientists who had stopped their work to watch the proceedings.

Trig, echoing Luci's actions, used an orb from their own belt to recreate the pair of revolving crossbows from their first Imperium encounter. They launched a volley of bolts toward the scientists, causing them to scatter, most opting to run for the room's exit.

Luci aimed again, this time at Sara. She fired another arrow which Sara easily rolled away from as she retreated toward the bridge.

***

Chauncey, whom no one was paying attention to, used the confusion to follow one of the scientists down the room's exit ramp. He snuck up behind his target and kicked at the back of the man's knee, causing him to tumble face-first into the floor ahead.

"Don't...Don't hurt me," the fallen scientist pleaded as he crab crawled away from his attacker.

"You needn't suffer the slings and arrows laddie," Chauncey replied. "So long as you impart upon me that, your most drab of vestment."

The scientist looked up at Chauncey, perplexed, "My what now?"

"Your coat! Your ugly ass lab coat laddie," Chauncey responded. "Give it to me and I won't hurt you."

The scientist acquiesced, providing Chauncey with his coat, knowing that such a move wouldn't be taken lightly by his bosses.

Chauncey used the coat to sneak around the room unnoticed to the vacuum tubes, taking up a stance behind them. While hidden, he started to unplug the various conduits that connected each of the tube's bases.

***

"Wordsmith...now! The switch is all that matters," ordered Scot.

"Scot, please," Marnie pleaded from her precarious position. "Don't do this. Nothing can be worth this." Her words cracked as she realized she had no say in her fate. But still, she continued to fight against her bonds and tensed up her body, attempting to hold off the violation that was coming her way.

"But dear sister, you haven't felt it yet," Scot replied. "You'll understand. You'll all understand." With the completion of these words, Wordsmith flipped the switch, activating the machine.

The aurora of Muse once more started to form in the spire's dome. Swirling as it formed into a tighter and tighter funnel, reaching down toward the menhir's face.

"This is it...finally...this is it," Scot cried in exuberance as he watched the cone of Muse form, getting ready to touch the stone.

The stone activated as the funnel touched it. The cracks and blemishes started to glow a brilliant blue, which gained intensity with each passing second.

"No this isn't right," Scot said, as he watched the light increase. "It should have discharged...this isn't right."

Scot's head turned toward the giant vacuum tubes which weren't glowing as expected. He watched as Chauncey disconnected one final tube. "What are you doing, you fool? You'll kill us all!" Scot shouted, just as an arc of concentrated Muse jumped out of the conduit Chauncey was holding.

The bolt of Muse sent Chauncey flying backward more than ten meters, causing him to crash into the side of the dome. Trig watched in horror as their friend fell to the ground, unconscious. They sprinted across the room hoping to find him still breathing.

***

"What's going on?" Marnie shouted from underneath the bridge, helpless. Her bracing expectation of a coming pain hadn't been met.

"I can fix this. I can fix this," Scot said as he looked at the damage Chauncey had caused. "Wordsmith, turn the machine off!" he commanded.

Scot glanced over at the switching mechanism to find that Wordsmith was also incapacitated, writhing in exhilaration after receiving a highly concentrated dose of epiphany.

"Scot, I'm not going to tell you again, you need to stop this," David pleaded, not sure if his words were reaching him.

Scot took three steps toward the switch before stopping cold in his tracks. "No...No...This can't be right...No...No...No...This is too much...No...This cannot be...What did he do to me?" Scot said, trying to comprehend what was happening to him. A panic crept over his face as a stream of blood started to flow out his left nostril. His eyes had changed color, becoming pitch-black. "This is too much...This is too much...This is too much," he kept repeating as he collapsed to the floor shaking.

"Scot!" David cried out as he ran across the room to check on the man he once called friend.

"What is it? What is going on?" Marnie pleaded from her bound position, "Tell me!"

***

Sara made an effort to cross the room toward her boss but was stopped short by another arrow from Luci's bow. She backed up until she was on the bridge. She then looked up to see the swirl of illumination starting to form again.

She looked from the lights to Marnie's bonds and back to the lights, pulling out a knife. Sara had come to the incorrect conclusion that removing Marnie from the equation would save Scot from the agony he was experiencing. She reached down and sliced at the bonds holding Marnie's arms to the stone.

Marnie screamed in terror as the right side of her upper body dropped into a dangle, still secured at the waist and one of her wrists. She was starting to feel another panic attack coming and began to hyperventilate. Her nerves were already fried from the previously absorbed blowout, greatly tempering the feeling, her mind still foggy from the experience.

Luci sent another arrow flying in Sara's direction. The projectile shattered into a million tiny fragments of light as it crossed the border of the atrium. The light fell like a waterfall, destined for the Wellspring below.

Sara looked on smugly, commenting, "Nice try. As a Geddes, you should have known that wouldn't work."

Luci sprinted toward the bridge, closing the gap between them, not giving Sara another chance to slash at Marnie's bindings. She took a swing at Sara with her bow.

***

Trig found Chauncey to be unconscious and commenced slapping him in the face in an effort to rouse him. It was a desperate act, one they would have enjoyed had he been awake and the current situation not been so dire.

"It's not time for school yet," Chauncey murmured. "Just ten more minutes."

Trig took another crack at his face, forcing him into alertness.

"Stop...stop," Chauncey commanded, as he rubbed the side of his face.

Trig wound up for one more hit, making hard contact and causing Chauncey to yell out once more.

"What was that for?" he screeched.

"That one was for worrying me...and being foolish," Trig replied.

"Careful...People might start to think you like me," Chauncey replied as he crawled his way up to his feet. His eyes scanned toward the bridge. "Marnie!... Luci!" he exclaimed with a tone of panic, causing Trig to turn their attention back to the chaos behind them.

***

"What's the matter...jealous?" Sara taunted. "We are about to complete that which your parents could not. A total consolidation of power. You should be happy."

Luci ignored the taunt and took another slash at Sara with her bow.

Sara sidestepped the attack as she pivoted around to Luci's back. She then grabbed hold of the weapon as it completed its follow-through arc. The pair were locked in a wrestle over the mass of metal and wood, their feet coming dangerously close to the edge. Sara made a twisting motion, causing it to lever its way out of Luci's hands. She then cast it aside allowing it to fall into the Wellspring below.

Sara retrieved another knife from a holster at the small of her back and lunged at Luci. Luci telegraphed the movement and moved out of the way, using the opportunity to pull out her own knife. She slashed at Sara's forearm, drawing blood as the blade glided through the air.

Sara ignored the cut as she pushed an advance into Luci's guard. She thrust the knife at her opponent's waist, a move which Luci was able to parry, dislodging the steel blade from Sara's hand. Luci then brought her knife over her head in a two-fisted stabbing motion, slashing downward in an attempt to hit Sara's carotid artery. Sara caught Luci's wrists in her palm and started to fight against the downward motion.

Luci and Sara spent a few moments locked in this position, both fiercely trying to gain control of the situation. Luci, thinking fast, took a calculated step back, creating space to wedge her foot between her and her attacker, using it to push Sara backward, creating space for her next attack. Luci took a sprint step toward her opponent, taking a final lunge with the knife.

Sara once more skirted the lunge as she grabbed hold of Luci's knife arm. She yanked the arm downward toward her right thigh as she rotated her body. This action forced Luci's body to connect to Sara's left side as she used the momentum to hip-toss Luci to the side.

Luci's eyes grew wide as she realized there was no longer ground beneath her feet. She fell without a sound into the darkness below, her eyes momentarily meeting Marnie's as she stared skyward as if to plead, "Do something." But there was nothing that could be done. *A heretic will fall at dawn's first light.*

Marnie watched on helplessly struggling against her bonds. The cold feeling of despair started to mix with her panic. Her body felt somehow hollow, not even being able to recognize the air that was filling her lungs.

Trig watched on in horror as Luci disappeared over the side. "No!" they gasped quietly before crying out, "Noooooo!" as they ran up to the edge of the atrium. They were unable to catch a final glimpse. The woman they had one day hoped to love, the woman this moment would tell them that they had already fallen in love with, had been consumed by the blackness. They turned their attention toward Sara, enraged, launching the remaining bolts in their crossbows. They watched as the projectiles exploded into light before getting sucked into the same nothingness that had claimed Luci.

Trig stood in silence as a hot fury crawled its way through their body. The purple glow of their veins had morphed into a crimson red. A fire mixed with tears as they focused their anger on Sara, turning their attention toward the mechanism used to rotate the menhir. Trig moved swiftly to the machine and started to operate the wheel, hoping to cast the Imperium foe into the same darkness that had claimed Luci. The thought of bringing Marnie to safety was now only secondary in their mind.

"Stop that!" Sara tried to command with desperation. She knew she wasn't in a position to bargain.

"Just die already!" Trig snarled back as they continued to crank faster.

Sara sprinted to the other end of the bridge leaping off moments before the slab reached a pitch her legs would be unable to cling to. She continued running to a wall of swords that Scot had on display.

"Chauncey get over here...help Marnie!" Trig yelled to their traveling companion as they gave chase around the outside of the atrium. "David a little help here mate!" they shouted, spotting him across the chamber still standing over a huddled Scot.

Marnie was still dangling over the abyssal darkness but was now at a vantage point to get a glimpse of the ensuing chaos. Feelings of anger mixed with pity as she caught sight of her brother convulsing on the ground. The cocktail of emotions she was dealing with had become volatile. She didn't know how much longer her body would be able to hold out.

***

Chauncey hesitantly stood up. He was still shaking from enduring the bombardment of Muse. It was a rush he had never felt before and left him with a squeamish feeling in the pit of his stomach. "If this is what people feel when they have a good idea," he said to himself, "They can have it."

As Trig dashed away, he crossed the room on unsteady footing, taking over the bridge crank to finish bringing Marnie to safety. With Marnie on a flat plane, he cut the remainder of her bindings and helped her off the menhir bridge. The pair headed to Scot, who was still convulsing on the floor. They hovered over him, not sure what to do.

Marnie looked at her brother, unable to make sense of his betrayal, unable to make sense of any of his actions in the short time since finding him again. She didn't know what to feel and her body was in no state to make the choice for her. This wasn't the Scot she knew, the Scot who disappeared so long ago.

***

Trig and David circled opposite sides of the atrium, performing a pincer move as they approached Sara who had taken up a defensive stance with a broadsword.

Trig reached into a pouch on their belt and pulled out another Muse orb. They held it in their right hand, deliberating for a moment on what they wanted to create. With a fiery rage, they crushed the orb in their fist, producing a flaming sword. They sprinted forward toward their opponent, arcing the sword through the air in an attempt to bring the entire might of their fury and despair down upon Luci's killer.

Sara brought her sword up into a crossed guard, glancing the blow off toward her right. "You'd do well to back down. You're in over your head if you really think you can get the best of me," she said, tauntingly.

"It was just a distraction," Trig answered as a sinister grin crept across their face.

David, who had been coming up behind her, swung his staff, connecting with Sara just under her left arm, right in her rib cage. An audible crunching sound could be heard as the Imperium marshal staggered to the side, turning their guard to face both attackers. With labored breath, she once more brought her sword into a protective stance. "Hardly a fair fight, two-on-one," she said. "David, is this really how you want to defeat me?"

David had on many occasions thought about what he would do if this situation ever presented itself, thinking he would have a final standoff like in one of Scot's action movies. Finally presented with the moment, an unexpected indifference crept over him as he replied, "What makes you think I give a shit how you go down?"

"You killed the only person that would have participated in the cliché of your so-called fair fight," Trig said through their glassy eyes, as they once more brought their sword to bear upon their enemy's weapon.

Sara once again parried the blow but it wasn't enough as David had swung his own weapon, connecting with the side of her head, knocking her unconscious.

Trig brought their weapon over their head for a final time, staring down at Sara's prone body, ready to deliver a coup de grace.

"Nooooooo," Chauncey yelled from across the room. Both he and Marnie stood watching. A terrified look crept over Chauncey's face. "This isn't you," he pleaded.

Trig looked over, seeing both of their faces before looking back at the incapacitated foe, deliberating whether they would let their rage win out. They wanted to end her. They wanted to make their pain go away.

"They're right," David said, "A quick death would be more than she deserves. She deserves to live with her failure. For her, there is no greater torture."

Trig considered his words for a moment, doing the math on what he had just said. They raised their sword higher still ready to take the final blow.

Chauncey and Marnie both looked away, sparing themselves from something they couldn't unsee.

Trig froze, letting their sword fall to the ground behind them and dash itself out of existence. They then crashed to their knees. Tears were rolling down their face, tears mourning all that could have been. Their fiery red glow shifted back to purple as the sputtered sound of gasped crying could be heard emanating from their hair-masked face.

Chauncey ran over to David and tossed him the cuffs previously used to bind Marnie before turning his attention toward Trig debating an attempt to console the inconsolable. He knew there wasn't much he would be able to do.

Sara's hands were promptly secured before Marnie, David, and Chauncey turned their attention back to Scot, who had started to murmur once more.

***

"Too much...it's too much," Scot said, as he continued to writhe on the ground. "What did he do to me?"

"Scot!" Marnie cried as she ran back to him, her anger and panic had faded away leaving only concern as she realized her brother wasn't in control of his actions, "What did who do to you?"

"What did he do?... What did he do?" Scot continued to murmur.

"What is happening? How can I help you?" Marnie once more pleaded as she reached down grabbing hold of her brother's arm.

"I'm not sure he can hear you lass," Chauncey said as he took up purchase to her right, staring at this man who had been the object of his quest.

Scot's body was anguishing under the heavy burden of a forbidden knowledge trying desperately to integrate with his mortal mind. Three years of mainlining raw Muse and the corruption that attached itself to him had made him ripe for this moment. Somewhere from the darkest recesses of his mind, Scot was trying to crawl to the surface and reason out what was becoming of him.

"Fight it Scot...Fight it," Marnie continued to beg, hoping her words were piercing through the madness.

She continued to stare as her brother's breathing picked up to the point of hyperventilation. He sat straight up, his black eyes rolling over to white as they started to glow. "I can see. I can see...everything," his voice spoke with ominence.

"Scot, you're scaring me," Marnie replied.

"The one you call Scot is no longer here," the being before her responded. "We must go now. We must go to the Wellspring. We must set her free."

Scot's body stood slowly and started to puppeteer itself toward the exit ramp, making its way toward the Ebony Wellspring. It was clear that whatever was piloting him wasn't used to controlling a body and it took very slow deliberate steps.

Trig, still in shock from Luci's death, just watched as he shambled off. Marnie, David, and Chauncey immediately jumped up to block his path.

"Set who free?" Marnie demanded, trying to look into her brother's eyes. "You're not making sense."

"She that is war and Fate," Scot's body replied. "The phantom queen."

"The Mórrigan," Chauncey whispered. The gravity of this quest hit him all at once. "This is not good," he said with an air of disquiet. He set his hands upon Scot hoping to hold him back.

A blast of Muse emanated from Scot's body, throwing Marnie, David, and Chauncey toward the ground. He continued his advance toward the ramp, using his newly gained power to form a wall behind him, trapping his would-be rescuers.

***

"We have to stop him," Trig said with a hollowed reserve, having barely gained composure after the blast of Muse rushed over them. The wave had provided a minimal fortification of their mind for what must come next

"I don't get it. I thought the Mórrigan was a myth," Marnie replied.

"Aye Miss Marnie, you spend enough time on the road, hear enough stories...You come to realize there's not much separating the fairy fact from the fairy fiction," Chauncey responded, "Least not in this world. This is serious shite. This brot'er o' yours may very well bring eternal darkness to Eternal Dawn...'Spectin' your where may not fair much better."

"What can we do?" David said desperately, a tinge of hopelessness was audible in his voice, "You saw the power he has now. That push, that wall. What match are we for that?"

Marnie looked at her three companions, unsure of what to do or say. The events of the day had been all too much for her. "What can we do against what he has become," she said echoing David's sentiment. Her words sat in the air for a few moments before the stillness they commanded was broken.

"I have a thought," Chauncey offered hesitantly.

Trig looked over at him, instinctively ready to chastise. They thought for a moment, biting their lip, ready for once to hear him out.

Chauncey searched through his bag, grabbing a sketchbook. He glanced over at Marnie. "Hope you don't mind but I couldn't help myself," he said as he skimmed the sketchbook. "This one...This one is intriguing," he said as he showed Marnie a page in her sketchbook.

Marnie looked at the image almost in disbelief. "But how would I..." she started to say before getting cut off.

"Think fast lass," Chauncey said as he removed a can of spray from his bag, tossing it to her before dumping the rest out onto the floor.

"Are you sure this is a good idea," Marnie replied, again looking at the image and then back to Chauncey.

"Of course not, lass," he responded. "In fact, I'm sure it's a bad one. That's why it's going to work."

Marnie picked up a few more cans and approached the wall blocking the group's exit. With a can of brown paint, she roughed in the outline of a two-and-a-half-meter-tall organic exoskeleton. One arm featured a large pincer claw and the other featured a large ram-like fist. She picked up a can of black and roughed-in articulation points at the knees and elbows and added texture to each of the limbs creating a branch-like appearance. She then used a can of green to create the appearance of moss and lichen growing on the outside of the exoskeleton's body. It was probably an unneeded detail but she couldn't be sure if a lack of commitment to the artistry would create an inferior machine. She sprayed in some foliage for good measure, using pages from her book to mask off the sharp edges of leaves. Marnie then picked up a can of silver and started to spray the suit's robot pilot next to the exoskeleton.

"Aye lass, what are you doing with that?" Trig interrupted, anticipating and fearing the response.

"Creating a driver?" Marnie responded, her voice echoing the uncertainty Trig's query had placed in her brain.

"Oh no no no lass," Trig warned, "'Tis not wise to create a golem. More often 'n not they pull in a nefarious conscious from the never. Erratic. Cannae be controlled. More 'n one Adept lost their life cause of that miscalculation. Unwritten rule of Musin' I'm afraid."

"What do you suggest we do then?" she replied as her eyes met Chauncey's in unspoken conversation, thinking back to the pickle-pocketed robot from the park. She then started to buff over the rough outline of the robot, not wanting to risk the possibility of bringing it into the world.

"I...I was kinda thinking you'd be pilot," Chauncey replied. "Be attuned to you after all. I mean I'd do it but it would take the gift that I'm lacking"

"If it were me, it would decay and fall apart before we caught up to him," David interjected.

"Don't know if you can tell, I'm a bit of a mess right now," Trig added, wiping away their still-flowing tears.

"Guess that settles it," Chauncey said as the group stared at Marnie.

Marnie stared back for a moment, not sure what to say. In the context of her world what she was about to do was unheard of, insane even. She turned around to face the wall and then placed her hands upon the wet parts of her creation. She focused for a few seconds on the intention of the piece, making sure to add in the details she had neglected for the sake of time. She shut her eyes and grabbed hold of two vertical branches which acted as grab bars for her to step up into the contraption. She then pivoted her body to take a seat in the suit's cockpit. She felt an immediate rush of epiphany as her mind melded with the machine. The rush had the added effect of flushing away some of the uneasiness left behind by the panic attacks she had been forced to endure.

Marnie opened her eyes to see that most of the machine was still on a flat plane. She instinctively took a step forward, peeling the remainder of her contraption away from the wall. It was a cathartic moment. She hadn't thought about the sketch in the five years that had lapsed between now and the night she had drawn it, the night Scot and David went missing.

David stared on in awe. Even in his time with Scot, he hadn't seen him attempt a similar feat.

Chauncey had a grin that stretched from one ear to the other as he crossed his arms with prideful satisfaction.

Trig made eye contact with Marnie, giving her a quiet nod of approval, the highest praise they had to offer as an Adept.

Marnie tested out the machine's functionality. She raised the pincer arm while simultaneously opening and closing its jaws. She then made a punching motion with the pummel. The motions were an extension of her being, flowing forth with organic smoothness. "This is brilliant," she said as she continued maneuvering the machine.

She then turned the machine around and locked eyes with the wall that was blocking her path to Scot. Marnie took a swing with the pummel arm, feeling an immediate give as a haptic shock wave crept up her arm. She took another swing, creating a sizable hole with which the group could pass.

"Bloody brilliant," Chauncey echoed. "Much better than David's door."

"What of Wordsmith?" David questioned, remembering the incapacitated former Master.

"Don't think she's going anywhere, laddie," Trig replied as they looked over, seeing her still writhing on the floor. "'Spect the bombardment's put her brain into some kind of feedback loop."

***

Marnie led the charge down the spire. Her appearance was intimidating to the Imperium soldiers that they passed. They were already in disarray, not knowing what to do without the authoritarian command of their leader, Sara. Many of them were still nursing wounds from the savaging they received at the hands of Chauncey, David, Trig, and Luci on their way up the spire. Some of them, sensing the end of their employment, were opting to rob the place blind.

"Good on ya mate," Chauncey called out to one such soldier who was walking away with a large decorative sculpture. He was giddy with excitement at the level of ruination being visited upon the evil corporation. Ruination that he had had a sizable hand in fomenting.

The building was in rough condition. Chauncey's act of sabotage had disrupted the normal flow of Muse within the building. Muse lights were flickering on and off as the artificial connections used in the building's construction were being severed and rerouted. The spiles that controlled the flow of water to the unnecessarily potted plants were running at full blast, flooding the walkways. Pixies that were kept as test subjects had been set loose and were running amok, causing wanton destruction to any object not bolted to the floor and some that were. Trig watched the proceedings with detached amusement, keeping their mind distracted from the fallen Luci.

In the wake of chaos, the group's passage to the citadel foundations would continue unhindered. The journey to the deepest level seemed to take forever as they navigated down fifty floors.

***

"I'm not sure I can go through with this," Marnie said, as the group stood outside the iron door to the lowest level of the old citadel, the doorway to the Ebony Wellspring. It wasn't a generalized panic she was feeling at this moment. Instead, there was a specific fear of hurting her brother. Her brother, who might still be buried deep down in the husk of the man who once called himself Scot.

"Deary," Trig spoke, "Not much for pep talks...but perhaps providence has brought you on this inexorable path as it has with us. As it did with..." their voice had formed a quiver, "Luci. If fate has dictated we should go no further our losses may be for naught. Maybe you were called here to save your brot'er. Maybe you weren't. Maybe you were called to save us from darkness. Maybe you weren't. Maybe it really is all for naught but maybe it isn't. Would you be able to live with yourself if you didn't try?"

Marnie took a moment to consider Trig's words, took a few deep breaths then wound back the pummel fist before following through into the door, knocking it clean off its hinges.

***

"Dear sister, you made it!" Scot's voice bellowed with an almost jovial aplomb. "I hoped you would. You're the key, you see. The key to her ascension. Our ascension. The ultimate novelty. The ultimate ephemera."

"Scot," Marnie pleaded as she walked through the door, "This needs to end."

The group of companions found themselves in a hollow channel. The outer ring of the atrium stood flush with the cells above. Fine dust layered the ground beneath their feet as they drew their gaze to the focal point of the room.

From her vantage point in the cell above, Marnie hadn't noticed that the Wellspring wasn't level with the floor, instead, there was a wall ringing it, one which stood a head taller than her at her normal height. She could just barely make out the blackness of the well from her perch in the machine.

The wall was coated with a blackness that undulated as drops of black goo oozed down its sides before being drawn back up over the rim. The goo didn't possess form as it did when being unleashed by the Green Men.

"Don't you see? Don't you see? He gave me her power," Scot replied. "For what else than to set her free? To make this all just a wistful memory. It's the only thing that makes sense."

"Who...who gave you her power? What are you talking about?" Marnie continued to entreat, trying to parse through the jumbled speech that belonged at once to her brother but also to someone or something else.

Scot looked at Marnie, confounded that she wasn't understanding the thoughts that were so clear to him. He spoke slowly, "Father of course."

"I...I don't understand," Marnie responded, as the blackness that had been welling in her stomach tied tighter knots. "None of this makes sense."

"It's no matter dear sister," Scot replied. "You will see...you will see...once she is free, you will see...Just climb out of that machine. We will go into the Wellspring together. We will complete the Masterpiece."

"You're going to hurt a lot of people," Marnie once more pleaded, though she was unsure if he was actually hearing her anymore.

David, Trig, and Chauncey looked on, unsure of what to do.

"Please Scot, listen to her," David finally managed. "There must be some part of you that can still hear us."

"Silence traitor!" Scot screamed, his booming voice knocking Marnie's traveling companions off their feet. "What are the lives of the mortal when measured against those of the gods?"

"I don't want to have to hurt you," Marnie begged as she continued her attempts at reason, hoping that a part of her brother was still capable of hearing.

"I had hoped you would come willingly, dear sister..." Scot replied. "...But it is no large effort to rend your paltry machine to shreds then drag you by your hair into the void."

Marnie watched as the weight of her brother's body settled into his right heel before springing forward into a sprint. Scot closed the thirty-meter gap between him and Marnie in seconds, giving her little time to form a strategy. Working on instinct, she swung the pummel arm in a sweeping arc that caused her brother to glance off to the side.

After flying nearly ten meters, Scot fell into a roll from which his body recovered with an unstaggered smoothness. His puppet master had clearly learned a lot about the human body in its fifty-floor descension. Scot used continued forward momentum to take another pass, this time coming up from behind. He shouted out in another void cry, pushing the exoskeleton into a stuttered step as he leaped through the air, intent on using his feet to force his sister to topple to the ground.

Marnie could feel the haptics in the suit indicating an impact on the shoulder blade area of the armor. The suit's feedback was accompanied by the sudden lunge of the machine. She instinctively put her right hand forward to catch herself as the exoskeleton tried to tumble forward. The pummel fist planted itself into the ground as she defensively swung her left elbow back in an effort to knock her attacker away. Scot was once more flung to the side.

"Scot, stop this now!" Marnie once more demanded as she commanded the machine to rise once more. She repeated, "I don't want to hurt you."

Both of their bodies had started to glow brightly.

"Hurt me?" Scot questioned before crowing, "You can't hurt a god." He rose to his feet once more as he stared at his sister with his achromatic eyes. The intensity of the light radiating from the two figures facing off had risen to a blinding white. He once more dashed forward to attack.

Marnie reached her claw hand forward, catching her brother before he could complete his strike. The jaws of the pincers closed around Scot, binding him at the waist as his arms flailed. Marnie brought his body into the air, leaving him helpless.

Scot attempted to shout down Marnie again as he tried to fight her grip. The effort had no effect. Marnie looked down at Trig and the others as if to ask, "Now what do I do?"

Trig considered their options for a moment. "You need to discharge him, deary," they said, "You need to force a blowout."

"I don't know if I can," Marnie replied.

"You have to try," Trig responded. "For the sake of us all...you have to try."

Marnie thought back to her experimentation at the camp. She concentrated on her anxieties, trying to lean in, trying to force a greater panic. No matter how hard she tried, she had come up empty. "I...I can't do it," she gasped, lamenting the inconsistent nature of her condition.

With a conditioned impulse, her body slunk over in failure. Scot saw his opportunity. As his feet touched the ground, he had the leverage he required to continue his fight. With feet planted, he grabbed hold of each arm of the pincer and used the force of his body to push them open. He continued the motion and forced the jaws past their neutral rest position, snapping the branches that formed the claw.

The suit shook, sending a shudder through Marnie's body as her mind struggled to maintain the haptic connections to parts of the suit that were no longer there. It was too late, Scot had grabbed hold of the pummel arm, breaking it over his knee with the ease of shortening branches for a campfire.

Marnie was left helpless as Scot, as promised, continued to rend her machine limb from limb. Within moments she was left under nothing more than a pile of branches.

David, Trig, and Chauncey trying to use Scot's focus on destroying his sister as a distraction, fanned out and made a rushing attack in an attempt to overwhelm him.

Scot detected the footstep of the new barrage and immediately brought his palms to rest on the ground, bringing forth tendrils from the void to lash down his would-be attackers.

With David, Trig, and Chauncey subdued Scot turned his attention back to the pile of rubble that was Marnie's machine. He bent down and grabbed his sister by her hair. He then started to drag her over to the Ebony Wellspring as a final payment to the void for the Mórrigan's freedom.

When the pair had reached the side of the well, Marnie regained her wits and once more tried to defend herself. She tried to grab at his throat. She tried to smack his arms away. She tried to stomp at his feet. She tried punching him. It was all for naught as all of her attacks went ignored. There was no reaction. It was as if she was punching a brick wall.

Scot then grabbed his sister by the waist, intent on hoisting her up over the nearly two-meter-high wall.

As she was being lifted, Marnie caught her first up-close glimpse of the inside of the well. Just as Wordsmith had described, it was a pool of black that reflected nothing; a blank space with no discernible pattern in its movement.

Feelings started to well up inside Marnie, feelings of despair that she hadn't had since she had first entered the Green Door to cross over to Eternal Dawn. Marnie made one more halfhearted attempt to foster a blowout but came up empty. There was no panic to be had. She was numb, burnt out, out of hope. She resigned herself to her fate. She had failed. The hope of her triumphant reunion had been dashed. There was nothing left to do but be taken by the void. Marnie closed her eyes in anticipation of the inevitable.

There was a long pause.

Scot had suddenly stopped his attempt to cast his sister into the well. Marnie looked down at him as he looked lost in thought. She attempted to struggle out of his grip but this proved to be fruitless. Ten seconds had passed before Scot seemed to snap out of his daze, his eyes refocusing as he continued to force his sister over the wall.

A flash of golden light entered Marnie's periphery. Scot once more stopped. This time he was fully distracted and lost his grip. Marnie crashed down on top of him, leaving the siblings as a tangle of limbs on the ground. The pair stared back at the remnants of the door that Marnie had destroyed moments before, unsure what had just occurred.

The golden light was blinding as it emanated from the broken doorway. Marnie and Scot looked on as a black silhouette crossed the door's threshold. They were both afraid but for different reasons. The source of the golden light followed the cloaked figure into the room, immediately heading toward Marnie's bound companions. The creature's light served to cast out the dark vines that were binding them to the floor.

A third entity then entered the room, sprinting toward Marnie. The creature's darkness existed in contrast to the bombardment of light being emitted from her companions' liberator. It was only at the moment it reached Marnie that her eyes adjusted properly. She realized what the beings were.

Marnie observed as the source of the golden light aggressively attacked David with affection. It was the creature she would come to know as the dog Brutus. The darkness that sprinted toward her flashed its ultraviolet light as it reached her forcing its immediate recognition as that of the Razor-Sith. All fear left Marnie as her eyes drew back toward the shadowed figure with whom she was unacquainted.

Marnie had only moments to contemplate the stranger before Scot was able to rise to his feet and grab hold of her. Paying no deference to the new intruders, he once more dragged Marnie up by her hair and began forcing her back toward the wall in an attempt to complete his mission.

"Scot!" the voice of the shadowed man bellowed, "Stop this."

"I must complete the Masterpiece," Scot replied, ignoring the command.

"Wishbone now!" the stranger's voice ordered.

At this signal, the cat leaped through the air and pounced at Scot, hitting him in the back, and causing Marnie to stumble out of reach. She recovered and scrambled back, putting some distance between her and her brother. The Sith paced between the pair, protecting Marnie.

"The work must be completed," Scot said as he rose to his feet once more, staggering toward Marnie.

"Stop this. This isn't you," the stranger pleaded.

"How would you know what I am, old man?" Scot replied. "You dare command a god?"

"You are no god, son," the stranger responded. "You are being used just as I was being used."

"You wouldn't know the first thing about it," Scot replied. "She will be free and you will see. You will all see!"

"I know more than you could ever fathom," the stranger said. "I did this to you. I made you into this...this thing. For that I accept responsibility. I accept responsibility for all of it. I have come in an attempt to make things right. To relieve you of your pain."

"Who...Who are you?" Marnie interjected as feelings of distrust crept up her spine. "What are you?"

The stranger approached Marnie, causing her to back up toward the well with Wishbone still pacing between her and her brother. He then reached up to the hood of his robes, dropping it to his shoulders.

Marnie stared at the stranger, feeling raw synapses fire in the deepest parts of her brain as she became overwhelmed by recollection. Her emotions grew to a peak as she recoiled, dropping to her knees.

"Marnie, I'm your father," Declan Murphy replied. A blinding flash filled the room.

Chapter Twenty-Three
"...brains do not make one happy."

Wave upon wave of Muse ejections emanated from Marnie's body as the young traveler was lifted off the ground and brought to a hover just above the center of the Ebony Wellspring. The intensity and reach of the Muse flood far eclipsed that of the one she birthed upon hearing the rumors of her father's demise. It was unknown to Marnie from deep in the bowels of the citadel but the blowout had reached every corner of Eternal Dawn, blanketing the land in darkness. Trig could feel the remaining Muse orbs in their belt shatter as they watched the light being pushed away on a wave.

Marnie had locked her eyes on her brother's as each subsequent pulse swept through him. She continued to watch as each wave pushed more and more of the corruption out of his body. A shadow creature was desperately trying to cling to his body but was gradually losing grip. First, the claws of its feet gave way, causing it to hang off his back like a cape. On the next wave, one of its three arms lost its grip. It continued to claw desperately onto Scot's shoulder as another wave pushed it off, causing it to get sucked into the abyss under her feet. Marnie saw Scot collapse to the ground, no longer under the creature's control.

As the waves continued, Marnie's vision was drawn downward toward the Wellspring. The waves acted almost as an X-ray, exposing the room below. She saw in one wave, the image of a young woman crowned by a wolf's head. On the next wave, the woman had been replaced by a giant raven. The subsequent wave would see the raven morph into a wolf, and then the crowned woman again.

David, Declan, Chauncey, and Trig stared up at Marnie, helpless to do anything. Fate had removed any capacity they had to influence the motions of the current proceedings. Wave after wave ejected itself from Marnie, her light growing with each swell of Muse. Mere moments had passed before the light finally became unbearable. The group could no longer make out Marnie's image and were unsure if she was still contained within the ball of illumination.

The waves stopped. Marnie had become unaware of her feelings, lost in the endless epiphany, a blanketed hug of pure unbridled love. As suddenly as the waves had started, all of the Muse light was pulled deep inside her body, leaving her floating in the nothing. She felt an immediate longing for the sensations she had just been feeling, a sucking ache inside her chest. She could feel a coldness overtake her as she was suspended in blackness.

She took a deep breath holding it for a moment as she cleared her mind. All at once light exploded out of her body in a singular final wave, flooding the darkest reaches of Eternal Dawn, revitalizing the luminescence that had diminished in the wake of the Dying of the Light.

Trig looked down at their skin seeing that their veins had returned to their pre-Dying splendor. They at once felt themselves to be who they had been before but somehow also more. They looked up at Marnie, seeing her still floating as she regained awareness of her surroundings. Her body had started to float downward.

"Do something!" Declan shouted as it had become clear that Marnie's body was on a course to enter the Wellspring. Fear had gripped him at that moment as he had briefly considered the Mórrigan words and her impending ascension. It would all be over if Marnie were to cross through the darkness into the Oraculum. He rushed to the well's edge, though he had no idea what he would or could do.

Marnie continued her slow fall, eventually coming to rest her feet on the surface of the spring. The darkness was unable to touch her as she walked across its surface.

The onlookers stared on befuddled. They weren't sure what to make of the events that had just transpired.

Marnie looked down once more, seeing through the darkness as if it were glass. She saw the image of the raven once more. It was just on the other side of the well. "It's trying to get me," she said. "The raven is trying to get me!"

"Get off of there deary," Trig commanded as they reached up to help Marnie down. They then turned to the well and laid their hands upon it, calling on a power that was growing from within. Focusing their intention, they formed a large iron door to cap the ten-meter-wide void. Giant padlocks secured hasps that lined its perimeter. The group watched as keys were extracted from each of the locks and floated through the air before shattering into a million fragments of light.

Chauncey looked at them smiling, realizing that Marnie's Flood had caused his best friend to become the very thing they had shown so much indignation toward, a Master. It was a fact that he hoped they would never be able to live down.

Marnie looked around at the people now in her presence. Chauncey, Trig, and David looked at her wordlessly, bowing their heads. "Luci..." Marnie started as she stared at Trig, her eyes welling. David and Chauncey gave Marnie and Trig a bewildered glance.

"Do not fret dear lass," Trig began. "In time, with mourning, these feelings may come to pass...and I will mourn that day as well."

Marnie then drew her gaze upon the man who called himself her father, unsure of what to think or do.

"I do not expect your forgiveness for the things that I have done...but I am truly..." he started to speak before being interrupted. Marnie had run into his arms, wrapping them around him as tears had started to roll down her cheeks. He silently reciprocated as his own tears began to form. They held this moment for what felt like an eternity, only being halted by the pained murmurings of Scot on the floor beside them. He was being circled by the Razor-Sìth, Wishbone who was unsure if the human still posed a threat.

"It's not over...We need to destroy the machine," Scot's coarsened voice managed to eke out. His thoughts weren't those of reunion but of the immediate danger his past actions now posed. "We need to disconnect the cuffs...All of them." Even as he spoke, a new cloud of Muse had started to circle in the atrium above. A funnel was forming, slowly reaching toward the iron door that now capped the Wellspring.

Marnie and Declan helped Scot to his feet. They didn't know what to say. They were still processing his words. Had the evil truly been cast out or was this just a ruse?

Scot's legs were barely able to support his weight as he staggered alone toward the door. The others looked on, not sure if they were capable of trusting the figure that had already put them in so much peril. "We don't have much time," Scot begged as he continued his plodding movement.

Trig watched as Scot hobbled out of the room. They considered all of the ill will they had stored up over the past fifteen years. Their scorn for the Masters. Their misplaced thoughts and firmly held prejudices against them...against Luci. They considered Luci, they considered Marnie, they considered the Vagabond that now stood before them...they considered themselves...all of them Masters, all trying to perform altruistically whether their attempts were misguided or not. They stared at the doorway considering their next action before running toward it to meet Scot and prop him up as they both limped their way toward the spiral walkway.

Those that remained looked at each other for a moment. Then in silent agreement, they followed behind. David sensing that he may be once again looking upon the version of his friend he had known before their journey to Eternal Dawn, ran up to Scot's other side, lending further aid as they tried to hastily make their way to the top of the spire.

***

"We need to reconnect the machine to shut it down," Scot said as the group walked into the room.

"Wait...How do we know you aren't having us on?" Chauncey asked suspiciously.

Marnie, Trig, and David stared at Chauncey in momentary disbelief.

"Haven't you been paying attention?" Trig replied, unsure of what Chauncey had thought when he saw the darkness being expelled from Scot's body. "Besides what's he going to do? His body's gone dark," they continued, making note of the distinct lack of Muse in Scot's body.

"David, you need to reconnect the conduits while I configure the shutdown sequence," Scot interrupted, his voice shaded with a pain that spoke of regret.

"Me?" David asked in surprise.

"Too dangerous for a Master. Especially ones at full strength," Scot replied. "And no offense but that one's talents are better suited to sabotage," he continued, gesturing toward Chauncey.

"None taken laddie," Chauncey replied, thankful that his talents were being recognized.

"What do I need to do?" David asked, looking at the mass of disconnected wires and tubes that had been Chauncey's work.

"It's all color-coded. Blue to blue. Green to green. Purple to purple. You really can't hook it up wrong as long as the colors match," Scot responded.

David looked down at the problem before him, seeing nothing but blue and brownish components. "In case you've forgotten, I'm colorblind, remember?" he replied.

"What about those goggles on your head?" Scot responded.

"What about them?" David asked quizzically as his fingers grazed Luci's goggles.

"Don't you wear them to correct your sight?" Scot responded, only realizing that the goggles hadn't belonged to David once the words crossed his lips.

"My sight?" David queried as he brought the goggles down over his eyes. "Holy shit!" he exclaimed as he started to scan his eyes around the room. He looked at the conduits and wires before him, observing each of the colors. He then looked at the Muse vortex which continued to swirl down through the atrium, picking up on the brilliant shades of greens, violets, reds, and blues. Tears had started to form in his eyes as a sense of epiphany filled him, being amplified by the funnel they were trying to shut down. "Is this what you get to see?" he murmured.

"We don't have time for this right now," Scot replied. "If we don't get the Musestrom shutdown right now, we are risking plunging both our worlds into darkness. That iron door can't hold her for long if the Black Door falls."

"Right," David said, snapping himself out of his momentary trance. He looked back down at the mass of connectors and started to reconnect them to the tall wall of components next to him, blues to blues, reds to reds, greens to greens, and what he assumed to be purple to purple while Scot went to work on coding in the shutdown sequence.

After a few minutes of work, David announced, "Okay I'm done."

"Okay, when I say so, I need you to turn the key in that console to the off position," Scot replied.

"Hey guys," Chauncey interrupted. "I don't mean to intrude but where is that psycho Sara and the Wordsmith?"

"Probably fled like the cowards they are," Trig interjected.

David's eyes glanced to the spot where Sara had been shackled, seeing the broken cuffs they had used lying on the ground. "I can't speak to Wordsmith but Sara...she's a lot of things but she's no coward," David replied.

"So nice of you to say, David," Sara said as she stepped out from behind the wall of components, grabbing him from behind and sticking a knife to his neck.

"Sara, you can put the knife down. He is not a threat," Scot commanded to his private army's commander.

"I'm sorry, did you think I was working for you?" Sara replied before adding, "Wordsmith, now!"

The group watched as a restored Wordsmith crept out from behind the wall. They had expected her to make some kind of grand attack but she simply ran toward the exit as Sara kept their leverage at knife point.

"Okay, she's gone now. Let me go, we need to get this machine shut down!" David nervously implored. He was truly shaken. A wave of recollection concerning his compromised position washed over him, cleansing him of the remaining epiphanous feelings that had been triggered by the goggles.

The funnel of Muse had reached down toward the Wellspring. The sounds of Trig's cap locks clanging against the sides of their shackles could be heard echoing up the atrium.

"After the trouble you caused me, do you really expect me to let you live?" Sara responded, not giving heed to his words as she withdrew the knife from David's neck. She wound her knife arm back, ready to plunge the blade into his spine.

She had started her forward thrust but froze. The knife, still in hand, hung in the air as a rushing blackness stormed its way toward her. The unseen Razor-Sith leaped from the nearby shadows, peeling her off David and casting her to the ground. Sara's pained screams of "No! Nooo! No! Nooooooo!" were silenced to a gurgle by piercing fangs as Wishbone rended her throat from her body.

The group stared on, stunned, as the self-satisfied cat sat back on its haunches and began to fastidiously clean its face. It paused mid-lick. "Go on shut the machine down," Wishbone said, knocking David and Scot out of their momentary stupor.

Scot and David turned back toward the machine and on the count of three, turned their keys. In nearly an instant, the funnel reversed its direction and started to climb back out of the atrium. The vacuum tubes of the machine had begun to glow with bright intensity and the floor had begun to shake.

"Scot, is this normal?" Marnie asked, shouting over the rising noise as the whole tower started to rattle.

A look of concern crept across Scot's face as the tubes continued to get brighter and brighter. Seeing that David was in the path of an imminent explosion, Scot sprinted toward him with the intent of knocking him out of the way. He took a flying leap through the air, much as he had seen the Sìth do just moments prior. He collided with David just as all of the tubes shattered at once. Muse ejected from each of the exposed ports on the wall, sending shock waves through both men as they flew through the air. In a matter of moments, the lights in the room dissipated and the funnel disappeared leaving only faint traces of the Muse aurora in the sky above.

***

Due to Scot's action, David had only taken a small amount of the hit and rolled away clean. He lay on the floor for a moment, surveying his body, before deciding to stand up. The rest of the group ran over, hovering over Scot who was writhing on the floor.

"It's too much. It's too much. Make it stop," Scot pleaded as his eyes stared blankly toward the sky. Multicolored light was coursing through his veins, trying to reactivate the burnt-out pathways in his body.

"What is it? What's too much?" Marnie begged of her brother, hoping her words could penetrate the madness in his head.

"Everything..." Scot replied, "...I can see everything. Make it stop. Make it stop." Tears had started to form in his eyes as every permutation of the future laid itself out before him. Unspeakable horrors were haunting his visions, things no one should bear witness to. The one power that had been left with the Mórrigan, the one that no mortal was capable of harnessing, the power that had been left with the godwitch had penetrated his mind.

"What do we do? What do we do?" Marnie pleaded as she looked at her father for answers. The pained cries of her brother echoed across the domed room.

"He must have been inflicted with the Mórrigan sight. The tubes. This machine. The Flood. It's all happening again. I...I don't know...I don't know what to do," Declan said out loud, though a thought had started to form inside his head. It was one he dare not speak. It was the same thought that had brought him to where he was now.

"Can't you make him forget?" David questioned, speaking the thought for the Master. He now fully understood the nature of what Declan had done, who his Forgotten Master truly was.

"Is that something you can do?" Marnie asked. "Make him forget?"

"I...I can't do it to him...Not again," Declan said, pleading with his daughter and David not to push him.

"Please Dad...please," Scot begged from the floor as he clutched his head tightly between his palms.

A moment passed before Wishbone's timbrous voice spoke with authoritative aplomb, "You must do this Declan Mhurchaidh. Not out of selfishness. Not out of hubris. Not out of vanity. You must do this out of compassion...Compassion, the false excuse you used to justify yourself so many years ago. You must spare him this torture."

"I...I can't do it to him. It would break his mind further. It would kill him," Declan said desperately, his words resting in the air.

Chauncey glanced at Declan, the gears in his head were in fast motion as he offered, "What if you had a vessel?"

"My mind...my mind is too broken," Declan replied. "I don't have much Muse left. I can't hold it together and do the transfer...would kill us both."

"No..." Chauncey responded, "Me...it has to be me. The person who holds this knowledge can't know they have it. You have to give it to me and make me forget. Forget you, forget Marnie, forget all of it. It never happened."

"This...this is stupid," Trig said. "There has to be another way. This is all you ever wanted. The grand adventure. World saving stakes. I can't let you give that up." They looked at their friend, then over to Declan before speaking, "Use me."

"I would tell. You know I'd tell. I won't be able to help myself," Chauncey pleaded. "It has to be me. With your new power, you'd be able to protect me. What would I have to offer you?"

Trig didn't say anything. Part of their desire to forget was to alleviate the pain of losing Luci. There was a moment of contemplation. "She deserves better," they finally thought. "She needs someone to remember the hero she was." They weren't about to leave that responsibility in the hands of Chauncey.

"The fool is correct," Wishbone chimed in. "It has to be him. We cannae risk leaving this responsibility to rest in the mind of a Master. We cannae risk another corruption."

"What about me?" David finally chimed in, throwing his hat in the ring.

"We cannae risk leaving this responsibility in the mind of a Master," the Razor-Sìth repeated.

David was left puzzled as he looked down at his arms seeing electric blue light coursing through his veins in contrast to his now glowing skin.

"Are you sure you want to do this?" Declan said, directing his question toward Chauncey.

"Of course I'm not sure," he responded, "but it appears we are out of options here, Sunny Jim."

Another pained cry emanated from Scot as he continued to writhe on the ground.

Marnie approached Chauncey and hugged him, not sure of what to say before finally offering, "I think I'll miss you most of all." She held the embrace for a moment.

"I wish I could say the same. This long strange trip has been something else," he said as he looked her in the eyes before withdrawing from her arms. He gave David a nod of respect which was returned in kind. He then approached Trig, "I suspect this will give you reason to be coarse with me again."

"I'll try to go easy on you," Trig replied. "No promises."

"None needed," Chauncey responded. He then took a lying position next to Scot. "Do it," he said as he closed his eyes.

Declan placed his hands on Chauncey and Scot's foreheads. He then focused his intention to draw the godwitch's power out of Scot's head. He took the sight and stored it in the recesses of Chauncey's mind, deep in his subconscious where he could never find it. He released Chauncey into a dreamless slumber, allowing his brain to build the walls around the hidden knowledge, forging a new Forgotten Master.

With a continued connection to his son, Declan took all of the corruption-tainted memories and buried them far down in the recesses of Scot's mind. They would come to live in the areas where dreams were forged. The places Muse would enter as it crossed from one plane to another. With any luck, when Scot awoke he would believe he had been in a coma for the last five years, unaware of the evil deeds he had been coerced into doing. Declan left Scot to sleep as he turned his attention toward his daughter.

"We need to cross back over before he wakes up. He cannot know this world exists," Declan said, still questioning in his mind if he was doing the right thing. "David, drop that door into the pit," he continued as he gestured toward the bridge.

"What? How?" David questioned as Declan approached him.

The Forgotten Master placed his palm on David's head and focused the last of his remaining Muse into his pupil's mind. David's veins shifted from a dark electric blue to ultraviolet.

"Oh," said David as he turned to face the bridge. Declan had spent his last vestige of Muse to drop one final wall, giving David an understanding of the true power he held, the reason his command of the Muse was the way it was. One that had been secreted from him so many years ago. One that would serve him well in the nights to come.

"It would seem the apprentice has become the Master," Declan said as he bowed his head to David.

David placed his hands on the rotation mechanism that had held the bridge in place. The support melted at his touch and the menhir swung downward, causing it to bounce off the sides of the atrium. The force imparted on the opposing support caused it to snap, sending the Green Door crashing down to the citadel foundations below.

"Can you make sure that room gets sealed off?" Declan asked Trig.

"Me?" Trig questioned as they pointed at themselves.

"Yeah, you. Someone is going to need to take charge around here. Better the person who never wanted it than the one who seeks it," Declan replied.

Trig considered the request for a moment. "How am I going to explain all of this to him?" they responded.

"You're your fathers' child. You'll figure it out," Declan replied. The reverence that colored his voice spoke volumes about the respect that he, the greatest of the Masters, had for Trig's parents, George and Gilbert.

Scot started to murmur as he often did in the minutes before waking up from sleep.

"We need to get out of here," Declan stated. "Marnie, a door."

Marnie walked to the nearest wall and reached into her bag, pulling out a can of black paint. She then proceeded to freehand a traditional Green Man on the wall. This piece was much more simplified than the ones Scot had painted, lacking the layers and visual flair that marked his style. The one she had drawn consisted of a face on a single acanthus leaf.

"What about the eyes?" she questioned of her father, having not yet considered the return trip.

Declan pulled out his chisel and used it to scratch a shape on the floor. He drew one circle with a single crescent moon on the inside.

"Of course," she said. "Terra and Luna."

Declan nodded as his daughter turned back to her painting to scribe in the last of the details.

Marnie finished the piece and turned toward Trig to say her final goodbye.

"You did good, lass," Trig said as they went in for a hug. Tears had started to well up in their eyes.

"I'll never forget you," Marnie said, knowing she could never come back to this place. While it was full of things to be feared, it wasn't without its allures, foremost among them were the friends she had made in Chauncey and his partner Trig. But even with her new friends, it would be much too dangerous, a single trace of her Muse being enough to free the ancient evil that continued to lurk below.

Marnie activated the doorway, allowing it to light up and the tentacle-like vines to grow. She found herself in control of the portal, keeping the appendages at bay until she was ready. Declan lifted his son into his arms and allowed himself to be taken through.

"David you're next," Marnie stated as she looked at her friend.

"I'm not coming back with you," David stated.

"David quit playing, you have to," Marnie replied.

"Marnie, this is my home," David responded. "It's always been my home. Don't you see I was just a visitor in yours? They're going to need me."

A sudden realization and feelings of epiphany washed over Marnie. All of his secrets. His singular attachment to Scot in the place she called home. His predilection toward the avoidance of danger where she and her brother were concerned. She wondered at that moment, "What had my father hidden from you?"..."What had you actually known?"

"But what if we need someone to watch over us?" Marnie asked, already knowing any further attempt to coerce his crossing would be in vain.

"Look for me in the witching hour," he replied. "When the night is its darkest and the walls are most thin. Ask what I would do...Then do the opposite. Throw some paint up on that wall."

"I love you...I'll miss you," Marnie said as she backed into the doorway, letting herself be taken for a final time.

David Almánzar stared on, tears streaming down his cheeks. His watch over the Murphy children had finally come to a close.

***

Marnie opened her eyes to find her father cradling the upper part of her brother's sleeping body in his arms as he sat on the living room floor of Scot's loft.

"How are we ever going to begin to explain this to Mom?" she asked as she looked into her father's eyes, breathing a sigh of relief.

"Marnie? Is that you?" a panicked voice spoke from one of the loft's bedrooms. The voice was followed by frantic footsteps. "Scot? Declan?" Diane eked out as she collapsed to her knees.

"What can one make of such a denouement?"

"It's been six months, why isn't the pit filled in yet?" Trig asked.

"In case you haven't noticed, a lot is going on right now," Chauncey replied. "I don't know why we're doing any of this anyway. What did Ærratum ever do for us?"

"For the thousandth time...when you caused the Dawnbreaker to remember her father in the woods, you set off a blowout that changed the very fabric on which the Muse flows," Trig replied. "You and you alone created a new Flood. This is our reward...or penance."

"And I went into a coma because of this?" Chauncey responded.

"Yes, you went into a coma," Trig responded.

"And Imperium is no more because of this?" he followed up.

"Yes, your actions defeated Imperium," Trig said, once more entertaining the endless volley of questions that exited their friend's mouth, already anticipating the one that would follow.

"And this girl Marnie...the Dawnbreaker, she dissipated into the Muse?" Chauncey asked.

"Yes, she was obliterated like her father before her," Trig replied.

"And you...you're a Master?" Chauncey said, completing his string of questions.

"Again, for the thousandth time, yes I'm a Master," Trig responded.

"I know. I just like to hear you say it," Chauncey replied.

Trig couldn't be sure if their companion's transformation into the Forgotten Master had stunted his short-term memory or if he was just having a laugh at their expense.

***

"That marks fourteen we know of still intact," David said as he surveyed the Seoin Menhir.

"He cannae sniff the stigma on this one," Wishbone said as the pair observed Brutus explore the perimeter of the large henge.

David let out a dejected sigh, "I wish the Vagabond hadn't taken knowledge of the doors when he sent me on the long watch. That was ten years I could have been studying."

"Don't worry laddie, we'll find the traitor Wordsmith. We'll figure out how she used the Dark Door," Wishbone responded to David's murmurs.

"Look's like Beàrnan Menhir is next," David said as he mounted the cyclocycle. He touched his hand to the fuel tank, causing it to come to life. The trio then set off for their next destination.

***

"Any more thoughts of moving out?" Diane said as she closed the pizza box that sat in front of her.

"Yeah...but I...I don't think I'm ready," Scot said, "My mind is still all jumbled."

"It will come in time son," Declan chimed in. "We just have to take it one day at a time. It will come in time."

"Where's Marnie tonight?" Scot asked, changing the subject. "Not like her to miss Friday night pizza."

"She's doing a mural on the side of the courthouse," Diane replied. "She warned me it was going to be 'provocative'. I don't want to know the world of shit I'm going to walk into Monday."

"Not as much shit as you had to go through explaining the re-emergence of your husband and son, I'm sure," Martin said, going in for a slice of his own. "You're lucky I have a good sense of humor...but please don't accuse me of murder again."

"I will never not be sorry for that," Diane said as she watched Martin try to hold back his laughter.

***

"Beep beep, boop," the pickle-pocketed robot said, as it finished chiseling through the Ebony Wellspring's iron cap, dropping into the oubliette below.

"Curious," the Mórrigan said, as she watched it hit the floor with a crash. Its telescopic arms pushed its body up to rest over its singular wheel.

The robot wheeled its way over to the seated Mórrigan.

"And who might you be?" she asked, staring at the creature before her.

At this, the creature extended its telescopic arm and brought them to bear against the side of its head. A crack began to form across its face as it wound up for another blow. Upon the second connection of its fists, the machine's head exploded, causing an escape of pure white light.

"Curious indeed," the Mórrigan said as she reached her arms out to grab hold of the essence. Darkened wings sprang forth from her back. She watched the rest of the light drain out of the robot's camera eye, its aperture closing forever as her own eyes drifted toward the undulating darkness above.

***

Marnie couldn't help but feel anxious being alone, painting the side of the courthouse building. Even though she had her mother's permission, somehow it still felt wrong.

"I do my best work in the witching hours," she muttered to herself as she stepped back to survey her latest work. "She is definitely going to regret letting me do this."

The piece Marnie had painted was a representation of Lady Justice. Lady Justice's pale marbled body had been depicted as with child. The blindfold once used to blind her eyes had been repurposed as a gag, allowing her to see but not speak.

Marnie had made Justice's sword oversized and integrated her balanced scales into its hilt. The dish on the right was filled with money while the one on the left was filled with feathers. The scale's dishes hung off the cross guard, unable to move freely, a false balance. Some chains led from the ends of the guard to the tip of the pommel.

These elements would have all been acceptable to Diane had it not been for how Marnie combined them. Lady Justice had been depicted as being crucified on her sword and scales. Blood poured out of the hand on the right soaking the money beneath it.

Marnie didn't expect this piece to have a long runtime but felt she was saying something that needed to be said. She hoped that the conversations that inspired the work would outlive the piece itself. With her brother home safe, she had learned to embrace the ephemera his tongue had so constantly espoused.

"Now where is my silver," she said, talking to herself. "Need to add the accents."

"Here use mine," a voice behind her whispered, startling her. Panic grew up Marnie's spine before quickly subsiding as she leaned into it.

Marnie caught the can as it rolled across the ground. She raised it to the piece and started to accent the eyes.

"Thanks," she said just before witnessing the silver accents fill with light.

Marnie turned her head to look at the person who had provided the paint, seeing a reflection of her freshly painted Lady Justice staring back at her.

The woman spoke, "So...where do your ideas come from?"

The End

Chapter Title Reference

Prologue - "What's past is prologue." - William Shakespeare, The Tempest

I - "The abyss gazes also into you." - Friedrich W. Nietzsche, Beyond Good and Evil

II - "Do not go gentle..." - Dylan Thomas, Do Not Go Gentle Into That Good Night

III - "...sincerest form of flattery..." - Oscar Wilde

IV - "...a house that tries to be haunted." —— Emily Dickinson

V - "...the crag of Scylla and dire Charybdis' vortex..." - Homer, Odyssey

VI- "...straight on till morning." - J. M. Barrie, Peter Pan

VII - "...six impossible things before breakfast." - Lewis Carroll, Alice's Adventures in Wonderland

VIII - "If the fact will not fit the theory...let the theory go." - Agatha Christie, The Mysterious Affair at Styles

IX - "...eddying darkness seemed to swim round me... - Charlotte Bronte, Jane Eyre

X - "A warrior will sooner die than live a life of shame." - Beowulf

XI - "It isn't what we say or think that defines us, but what we do." - Jane Austin, Sense and Sensibility

XII - "...that dare not speak its name." - Lord Alfred Douglas, Two Loves

XIII - "Ships that pass in the night." - Henry Wadsworth Longfellow, Tales of a Wayside Inn

XIV - "...barefoot from distant travel..." - Charles Dickens, Great Expectations

XV - "...making the darkness conscious." - Carl Jung, Psychology and Alchemy

XVI - "...awoke one morning from uneasy dreams..." - Franz Kafka, The Metamorphosis

XVII - "I defy you, stars! " - William Shakespeare, Romeo and Juliet

XVIII - "Unfortunately the cave contained a lion." - Aesop, Aesop's Fables: The Stag and the Lion

XIX - "What hath night to do with sleep?" - John Milton, Paradise Lost

XX - "...this bitter world where vice is king..." - Molière, The Misanthrope

XXI - "How did I escape? With difficulty." - Alexander Dumas, The Count of Monte Cristo

XXII - "...then in the following one it should be fired." - Anton Chekhov

XXIII - "...brains do not make one happy." - L Frank Baum, The Wonderful Wizard of Oz

Epilogue - "What can one make of such a denouement?" - Arthur Conan Doyle, The Valley of Fear

The Orb Mongers

"Why do you insist on wearing those ridiculous clothes? We're on a mission for crying out loud." It was a question Trig had asked on countless occasions, a castigation with rhetorical foundations. They knew it would not be heard as such.

Chauncey had formed a repertoire of answers that he believed to be of sound reason. He scrolled through the Rolodex in his mind before offering, "What we do tonight, dear Trig, is fraught with danger. If I'm going to go out, I'm going to go out in style. Leave a good-looking corpse and all that."

"And who, pray tell, would come 'round to mourn you?" Trig chided. "I'm your only friend and I barely tolerate you."

"So we're friends now, are we then? A rare admittance indeed. I'm going to have to mark this one down," Chauncey quipped. Though Trig would be hard-pressed to admit it, Chauncey always suspected that they held a spot in their heart for him. "Why are you so concerned with my clothes? It's not like they hinder my movements...see?" The tallish elf-like man with dandy flair crouched down before immediately popping up to his feet. He then threw out a few leg kicks for good measure. "See, full range of motion. I had a good tailor after all."

"For the last time, I'm not your bloody tailor," Trig responded before adding, "If you're going to waste your orb on something as stupid as clothes, they should at least have some function." They had become aggravated. Their glowing purple veins started to pulse. "Can we just focus on the task at hand?"

"Hey..." Chauncey started, unsure as to why Trig had become flustered, "...you're the one that brought it up."

"A fresh regret indeed," Trig said as their eyes drew down to the old mill at the base of the hill upon which they found themselves perched.

A field of glowwheat stretched down the hillside, filling in the gap between their hide and the target ahead. The Lonely Sister bathed the area with a crimson moonbeam which mingled with the gold of the field to produce an orange hue. Trig thought of smoldering embers as they watched the stalks move back and forth in the warm autumn breeze. They brought the hood of their cloak up to cover the shock of electric blue hair that sat atop their head and they beckoned Chauncey to do the same. "Okay exactly as we planned...No diversions."

"No diversions," Chauncey echoed.

***

Three Nights Prior

"Why do you suppose he calls it 'Lance's Dance Hall'?" asked Chauncey. "I've never seen anyone dancing...and his name's not even Lance."

"Because 'shithole where reprobates go to gamble and cheat on their partners' is too much of a mouthful," Trig replied. They waited a moment before letting out a slight sigh, adding what they rightly assumed was the real reason, "...some times people shoot for the stars and have to settle for the moon."

"Oh really, which one?" Chauncey said.

Trig glared at him, unsure if he was attempting to make a joke or if he was actually confused. They were about to clarify the statement before being cut off by an interloper.

"Did someone say gamble?"

"Go away Todd, I don't have the patience for your nonsense tonight," Trig replied.

"No need to be hostile my friend," Todd replied.

"We-are-not-friends," Trig said, careful to enunciate every word so there would be no mistaking their position.

"Besides, with what I have to wager you may very well change your tune," Todd said. A sly grin crept across his face, one that indicated that he may, for once, have something worthwhile.

Chauncey, much to Trig's chagrin, was quick to take the bait, "Really, what do you have? Something good I hope."

Trig rolled their eyes, their mind was already forming the words to send Todd on his way.

"Information, orbs, at least thirty of them," Todd quickly blurted out, trying to preempt further rebuttal.

Trig thought about the prospect for a moment. Thirty orbs would fulfill the Drumlocke order. *Could Todd have known?...No, there was no way. Pherson is known for bouts of imprudence but he can't be this careless, can he?* Trig would decide that the spatial math didn't add up. Todd, in all truth, rarely left the confines of Olde Towne, and if he did it was to cross the city wall in an attempt to skirt his ban from the Violet Huntress. Most taverns in Ærratum frowned on open gambling, especially if, like Todd, one didn't have the courtesy to give the bartender a proper rake of the winnings. No, Todd would not have known about the duo's illicit contract, this was just a happy coincidence—or if you're Trig, an unhappy one.

"OK, I'm listening," Trig said, careful to make sure that their voice was not shaded by eagerness. In truth, it was effort wasted, nobody would have recognized what passed for eagerness in Trig's voice anyway.

"Let's discuss your side of the wager first," Todd replied. "Same ask as last time?"

"Gross," Trig said before relenting, "Fine, same as last time."

"And you're sure you can make something like that? Texture, ooze, and what-not?" the gambler asked.

Trig looked at Todd dejected by the prospect of their talents being tragically misused if they were to lose. "Yes, I assure you, I am more than capable." Disgust was something that was recognizable in their voice as they briefly let their mind consider the use Todd would have for such a device.

"Okay then!" Todd exclaimed. "What's it going to be then?"

Trig thought for a moment and said, "Darts or thirteen vulgar stones." They said this knowing that neither game would suffice for their opponent. These were games of skill. Todd, they knew, was a gambling purest but it never hurt to try.

"Oh, come now Trig, you know my Upland heritage wouldn't allow me to agree to games that can be beaten with practice. No, no, no, no, no—Nothing less than pure luck will sate my appetite this eve," Todd replied. "How 'bouts we let the spectator decide? Chauncey, what will it be then?"

Trig glared at Chauncey, trying to project thoughts into his head, desperately trying to force him to pick a game that could be gamed in some way, something with a hidden layer of skill, something that could be exploited. They knew it wouldn't work. Even if the Readers weren't all but extinct, Chauncey would be the last person to be suspected of possessing such a gift.

Chauncey's eyes didn't even meet Trig's as they drifted toward the ceiling, trying to pull something from the top of his brain. The decision didn't warrant the consideration he was giving it. This only served to add to Trig's agitation as they continued to glare at him. "What about Witchell?" he finally offered.

"Of course he'd have to choose that one," Trig thought. Witchell was one of the few games that Chauncey had ever been able to best Trig in. It was a game that, to Trig's chagrin, honored the bygone Masters. It was not a game that could be gamed indeed. They attempted to protest, "We don't have a board...or pieces. Can't we just flip a coin, get this over with already?"

"Dear Trig, where is the fun in that?" Todd said as he pulled up his sleeve to reveal the leather cuff attached to his arm. The cuff contained a clockwork mechanism flanked by two small wire-wrapped tubes, each of which possessed a soft blue glow. Flashing lights peaked out from under the gears as an indication of the computations and communications being made within. "It's no worry I still have a few charges."

Trig watched in continued revulsion as Todd pressed a button on the side of the device. With his palm hovering over the table, his eyes rolled back into his head, and a detectable shiver ran through his body. A smile crept across Todd's face as a circular copper game board appeared between the pair. The board was coated with a greenish patina. This, Trig knew, was unintentional, a sign of an unskilled Muser.

From the dingy board grew fifteen pairs of matching pieces. There was one set per side. Each piece represented one of the fifteen Masteries. Trig lifted a piece to inspect it and was half surprised that it was not affixed to the board. The pieces were not of quality construction, possessing blocky unfinished appearances and the potential to cause splinters in the hands of the players who wield them. Looking at the condition of the game it was immediately clear to Trig why Todd did not want to produce the device that would be the fulfillment of their end of the wager.

"So they got their hooks into you too," Trig stated, commenting on the cuff. "Why am I not surprised?"

"We're all going to have to come around eventually. Way of the world in these uncharted times," Todd replied. "So, what's it going to be Outland or Upland rules?"

"Outland..." Trig responded. "I don't want this taking any more time than it needs to."

"Outland it is then," Todd said as pulled a pair of bone dice from his pocket, ready to hand one of the pair to Trig.

To Trig's surprise, Chauncey reached out to grab Todd's wrist, arresting the action. "Now now Todd, you know Trig doesn't trust your dice." Chauncey had learned to expect the objection their partner would have and was already working to rectify the situation. He yelled over to the bartender, "Oi! Rory, can we get a set of untainted bones over here?"

A pair of dice came flying at Chauncey's head, "How many times do I have to tell you? When I'm behind the bar, the name's Lance, jerk-o."

"Sorry Mr. Jerk-O. I'll try to remember," Chauncey replied before reaching down to pick the dice up off the floor, rubbing the side of his face they had impacted as he handed them to Trig.

"His name's not Jerk-O," Trig started before relenting, "You know what, never mind." They turned their attention to Todd and said, "Just roll."

The Outland rules for Witchell were simpler than the Upland variation. Each player sets their pieces up in any configuration they want within the fifteen discs that bordered the outer edge of their hemisphere of the board. The players each roll a die and count the result from the leftmost piece to the right, looping back if needed. Those pieces then 'duel' based on a situational and convoluted set of piece rankings. The victor reclaims their piece and the loser sets theirs aside in the 'graveyard.' Play is over once one side has been wiped out.

The Upland rules added five more dice to be split between the players each round based on piece rankings. There is then a two-out-of-three dice roll battle. The only purpose for the added rules, as far as anyone knew, was to allow more time for drinking.

There had been an attempt at popularizing a simple hand gesture version of the game but it only contained signs for three Masteries. Lack of history and ceremony caused it to fizzle out quickly.

Trig and Todd each rolled a die to see which pieces would battle first.

"Ahh, the classic battle of the Poet and the Critic," Todd said as he withdrew the Critic to its starting position.

Trig moved the Poet to their graveyard and they each rolled again. The game saw a few more of the 'classic' match-ups, the Storyteller and the Comedian, the Librarian and the Professor, the Dancer and the Siren.

Todd had the good fortune of pulling the Gambler early and giddily exclaimed, "Oh what luck, my favorite piece." It was a piece that had no rank and allowed the player to leave it in the arena as long as they wanted. A single competing dice roll then decided fates. Todd was able to use the Gambler to take Trig's Engineer, Seer, and Librarian before his piece was claimed by the opposing Gambler which was quickly defeated by his Destroyer. On the next turn, Trig's own Destroyer faced down and took Todd's Seer in another of the 'classic' match-ups.

Trig saw no need to converse with Todd more than was required and Todd, having played his opponent more than once before, knew that his normal chatty style of gameplay would be met with stern silence so he didn't waste his breath save for the occasional outburst when one of his pieces found itself to be the victor.

Play lasted seven minutes before Trig and Todd's piece counts were depleted to just three and five respectively. It was at this point that Trig did some mental math and noted that their chances for victory were very close to being dead.

On the next round, Todd pulled the Architect, a piece that could have bested two of Trig's three remaining pieces and possibly the third depending on what the fates had in store. His eyes were alight with the expectation of his pending victory and more so, his pending reward.

Trig rolled their die. It spun on its axis for a moment before settling on a six. Fate had caused their roll to land on the Vagabond. The slightest of smiles formed at the corners of their mouth. Their chances had slightly improved and they allowed the smallest bit of hope to creep in.

The Vagabond was a sacrificial piece allowing for the return of another piece from the side of the board. Per Witchell's rules, Todd lined up Trig's defeated pieces in the order of his choosing. He didn't really have a strategy but did make a show of reshuffling them five times before letting them be. The shuffling, he knew, only served the purpose of agitating his opponent and would perhaps cause them to channel bad luck into the die.

Trig then rolled their die three times, adding up the pips as they went. Two fives and a three, a total of thirteen. A feeling of dread crept over them as they zeroed in on the piece that would come back to play. They made a show of placing their fingers on each piece as they counted down the row, cycling back to one once they hit the end, trying to delay the inevitable. Their finger was resting on the Engineer. They put the Engineer in the center and knocked it over, resigning the game to Todd, knowing their last two pieces were guaranteed losers against any of Todd's pieces in the next rounds.

Trig's eyes drew up from the board to see no joy in Todd's. They looked over to Chauncey to see elation in his. "What, what is it?"

"Trig, you won!" Chauncey exclaimed.

"What? You fool, no I didn't. Architect beats Engineer," Trig replied.

"I hate to say it but your friend's correct," Todd offered. "Last War rule."

"The what?" Trig responded.

"The Last War rule," Todd stated. "It was added a little over ten years ago. If the Engineer is resurrected by the Vagabond causing a situation where the Engineer faces down the Architect, the player who possesses said Engineer immediately wins the game. It was done as a tribute to the Coimín lineage's triumph over the Geddes and to honor the Vagabond Master's sacrifice. I've never actually played a game where it's happened. The luck in seeing it almost makes the loss worth it. Take this as a good omen. Fate smiles upon you."

"Yes what luck," Chauncey said, mirroring the gambler. "Surely this is a sign that we are about to embark on a grand adventure."

Trig's mind exploded with feelings of epiphany as a warmth radiated down their spine and through their appendages. The feeling helped to mask a sadness they knew should have been in its place, a sadness that always followed mention of the Last War and the Masters that the game pieces represent. Trig rolled their eyes, "There is no room left in this world for luck or fate. They are simple constructs of simple minds." Their eyes drifted from Todd to Chauncey then back to Todd. "Spill it."

"Sure you don't want to make it best of three?" Todd asked in jest, though there was a part of him that hoped Trig would agree.

Trig swept their arm across the table, knocking the Witchell pieces to the floor. Not a single figure was left intact as they crumbled like under-baked pottery upon impact. They weren't sure if they fell apart due to Todd being a poor Muser or if it was the substandard nature of objects produced by cuffs. Truth be told they didn't know if the cuffs were capable of producing quality items as they didn't know of an Adept Muser willing to try one. The cuffs were seen as a debasement of the art form. They couldn't help but feel a little hypocritical at this moment; not so long ago, the use of Muse Orbs was seen in the same light. The feeling was fleeting. Their eyes shifted to a glare as they drew them back to Todd.

"Alright, alright, alright," a flustered Todd started. "I may have heard from a guy, that heard from a gal, that knows someone who works in a certain house, that someone has a horde."

"Well Todd, I think we knew that already," Trig replied.

"Did we?" Chauncey questioned.

Trig's glare traced itself over to their partner. They didn't know whether to be annoyed or sorry for him, "Haven't you been paying attention?"

"I thought he might have them on him," Chauncey replied.

"He told us it was information he was peddling," Trig said. They may have been giving Todd too much credit but figured he also knew the cardinal rule of grifting. *You never do more than one illegal thing at a time, unless of course, the subsequent illegal thing was in service of the first illegal thing.* Gambling, strictly speaking, wasn't exactly legal.

"Oh right," Chauncey said as his eyes moved over to Todd, threatening, "Yeah, where are they jerk-o?"

"Relax...relax, I was going to tell you. Man of my word after all," Todd said. He glanced over his shoulder for eavesdroppers. Trig's instincts caused them to do the same. Chauncey also took the opportunity to look around but was not as inconspicuous as his tablemates. He craned his neck rapidly from side to side and in all manner of angles. Trig kicked him under the table, causing him to roll his head back. He once more attempted to be inconspicuous as he pretended to work out a crick in his neck.

Todd continued, "So, as I was saying, I know a guy, who knows a gal, who knows someone that works for Vernon Kesley. Yes, that Vernon Kesley. Word is he's got a stash. Doesn't really have a purpose for them, just keeps 'em on a shelf in his study. Likes to bask in their glow every evening I guess—Told he does it in the buff too. Might think it'll give him his power back."

Before the Flood, Vernon Kesley was the Master Poet. He was said to be capable of making someone weep with less than six words, or so his legend goes. He also made up one-fifth of a cadre of Masters known as the Laureates, the propaganda arm of the Geddes regime. Many in Eternal Dawn still held the surviving Laureates in esteem but there were just as many that would see him cast out, never to return. He didn't have much to fear from the latter. They were the more educated of the two groups. They had logic on their side and were still prone to proper etiquette. Trig, being of the later group, save for the etiquette, despised him and all that he had done. Hearing that he would be the object of their next act of larceny sent more feelings of epiphany down their spine, leaving their body warm and tingly. It felt like a second victory.

"He still live in that garish house in Center District?" Trig asked.

"It's called Imperium District now but yeah, same one," Todd said.

"Don't remind me," Trig replied, knowing that they would never use the new name. With that, Trig rose from the table and exited the bar with Chauncey in tow.

Todd was left looking at the crumbled Witchell pieces then to his cuff, thinking about the prize that got away, wondering if he should take a gamble on a second attempt to produce it himself. He remembered the embarrassing trip to the clinic that his previous attempt required and thought better of it, deciding to bide his time until he could sucker another Adept into a game of chance.

***

"You think Gamblin' Todd can be trusted?" Chauncey asked as they started walking down the road to Olde Towne toward the abandoned house that had become the pair's latest residence.

"The information itself?—Yes," Trig replied. "That we were the only ones he's shared this information with, definitely not."

"What are you thinkin'?" Chauncey asked.

"I'm *thinkin'* that I have to do a little more thinking," Trig responded.

The pair made their way back to the squat. Chauncey crashed on the couch with Trig looking on from a chair, forming a plan for this, their latest grift. It wasn't long before they too fell asleep.

***

Chauncey and Trig awoke as the purple moon Uther was breaking the horizon. A new night of possibilities had laid itself out before them.

"So, what's the plan then," Chauncey opened. As he stared at Trig, he started to get the impression that they had not made the progress they had intended. Seeing this as an opportunity, he chimed in, "It's on Chauncey then is it?...Okay, how 'bout this? We wait until the Poet throws a party then we go in disguised as catering or better yet, maids—You know, someone who is supposed to be there. Then when nobody's looking, wham boom, we dip into the study, take the goods, then repel out the window. Bango, contract fulfilled."

Trig looked blankly at Chauncey, thinking that it was too early for this level of nonsense. Sleeping upright in a chair had done them no favors. They would have much preferred a bedroll in the forest to sleeping in the abandoned house.

Sensing their disapproval, Chauncey launched into another proposal, "What if we get into a box and mail ourselves to him? That could work—right?"

"I'm going to need a cup of coffee before I respond to this blackened well-spring-bound idiocy," Trig said. They may have been on the wake but their Chauncey chastisement impulse still appeared to be sleeping and more importantly, so too was their focus.

Chauncey made one more attempt, "The 'no plan' plan then? A classic grift? Knock on the front door? Classic ransacking?" He knew his ideas weren't great. It was the way of the world. Trig's brilliance only shined as bright as it did when they had someone to contrast against. Chauncey was more than happy to be that contrast. At the very least he thought his ideas might spur some of Trig's brilliance.

"Let's get out of here," Trig said. They were not yet able to conjure a witty retort. The call of a dark roast was much too great.

"Can't I change first? Can't wear the same outfit twice in as many days. Fashion faux pas and whatnot, " he replied.

"Fine."

***

Trig waited until they were inside the city walls before acquiring the beverage they so desperately craved. They had once sampled the swill served in Olde Towne and

313

decided that the intestinal distress it inflicted was enough for them to swear off the entire district.

They downed half the cup before they felt that their mind was spinning at their normal rate. "First thing's first," they started, staring at Chauncey who had draped himself in a purple velour suit, complete with cravat. "We have to case the target. Figure out if the pillaging has already been done. See who else is camping the spot. See who else has beaten Gamblin' Todd recently."

"Right-o, sounds good. Think we'll get to meet him? Never met a Master before. He's not one of my favorites, entanglement with the Geddes and all, but still a Master," Chauncey replied with eagerness.

"Ex-Master and war criminal," Trig corrected, scorn once more tinged their voice at discussion of the Masters. "Your heart should hold no quarter for the Poet."

"I'm guessing that's a no then?" said a slightly dejected Chauncey.

***

The pair made the nine-block walk to Baird Park. It was a lightly wooded area that bordered Imperium Spire. This proximity to the tower allowed the forest to glow resplendently, hearkening back to the luminescence of the Outland forests just five years prior. Seeing the park triggered a yearning in Trig, an almost sadness as they wondered if the forests in the reach would ever regain their splendor.

Across the park from the imposing monolithic spire, Trig and Chauncey could see the homes of Ærratum's gentry. They were not so much homes as much as they were manors, belonging to Imperium executives for the most part. The manor that stood out the most was a three-story dwelling formed out of a series of moonlight yew trees. This building, as with most of the older buildings within the city limits, was not constructed of hewn timber but was a living structure, grown out of the ground, pruned and trained by arboreal-architect Musers when the Muse still flowed abundantly enough to allow for such things. Between the Last War and Eternal Dawn's latest plague of darkness, the building style and profession that created them had all but vanished.

The branches that stuck out of the building's sides were covered with bright multicolored silk scarves. Various adornments hung from thick gold chains with aimless intention. There was a glass sphere that looked to contain a trapped fairy, though it was just an illusion. There was the carved head of a trompf, a giant moose-like creature possessing razor-sharp antlers. There was also a carved wolf's head flanked by the wings of a raven.

"That's the one right there. The garish one," Trig said as they pointed it out to Chauncey.

"I think you mispronounced classy. Just look at it," replied the traveling companion. He was in awe. To him it was spectacle.

Trig rolled their eyes, immediately turning their attention back to the park, searching for a tree that had good enough purchase to see inside the Poet Kesley's house and perhaps get a glimpse of the orbs they sought. They spied a giant six-story ageless oak just beyond the park's fence line. The branches of the old tree reached out in every direction making it the perfect climbing tree. There was one very thick lower branch that needed to be propped up by younger trees growing beneath it, otherwise it would have broken off.

Other than proximity to their target, the tree had another advantage. Due to its age, the bark was exceeding thick, muffling the light that flows through the trunk's phloem and xylem, carrying Muse to the tree's leaves. This meant that, with the donning of dark robes, the pair could climb mostly unnoticed, which they did.

***

"Which window do you think belongs to the study?" Chauncey asked.

"Your guess is as good as mine," Trig replied, knowing that it wasn't. Trig knew how the Master mind worked, or their cynicism made them at least think they did. They knew that vanity and hubris were what drove them. A Poet's most important room is going to be their study. It would be the focal point of their whole house. It's going to be the one with the best view from outside and be the most opulent on the inside. It was also going to be the room containing a desk. Their eyes drew directly to the center of the third floor. There was a large circular window. The tree branches that surrounded it had been carved into with grotesques representing Eternal Dawn's mythical creatures. Most prominent of them were the Nuckelavee, the Mórrigan, and the Razor Sìth, the last of whose mythological standing was still up for debate. This, Trig thought, was the study.

At Trig's insistence, they went up the tree first. The reason behind this was twofold. For one, they didn't want a face full of Chauncey due to a misplaced foot. This is at least how they rationalized it when they made their case. They knew Chauncey to be the better climber and secretly knew he'd be able to catch them if they were the one with the misplaced foot. The second more important reason was that it had been a few weeks since either of them had had a proper shower. Sure they had occasion to take an impromptu rinse in the latest rain storm but it wasn't like they had a bar of soap handy when it happened. The pair's feet possessed an acrid stench. It was hard to notice at nose level when standing but their proximity in the tree would surely send the oniony odor of Chauncey's soles wafting through the air. It wasn't like they were high folk wearing shoes at some formal engagement, it would be foot to face the entire climb.

Trig maintained a nimble pace going up the tree but it still wasn't quick enough for Chauncey who was easily twice as fast as them. He took every opportunity to tickle their dangling foot as they surveyed the next branch for safety. On more than one occasion his head had to dodge an incoming stomp.

The pair climbed a little over three stories to a large branch that looked slightly down at the round window.

"What was that with the tickling?" Trig barked in chastisement. "I could have tripped."

"Dearest Trig, I would not have let that happen. It was just a spot of fun," Chauncey replied. "If you take the fun out of adventurin' what's the bloody point?"

Trig stared at Chauncey as he finished his climb up to the meter-wide branch they were perched upon.

"Okay...What now?" Chauncey asked.

"Now we wait to see if the rumors are true," Trig replied.

***

The pair waited for hours. They watched as the moon Uther and Uther's moon Arthur fell beyond the horizon. It wasn't until the Lonely Sister was threatening to leave the sky that movement could be detected from within the house.

Trig had dozed off for a moment, the effects of their morning coffee had long since subsided. They were shaken awake by Chauncey, almost slipping as they regained their balance, having nearly forgotten they were precariously perched in a tree.

A smartly dressed man walked into the room they were surveilling. He was a little tipsy, apparently having imbibed one substance or another that lends itself to such states. The pair watched as the man undressed. He became entangled inside his clothes and fell over. He finished shimmying out of the garments before picking himself up off the floor and wandering over to a built-in cabinet. He reached up with both hands to tug on a set of rope pulls and swung the cabinet doors open with abandon. The nude figure was instantly bathed in white light.

"So the orb bathing thing was true?" Chauncey questioned. "I thought Todd was making it up."

Trig was surprised by the comment. Chauncey had a penchant for being a little too trusting and gullible. "Guess so," they replied.

"Think it works?" Chauncey said.

Trig's surprise faded. They readied a retort and just as they opened their mouth to speak, they heard a branch snap fifteen feet above their head. The sound was immediately accompanied by a "ssshhh" and some muffled speech. It was clear at that moment that they were not alone. "Todd you asshole," they muttered as their gaze moved from the naked visage in the round window to the branches above.

They could just make out two amorphous black blobs perched on one of the tree's narrower boughs. The figures were clearly wearing cloaks to hide their glow. Trig shook their head in disappointment and turned their attention back to the window, hoping to give whatever competition rested above the false hope that they had gone unnoticed. "Hmm, I doubt it," they said, replying to Chauncey's query. "If it did, I suspect the light from the orbs would have dissipated by now. Have you ever seen an empty orb?"

This was a rare treat for Chauncey who had not heard the chatter above. Trig had apparently grown bored enough to entertain a speculative conversation on the nature of Muse Orbs. He was not about to let the opportunity go to waste.

"No, I guess I haven't. Do you think it would work though? Could you charge yourself off one of those? I mean if you smashed it first of course."

Trig thought for a moment, knowing that they would have to drag out the conversation a little more to sell the notion that they didn't know they weren't alone. "No, it wouldn't," they replied.

Chauncey knew Trig was telling the truth and not just trying to end the conversation. There was something in their tone that seemed experiential but also somewhat dour. To Chauncey's surprise, Trig actually started to elaborate rather than follow their usual mode of making a brief blunt statement and leaving it at that.

"Ever hear of vasoimpedance?" Trig asked.

"Vaso what now?" Chauncey replied.

"Vasoimpedance," they continued. "You know how Muse isn't evenly distributed around the body?"

"Right..." commented Chauncey in a tone that echoed his agreement but begged for more.

"Well, vasoimpedance is what happens if Muse is pooled in any single part of the body. It's why if it's concentrated in your feet you don't absorb as much from the ground. It creates a blockage. If you were to attempt a cycle charge by breaking an orb and it found one of these blockages it would flood the vein and cause it to balloon up. Veins aren't very elastic, so pop," Trig exploded their fingers away from their palm in demonstration.

Chauncey's eyes grew wide. He was curious about how Trig knew so much about it but knew better than to ask as it would be a question of their history. He instead asked, "Well what if there was no Muse left in the body?"

Trig considered the question for a moment, wondering how much longer they had to keep up the ruse to ensure the competing mongers above didn't know they had been seen. "Well, what you're talking about would require a blowout, a very powerful one. The dark wash would need to extend at least a couple of miles. If that were to happen—and if any of the orbs you might have on you survive—I suppose then you could do it. But if even a small amount of essence was in your body at the time, the blowout wouldn't be the only thing turning off the lights that night, if you catch my drift. It's all speculation of course. There hasn't been an event like that since the Flood and we know how it turned out for the guy at the center."

Chauncey nodded his head and touched the side of his index finger to the middle of his forehead, slightly bowing as he did it. A show of respect for a fallen Master.

Trig rolled their eyes at the display, "Well, enough of this, I've got to go use the loo. Keep your eyes on the Poet. I want to know if he does anything funny."

"I suppose you mean something funnier than trying to get moonburns from the orbs, right?" Chauncey replied.

Trig didn't even acknowledge the question as they started to climb down the branches.

***

The competing mongers were perched above Chauncey in silence. Gilly and Rhodes Stoat had thought for a moment that they had been discovered but Trig's forced conversation had served its purpose in easing the pair's concern. They now looked down at the solo Chauncey with the gleam of murder in their eyes. The twins each unsheathed a dagger. These blades were twins in their own right, having been forged from the remains of the fabled sword the Moonlight Crow. The child blades did not have names. Their authors had done nothing worthy of the bestowment of such honors.

The pair, brandishing their weapons between their teeth, moved in unspoken unison toward their prey. It was a slow deliberate pace as they tried to avoid breaking another branch. Their black robes served to obscure them, keeping their forms amorphous. An onlooker would be confused to find that the moving shadows in the tree were not some form of ooze weeping between the branches.

The twins had closed the gap between where they were and Chauncey to a matter of yards. They balanced on two thick branches which hung in the air on either side of their target.

Chauncey's gaze was still fixed on the man in the window. He had not detected that anything was out of place. He chuckled a little as his own prey started to dance. The light of the orbs created interesting forms on the walls of the room as the Poet moved, creating an abstract shadow-play.

The Stoat twins paused for a moment. Chauncey's laughter had served to briefly break their concentration. Gilly rebalanced her feet on her branch. A slight creak emanated from the tree's appendage as it rubbed up against another. Her eyes caught her brother's as she looked for the signal to pounce. He gave a quick nod of the head which caused her to rise to full extension. She pulled the knife out of her mouth with her left hand and brought it up overhead where it met her right. She leaned forward slightly, ready to fall onto the unsuspecting victim below.

Suddenly there was a loud snap from above. All three of the tree's occupants turned their gaze skyward.

Chauncey caught sight of the would-be attackers and let out an audible, somewhat lackadaisical, "Heeey," as he pointed a finger at Gilly then another at Rhodes. His fingers traced the attacker's movements as they each fell backward in quick succession. Their bodies bounced off the branches like pachinko balls as they made their way to the ground below. Chauncey's mouth was agape, unsure of what had just happened. His eyes traced their way upward as another cloaked blob made its way toward him. "Don't...don't kill me," he tried to bargain.

"Don't be so dramatic," Trig said, coming into view, their face peeking out from beneath the hood of their black robes. They cast the branch they had used as a club aside being sure there was no chance of it hitting their partner.

"My hero," Chauncey uttered before thinking for a second. "I guess that's a life debt I owe you. Now you'll never be rid of me."

"You're telling me there was an option before?" Trig offered dryly. Their gaze then moved beyond Chauncey to the round window. Their expression became one of worry. The Poet was staring at their position. "Don't move," they commanded.

The Poet's head swiveled from side to side, scanning in the pair's direction. He then moved to the far side of the window in an attempt to try for a better look.

Trig, thinking fast, focused as much Muse into their face as they could. They then moved so their face would be obscured by the leaves of the tree's denser branches. They started to swivel their neck as they bellowed, "Whooooo, Whooooo, Whooooo."

The Poet could barely make out the sound of Trig's charade from behind the glass but was more than convinced that he had just caught the sight of a glowl who had recently happened upon some helpless prey. Satisfied, he set his sights back on the orbs. He had at least another hour of "absorption" planned before calling it a night.

Once the Poet turned his back, Trig beckoned Chauncey to climb down out of the tree.

"Are they dead?" Chauncey asked as he looked at the Stoat twins in their tattered cloaks.

"We could only be so lucky," his partner replied as a pained moan emanated from Gilly. Trig grabbed the twin daggers to preclude the possibility of another attempt at attack. "Get up you weasels," they said as they nudged Rhodes in the ribs with the heel of their foot. A cry of pain escaped his mouth.

The twins took a moment to survey their bodies as they found their way back to consciousness. After a few moments of labored breathing, they were able to laboriously claw their way up to their feet.

Trig could see that they were in no position to fight and moved forward to drop their hoods, "The Stoats, I should have known."

Gilly's words were pained as she replied, "You seem to have us at a disadvantage."

Against Trig's better judgment, they dropped their own hood.

Panic crept across the twin's faces. It was as if they had seen a ghost. Gilly pleaded, "Had I known, I would'a never. Please—please just let us leave with our lives."

Chauncey stood by, silently watching the proceedings. He had never seen Trig stoke this kind of reaction in someone. He had a million and one questions. He knew it wouldn't be the night for answers. He was not sure if any night would be the night for answers. He knew he could be annoying but also knew well enough where the lines were drawn. Looking at the Stoat's terrified faces, Chauncey knew that this was a line that could not be crossed. It was for Trig to share, not for him to pry.

Trig stood in mock judgment, feigning the weighing of the pair's fate in their mind. After thirty seconds they relented, "Fine, you may live...Now go."

A look of relief found its way across the faces of the Stoat twins. Rhodes pulled Gilly's arm over his shoulder to prop her up, and with great effort, they hobbled away.

"Hey," Trig barked toward the pair, causing them to turn their attention. "If you find your lips telling tales of what you found yourself doing tonight—or of who you met—you might just find these daggers delivered back to you...Nod if you get me."

The twins nodded. And with the warning, their pace seemed to quicken.

Chauncey didn't know what to do. This was a side of Trig with which he had not been acquainted. He knew their anger but he did not know their rage. He didn't know what to think as he wondered if the threat against his body was the reason it had been so intense; if Trig not only tolerated him but did indeed hold a piece of him in their heart as well. Chauncey waited for what felt like the appropriate amount of time before asking, "Now what?"

"Now we do what we always do," Trig replied.

"Right. Put in an anonymous report and let the Constabulary do the hard part?" Chauncey said.

"Right," Trig confirmed.

Normally Chauncey would have objected and subsequently attempted to campaign for a classic breaking and entering. Tonight he would not. Having had just enough adventure to sate his appetite, he was not looking to push his luck for once.

As the pair walked out of the park, Trig dropped the twin daggers down a nearby well into the waters of the city's cisterns below.

***

Trig and Chauncey waited the entirety of the next day for the Constabulary to execute their raid. There was paperwork to file and red tape to cut. Going after a former Master was no easy feat no matter how marred their name may be. The pair had watched the gears of justice slow over the last year. The supply of orbs was running thinner by the day. Knowledge of the methods concerning their creation had died with the Geddes at the end of the Last War. With the rise of Imperium and the advent of their cuffs, the demand side of the market had dwindled as well. Only holdouts to Imperium's influence in the reaches were still making requests. While it was still a crime to possess them, there wasn't the government fervor surrounding the orbs that there once was.

The pair waited. It wasn't until the moons Uther and Arthur were in fall that they would see the constables knock on the Poet's door. The fallen Master put up a fuss and said he did not engage in such illegal dealings. It was too late for him though; the investigators had brought along a hollyhog. A hollyhog was a pig-like creature trained to suss out anomalous Muse activity. This particular hollyhog alerted the moment it reached the front door and attempted to go through the Poet's legs as he opened it. This was more than enough evidence to give the constables just cause for a search.

The two investigators would follow the hollyhog upstairs and find the Poet's stash. There was no jail time to be served for the crime of possession. The confiscation of contraband was more than sufficient punishment. The fine was the time that would be wasted going to court and the public humiliation that went along with it. The real crime when dealing with orbs was in theft and distribution. Trig and Chauncey would be hemmed up for at least a couple of years if they were to be caught.

The pair of thieves watched as the investigators exited the former Master's manor. One was holding a rawhide duffel. Judging by the size, Trig assumed that it contained a few more than the thirty orbs required for their job. If that were the case they would be more than happy to replenish their own depleted supply.

Trig and Chauncey watched as the cops handed off the bag to a half-light messenger. Half-light messengers were who one went to if they needed to secret property from one place to another without drawing suspicions. They were experts at their craft and they were bonded. They were also deadly. To Trig this proved to be a good sign. The orbs were being taken somewhere the Constabulary feared to go. This was not saying much as the Constabulary had feared to go anywhere outside of the city limits due to their newfound relationship with Imperium, who many saw as an evil worth doing battle with. Trig had heard that the last of the destruction depots within the city wall had been shuttered a few months back but had been unable to confirm the rumor until now. The fact that the service was bonded also meant that there would be punishment for the messenger if they were to get light-fingered. Trig could be assured that the orbs would make it safely to their destination.

The two investigators took the hollyhog and headed west toward their precinct. The half-light messenger placed the duffel in a large canvas rucksack before heading south. Chauncey glanced up to the circular window above, watching the Poet looking down on the messenger with anger. He would then see the former Master turn toward his desk. He did not know that the Master was eyeing a pen and quill, readying himself to create. The two thieves raised the hoods of their robes.

***

The pair was able to keep pace with the half-light messenger. Trig could tell he was new to the job and that the road had not yet hardened him to be the deadly instrument that the work required. The messenger had a single-minded focus on getting to his destination and didn't even bother to keep an eye out for a tail let alone glance at his surroundings. Trig and Chauncey were much too practiced to be seen but that didn't stop Trig from thinking that this poor sap would not last long.

They continued to follow the messenger outside the city gates and on to one of the old paths which had fallen out of use with the advent of the Geddes Road. The pair would continue their stalking for another five miles into the western woods before coming across a clearing where the road went downhill toward an old mill perched in the middle of a glowwheat field. Trig and Chauncey made an immediate left upon reaching the clearing and followed the tree line along until they had sufficiently distanced themselves from the road. They watched as the messenger entered the building.

Trig and Chauncey would observe the mill from moonset to moonrise, casing the building, getting ready to execute their raid.

***

The Lonely Sister had not quite reached her apex when the pair saw the focus of their earlier stalking leave the building. He was carrying an empty pack on his back and a piece of glowing fruit in his hand. Ten more minutes would pass before the half-light messenger was out of sight.

Trig waited for another fifteen before offering, "Okay exactly as we planned.. .No diversions,"

"No diversions," Chauncey echoed as he followed Trig in raising the hood of his cloak.

The pair had not seen anyone other than the messenger enter or leave the building. Trig knew better than to think that the mill would be empty. There was always one or two dark adepts overseeing and guarding the process.

Snuffs, as they were pejoratively known, were the result of an adept losing their ability to absorb Muse. There were more than a couple of reasons this could occur and very few of them were the result of altruistic behavior. The most common mechanism by which an adept became a snuff occurred during the Last War and was the result of the misuse of Muse orbs. There was a grenadier technique that adepts used requiring a single Muse orb to create a small blowout. The adept simply had to throw the orb with the intention of having no intention. Once the orb struck the ground it would break, creating a vacuum effect that would suck in all Muse from the surrounding area before ejecting it outward, pushing the remaining Muse in the area away on a shock-wave. This nullified the target's ability to pull in the essence themselves, leaving them vulnerable. Problems could arise in the interval between release and contact. If the adept formed any kind of intention between committing to their action and the orb hitting the ground, their body would suffer a Muse receptor burnout. Enough burnout would leave them snuffed.

There was also the more common cause of the condition whereby the adept attempted to throw multiple orbs with no intention to maximize the size of the blowout's dark wash shock-wave. It was a more dangerous technique and prone to blowback, completely frying every Muse receptor in the adept's body in a matter of moments.

The condition turned the adept's normally glowing veins black, marking them and turning those who did not repent into outcasts. The repentant snuffs were absorbed by the Constabulary to perform orb destruction. There was no longer any risk of them using the orbs for nefarious purposes and little risk of them harming themselves. They had already done the worst possible damage. Most Snuffs were more than willing to destroy the devices that had caused them so much hardship.

***

Chauncey and Trip crept over to the pathway leading to the old mill. They didn't want to risk going through the field. Their dark appearance would provide enough contrast against the orange-tinted glowwheat to blow their cover to any onlooker. There was also the matter of the path that would be left in their wake when they undoubtedly trampled the tall grass, cutting the vegetation off from the Muse that gave it its light. The pair had barely reached the pathway when there was a light ejection from the building.

"Shite, they've already started," Trig said as a shock wave passed through them. They looked at the veins in their arms noticing no diminishing of their light. They glanced at the surrounding field before remarking, "This snuff must be completely drained, look they've barely bled the field."

Chauncey's eyes scanned the grasses surrounding the mill, "This is going to be easier than we thought."

"Oh no," Trig uttered with something akin to instinct. "You just had to say it didn't you?"

"Say what?" Chauncey replied with confusion.

"You never say a job is going to be easy. You only ever say a job *was* easy," Trig said.

"Hey, aren't you the one who is always saying, 'Superstitions are for the weak of mind'?" Chauncey responded, knowing he had made a rare point.

"Don't confuse overconfidence for superstition," Trig said, taking some of the wind out of their partner's sails. "Confidence breeds complacency." They watched as a smile of victory faded from Chauncey's face, knowing that their other overused phrase had hit its mark. "Now quiet, we don't want whoever is inside to hear us."

Chauncey put a finger to his lips as an indication of his compliance. The pair continued to move closer and closer to their target.

***

The pair were able to cover the distance between their hiding perch and the mill unseen, finding themselves under a window, listening for voices.

"I think it's just one of them," Chauncey whispered as another wave of light passed through the pair.

"Shite, they're going to destroy all the orbs before we can liberate them," Trig said.

"Is that what we are calling it now? Liberation?" Chauncey quipped.

Trig rolled their eyes and inched their way over to the door.

Chauncey followed along and took up a post a few meters from the door, setting back into his foot with the intention of executing a shoulder ram. He took his first step but his partner stepped out in front of him.

With their palm pointed at the ground, Trig waved their hand up and down beckoning him to stop. They then reached for the doorknob and twisted it. The knob turned without resistance and they gave the door a gentle nudge, finding it capable of swinging freely. They glanced back at Chauncey with a look that said, "When will you learn?" They then attempted to open the door carefully but only just a crack so they could obtain a proper peak. Just as they did, another ejection of light appeared from within the room and passed right through them. Their proximity to the source was closer than before, causing the intensity to be much greater, almost blinding. Trig's head swiveled as they looked over their shoulder, trying to soften the deluge. The bombardment of light was almost too much. They looked down at their veins, not seeing any light emanating from them. Concern grew in the pit of their stomach. Had they become a snuff? They kept staring at their arms hoping for a change. It was almost a minute before they realized the latest flash had affected their visual acuity. The contrast between their glowing vessels and their skin started to bleed back into focus. They breathed the smallest sigh of relief and they looked at Chauncey to give him the signal to rush the room.

Trig nudged the door the rest of the way open and Chauncey charged into the room yelling, "Beeees, beeees, they're everywhere! Make it stop! Oh, venerable Masters make it stop." He started running around the room in a feigned panic.

Trig crouched and crept into the room, hoping to remain unseen and allow themselves to size up the surroundings. To their surprise, there were panels and canvases everywhere. Toward the center of the room, there were multiple buckets of paint in various colors. It was an odd sight for sure. It was well known that due to their condition, dark adepts lost their creative prowess.

Trig's eyes eventually fixed themselves on the snuff in question. He was an alarming sight. The man stood at least six foot six inches. He was wearing baggy harem pants without a top. His black veins could be seen in vascular relief across his bare chest and down his muscular arms. His eyes were blackened. Void eyes were another hallmark of the dark adept's plight. In his hand, he held an orb that had been freshly dipped in bright green paint. The snuff watched Chauncey with concern.

In that moment it dawned on Trig that the snuff was trying to create art. The feeling of epiphany flooded their brain and caused their own veins to illuminate.

The snuff's eyes darted over to Trig to size them up and the concern immediately dropped off his face. The former adept then wound up and threw the orb as hard as he could at Chauncey, leading him slightly as he continued to run.

Chauncey was still attempting to create a distraction. The orb hit the smartly dressed rogue square in the chest. It shattered upon impact, creating another wave of light. The snuff's lack of ability to apply the intention of having no intention meant that his blowouts were devoid of the dark wash that tempers Muse absorption.

Chauncey tried to survey the damage that he was sure had befallen his vestments but was instantly greeted with a violent flash of pure white light. He had always wondered what it would have been like to be close to the Vagabond Master's Flood. In his momentary blindness, he was struck by the thought that this might be the closest thing to it. He reached for his chest as a dull ache had radiated out from the impact site. His hands were greeted by a warm gooey liquid. It took him a moment to realize that it was paint covering his fineries and not blood.

Trig anticipated the snuff's actions and threw their arm up to block the light. Even though their eyes were buried in the crook of their elbow, light was still able to penetrate their flesh. Trig could swear they were able to see the bones of their arm from behind their eyelids.

Chauncey was dazed, he immediately reached up to cover his eyes and was vigorously waving his other arm out in front in an attempt to find his bearings. "Hey mate...We mean you no harm, we just want the orbs and we'll be out of your hair," he said trying to calm the developing situation, completely ignoring the fact that the snuff was lacking hair, alopecia being yet another side effect of his attacker's muted condition.

The snuff was incensed, taking Chauncey's words as a slight. "You're the interlopers here. It is well within my duty as a functionary of the Constabulary to rend your heads from your body. Leave now or it's your lives."

"Whoa, settle down there Sonny Jim. We mean you no harm and capital punishment's been illegal since the war...Don't know if anyone's told you but it's been over fifteen years," Chauncey tried to reason, knowing he would be no match for the man who was half a head taller than he and probably weighed twice as much. With Trig standing much shorter than himself and being even slighter, Chauncey knew they would similarly want to avoid the potential of a fight.

Trig stood up from their crouched position but maintained a dynamic stance. Their weight was planted firmly in their back foot, ready to spring in whichever direction the developing situation required. They couldn't help but feel slightly empathetic toward the snuff. The feeling was fleeting. They took less than a moment to consider the source of his plight and who he would have planted his flag for in the Last War. Their mind then drifted to the Stoat twins' twin daggers, wondering if they had been too hasty in dropping them down into the city's cisterns. They were used to finding frail darkened adepts at the end of an orb quest, not someone who looks like a number one contender for the caber toss at the Outland games.

The burly snuff darted his eyes between Chauncey and Trig, not convinced that either posed a threat. "This is your last chance. Leave now and all can be forgotten," he said. He knew that further altercation might require an incident report which would invite questions about his non-standard means of orb destruction. These would be uncomfortable questions to answer.

The thought crossed Trig's mind that the dark adept would not be fighting to wound and judging by the scars on his body he was no stranger to violence. They gave a momentary thought to calling the heist quits but thought about the contract. It would take them at least another three months to gather the number of orbs they saw in the room. Drumlocke had already been waiting too long for them. They pondered their options for a moment, deciding that their plan hadn't yet gone completely upside down, and yelled, "Chauncey now!"

Chauncey paused for a second to glance at Trig with an "Are you serious" look on his face. He was supposed to be the one with the bad ideas.

Trig gave an urging nod toward the attacker, trying to signal Chauncey to continue with their original plan.

The snuffed adept's eyes kept darting between the pair. The thieves had not heeded his warning. A blood lust started growing from the pit of his stomach. It was a feeling he hadn't felt in fifteen years, one that he had hoped to never feel again.

Chauncey removed his green paint-speckled robe and balled it up in his hands, drawing the snuff's focus. He then took a feigned step toward his target and watched as the dark adept settled his weight back into his right leg getting ready to pounce. "Now," Chauncey yelled as his feigned step turned real and he threw the robe into his target's face.

The dark adept reached toward his face in an attempt to remove the obstruction. Trig took this opportunity to sweep their planted leg, knocking them to the floor before darting toward the table that held the objects they sought. The snuff reacted quickly by tucking into a ball as he fell, attempting to prevent any injury that could be sustained by landing awkwardly on a misplaced limb. It wasn't something he was taught, it was instinct. He lay on the ground pretending to struggle with the cloak as he listened to the sounds of the thief's footsteps. In his struggle, he made it a point to knock over a couple of canvases in an effort to sell his mock disadvantage.

Trig watched and was satisfied their sweep had had the desired effect. They took the moment of disorientation to shuffle their way to the table containing the orbs. Taking a quick stock, they estimated there to be a few north of thirty orbs; just enough to satisfy the Drumlocke job with a few to spare.

The snuff rolled over onto his hands and knees, removing the robe from his face as he did. He was facing away from Chauncey as he took a crouched position reminiscent of a runner in the starting block position. He threw a leg back, which connected squarely with the taller rogue's stomach.

Chauncey doubled over as pain radiated from the impact site, through his limbs, and up his spine. He tried to gasp for air, only being able to suck in the tiniest of amounts. The pain grew to be too much and he toppled to his side. A feeling of shame mixed with his pain. He knew he had one job and he had failed to do it.

The dark adept then set to aiming himself at Trig who had seemingly become too transfixed by the orbs to pay much attention to the goings on behind them.

"Look out!" Chauncey was barely able to gasp as the attacker pounced.

Thinking fast, Trig spun around to face their attacker. Their body looked like it was acting as a centrifuge for the Muse contained within. Light could be seen rushing out of Trig's legs, left arm, head, and torso, as it shot down their right arm, pooling in their hand just as they released an orb. The luminescence jettisoned from their hand and followed the orb like the tail of a comet as it crossed the eight-foot gap between them and their attacker.

The snuff was mid-sail through the air, parallel to the ground with their arms stretched out in anticipation of wrestling Trig to the ground. Time seemed to pass in slow motion as he watched the orb fly toward his face. He attempted to pull his arms in to block it but he was just shy of being quick enough. The orb made contact with his forehead and exploded as he fell to the ground and skidded across the floor. He came within inches of knocking his head against the back wall under the table where the orbs sat. His hands managed to make it to his face. He was anticipating needing to stanch the bleeding from the cuts the shattered glass of the orb was sure to have inflicted, but there was none. Instead of blood he felt the texture of hempen rope wiggle its way between his fingers. The rope traced its way around the back of his neck and down his arms.

Chauncey watched as a fishing net weaved its way over the snuffed adept's body, carefully knitting itself together as it grew from head to toe. "That might be your best one yet," he remarked.

The snuff was captive to the net. He attempted to struggle against the constriction but all of his strength proved to be of no use. He was defeated and he knew it. All he had left to do was plead, "Please don't take them all...please." There was an air of desperation in his voice fueled by his desire to create...to find just a taste of the power he once wielded.

Trig attempted to pay no mind to the mutterings of the floored foe. They pulled out a single oversized pouch and shoved the orbs into it before placing it in their rucksack.

"You...you don't understand. This is all that I have left," the dark adept continued to plead.

Trig turned their gaze to the room, scanning it, taking the time to see the abstract paintings that rested against the walls and furniture. They considered the waste of resources before their eyes moved back to the netted figure on the floor, scanning his incapacitated body and meeting his voided-out eyes. They couldn't help but feel sorry for this person who was once their enemy, this Muse junkie who was just trying to get the tiniest of fixes.

Trig looked at the table. Two orbs remained. They placed one in their pocket. The other would remain on the table as the orb mongers exited the old mill. It was a rare act of mercy on the part of the shorter rogue, a decision they hoped they would not come to regret.

***

The pair walked up the path toward the woods from which they emerged. It would be another three-hour walk before they would reach a fork in the road. There was a feeling in the air. The crossroads that Trig and Chauncey found themselves at was more than physical. The orb trade was waning. This could very well be their final trip to Drumlocke. Trig thought for a moment about keeping the orbs. They could be invaluable in the establishment of a new career. They looked at their partner Chauncey and wondered if he might be thinking the same before wordlessly taking the southern route toward the artisan city where the treasured objects belonged.

Trig pulled out the orb they had stashed in their pocket, asking, "So what genius idea did you have in mind for this?"

Chauncey was briefly taken aback, thinking that the orb that was left behind was meant to be his. He thought Trig was punishing him for not subduing the dark adept quickly enough. He thought a moment longer and stared down at his paint-covered suit before asking, "How are you with brocade?"

About the author

A.B. Charles likes to write, the book in your hands should attest to that. They would like to write more if you'll allow them. Their love of nature should be evident with the turn of each page. They are an avid distance and trail runner, piano player, and reader. They live with their partner, Laura, and two cats, Toothless and Kira, in Corning, NY.